THE BLACK SHEEP

A Learning Experience - Book III

Book One: A Learning Experience
Book Two: Hard Lessons
Book Three: The Black Sheep

CHRISTOPHER G. NUTTALL

Printed in the United States of America.

ISBN: 152343287X
ISBN 13: 9781523432875

http://www.chrishanger.net
http://chrishanger.wordpress.com/
http://www.facebook.com/ChristopherGNuttall

All Comments Welcome!

PROLOGUE

Datanet Discussion Forums are buzzing after Captain Hoshiko Stuart stated, publicly, that the Solar Union should not consider intervening in the ongoing civil war on Earth. Her comments have been repeated by a number of other 'Solarians' who feel that the affairs of our former homeworld are none of our concern…

-Solar News Network, Year 54

"Admiral," Lieutenant Marie Campbell said, over the communications network, "Captain Hoshiko Stuart has arrived."

Admiral Mongo Stuart, Commander-in-Chief of the Solar Navy, looked up from his desk, keeping his face impassive despite his inner dismay. He knew how to reward good performance and he was an expert at chewing out the incompetent or criminally stupid, but dealing with someone who had crossed the line without *quite* doing anything against the Solar Navy's regulations was a little harder. The whole affair left a sour taste in his mouth. He'd seen enough good men and women railroaded by the former United States Navy on Earth, all for political reasons, to hate the thought of doing it himself. But there was little choice.

"Send her in," he ordered. "And then hold all my calls unless they're urgent."

"Yes, sir," Marie said.

Mongo sat upright as the hatch hissed open, revealing Captain Hoshiko Stuart. She was third-gen, the granddaughter of Steve Stuart - Mongo's brother - himself, the closest thing to outright royalty in the Solar Union. Not that she or anyone else in the Stuart family had been allowed to *think* of themselves as royalty. Hoshiko had earned her stripes, as surely as any of her peers in the Solar Navy; no one, not even the handful of politicians who argued the Stuart family exercised undue influence within the Solar Union, questioned her *competence*. But that hadn't stopped them from using her words as a talking point.

"Admiral," Hoshiko said.

Mongo studied her for a long moment, allowing the silence to lengthen. She was tall, her features a mixture of Caucasian and Japanese, her skin tinted and her almond eyes dark and expressive. Like all third-gen children, she had the genetic modifications that ensured both a natural lifespan of over two hundred years and an immunity to disease, most poisons and even tooth decay. She could have turned herself into a goddess, if she'd wished - most teenagers went through a stage of changing their looks on a daily basis - but she'd stayed with the appearance her parents and grandparents had gifted to her. At thirty-five, she looked twenty-one. And she held herself with the poise of a seasoned veteran, waiting for him to speak.

Her file flashed up in front of his eyes, prompted by a mental query to his implants. Born in Year 19, entered the Solar Navy in Year 35 - the youngest possible age - and graduated from Sparta Military College in Year 39. Assigned to a destroyer, then to a light cruiser; assigned to command an alien-designed battlecruiser during the Battle of Earth, where she acquitted herself well. No black marks in her file until two weeks ago, when she'd made a number of statements to the Solar News Network that had ignited a political firestorm.

And she's certainly bright enough to understand what she's done, Mongo thought, as he directed his attention back towards Hoshiko. *The only question is why?*

"Captain," he said, coolly. He might be her Great-Uncle, but he wasn't going to do her any favours and she had to know it. "Do you know why you're here?"

"Yes, sir," Hoshiko said.

"Explain," Mongo ordered.

"I gave an interview to the Solar News Network," Hoshiko said. Her voice was very flat, suggesting she was either keeping it under tight control or using her implants to ensure she betrayed none of her internal feelings. "I expressed my feelings on the planned intervention on Old Earth. The interview went viral and spread through the datanet."

"Correct," Mongo said. He cocked his head to one side. "Why did you give that interview, Captain?"

Hoshiko, for the first time, showed a flicker of animation. "I was asked for my opinion, sir," she said, "and I gave it."

Mongo lifted his eyebrow, inviting her to explain further.

"I am a Solarian," Hoshiko said. "My parents may have been born on Old Earth, but I was not. I grew up on an asteroid colony, sir, with all the boundless wealth of space all around me. My fellows and I enjoy a freedom that none on Earth can even comprehend. The problems of Old Earth do not concern us. They are free to move to the Solar Union, if they wish, or continue to live amongst the dirt. The social and political breakdown on the planet is none of our concern. We certainly do not wish to spend blood and treasure trying to save the Earthers from themselves."

"And that was what you told the reporters," Mongo said.

"Yes, sir."

Mongo had to admit, if only in the privacy of his own thoughts, that she had a point. The Solar Union's invitation to everyone on Earth remained open - and would remain open for as long as the Solar Union itself endured. Leave the gravity well and live in space, where even a low-paying job could ensure a decent lifestyle. Hoshiko, like so many of her peers, couldn't comprehend just why so many Earthers were scared of implanting technology, let alone genetic splices and fixes, into their bodies. Hell, *Mongo* found the concept scary at times…and, without the nanotech and automated doctors they'd captured from the Horde, he knew he'd be dead by now. But there were other concerns.

"Many of us have ties to Earth," he pointed out. "Don't you feel we might have legitimate concerns?"

"No, sir," Hoshiko said. "The Solar Union was founded on the concept of *escaping* Earth, of escaping governments that were too controlling to allow true freedom. I see no value in looking back to our roots."

"You have relatives down there," Mongo pointed out.

"I don't know them," Hoshiko countered. "Surely they could come up here, if they wished?"

Mongo gave her a long considering look. Hoshiko had never seen the Stuart Ranch, where Mongo and his brothers had been born and raised. She was used to controlled environments, not the beauty of Earth. But, at the same time, he knew she had a point. The American melting pot had only started to come apart at the seams when it had become easy, too easy, to remain in touch with the Old Country, for old grudges to cross the oceans and infect the United States. Mongo still mourned the country he'd served, even though it had left him behind a long time before the Solar Union had been formed. It was hard for him to say goodbye.

"Military officers are not supposed to talk to the press," he said, instead. "You should not have given that interview."

"Military officers are supposed to speak their minds, as long as they can back up their statements," Hoshiko countered. "Can I speak freely, Admiral?"

"You may," Mongo said.

"Am I in trouble because I'm a military officer who spoke to the press," Hoshiko asked, "or because I'm a *Stuart* who disagreed with the family line?"

"The family does have an interest in its property on Earth," Mongo said.

"Which it shouldn't have," Hoshiko said. "It provides a tie to the planet we sought to escape, sir. The older generation may want to keep it, but the younger generation sees no value in it."

"No, you wouldn't," Mongo agreed.

He cleared his throat. "Yes, you *are* in trouble because the family can no longer present a united front," he admitted. "Our opponents in the Senate have not hesitated to capitalise on your remarks."

"The united front did not exist," Hoshiko pointed out, coolly. She waved a hand at the walls, where a number of images from the Battle of Earth were prominently displayed. "You may want to try to recover territory on a single world; *we* want to get out there and build empires, carry the human race to heights unmatched even by the Tokomak! There is nothing to be gained by becoming involved with scrabbles on Earth when there's an entire universe out here, just waiting to be seized. Our manifest destiny is out there, Admiral!"

"We are one small system, with a handful of allies," Mongo said. "There is no way we can hope to conquer the entire galaxy, let alone the universe."

"Not now, no," Hoshiko said. "But we seem to have a choice between building an empire - call it what you like, Admiral - of our own or taking the risk that someone *else* will build an empire. The Tokomak still have *millions* of starships under their command, sir, and we're not the only ones who can innovate. Even if the Tokomak Empire falls apart, sir, one of the successor states may pose a greater threat. We don't have time for narrow-minded people who look at the prospects before us and flinch away."

Mongo took a second to place firm controls on his temper before speaking. "You present us with an unusual challenge," he said. "If you were to be court-martialled for your actions, it would require open discussion of the issue, which would not rebound to anyone's credit. But if you are *not* punished, it will look as though the family name has protected you from the consequences. I've decided to take a third option."

He waited for a long moment. Hoshiko said nothing.

"We have been asked to establish a military and trader base in the Martina Sector," he explained. Hoshiko closed her eyes for a moment, clearly consulting her implants. "This base will have a battle squadron of heavy cruisers attached to it, as well as a handful of support ships and intelligence personnel. You will be reassigned to *Jackie Fisher* as her commanding officer, but you will also be in overall command of the detachment and roving ambassador to any local alien powers. I'll assign a steady hand to serve as your XO. You're going to be very busy."

"That's six months away," Hoshiko said, shocked.

"Yes," Mongo said. He hid an amused smile. The rest of the assignment clearly hadn't sunk in, yet. "You and your squadron will be on a five-year deployment. During that time, you will have considerable autonomy, as long as you stay within the standing orders. Assuming all goes well, you will be relieved by another squadron at the end of your time on station. By that point, one would hope the political crisis here will be resolved, one way or the other."

It was, he thought, a neat solution. Hoshiko couldn't remain in touch with anyone in the Solar Union, not when it would take at least a year for her to send a message and receive a reply. If anyone questioned her deployment, he could point to it and say it was a punishment, but if she did well, her career could resume its more normal course after her deployment came to an end. A court-martial, on the other hand, would terminate her career even if she was found innocent.

"You'll receive a full intelligence brief, what little we know about the sector, once you reach your new command," he told her. "Martina itself is a shared world, thanks to the Tokomak, but there are several alien races nearby that may pose a threat. There's also a large number of humans, descendents of alien slaves, living within the sector. We'd like you to try to build ties with them, as well as protect shipping and generally represent the Solar Union to the locals."

"Yes, sir," Hoshiko said. She snapped off a tight salute. "I will make you proud."

"See that you do," Mongo warned. "You're going to be on your own out there. Good luck."

ONE

Fighting broke out again in California as the Mexican Independence Front, with armoured support from Mexican tanks, attempted to push north against the United Farmers Alliance, who have been receiving support from Texas. The Governor of Texas stated that she would not hesitate to support her fellow Americans in their struggle against the Mexican threat.

-Solar News Network, Year 54

Hoshiko didn't want to admit it, not even to herself, but she was bored.

She was the kind of person who always wanted to be *doing* something. She'd *always* been a very active person, even as a young girl growing up on Stuart Asteroid. Hoshiko had been first to take a spacewalk, first to explore the nooks and crannies of the asteroid without parental supervision, first to use a neural interface and plunge into a virtual world, first to lose her virginity and first to apply successfully to the Naval Academy. The thought of just sitting in orbit around Martina was horrifying, yet she'd been stuck there for over six months. There were only so many tasks for the squadron and she was privately surprised that morale had held up as well as it had.

Because we're pretty much isolated out here, she thought, as she paced her cabin and scowled at the near-orbit display. *And there's very little to do.*

She glowered at the blue-green planet at the centre of the display, surrounded by hundreds of starships, orbital habitats and industrial nodes. Martina was a shared world - there were over twenty different races living in near-harmony on the surface - and there was almost nothing in the way of planetary authority. No one had been able to muster the authority to tell her she couldn't establish a naval base in the system, but no one had been able to meet her for more substantive discussions either. She hoped, for their sake, that no one ever decided to view the system as a target - there was no unified defence force - but she knew the peace surrounding the planet wouldn't last. Martina had no less than *nine* gravity points orbiting the local star, each one a money-making bonanza for a military power strong enough to demand passage fees.

And they'll get them too, she reminded herself. *Interstellar shippers will pay whatever it takes to get through a gravity point, cutting hundreds or thousands of light years off their trips.*

She picked up the datapad containing the latest set of readiness reports, then put it down again unread. There was no point. The squadron had exercised regularly, both to ensure their skills were kept up to par and show off humanity's military might to potential threats, but they hadn't fired their weapons in anger since a brief encounter with a pirate ship two months ago. Her *real* problem was keeping her crews busy and entertained, ensuring they didn't slip into VR worlds or sneak down to the planet and desert. There was a small human community on Martina after all, descended from men and women who'd been taken from Earth centuries ago. An enterprising crewman could probably make a few local contacts and vanish if he wished. Somehow, Hoshiko doubted the local authority would help to search for a missing crewman.

"And if Uncle Mongo wanted to punish me," she muttered to herself, "he couldn't have found a better way."

She glowered at the display, again. The squadron was so far from Earth that everything they heard was second or third-hand, passed on by a handful of supply ships and freighters that had made their way to Martina, hoping to open up new trade routes into the sector. Hoshiko didn't blame them for trying - having dinner with the trader captains was one of the few highlights of her position - but so far their results had been very poor. The sector didn't have anything unique or interesting…and it *was* very far from Earth. She was surprised the freighters kept coming.

Probably trying to buy more starships, she thought, crossly. *We can never have enough.*

Her intercom buzzed. "Captain, this is Ensign Howard on the bridge," a voice said, nervously. He clearly hadn't managed to overcome his fear of interrupting his commanding officer, who would *doubtless* be doing important work in her cabin. "We have five ships inbound to Martina at FTL speeds."

Hoshiko frowned. Ensign Howard was so young she was marginally surprised he wasn't still in diapers. *Jackie Fisher* was his first assignment, right out of the Academy; he was simply too inexperienced to realise that few captains would be angry if they were disturbed, not even if it turned out to be nothing. Better safe than sorry was a lesson the Solar Union had drummed into its citizens from a very early age. Asteroids, even with modern technology, were hardly *safe*.

"Five ships," she repeated. Every day, there were hundreds of starships passing through the system. She tried to keep her voice calm. "Why do you think this is important?"

There was a pause. "Captain, two of them read out as *Livingston*-class freighters," Howard said, finally. "The other three seem to be warships - and they're in hot pursuit. They're practically right on top of the freighters."

Hoshiko's eyes narrowed. *Livingston*-class freighters were unique to humanity, as far as she knew; there were only a handful in the sector, all of which were registered with the Solar Union. Two of them flying in unison almost certainly meant a trade mission…and, if that was the case, the pursuing warships were an ominous development. She sent a command through her implants into the cabin's processors, getting them to display the live feed from the gravimetric sensors. Howard was right. Five ships would not be flying so close together if three of them weren't trying to run the other two down.

"I'm on my way," she said. Assuming the freighters were heading for the base she and her crews had painstakingly established, they'd drop out of FTL within two hours. "Sound yellow alert, then inform the squadron to prepare for combat manoeuvres."

"Aye, Captain," Howard said.

It was probably nothing more than pirates, Hoshiko told herself as she checked her uniform in the mirror before striding out of her office and down towards the bridge. But she couldn't help feeling a thrill of excitement anyway. The pirates wouldn't be expecting to run into *nine* heavy cruisers, not at Martina. There wasn't even a formalised out-system patrol force to fend off pirates who might come calling. Even the ground-based defences weren't as formidable as they could have been.

She stepped through the hatch and walked to her command chair. No one saluted - yellow alert protocols insisted that crewmen had to watch their consoles at all times - but she saw a number of backs stiffen as Ensign Howard practically leapt out of the command chair and snapped to attention. Hoshiko gave him an approving smile, then nodded towards the tactical console.

"I have the bridge," she said, firmly.

"You have the bridge, Captain," Ensign Howard said. "Intruder ETA is now 97 minutes…"

"Assuming they drop out at your predicted endpoint," Hoshiko said, cutting him off. She didn't blame the ensign for assuming the unknown ships were heading for the base, but there was no way to be sure. "Squadron status?"

"Yellow alert," Ensign Howard reported. "Combat datanet is standing by, ready to activate; tactical communications net is up and running. No signals from the planet as yet."

"Unsurprising," Hoshiko said. She took her seat and studied the tactical display for a long moment. "Take your console, Ensign. Let's see what's coming our way."

She heard the hatch opening again behind her, but said nothing as her XO, Commander Griffin Wilde, stepped into view and took the seat next to her. Wilde wasn't a bad man, she had to admit, yet he was easily twice her age - he remembered living on Earth before his parents had emigrated to the Solar Union - and he had almost no imagination at all. Hoshiko had a feeling that Wilde had *actually* been assigned to the squadron to keep an eye on her, or at least try to dampen her more ambitious schemes. But if that were the case, it was hardly necessary. The opportunities she'd hoped would appear, when she'd led the squadron through the gravity point for the first time, had never materialised.

"Captain," Wilde said.

Hoshiko turned and gave him a tight smile. He even *looked* old, with grey hair, although she'd seen his medical report and knew he was physically fit. Choosing not to make himself look like a young man was a statement, just as much as her refusal to alter her looks was a statement, although she didn't understand it. Some men, she'd been told, were just born old, without the mindset that would allow them to have fun. She didn't understand that either.

"Commander," she said. "We may be in for some excitement."

She leaned back in her command chair, watching the reports flowing in from the remainder of the squadron, as the unknown ships came close. Tracking did their best, but apart from estimates regarding the size and power of the warships they weren't able to add much else, certainly nothing solid. Hoshiko rehearsed the engagement in her mind, contemplating the different weapons mixes they might face and waited. At least, now there was a prospect of action, she could wait patiently.

"Captain, they're altering course slightly," Ensign Howard said. "They're now angling directly towards the station."

"Understood," Hoshiko said. She contemplated, briefly, detaching two of her ships to take up a different position, but decided it would probably be futile. A few seconds in FTL would put the incoming ships millions of kilometres from the waiting ships. "Hold position and wait, but prepare to move us when they arrive."

"Aye, Captain," Lieutenant Sandy Browne said. The helmsman had been running tactical simulations of his own. "Drives are ready and free; I say again, drives are ready and free."

Hoshiko nodded, then waited as the last minutes counted down to zero, knowing that there were too many uncertainties. There was no way to *know* the ships were heading for the base, for her squadron; they could easily be planning to skim around the planet's gravity well and try to lose their pursuers. Or they could be planning to plunge into a gravity point at speed, hoping to escape through sheer nerve. They'd be vomiting on the decks, if they survived, but it might be their only hope. Did they even *know* there was a human squadron at Martina?

"Contact," Ensign Howard said. "They just dropped out of FTL. Two freighters, *Livingston*-class; I say again, two freighters, *Livingston*-class."

"Raise them," Hoshiko ordered.

She took a long breath, knowing they had bare seconds before the warships arrived and announced themselves. Thankfully, there shouldn't be any problems establishing communications with human ships... unless, of course, something had wrecked their communications systems. The Tokomak had done their best to ensure that everyone spoke the same language, at least during interspecies communications, but even they had never succeeded in making the handful of artificial languages universal.

And a good thing too, she thought, remembering her lessons at the Academy. *Those languages were carefully designed to dampen individual thought.*

Three red icons popped into life on the display. "Contact," Ensign Howard said, again. This time, he sounded almost panicky. "Three warships, unknown class. Database comparison suggests they're light cruisers."

"Sound Red Alert," Hoshiko ordered. "Raise shields. Charge weapons."

She frowned as more data flowed onto the display. Most alien races used starships based on Tokomak designs, knowing them to be reliable even though they were hard to modify or rebuild. They were, quite simply, the most prevalent ship designs in the galaxy. Even the Solar Union, which was ramping up its own design and building process as fast as it could, still used thousands of Tokomak-designed ships. But facing a whole new design…there was no way to know what she might be about to encounter. If humanity could invent a weapons system that smashed battleships as if they were made of paper, who knew what another race could design and put into operation?

"Unknown ships are scanning us," Ensign Howard reported.

"No word from the freighters," Lieutenant Yeller added. The communications officer was working his console frantically. "The unknown ships are attempting to hail us."

"Put them through," Hoshiko ordered.

There was a long pause, then a dull atonal voice - the product of a translator - echoed through the bridge. "We are in pursuit of criminals," it said. "Allow us to capture the criminals or you will be fired on."

Hoshiko blinked in surprise. The unknown ships had defied communications protocols that had been in existence long before humanity started building anything more complex than stone axes and rowing boats. Every spacer in the known universe used the protocols, save - perhaps - for the race in front of her. Could they be completely new? Her heartbeat raced at the thought, although she knew it was unlikely. The Tokomak had held the sector in their grip for thousands of years. They'd know every power in the sector intimately.

"Those ships are human ships," she said. She had strict orders to defend human shipping, if nothing else. Besides, she had no idea just what was going on. "Allow us to take them into custody and investigate. If they are criminals, they will be dealt with."

"Enemy ships are charging weapons," Lieutenant-Commander Rupert Biscoe snapped. "They're locking targeting sensors on our hulls."

"Return the favour," Hoshiko ordered. *No one*, unless they had almost no understanding of the ships they controlled, *allowed* anyone to see their weapons being charged unless it was a deliberate threat. Just what was going on? "Try and raise the freighters again…"

"Incoming message," the communications officer said.

"This matter is none of your concern," the atonal voice said. "Stand down or be fired upon."

Hoshiko took a long breath. "We will take the ships into custody and investigate the crews," she said, tartly. "Should they be confirmed as criminals, they will be returned to you. We..."

Jackie Fisher rocked, violently.

"Enemy ships have opened fire," Biscoe said. "Standard directed-energy weapons. Shields held. No damage"

A warning shot, Hoshiko thought. She fought down the urge to simply return fire, even though she was sure she held a considerable advantage. *Are they mad?*

"Picking up a message from the lead freighter," Yeller reported. "It's very weak."

"Put it through," Hoshiko ordered.

"This is Captain Ryman of SUS *Speaker to Seafood*," a voice said. Hoshiko hastily launched a query into the datanet, trying to confirm Ryman's identity. Moments later, a voiceprint match popped up in front of her. "We have a cargo of refugees from Amstar. We need help..."

"Enemy ships are locking weapons on the freighters," Biscoe reported.

"Move us forward to shield them," Hoshiko ordered. Refugees from Amstar? Her implants told her it was a star system thirty light years from Martina, but there was little else current in the datafiles. Like Martina, Amstar was a shared world, peaceful and boring. Why would refugees be fleeing to Martina, on human ships? "Tactical..."

"Enemy ships are opening fire," Biscoe reported. "Freighter Two is taking heavy damage."

"Open fire," Hoshiko snapped. Human-designed freighters carried better shields than the average Tokomak-designed freighter, but they weren't strong enough to stand up to a full barrage from the light cruisers for long. "I say again, all ships open fire."

She expected the enemy vessels to turn and run, but instead they accelerated *towards* the human ships, one of them firing a final spread of missiles in passing at Freighter Two and blowing her into an expanding cloud of plasma. It didn't *look* as though anyone had managed to get to the escape pods, Hoshiko noted; the ship had been lost with all hands. She swore under her breath as one of the alien ships exploded, followed rapidly by another; the third kept on towards *Jackie Fisher*, firing every weapon she had, until her shields were finally overloaded and a handful of missiles slammed into her hull, disabling her drives.

"Prepare a marine boarding party," Hoshiko ordered. If the third ship had lost power completely, they should be able to teleport an assault force over to the enemy ship rather than dispatch a shuttle. "Get them suited up and…"

The third icon vanished from the display. "Enemy ship destroyed," Biscoe reported. "That wasn't our fire, Captain. They self-destructed."

"Belay that order," Hoshiko said. Judging from the blast, it was unlikely there would be anything worth recovering. The enemy ship had been completely atomised. "Ready a marine party to examine the freighter instead."

She sucked in her breath, thinking hard. Who the hell were they facing? The Horde might have launched a suicide attack, but the Horde rarely dared face anyone who actually knew how to use their ships. God knew the Horde had been so criminally ignorant that a bunch of humans, from a low-tech world, had taken their ship out from under them. Anyone else…surely, they would have assessed the balance of power and backed off. If the freighters *had* been carrying criminals, she would have had no choice but to hand them over.

"Order the freighter to be ready to receive boarders," she said, grimly. At least she wasn't bored any longer. "All ships are to remain on yellow alert until we get some answers."

She glanced at Commander Wilde. "Accompany the marines," she ordered. "I want to speak to Captain Ryman as soon as he's cleared to board *Fisher*."

"Aye, Captain," Wilde said. He rose. "Ensign Howard, with me."

Hoshiko felt a flicker of envy, which she rapidly suppressed. *She* was the Captain-Commodore of the squadron, as well as *Jackie Fisher's* CO.

There was no way she could leave the bridge, not when they might be at war. All she could do was wait and see what her crew found…

…And pray, silently, that she wouldn't wind up wishing she was bored again.

TWO

Washington saw a second night of heavy fighting between soldiers of the Tenth Mountain Division and civilian militias as martial law, in place since the coup, was extended for a further sixth months. Morale in the military is believed to be poor and rumours of mass desertions cannot be ruled out.

-Solar News Network, Year 54

"Gently does it, Ensign," Major Bjørn Hyldkrog said. "We don't know what might be waiting for us."

Ensign Thomas Howard nodded, fighting to keep his hands from shaking. The marines had never said anything threatening to him, but he couldn't help finding them far more intimidating than anything else he'd encountered. Four years at the Academy hadn't prepared him for rough men and women who practically carried knives in their mouths or strode around the ship as though they owned the vessel. He was sure it was *technically* against regulations for the marines to pick on him - and they hadn't - but they still scared him more than he cared to admit.

He watched through the shuttle's hull-mounted sensors as he carefully guided the craft towards the freighter. The hulk had clearly taken a beating, he noted; carbon scoring criss-crossed the metal, burning off the paint and sensor blisters alike. Someone had done some intensive patching, probably while the vessel was in FTL. Humanity built good ships, he'd been told, but it was a minor miracle the freighter had survived long enough to reach Martina and find help. Judging by the emissions from the rear of the ship, she'd be unable to go FTL without a complete refit. It might be cheaper to scrap the hulk and buy a new ship.

"There's a standard hatch towards the prow of the vessel," he said. *That* wasn't a surprise. The Tokomak had insisted on a degree of uniformity among interstellar shipping and what the Tokomak wanted, they got. Even humanity had seen the advantages in copying the Galactic model. "Do you want to dock there?"

"Yes, please," Hyldkrog said. He seemed to be in command of the mission, even though the XO himself was accompanying the marines. "Put us up against the hatch, then latch on."

"Maintain standard security procedures at all times," the XO added. "We do not want someone slipping a piece of malware onto the shuttle."

"Yes, sir," Thomas said. The XO was old enough to have served in the wet navy, long before the Solar Union had been anything more than a dream. "The shuttle computer cores are isolated from the hatch processors."

He sucked in a breath as the freighter came closer, wondering if the next second would be his last. If it was a trap, if the freighter was playing possum for some inexplicable reason of its own, they'd be fired on the moment they came within point-blank range. Or the vessel might be crewed by pirates, intent on swarming the shuttle and using her to force their way onboard *Jackie Fisher*. A shiver ran down his back as he looked at the marines, carefully checking their weapons and suits of armour; for once, he was grateful to have them along. They'd know what to do if it really was a trap.

"Docking in ten seconds," he said. "Hatch cycling now..."

A dull thump ran through the shuttle as it made contact with the freighter. The gravity field flickered, just for a second, as it merged with the human-standard gravity field projected by the freighter, a subtle confirmation that the ship was probably still in human hands. Unless, of course, the Horde or another race of low-tech interstellar barbarians had somehow managed to gain control of the ship. They probably wouldn't dare to fiddle with the artificial gravity, even assuming they'd known *how*. One mistake at the worst possible time and they'd be smashed against the deck, if the compensators failed. They wouldn't even have a chance to realise what had happened before it was far too late.

"Contact," he said. He heard the marines moving forward as the hatch began to open. "Sir…"

"Remain behind until the marines have secured the ship," the XO ordered, calmly. "They know what they're doing."

Thomas nodded, then gagged as a foul stench blew through the hatch and into the shuttle. He hastily clicked the air fresheners to full, then triggered his implants and ordered them to dim his sensitivity to the smell. What had *happened* on the freighter? It smelled worse than the dorms at the academy! He'd been told, by some of the newcomers from Earth, that the planet smelled bad, but surely it wasn't as vile as the freighter? How could the human race have survived?

"They've overloaded their life support, sir," Senior Chief Brian Siskin said. He'd somehow wrangled his way onto the mission, even though Thomas wasn't sure why the Senior Chief was considered necessary. Maybe his job was to keep an eye on the young ensign. "That's the smell of too many bodies in close proximity."

"Reminds me of Haiti," the XO said. He didn't sound pleased. "Have the shuttle cleaned *thoroughly* once we return to the ship."

"Yes, sir," the Senior Chief said.

Thomas kept one eye on the live feed as the marines moved through the freighter, securing the bridge, life support system and engineering compartment with practiced efficiency. There didn't seem to be any resistance, merely a string of remarks about helpless people. The XO rose as soon as the ship was secured and motioned for Thomas and the Senior Chief to follow him through the hatch. Thomas checked the pistol on his belt - he'd spent *hours* on the range, as per regulations, but he was no expert marksman - and locked the shuttle's controls before rising. If the freighter *was* a threat, the crew would be unable to turn the shuttle against her mothership.

"Remember to set your implants to record," the Senior Chief muttered, as they stepped through the hatch. "You might find yourself giving evidence later."

"Yes, Chief," Thomas said. "A full-spectrum recording?"

"Yes," the Senior Chief said. "You never know what might be important."

He cocked his head as he sent the commands to his implants, even though it bothered him on a very primal level. What was in his head should *stay* in his head. The cadets at the Academy had suspected that their superiors could access their implants at will, even though hacking a person's implants was a guaranteed death sentence once the perpetrator was caught. He'd certainly been told there were times he'd have to share his recordings, no matter what rights he thought he had. Joining the military meant giving up a few rights to protect everyone else's rights.

Warning icons flashed up in front of his eyes, informing him that the atmosphere in the freighter was barely breathable for unenhanced humans and compatible races. The Senior Chief had been right, Thomas realised; the freighter's life support had been pushed right to the limits. Judging by the number of contaminants in the air, it might well have gone *over* the limits. It was a frightening thought - Thomas knew just how much over-engineering was worked into life support systems - but for the moment it posed no threat. His augmentations would be more than capable of ensuring his survival.

He sucked in his breath as they passed through a solid metal airlock and into a long corridor leading towards the bridge. It was crammed with people; men, women and children, all staring at the three Solarians with terrified eyes. Thomas wasn't sure where to look; his gaze moved from refugee to refugee, even though he wanted to look away from them. There was a mother, sitting against the bulkhead, rocking her child against her breast; there was a young girl and boy, holding hands as they stared at the newcomers, terror clearly visible on their pale faces. The XO looked neither left nor right as he made his way through the mob of desperate people; the Senior Chief showed no visible reaction, but his stiff back suggested he was just as horrified as Thomas himself.

"Contact the ship," the XO ordered, as soon as they passed through a second airlock. "Tell them we need additional life support and ration packs, now."

"Aye, sir," Thomas said, relieved to have *something* to do. "Do you want them teleported over?"

"Teleport them onto the shuttle," the XO said, after a moment. "We don't know if there's any clear space on this damned freighter."

Thomas hastily keyed his wristcom, forwarding the XO's commands, as the next hatch opened. The XO led the way through another hatch and onto the bridge. Thomas looked around with interest, taking in the number of jury-rigged modifications to the original design. He'd been taught the basics of Galactic technology, back at the Academy, but he'd never seen *any* ship that had been so obviously modified by her owners. A handful of sleeping rolls lay against one bulkhead, as if the crew had been confined to their own bridge. If the remainder of the ship was crammed with refugees, Thomas told himself, they might well have been.

"Mr. XO," Hyldkrog said. "Allow me to present Captain Ryman of the *Speaker to Seafood*."

Thomas stepped back as Captain Ryman nodded tiredly to the XO. He was a tall man, clearly a second-gen Solarian judging from the way he held himself, but he looked almost unbearably tired. It was evident, from the way his eyes were darting left and right, that he was running on coffee, energy pills and implant stimulation. There was a reason, Thomas recalled, why abusing energy pills and implants was against regulations, certainly on active duty. After a few days without sleep, Captain Ryman had probably started having hallucinations. He was lucky that his heart hadn't given out, despite all his augmentation.

"Captain Ryman," the XO said. "I'm Commander Wilde, XO of *Jackie Fisher*."

"Pleased to meet you," Captain Ryman said. His voice sounded slurred. "They killed Kenny, didn't they?"

The XO frowned. "Kenny?"

"Captain Kenny Rogers," Captain Ryman said. He yawned, suddenly. "My partner. Commander of *Speaker to Morons*."

"I'm afraid they did," the XO said. "There are no survivors from the other freighter."

He cleared his throat. "With your permission, Captain, we will bring a team of medics over to your ship to assist your crew and passengers," he added. "And we can teleport you back to our sickbay for examination. We can even start on basic repairs."

"Too much to do," Captain Ryman said. "I..."

He stumbled, then toppled forward. The XO caught him before he hit the deck; a pair of marines hurried forward, pressed a sensor against Captain Ryman's neck and then lowered him to a blanket on the ground. His crew, Thomas noted, didn't look in any better shape; a teenage boy had fallen asleep at his console, a pair of middle-aged men were eying the newcomers warily and a young girl, barely entering her teens, was cowering back against the rear of the compartment, her eyes wide with terror.

"Give them all a sedative, then take control of the vessel," the XO ordered. He turned to look at Thomas. "Update on our support?"

Thomas hastily checked his implants. "The engineers are beaming over now, sir," he said, "along with additional marines. There's a pair of medics waiting to be teleported."

"I can work on the life support, sir," the Senior Chief offered. "We really need to get some of the refugees off the ship, though. There are just too many of them to be transported safely."

"See to it," the XO said. He looked at one of the middle-aged men. "Can you give us the control codes for your processors?"

The man looked doubtful - Thomas knew it was rare for a starship crew to *willingly* hand over their control codes to outsiders - but cocked his head, sending commands to the bridge's processors. A moment later, a new icon popped up in front of Thomas, informing him that the local computer network had just unlocked itself. The XO thanked the man, then nodded to the marines, who administered the sedatives. Thomas suspected, as he helped to prep the crew for teleport, that they were grateful they finally had a chance to *sleep*.

"That girl may have been molested in some way," one of the marines commented. "I'd advise keeping her sedated until we speak to her parents."

"Understood," the XO said. He glanced at Thomas. "See if you can download the ship's logs."

"Aye, sir," Thomas said.

He sat down at the nearest console and keyed commands into the system. It was an odd combination of human and alien technology, as if the freighter crew hadn't been able to obtain a number of subsystems from Earth. Given how far they were from the Solar Union, they'd probably been forced to jury-rig a great deal more than just the control consoles. He would have been impressed, if the system hadn't been so clunky. Half the files spat out by the damaged system had nothing whatsoever to do with either operating a starship or whatever had forced Ryman and his crew to run for their lives, carrying thousands of refugees and chased by three warships.

"We just completed the headcount, Commander," one of the marines said. "There were six *thousand* refugees, mainly human, crammed into the hulk. At least nineteen died in transit, sir, and thirty died when a shield generator exploded. I honestly don't know how they survived as long as they did."

"We'll have to ship them over to the base or down to the planet as quickly as possible," the XO said, slowly. "Inform Captain Stuart that we may need to request support from the local authorities."

Thomas shook his head in horrified disbelief. *Speaker to Seafood* was seven hundred metres long, one of the largest ships that could land on a planetary surface, but cramming six thousand humans into the hull would have been damn near impossible. They'd have to be crammed into the ship like sardines in a can. What the hell had they been running from, he asked himself as he drove further into the computer network, that impelled them to take the risk? Losing only nineteen passengers to suffocation - or whatever - had been amazingly lucky.

A new file popped up in front of him. "I think I've found something, sir," he said. "It's not the logbook, but it *is* a personal diary."

"Skim the last few entries and summarise them," the XO ordered. "Can you tell who wrote it?"

"I'm not sure," Thomas confessed, after a few moments. "It reads like it was written by a young person, but there's no way to be certain."

"Never mind, for the moment," the XO said. "What does it say?"

The girl wrote it, Thomas thought, as he brought up the last few entries and skimmed them as quickly as he could. He couldn't help feeling as though he was intruding on her privacy - she talked about video stars she liked as well as her feelings for someone who remained nameless - but there was no choice. *Why doesn't she say anything useful?*

He paused as he read the last entry, dated three weeks ago. "She talks about the ship landing on Amstar," he said, slowly. "There's a long section in which she complains about being confined to the ship, about being told she can't even cross the landing pad to visit her…her friend on the other freighter. The grown-ups are apparently talking about something she's not supposed to know about, then…"

The XO leaned forward. "And then?"

"Nothing," Thomas said. "That's the last entry, sir, but assuming they made all speed from Amstar to Martina they'd have been in transit at least a week. What happened between the last entry and their departure must have been bad."

He glanced back over the prior entries, but saw nothing remarkable. The girl had hoped to be a trader herself, he noted; her parents were teaching her the tricks of the trade, in-between making sure she had a well-rounded education. He couldn't help feeling a stab of envy - he'd grown up on an asteroid himself; he hadn't seen an alien until he'd enrolled at the academy - at the life she'd led, before dismissing the thought. Whatever she'd experienced on Amstar had traumatised her.

"No doubt," the XO said. "Continue searching for files, Ensign. If you find anything useful or informative, let me know. The intelligence staff will want to take a look at them too."

"Yes, sir," Thomas said. He moved away from the personnel files and glimpsed into the engineering records. Years ago, he'd been shown how to interpret the different files and put them together to build up a picture of what the ship had been doing. Now…he frowned as a number of automated statements suddenly fell into place. "Sir?"

"Yes, Ensign?"

"I think the freighter went FTL while she was still in the planet's gravity well," Thomas said, slowly. It was impossible to be sure, but why else would they have expended so much effort compensating for outside gravity fields? And yet, it was generally agreed that *trying* was certain death. "They must have been frantic."

He pulled up the dates and checked them against his internal logs. *Speaker To Seafood* had gone FTL barely a week ago, suggesting she'd been running constantly since then. Given the damage to the drive, Ryman must have feared being unable to go FTL again if he stopped for repairs - assuming, of course, he'd been able to evade his pursuers. His partner hadn't been lucky enough to survive.

"Sir," he said, "what were they running from?"

"Good question," the XO said. "I have no doubt Captain Ryman will be happy to tell us, when he wakes up. Until then…"

He pointed at the console. "Back to work, Ensign."

"Yes, sir," Thomas said.

THREE

In a landmark statement last night, the Houses of Parliament in London declared the adoption of Islamic Law throughout Great Britain and its own dissolution and replacement by a council of clerics. Since then, thousands of refugees have been making their way to Scotland or the Solar Union.

-Solar News Network, Year 54

"There's nothing wrong with Captain Ryman, save for exhaustion and fatigue poisons," Doctor Shari Carr said. "I've given him a booster, for the moment, but he really needs at least a day or two of sleep. Once you've spoken to him, Captain, I want to put him back under."

"Understood," Hoshiko said. She'd had her staff drawing information from the freighter's computers and intelligence from the refugees, but she wanted to hear Captain Ryman personally. "Can I speak to him now?"

"He's awake," Shari said. She ran her hand through her short blonde hair. "Like I said, though, he really needs to go back to sleep. I wouldn't have woken him if I hadn't needed to place his implants in stand-by."

Hoshiko nodded and followed the doctor through the hatch into the private room. Captain Ryman lay on a bed, his arms hooked up to a life support machine. He looked tired, Hoshiko thought, despite the brief period of enforced sleep. She privately resolved to take as little time as possible as she sat down beside his bed, studying him closely. He looked back at her, his eyes very tired.

"I'm Captain Hoshiko Stuart," Hoshiko said. "Commanding officer of this squadron."

"Stuart," Ryman repeated, as he sat upright. "One of *those* Stuarts?"

"I'm afraid so," Hoshiko said, stung. Was there nowhere she could get away from her family's legacy? "I'm afraid I have some questions I need answered."

"I understand the routine," Ryman said. He gave her a tired smile. "But you'd better ask quickly before I fall back into blackness."

"It's a simple question," Hoshiko assured him. "What *happened* on Amstar?"

Ryman laughed, harshly. "That doesn't have a simple answer," he said, after a moment. "Let me see..."

He took a breath, clearly composing his thoughts. "Captain Rogers and I have been partners ever since we bought our own freighters and set off to explore the galaxy," he said. "We had an...*understanding* with both the Deep Space Corporation and the Independent Traders Association; they'd underwrite some of our expenses in exchange for a detailed report on trade prospects within this sector. The ITA, in particular, was very interested in making contact with human settlements, believing they would serve as a way to defeat the trade cartels that dominate a number of sectors. That was two years ago."

"Before the Battle of Earth," Hoshiko commented.

"Barely," Ryman agreed. "We only heard rumours until we got a message packet from home...anyway, by that time, we had managed to make a few contacts with human settlements, including a number of communities on Amstar. They were quite friendly to us, Captain; my crew enjoyed their times there. It's one of those worlds where hundreds of different races rub shoulders frequently. It was a good place to gather intelligence as well as pick up trade tips and make new contacts.

"But we couldn't stay on Amstar, so we more or less made it our home base as we wandered the sector, buying and selling trade goods of all descriptions. Most of the cartels collapsed when the Tokomak withdrew... life was good for independent freighters, particularly as the cartels had forgotten how to turn a profit. We were actually taking on apprentices from Amstar, all human, and thinking about investing in more ships. I was looking forward to the future when we landed on Amstar once again, three weeks ago. But things were already changing."

He shuddered and lay back on the bed. "Amstar is - was - ruled by a cooperative council, set up by the Tokomak when they colonised the world," he explained. "Every race with more than ten thousand sentient inhabitants was allowed a seat on the council, including human settlers. It worked fairly well as no one wanted the Tokomak to take direct control of the planet or turn authority over to one of the races that serve as their bully-boys. Most races did what they wanted as long as other races weren't involved. But a week after we arrived, the Druavroks launched a coup."

Hoshiko took a moment to consult her implants. The Druavroks were listed as one of the bully-boy races, like the Varner; a race that served as enforcers for the Tokomak and, in exchange, were allowed to lord it over everyone else in their sector. There wasn't much else in the files, save for the observation that the Druavroks were a lizard-like race that laid eggs and had a major population problem. She would have been surprised if anyone on Earth had given any thought to the Druavroks. They were six months away, after all.

"They snatched control of the orbital defences, then took the council building and declared themselves the sole rulers of Amstar," Ryman continued. "That alone wouldn't have been so bad, but they insisted that everyone else had to ritually submit to their rule or face the consequences. The submitted have no rights, Captain; the Druavroks think nothing of *eating* their slaves or butchering them for fun. A number of other races flatly refused to submit; the Druavroks bombed isolated settlements from orbit, then sent in ground troops to cleanse the cities. They're bent on committing genocide on a colossal scale."

Hoshiko sucked in her breath. "And what happened to you?"

"We were down on the planet when they took over," Ryman said. "They told us - Kenny and I - that we had to submit or face the consequences. I submitted, while making contact with some of our friends. We smuggled over ten thousand refugees into the spaceport, loaded them onto the ships and took off. They opened fire on us once we were in the air, so we went FTL as soon as we could. The drive was badly damaged, but we made it out. We'd heard there was a human presence at Martina…I decided to gamble and run for help. And when we dropped out of FTL…"

His voice trailed off. "I understand," Hoshiko said. "You encountered us."

"The sensors were so badly battered I didn't realise just how closely they were following us," Ryman confessed. "I didn't mean to lead them right to you."

"We survived," Hoshiko said. "What are they *doing* on Amstar?"

"They're killing everyone who refuses to submit," Ryman said. "Perhaps they would have dealt with us earlier, but they were rather occupied. It's like bloody Paris in some of the giant megacities, Captain. Everyone is fighting like mad bastards because they *know* they're all going to be killed. I heard of children being gassed, men and women being firebombed…the only thing keeping them from destroying the cities from orbit is the presence of their own settlements. But I don't see how the defenders can hold out for long. They didn't have many weapons when the Tokomak withdrew and hardly any time to build up an arsenal since. No one expected a coup."

He shuddered. "They have some people fighting on their side," he added. "One of them…one of them hurt my daughter. I could do *nothing* to help her."

Hoshiko forced herself to remain calm. "How did you get so many people here safely?"

"Everything we could think of," Ryman said. "Used sedative gas to keep them quiet and content, recycled damn near everything we could to feed ourselves…built makeshift air scrubbers out of spare parts and jury-rigged everything else we could. How many did we lose?"

"Nineteen on the trip," Hoshiko said. She decided not to mention the refugees who'd been killed when the freighter was attacked. "We're having the refugees shipped down to the planet now."

"The Druavroks will come after them," Ryman said. "I don't think this is a localised uprising, Captain. They didn't have sole control of the Amstar Defence Force before the coup. Those ships might have come from their homeworld itself."

"And with the Tokomak gone, they might be thinking of a little empire-building of their own," Hoshiko said. It was a chilling thought. She had a duty to preserve human lives and now human lives were under threat. "Taking Amstar and its gravity points will give them a stranglehold on economic development throughout parts of the sector."

"Taking Martina will do the same," Ryman pointed out. "But I think they're more interested in genocide, Captain. Those bastards slaving for them are likely to be the last to be eaten, but they *will* be eaten."

"That is probably true," Hoshiko said. Where did her responsibilities lie? She had a duty to preserve human life...and humans were under threat. And, if other races were *also* under threat, there was an opportunity in the midst of tragedy. She had orders to find new allies for humanity, if she could. "Thank you for your time, Captain."

"My ship," Ryman said. "What will happen to her?"

"She really requires a full-scale refit," Hoshiko said. The bean-counters would probably insist on Ryman buying a new freighter and scrapping the old one, even though she'd managed to get her master and commander out of a lethal hole. "My engineering crews have secured her, for the moment, but it would take months to repair her."

"I'm not giving her up," Ryman insisted, firmly. "She's come a long way."

"A very long way," Hoshiko agreed. She understood the overwhelming impulse to protect one's ship, even though cold logic insisted that repairing the older ship was pointless. "She will be turned back to you, after you recover. After that...what you do is your own choice."

Ryman nodded and yawned, loudly. Shari hurried over to him, inspected the life support machine, then jerked her head towards the hatch. Hoshiko understood; she rose, nodded goodbye to the older man, then turned and walked out of the compartment as Shari put Ryman back to sleep. He'd have at least two days of uninterrupted sleep before she woke him. After that…

He can stay with us or go back to Sol, she thought, as she waited for the doctor. *I can arrange for free passage back to the Solar Union, if necessary. He won't owe us for that.*

She closed her eyes and accessed her implants, sending copies of her recordings to her senior staff. They'd have a chance to review them before she called a staff meeting to decide what, if anything, they should do about the crisis. There would probably be a long argument, Hoshiko knew, but she had no intention of allowing anyone to dissuade her from following her first impulse. She had a duty to protect humans and humans were at risk. Taking her squadron to Amstar was the only logical response.

"Captain," Shari said, as she emerged from the compartment. "Captain Ryman will remain asleep for at least three days. It should be long enough to purge his body and refresh his mind."

"Good," Hoshiko said. "And the rest of his crew?"

"The daughter was raped," Shari said, flatly. "Thankfully, she had a contraceptive implant so there was no danger of an unplanned pregnancy. Physically, she's fine; mentally, she's a little shaken up. I've left her sedated, for the moment, but she will probably require a considerable amount of help before she's fit to re-enter society. It isn't just the rape, Captain; it's the sudden awareness that her father was unable to protect her, that she could be just…used…that she could lose all control of her body."

Hoshiko shuddered. Violent rape was rare in the Solar Union. Between genetic enhancements, augmented strength, implant recordings and lie detectors, a woman had an excellent chance of fighting off a man, summoning help or - if nothing else - ensuring a conviction afterwards. Besides, anyone who felt the impulse to get his or her kicks through violent sex games could find a willing partner on the datanet or simply lose himself in VR simulations. But rape was prevalent on Earth, all the more so as society broke down and law enforcement agencies stopped functioning. She'd heard enough horror stories to know that it wasn't safe to go into a city on Earth without powered combat armour and a marine guard.

"Take care of her," she said, firmly. "Can we track down the rapist?"

"Probably not," Shari admitted. "She cleaned herself thoroughly, Captain, probably more than once. That's not uncommon among rape victims, but it destroyed the evidence. The only DNA I found on her was her own. She may be able to identify the bastard, if she sees him again..."

"We can try," Hoshiko said. "And the others?"

"Mainly tired, although the younger ones managed to get some sleep on the flight," Shari said. "I think they would have been in real trouble if the flight had lasted much longer, Captain - there's a limit to how far genetic enhancement goes - but thankfully we caught them in time. I've had them all sedated, for the moment; I imagine they'll be glad of the rest."

"No doubt," Hoshiko said. They *were* citizens of the Solar Union, after all. Protecting them was her job. "And the refugees?"

Shari's face darkened. "I haven't seen them personally, Captain, but I've been following the reports from the medics. These people have been through *hell*. They were half-starved before they were loaded onto the freighter and the food processors simply couldn't keep up with the demand for food. I haven't seen so many cases of bad nutrition and genetic problems since I was working on one of the intake asteroids, just after I qualified as a doctor and we were getting yet another flood of refugees from Earth. I'd be surprised if some of the children don't wind up dead within the next couple of weeks anyway, no matter what we do."

Hoshiko winced. "Is there nothing we can do for them?"

"I've put the worst cases in stasis, but I've already run out of stasis pods," Shari said. "They really need extensive nanotech-treatment,

Captain. I can work on them one by one, once we have the rest of the refugees under control…"

She shook her head. "They really need better facilities," she admitted. "We're not set up to handle so many casualties. Ideally, we need to keep them in stasis until we get them back to Earth or a fleet base. The facilities on Martina may not be sufficient for the task."

"Thanks to the Tokomak," Hoshiko said, sourly. *Humanity* had been able to unlock the full potential of nanotechnology, but the Tokomak had made damn sure that the nanites they supplied to their client races were deliberately limited. Having made themselves effectively immortal, they'd been determined to make sure that no one else lived so long. "Can we adapt a local autodoc?"

"Probably not," Shari said. "The Tokomak made certain the base codes couldn't be altered without special access permissions. Trying would merely render the autodoc useless."

"And we don't have a full-fledged AI on the squadron," Hoshiko muttered. It was the one concession to the Tokomak fear of artificial intelligence, although humanity's homemade AIs hadn't become monsters. The Tokomak must have had a bad experience with AI somewhere back in the mists of time. "Cracking the base codes would be beyond us without one."

"Yes," Shari said. "Those limitations are hardwired into the base codes."

The Tokomak might have had a point, Hoshiko conceded, privately. Immortality had turned the Tokomak into a stagnant race, unable to advance because of the growing population of oldsters who kept a firm lock on the levers of political power. Her grandfather, Steve Stuart, had departed the Solar Union because he feared what would happen if he remained as President indefinitely, but there were others who were growing older and older…and not dying to allow the younger officers a chance to claim the highest positions. Great-Uncle Mongo was *still* fleet commander despite being in his second century…

But we're expanding, she told herself, firmly. *There will be room for all of us for thousands of years to come.*

Great, her own thoughts answered her. *I'm sure the Tokomak thought the same when they cursed themselves with near-immortality.*

It was a chilling thought. The Tokomak Navy was the finest in the universe...when it came to parades, formation flying and stately advances towards its few targets. It hadn't been prepared for anything outside its understanding of warfare, let alone how a determined and innovative race could actually produce newer and better weapons. Could the Solar Navy end up that way, one day? Humanity had had long periods of stagnation on Earth, after all...

She pushed the thought aside, angrily. "Do what you can for them," she ordered. By now, her officers would have reviewed the recordings she'd made. "Have a report on their condition uploaded to the datanet by 1700."

"Aye, Captain," Shari said. She cleared her throat as Hoshiko turned to go. "Do you expect the locals to play host indefinitely?"

Hoshiko sighed. The human settlements on Martina had agreed to allow the refugees to land, thankfully, but they'd insisted on being paid in advance. Hoshiko had paid out of her emergency expenditure fund, yet she knew it wouldn't last indefinitely. Galactic currency was no longer worth what it had been, two years ago, and human currency was barely recognised outside Sol. It was just another reason to be confident that life in space was far superior to life on a planet.

"I don't know," she admitted. "We may have to arrange transport to Sol. Or see if they can find homes here. But as long as they're safe, for the moment, that's all that matters."

"Yes, Captain," Shari said.

FOUR

Heavy fighting broke out on Intake Asteroid Five between two separate groups of refugees with Earther grudges. Solar Marines moved in, separated the combatants and deported them back to Earth. Their families seemed relieved to be rid of them.
-Solar News Network, Year 54

If he were forced to be honest, Commander Griffin Wilde would have had to admit that he cordially disliked his commanding officer. She was young, the granddaughter of the Solar Union's founder...and given command of a squadron as a punishment - or a reward - for shooting her mouth off in public. Griffin, who had seen too many half-trained officers be promoted for being well-connected or 'diverse' in the United States Navy, didn't like the idea of such dangerous ideas infecting the *Solar* Navy. She wasn't an idiot, he had to admit, but she didn't always think before she acted. It would have been better if she'd been broken of such dangerous habits before she reached flag rank.

But it wasn't *quite* flag rank, Griffin thought, as he stepped into the cabin. Admiral Stuart had given his grand-niece a ship command *as well* as squadron command. Hoshiko should have insisted on a promotion to Commodore, and being assigned the staff she needed to serve as the squadron's commanding officer, instead of trying to split her time between serving as a starship's commanding officer and serving as the squadron commander. Griffin was honestly unsure if Hoshiko, determined to keep command, had insisted on the arrangement or if her great-uncle hadn't been bothered to make a final judgement. The only thing he could say in her favour was that she hadn't expected *him* to serve as captain while only drawing a commander's pay.

"Commander," Hoshiko said. She was seated on a sofa, sipping tea from a cup. "Please, take a seat."

"Thank you, Captain," Griffin said. He sat down facing her and rested his hands in his lap as the steward appeared, carrying a mug of coffee. "The freighter has been completely emptied, for the moment, and we've stripped out the computer cores for analysis."

"Good," Hoshiko said, as Griffin took the coffee from the steward. "Did you decompress the ship?"

"I'd prefer to wait until her crew decides what they want to do with her," Griffin said. "The ship really needs to be scrapped, Captain, but they may have other ideas. *And* there are probably personal possessions onboard that need to be recovered."

"Understood," Hoshiko said. She wasn't overruling him on a whim, at least. "And our crews?"

"Returned to the ship, Captain," Griffin said. He frowned, inwardly. There had been something in the way she'd spoken that worried him. "The freighter is currently abandoned and depowered, save for a single beacon."

Hoshiko nodded, slowly. Griffin studied her, feeling a tangle mixture of impatience and resentment. She wasn't just young, she *looked* young, like so many of her peers. They'd embraced the fantastic potentials of technology while many of the Earth-born had shied away from them. And they saw no limits in the universe around them. But there *were* limits, Griffin knew, and some of those limits were deadly.

A low chime echoed in the room. "It's time," Hoshiko said. "Are you ready?"

Griffin wanted to roll his eyes as the first holographic image popped into view, followed by eight more. Hoshiko had eight captains under her command, rather than the regulation nine; it wasn't the least of the problems facing the squadron that Griffin, a mere commander, had a vote if it came to a council of war. Admiral Stuart should really have kicked his niece upwards, into flag rank, and allowed someone else to take command of *Jackie Fisher*. It would have made the discussions a little less awkward.

"Gentlemen and ladies," Hoshiko said. "Thank you for attending."

There was a brief pause as the holographic images organised themselves. Griffin sighed, inwardly; there was a *reason* most meetings were meant to be face-to-face, rather than via hologram. The captains could be using holographic masks to conceal their true feelings; hell, they could be completely naked and no one would know, as long as they had the common sense to ensure their images wore a mask. Hoshiko might be a child of the Solar Union, but even *she* had good reason to appreciate personal meetings. She must have a motive to insist on holographic communications for *this* meeting.

"I trust you have reviewed the data," Hoshiko continued, after a moment. "The interview with Captain Ryman, the debriefing of the refugees, the intelligence recovered from the freighter's databanks...is there any doubt over what's happening on Amstar?"

Griffin shook his head. The evidence was overwhelming. No one would have expended three warships and an entire freighter, to say nothing of risking a shooting war with the Solar Union, just to set up a trick of some kind. The idea of one alien race trying to exterminate everyone else...humans hadn't found it hard to come up with justifications to commit genocide against their fellow humans, why wouldn't an alien race come up with a reason to slaughter billions of *different* aliens? God knew there were humans who had advocated, in all seriousness, exterminating the Hordes in response to their crimes against humanity.

"I have very little information on these...*Druavroks*," Captain Hamish Macpherson said, curtly. "My datafiles are curiously scanty."

"I have put in a request for more information from Martina," Hoshiko said. "But, from what little we know, it seems they now want an empire of their own, instead of holding up someone else's empire. Taking Amstar makes sense from an economic point of view, but outright genocide..."

Her voice grew very cold. "I intend to take this squadron to Amstar and put a stop to it," she added. "It is our duty."

There was a long pause. Griffin felt his blood run cold. He understood the impulse, he understood how far their standing orders stretched, but it could be a terrible mistake. The Solar Union had no treaty with anyone on Amstar, nor was it directly threatened by the Druavroks. It was hard to escape the feeling that they were about to commit a direct violation of their orders.

He cursed Admiral Stuart under his breath. As a captain, it was his right and duty to argue with his commanding officer, if he believed it necessary, even in front of other captains. But as a commander, he couldn't argue in front of the senior officers. He was supposed to present a united front with his captain, even as he disagreed with his commodore. There wasn't anything in regulations for a semi-permanent arrangement where the captain and the commodore happened to be the same person.

"Captain," Captain Joanne Mathewson said, finally. "Is this actually *wise?*"

"There are times when wisdom will not serve," Hoshiko said. "Our orders say, basically, that we are to protect human settlements throughout the sector - and, in more general terms, throughout the galaxy. Humans are being threatened with extermination by the Druavroks, along with countless members of over twenty other races. It is our duty to respond, to save them from certain death. It's the right thing to do."

And you weren't interested in intervening to prevent the fighting on Earth, Griffin thought, coldly. He didn't actually disagree with Hoshiko's stance - Earth was reaping what it had sown over decades of mismanagement - but she lacked even basic comprehension of how everyone else felt about the affair. *What makes this different?*

"There's another issue," Hoshiko said. "We have orders to find allies, to meet strange new races and make friends."

"And boldly go where lots of people have gone before," Captain Abdul Hassam said, deadpan.

"Yes, but they live here," Macpherson said. "They don't count."

Hoshiko ignored the byplay. "The point is this," she said. "Humanity is not the only race under threat. If we intervene to save members of other races, we may win new allies."

"And start a war with the Druavroks," Griffin pointed out. "Captain, with all due respect, we don't know the slightest thing about what we're getting into."

"We know they're murderous bastards," Hoshiko said. If she was angry at his comment, and she had every reason to be, she hid it well. "They're killing humans, Commander."

"We have no idea how many starships they have," Griffin said. "They *may* - they *may* - back off when they realise the humans in this sector have powerful protectors, but it is far more likely they will see our actions as a declaration of war. We are *six months* from Sol, Captain. There is no hope of receiving reinforcements in less than a year - and that assumes Admiral Stuart sends them when Sol needs protection itself."

"They've already declared war on us," Hoshiko pointed out. "Slaughtering humans cannot be allowed, Commander."

"Perhaps we should ask for orders from Earth," Captain Patrick Faison said. "Our standing orders call for the defence of humans, Commodore, but also to avoid conflict with powerful alien races."

"It will take a *year* to send a message to Earth and receive a reply," Hoshiko said. She sounded angry for the first time. Griffin didn't really blame her. "By then, Amstar will be a graveyard and the bastards will have moved on to a new target - Martina, perhaps. We have to act *now*, while the humans on Amstar still have a chance."

She tapped the table. "Our standing orders are to protect humans, make friends and spread the reputation of the Solar Union," she added.

"Going to Amstar and preventing genocide will accomplish all three. It isn't as if *most* races will go to the wall for another race."

Griffin nodded, conceding the point. The Tokomak had never tried to foster any sort of pan-species unity, perhaps suspecting that - once unified - their subject races would turn on them and demand change. Indeed, there were few races in the galaxy that would cross the road to piss on another race, if he happened to be on fire. They'd be far more likely to view the whole affair as a kind of spectator sport, rather than something that involved *them*. But humanity…if humanity made a stand against genocide, who knew where it would lead?

"It is unlikely the Druavroks have technology to match ours," Hoshiko continued. "They were probably not encouraged to innovate, any more than the Varner were. Their technology is almost certainly second-line Tokomak gear, rather than anything new."

"But they will have a *lot* of it," Griffin pointed out. "Our supply line is a shoestring, Captain, if that. Our supply of missiles is *very* limited and we have no Hammerhead Missiles. We could kill one of their ships with every missile we fire and *still* lose the war."

"I admit there are risks involved, Commander," Hoshiko said, curtly. "There are *always* risks involved. Standing up to the Tokomak was a risk. They had - and still have - hundreds of thousands of starships. But if we allow the prospect of *risk* to blind us, we will have no hope of doing *anything* beyond sitting in orbit until we are attacked again. This is a chance to take a stand against genocide and, by doing so, win friends and influence opinions."

She paused. "The decision is mine," she added. "The squadron will depart Martina in two hours, which should be long enough to prepare the base for independent operations. If any of you want to file an objection, please inform me and it will be noted in my log."

Griffin kept his face impassive with an effort. Technically, he could challenge her, call for a full council of war and a vote, but he knew he might well lose. And losing a challenge would mean court-martial when he returned home, with the verdict a foregone conclusion. No board composed of commanding officers would countenance a challenge with so little evidence against its target.

"I have reservations," Captain Faison said. "But we cannot with honour allow genocide to proceed unhindered."

The hell of it, Griffin knew, was that Faison had a point. Griffin was old enough to recall hundreds of small genocides carried out on Earth, each one watched by outside powers with overwhelming firepower and no will to intervene. By the time something was done - if it was - the genocide was nearly completed and hundreds of thousands of people were dead. And yet, the only problem had been lack of political will. Stopping the Holocaust had required a full-scale war against Nazi Germany and it had been too late to save millions of victims. The Nazis would have ignored a string of protests from the outside world as they completed their grisly task.

But we don't know what we're going to encounter at Amstar, he thought. The Solar Union had stopped a Tokomak fleet dead in its tracks, but who knew how powerful the Druavroks actually were? Hoshiko might be right - they might not have been able to improve upon Tokomak technology - yet there was no way they could take that for granted. *This might be the first shot in a whole new war.*

"Good," Hoshiko said. "Prepare your ships for departure. If your crews have messages they wish to send, have them uploaded to the base before we leave. I'll be sending a standard report to Sol informing them of our discoveries and my intentions."

And they won't be able to tell you to stop, Griffin thought. *The year it would take for any message to reach you would be more than long enough for you to start a war.*

"Dismissed," Hoshiko said.

The holographic images vanished. Griffin wondered, inwardly, just how many of the commanding officers *agreed* they had to intervene, but there was no way to know. Hoshiko was right, after all; regulations insisted that they had to do everything in their power to protect human lives, even humans who weren't Solarians. And besides, it *was* possible they'd make a few friends and allies at Amstar.

"You don't approve," Hoshiko said, flatly.

"No, I don't," Griffin agreed. "Captain, there are too many unpredictable elements here."

"That's always true," Hoshiko said.

"Yes, it is," Griffin said. "The problem here, however, is a matter of practicality. Do we have enough firepower to compel the Druavroks to abandon Amstar? If so, are they going to take the defeat lying down or will they launch a counterattack? And if they do, can we stop it?"

"They're hardly going to dispatch a full-sized fleet to Sol," Hoshiko pointed out. "It would be a blunder on the same level as dispatching a fleet and army to Sicily in the middle of the Peloponnesian War. Their rivals will be delighted."

"If they *have* rivals," Griffin reminded her. "Our intelligence concerning changes in this sector is sadly lacking."

"Then it's high time we learned," Hoshiko said.

Griffin took a breath. "There's another issue, Captain," he warned. "One that you have to consider carefully."

Hoshiko lifted a single eyebrow.

"We have an...emotional revulsion at the thought of genocide," Griffin said. "The idea of committing mass slaughter of helpless innocents is bad enough, but exterminating every last member of a given race, or an ethnic group, is repulsive to us. And that's how it should be.

"But such emotions can also blind us to the *practicalities*," he added, when she said nothing. "We are one squadron of ships, Captain; nine heavy cruisers and a handful of support vessels, facing an alien empire of unknown power. We may be about to bite off more than we can chew. I understand the impulse to stop the genocide, but we also have to be aware of the dangers. The Druavroks may not even be capable of understanding that genocide is wrong. We could wind up going to war to impose our own view of the universe on them."

"One shared by the Tokomak," Hoshiko pointed out. "They banned indiscriminate planetary strikes on pain of death and destruction."

"But clearly not by the Druavroks," Griffin countered. "And the Tokomak are no longer around to enforce the rules."

"I understand the risks," Hoshiko said, after a moment. She sounded almost pensive as she studied the remains of her tea. "But they have to be faced."

She cleared her throat. "I want Captain Ryman and his crew to remain onboard, for the moment," she added. "*Speaker To Seafood* is to be turned over to the base - they can look after her until we return to Martina. It's a five-day flight to Amstar at best possible speed, so Captain Ryman should be able to assist us by the time we arrive."

"Aye, Captain," Griffin said.

"I'll record a message for Fleet Command now," Hoshiko said, as she finished her tea and placed the cup on the table. "If you wish to record a message of your own..."

Griffin shook his head. He did have his doubts, but there was no point in airing them to Fleet Command. By the time they decided what - if anything - to do, the situation would have already moved on. Hoshiko's orders were so vague, at least in part, because there was no way she could call home and ask for clarification. Her great-uncle had given her, quite literally, the power to bind and loose. She could form an alliance with alien powers if she wished without ever overstepping the bounds of her authority.

"That won't be necessary, Captain," he said. He finished his own coffee and rose. "With your permission, I'll see to the freighter and her crew."

"Thank you," Hoshiko said. She gave him a smile. "And thank you for your honest opinions too."

But you're not going to listen to them, Griffin thought. Hoshiko *was* the CO, after all. The buck stopped with her. *I tried.*

He left the cabin and headed down to his office. There was work to do.

FIVE

Heavy fighting spread across Bavaria for the first time in three months, following the effective collapse of the German Government. The Bavarian Government has declared its intentions to preserve a little of Germany and its willingness to accept refugees of Germanic descent only. Non-Germans are warned that they will be shot out of hand if they attempt to cross the border.

-Solar News Network, Year 54

"It's hard to imagine," Max Kratzok commented, "that there are other ships out there."

Hoshiko nodded as she entered the observation blister and stepped up beside him. There was literally nothing to see in FTL; nothing, save for an endless darkness that had been known to drive grown men into panic attacks. It scared Earthers, who expected to see stars streaking past, but the Solarians saw nothing to fear. They grew up surrounded by the endless darkness of interplanetary space, after all. She peered into the darkness for a long moment, then turned to look at him. The reporter was young, his brown hair cut close to his scalp and his features sculpted into a reassuring handsomeness that was too bland to be natural. She couldn't help thinking that he hadn't - yet - learned the value of individuality. But then, putting people at their ease so they would talk to him was part of his job.

"They're wrapped in their own bubbles of compressed space-time," Hoshiko said, as she sat down on the loveseat. Traditionally, couples could use the observation blister for making out - assuming, of course, that they weren't on duty. "They can't see us any more than we can see them, but they're out there."

"FTL sensors can pick them up, I assume," Kratzok said. "There's no risk of an accidental collision?"

"The squadron is spread out," Hoshiko confirmed. "Even if we were flying in formation, Max, the odds of an accidental collision would be very low. It takes deliberate malice to ram one starship into another at FTL speeds."

Kratzok shrugged. "I spoke to John Ryman," he said, as he turned to look at her, leaning against the transparent bulkhead. "The picture he painted wasn't pretty."

"No," Hoshiko agreed. Captain Ryman's son had been in line for a command of his own, before he'd landed on Amstar. Now...he was badly shaken by his sister's rape, their narrow escape and the deaths of his friends. "It wasn't pretty."

"And we're heading to Amstar to intervene," Kratzok added. "Is that a good idea?"

Hoshiko gave him a long look. "On or off the record?"

"Whatever you want," Kratzok said. "I assume you're recording the conversation yourself."

"I am," Hoshiko confirmed.

She smiled, rather tightly. One advantage of implants that few Earthers realised was that *everything* could be recorded. If Kratzok decided to publish a version of their conversation that was at odds with reality, she could upload her own version to the datanet and demand compensation for being misquoted. Her grandfather had loathed reporters - or, at least, he'd loathed their editors - and he'd insisted on writing strong laws prohibiting the kind of bullshit, as he'd put it in his *Commentary*, that had brought the American media establishment to its knees. Not that she'd *need* the recordings, if push came to shove; she could merely object to the quote and force them to prove she'd said what they claimed she'd said. And if they couldn't, she could collect some pretty heavy compensation. Most media outlets in the Solar Union knew better than to take the risk.

"Call it off the record, for the moment," she said, carefully. "I may change my mind later."

Kratzok nodded in understanding. "Do you think we're doing the right thing?"

Hoshiko took a moment to think before answering the question. It galled her, although she would never have admitted it, that she had no idea why Kratzok had requested the assignment to the *Jackie Fisher*. The Solar Union Navy had no problems with embedded reporters, as long as they respected the limits, but *her* squadron had been dispatched so far from Sol that Kratzok's reports wouldn't reach home for months. She had wondered, absently, if he'd managed to get into trouble with his superiors too, yet there had been nothing in his file suggesting that he was anything other than a roving reporter in good standing.

And yet all of his followers will be discomforted by the lack of updates, she thought. Like most roving reporters, Kratzok had a private following of hundreds of thousands of people who read his reports. They wouldn't be his exclusive fans, of course, and he had to work hard to keep their interest. *He may lose them all before he gets home to start putting out new copy.*

"I think we don't have a choice," she said. She'd spoken briefly to the crew, once they'd departed Martina, giving the same rationale she'd given her captains. Their standing orders called for them to protect humans and win allies and intervening in an ongoing genocide would serve as a way to do both. "*Someone* has to do something."

Kratzok met her eyes. "Why us?"

"We're the ones on the spot," Hoshiko said, simply.

She smiled to herself as she remembered one of her few meetings with her legendary grandfather, when he'd slipped back into the Sol System as a private trader. He'd been full of stories about men who'd passed the buck further and further up the chain of command instead of taking action for themselves, which ensured that the situation constantly worsened and that the superiors *themselves* had to demand orders from *their* superiors. Hoshiko had no idea why *anyone* would fight in a shit-tip like Afghanistan when the solar system was ready for the taking, but the principle was the same. Nipping a problem in the bud tended to be cheaper, in the long run, than allowing it to fester.

But then, her grandfather had been used to a world where he could call Washington and expect an answer within minutes. *She* lived in a universe where it could take hours to get a signal from one end of the solar system to the other, days to get a courier boat from Sol to the nearest inhabited star…and six months for a one-way trip from Sol to Martina. The vast authority she'd been given - she'd gone over her orders very carefully when she'd first been assigned to *Jackie Fisher* - was *necessary*. It was unlikely that any problem would agree to wait for a year while she sent a request for orders to Sol and waited for a reply.

If, of course, I don't get summarily dismissed for gross incompetence and stupidity, she thought, ruefully. *They wouldn't have sent me out here if they didn't have faith in my ability to use my own judgement.*

"So we are," Kratzok agreed.

Hoshiko shrugged. "There's no one else in the sector I can ask for orders, or even for advice," she said. "I am ambassador-at-large as well as commander of the squadron and this ship. The buck stops with me and I say yes, we have to put a stop to attempted genocide. I hope you'll explain that to the folks back home."

"They may not care about events so far from Sol," Kratzok pointed out. "Earth's collapse is absorbing most of their attention."

"Idiots," Hoshiko muttered.

She shook her head in disbelief. A vast universe just waiting for humanity, enough space for every living human and the Solar Union was worried about affairs on a planet crammed with people too stupid to take advantage of the chance to leave. It wasn't as if emigrating to the Solar Union was difficult, not when there was no shortage of receiving stations scattered around the globe. And if the local governments tried to stop their people from fleeing, the Solar Navy could hand out a beating in an afternoon that would make them think twice. No, the only thing stopping the locals from leaving was their own stupidity.

But then, in the Solar Union, you are expected to work and follow the rules, she reminded herself. *It isn't as if they're hard rules to follow too.*

It was hard, very hard, to believe that Earth was anything other than a cesspit. She'd been told that there were places on Earth where women were little better than slaves, places where great mobs of ill-trained idiots only survived because the government fed them, where criminals pleaded mental disorders and were let free, places where being the wrong colour, or the wrong religion, or the wrong…well, *anything*…could lead to certain death. Hoshiko found it hard to wrap her head around the concept of women being automatically inferior, let alone any of the other issues. Surely, such a world would have collapsed into anarchy a long time ago. Her teachers *had* to have been exaggerating…

…And yet, if they weren't, why weren't far *more* people fleeing into space?

"Many of them have ties to Earth," Kratzok pointed out. "And even if they didn't, Earth represents a pool of untapped manpower."

"Which could move to the Solar Union at any point," Hoshiko noted. Her grandfather had talked about self-selection, about how the best immigrants were the ones who were prepared to move and put in the hard work to earn money and blend in. "And problems on Earth don't concern us."

Kratzok gave her a droll look. "And problems on Amstar *do*?"

"*Touché*," Hoshiko conceded. "The difference, though, is that humans are not trying to slaughter other humans, but being slaughtered themselves by another race. We are the protectors of humanity against outside threats."

"And internal threats can go hang?"

"If an alien force attacked Earth for the third time, I would die in its defence," Hoshiko said, dryly. She *had* been at the Battle of Earth, after all. "But there's a limit to how much we can do to save Earth from itself."

She looked past him, out into the darkness. "We made a very deliberate decision to cut our ties with the past," she added, slowly. "To step *away* from Earth and its corrupt and inefficient governments, its hang-ups about proper behaviour and the right way to live. I see no point in looking back. If they want to wallow in squalor, let them."

"Some people would say that was cruel," Kratzok noted.

"And what," Hoshiko asked, "would they have us do?

"We offer to take anyone who's willing to work; hell, we even make sure that local governments can't keep people from leaving. It isn't as if the Earthers don't have access to the datanet. Beyond that, what are we supposed to do? Send in the troops, crush the local governments and rule the planet ourselves? We'd have to create a police state infinitively nastier than anything that ever existed in human history just to root out the irredeemable bastards and condemn them to permanent imprisonment. And what would creating such a state do to *us*?"

Hoshiko shuddered at the thought. Her grandfather had been a great man, but his *Commentary* had talked, with a certain amount of fear, of the prospects for abusing Galactic Tech. It was possible to strip privacy away completely, to monitor an entire population 24/7....and, with AIs to do the monitoring, escape would be completely impossible. Hoshiko had grown up without many of the taboos that were taken for granted on Earth, but even *she* disliked the thought of being under constant observation. And who knew what having so much access would do to the watchers?

Maybe that's why so many religious people become fanatics, she thought, grimly. *They believe that they are being watched every hour of every day from birth until death.*

And constant inescapable surveillance was only scratching the surface. *She* had no fear of having implants installed in her brain, yet a redesigned implant would be enough to steal her independence and turn her into a drone. A *Borg*. Even the *worst* of criminals weren't fitted with control implants, no matter what they'd done. Stealing someone's independence of mind was a taboo so strong that the merest hint of it was enough to start a full police investigation. And if someone was discovered to be hacking implants or controlling unwilling victims, the Solar Union would never be satisfied with mere death. Their revulsion would be so strong that the usual prohibitions against cruel and unusual punishment would be forgotten.

Kratzok cleared his throat. "A debate for another time, perhaps," he said. "What do you intend to do when we reach Amstar?"

"Warn the Druavroks off, if I can," Hoshiko said. "If they won't leave, I'll have to engage them before they can turn their weapons on the planet itself."

"And once you hold the high orbitals?"

"Try to impose a peace on the planet," Hoshiko said. "There are human and alien factions on the surface who will support us, I think. The trick will be preventing them from committing genocide themselves, against the Druavroks. Revenge is a very powerful human motivator."

Kratzok leaned forward. "And then?"

"I don't have any solid long-term plans," Hoshiko admitted. "Our information on the sector is very lacking, Max. If we're lucky, we can put together an alliance of other races and...*convince*...the bad guys to stand down. If not, we may have to make up a new plan on the fly."

"I'd like to go down to the surface, if I can," Kratzok said. "A full set of sensory recordings will be needed, Captain. They'll do better than a thousand pictures at explaining the current situation."

"Assuming the situation is not resolved, one way or the other, before the recordings reach the Solar Union," Hoshiko said. She'd never cared for full sensory recordings herself - it was a little like living through someone else, rather than living her own life - but she understood their value. Everyone who accessed the sensory recordings would be assaulted by *everything* the reporter saw, not just the sights and sounds. It was almost as good as actually being there, she'd been told, but she had her doubts. "There's no way to speed up the signal, I'm afraid."

"No," Kratzok agreed. "There should be some interesting stories to tell, Captain."

Hoshiko looked at him. "Why are you here? I mean...why are you on the squadron?"

"There aren't many true scoops these days," Kratzok said. "The reporter who breaks a piece of news, Captain, is often overshadowed by other roving reporters or armchair analysts who are happy to elaborate on The Meaning Of It All. Getting the sort of fame I want isn't going to happen in the Solar Union. There are just too many competitors."

He sighed. "And then there's the rush to get your recordings and articles online before someone beats you to the punch," he added, "and then you make a tiny little mistake and your career is blown out of the water. Being *here*, Captain, limits the competition's ability to put out their own stories."

"Except you didn't *know* something was going to happen," Hoshiko pointed out.

"I was losing readers," Kratzok said. "A couple of my rivals had lucky scoops, a couple of others..."

His voice trailed away. Hoshiko understood. Being a reporter - or an artist - in the Solar Union meant an endless battle to stay in the public eye. Losing subscribers to his mailing lists, online sites and suchlike indicated that a reporter was slowly sinking into obscurity - and, once the downward slide began, it was very hard to stop. Gambling that *something* would happen he could use to rebuild his career had been his only reasonable option.

She smiled. Being the sole reporter in the Martina Sector would give Kratzok a lock on all articles and recordings, at least until another reporter arrived. And none of his rivals would know there was anything that needed covering for at least six months, giving Kratzok an edge they'd find hard to beat. Kratzok would have ample time to make all the contacts he needed before anyone else arrived.

"You'll have plenty of exclusives here," she said, thinking hard. "I may even be willing to offer you an interview with myself."

Kratzok blinked. "You would?"

Hoshiko smiled at his confusion. She'd declined his first interview request, when he'd first arrived on station, and rarely spoken to him until the refugees had arrived. And ambushing someone to demand an interview, even a serving government officer, was the kind of conduct that could get a reporter slapped with a heavy fine or a restraining order. But now, he could help her as much as she could help him. The Solar Union would find it harder to condemn her if public opinion supported her actions.

Because my orders are a little vague, she thought. *If they feel I overstepped myself, they can find grounds to condemn me.*

"All I ask is that you explain why we're doing what we're doing as well as *what* we're doing," she said. He'd understand the unspoken part of the offer. *You scratch my back and I'll scratch yours*. He'd know what she was asking him to do, but it worked in his favour as well as her own. "The public needs to know the truth."

"Of course, Captain," Kratzok said. He gave her a long considering look. "When can we hold the interview?"

"After we reach Amstar," Hoshiko said. "I have too much work to do to sit down with you before then. But you can watch from the bridge as we enter the system."

"I look forward to it," Kratzok said. He paused. "They'll see us coming, won't they?"

"Yes," Hoshiko said. It wasn't easy to fool gravimetric sensors. The Druavroks would see her squadron as it lanced towards the system. She'd thought about having her warships towed by freighters, but there hadn't been time to organise it. "But we'll do our best to keep them guessing."

SIX

The Swiss Government declared a state of emergency after armed militia bands tried to cross the border into Switzerland from Austria. Martial law has been declared. Members of radical Islamic groups have been rounded up and marked for deportation.
-Solar News Network, Year 54

"This," Thomas muttered, "is incredibly frustrating."

He wasn't sure if the XO had assigned him to the task because he wanted a fresh pair of eyes or he merely wanted to give a young and inexperienced ensign a task that would keep him busy for several days, but either way he hadn't been able to pull anything *useful* out of the datafiles they'd obtained from Martina. Either there *wasn't* much on the Druavroks, which struck him as unlikely, or the local settlers had deliberately decided to withhold information the squadron could actually *use.* Their homeworld was clearly identified, their history as yet another race of bully-boys was discussed, but there was very little else. There was certainly nothing that might suggest why they'd suddenly decided to declare war on the rest of the known universe.

Or maybe it's just the bastards on Amstar, he thought, as he flipped through the remaining files. *The rest of the Druavroks might have no intention of fighting a war.*

He puzzled over the thought for a long moment. The Tokomak had spread millions of settlements of every known race right across the galaxy, mixing hundreds of races together in melting pots that hadn't been anything like as effective as the Solar Union. He'd been told at the Academy that they'd probably hoped to play divide and rule. They'd certainly not bothered to do more than the bare minimum to ensure that everyone got along. Given that some races rubbed others the wrong way, fighting and ethnic cleansing on a galactic scale was perhaps inevitable.

But we took in aliens and invited them to live with us as equals, he added, silently. *The Tokomak had far greater resources. Why couldn't they do the same?*

The Academy had had some pretty sharp things to say about the Tokomak, he recalled. They were the masters of the known universe - had *been* the masters of the known universe - but they'd been sluggish, slow to move and unwilling to recognise that other races moved at a faster pace. Maybe it had been so obvious to them that races should work together that they hadn't realised that other races might disagree. Or, perhaps, they'd *hoped* there would be war as a way to stay on top. They'd certainly played favourites among their subject races.

He sighed and turned his attention to the holographic display showing the local sector, including five hundred settled systems and nineteen homeworlds. The Druavroks came from the far side of the sector, he noted; Amstar was in the rough centre, surrounded by a number of other multiracial worlds. There was surprisingly little data on all of the worlds, save for charts showing gravity points and pre-war trade routes. God alone knew what half of them looked like now. The squadron had collected a great deal of intelligence, but most of it was contradictory. It was impossible to tell what might be waiting for them at Amstar.

The hatch opened. He turned and straightened in his seat as the Senior Chief entered, then rose. Technically, as a commissioned officer, he was Siskin's superior, but only a complete idiot of an ensign would take that for granted. The Senior Chief, like the XO, dated back all the way to the pre-Contact wet navy. He had more practical experience than all of Thomas's graduating class put together.

"Ensign," Siskin said.

"Chief," Thomas said. He hesitated, unsure if he should ask for help or not, then took the plunge. "I can't draw anything else useful from these files."

Siskin gave him a considering look. "You can't get into them or there's nothing *important* in them?"

"There's very little important in them," Thomas said. "I thought the Tokomak had a *fetish* for recording everything."

"They do," Siskin said. "Natural bureaucrats, the lot of them. Everything must be signed and dated in triplicate before they'll get off their butts and do something. But that doesn't mean they'll share everything they know with the peons. Can't have the peons knowing *too* much about how the universe works, can we?"

"No, sir," Thomas said.

"Wrong answer," Siskin said. He smiled, rather dryly. "Maybe you're looking in the wrong place."

"I don't know where to look," Thomas confessed. He rubbed his eyes, tiredly. "I'm not even sure why the XO gave me this job."

"To see what you did with it," Siskin said. "If you needed to know something, Ensign, how would you find it out?"

Thomas frowned. "Look it up online," he said. "The naval database has *lots* of data."

"So it does," Siskin agreed. "And what would you do if the database doesn't include information you need? Like, perhaps, how to slot a missile launcher into a modified casing?"

"Oh," Thomas said, remembering. It had been one of the tests for young officers, back when he'd boarded the ship and he had a feeling he'd failed it, although no one had given him a definite answer. There had been nothing in the files, but when he'd asked the Senior Chief in despair he'd been told that the launcher needed to be adjusted manually when it was halfway into the casing. "I'd ask someone with more experience."

He looked down at the deck for a long moment. "But who on this ship has...oh."

"Oh, indeed," Siskin said. "Why don't you ask Captain Ryman?"

Thomas looked back at the files on his screen. "I thought I was meant to find out what the files said..."

"You were told to learn what you can about the Druavroks," Siskin corrected. "Did the XO specifically *tell* you not to ask Captain Ryman or his crew? They have something no one else on the ship has, Ensign: direct personal contact with our potential enemies. You should ask them before we reach Amstar."

Thomas glanced at the wall-mounted display. They'd spent four days in transit, with three more to go before they arrived at their destination. He'd hoped he'd find something useful in the files, something that would make the XO notice him as more than just another wet behind the ears ensign, but nothing had appeared. Indeed, the ship's intelligence staff had probably already come to the same conclusion.

"I'll ask the doctor if I can speak to Captain Ryman," he said. "Thank you, chief."

"Make sure you don't waste the opportunity," the chief warned. "You won't get a second one, I suspect."

"Yes, sir," Thomas said. He hastily activated his implants, uploading the request to the doctor's office, then looked back at the Senior Chief. "Can I ask a question?"

"You can ask any question you like," the Senior Chief said. "Just remember that such questions are always a learning experience."

Thomas paused, trying to organise his thoughts. "The intelligence staff must have already gone through the files - and interrogated Captain Ryman," he said. A message popped up in front of his eyes, informing him that the doctor had cleared his visit to the freighter captain, provided he was quick. "Why ask me to do it too?"

"I could give you two possible answers," the Senior Chief said. "First, having a number of different eyes on a problem makes it more likely that a solution will be found. The intelligence staff are good at their work, but they're not always good at understanding the real universe. Second, the XO gave you the task to see what you would do with it. Sure, you *could* have spent the next three days trying to get actionable intelligence out of some very thin files…instead, you thought outside the box and found a new angle of approach."

"After you helped me," Thomas said, slowly. He shook his head morosely. "I should have thought of it for myself."

"It isn't a crime to want to ask for help," the Senior Chief said. "And it isn't against regulations to ask for information one of your comrades or subordinates possesses. You never know just how much your comrades know until you ask them."

He shrugged. "But it is a crime to hit a dead end and then continue to pick through the intelligence, rather than admitting that there's nothing to find," he added. "That caused no end of problems with intelligence officers, back in the day."

Thomas looked up at him. "Can I ask a question? I've looked at your file - the sections that were open to me, at least. Why did you never switch to command track? They'd have fast-tracked you through the Academy and made you a lieutenant as soon as you graduated."

Siskin considered it for a moment. "I've been a chief on a dozen vessels," he said, slowly. "I was a chief on the *Enterprise*, the aircraft carrier, long before I joined the Solar Navy and left Earth behind. I grew to enjoy supervising crewmen and mentoring promising young officers, but it wasn't a task I could do properly back when I was younger. Too much political interference. Here…I can do it properly *and* enjoy passing my wisdom on to older officers smart enough to listen."

"I see, I think," Thomas said. "Why would anyone interfere, politically?"

"You're not a senior officer," Siskin said, "but you are someone who could grow into one, someone who could influence the future direction of the navy. People who think about *anything* other than the long-term good of the navy try to influence selections and promotions in the hope of appeasing a political agenda. And the fact you don't understand what I'm talking about shows just how far the Solar Union has come."

"Yes, sir," Thomas said, privately resolving to look it up in the history files. "Are you going to accompany me to see Captain Ryman?"

The Senior Chief gave him a *look*. "Do you need your hand held?"

"No, sir," Thomas said, quickly. "I'll record the meeting for later analysis."

He nodded to Siskin, then headed out of the hatch and down towards sickbay. A note popped up in his implants, ordering him to report to the XO at 1900; he placed a reminder in his calendar and then swore, inwardly, as he realised he'd be going on duty directly after his interview with the XO. Unless the XO had decided to tell him that there had been a terrible mistake and his assignment to *Jackie Fisher* had been revoked. He'd sometimes wondered, when he'd been feeling terribly inadequate, if he truly deserved his rank.

Doctor Carr met him at the hatch, her stern gaze making him feel around ten centimetres tall as he came to a halt and saluted. She wasn't in the line of command, technically, but only a fool would treat the ship's doctor lightly. Thomas wasn't the only ensign who was scared of a woman who could relieve the *captain* of duty, let alone a junior officer on his first deployment. And being relieved would look very bad on his service record.

"Ensign," she said. "Captain Ryman is currently awake and reasonably healthy, but if he gets tired or agitated I want you to stop the interview at once. Do you understand me?"

"Yes, doctor," Thomas said. The next question popped out before he could stop himself. "I thought he would have implants to compensate..."

"He's pushed them to the limit," the doctor said, cutting him off. "Implants can give your system a boost, ensign, but they can't compensate for *everything*. He really needs a long period of rest and relaxation, so don't push him too hard."

She stepped back and pointed to a hatch. "He's in there," she said. "He said he would talk to you, so...good luck."

Thomas swallowed as he walked up to the hatch and pushed the buzzer, unsure if he should just walk in or not. Back home, entering a person's private apartment without their permission was a gross breech of etiquette, but in sickbay? The doctor could walk in and out at will, he was sure...the hatch hissed open, cutting off that train of thought. Bracing himself, Thomas stepped into the private compartment. Captain Ryman was sitting on his bed, reading a datapad. He looked up and smiled, then nodded to the hatch. It hissed closed behind Thomas.

"The doctor said you wanted to ask me a few questions, young man," Captain Ryman said, as Thomas saluted. He certainly *sounded* better than he had on the bridge of his ship. "I am at your disposal."

"Thank you, sir," Thomas said. He pulled up a chair and sat down. "I've been asked to gather as much information as I can about the Druavroks before we meet them in battle, Captain. There's frustratingly little in the files."

"I had that problem too," Captain Ryman said.

"But you've met them," Thomas said, feeling a flicker of panic. What if the whole interview turned out to be a waste of time? The XO would have a few sharp things to say about it - and more, perhaps, if Captain Stuart found out. "You must know *something* about them!"

"I do," Captain Ryman said. He leaned backwards, as if the subject was somehow distasteful. "I just didn't learn about them in the files."

He paused. "I don't suppose you managed to smuggle a box of cigarettes in here?"

"I'm afraid not," Thomas said, wondering if he were being teased. He had to consult his implants to find out what cigarettes were, leaving him wondering why people smoked when they could just use electronic brain simulation instead. "I might be able to find a packet in ship's stores, if you like."

"No worries," Captain Ryman said. "The Druavroks."

He leaned forward, resting his hands on his lap. "I don't know much about their history, certainly nothing more than you'll have found in the files," he said. "What I *do* know is that they're an immensely aggressive race - even-tempered, you might say; mad all the time. The Druavroks picked the most fights with everyone else on Amstar long before the

Tokomak pulled out and abandoned them to their own devices. Look at a group of Druavroks funny and you'd be fighting for your life seconds later. They even picked fights with each other when there was no one else to fight.

"I actually saw two of them fight in a mixed-race bar on Amstar," he added, his face twisting in dismay. "They just flew at each other, claws out; the peace force had to stun them to get them to stop. They're not the sort of people who'll use the bureaucracy to screw you, to be fair, but they'll hammer you into the ground if they think you're not treating them with sufficient respect. Most folks of all races tended to avoid them as much as possible, or only deal with them over telecommunications lines. It was safer than perhaps winding up in an autodoc after being beaten half to death."

He paused. "And yet, it was rare for them to actually *kill* someone."

Thomas frowned. "Wouldn't killing someone have been a great deal more serious?"

"They were the local enforcers," Captain Ryman pointed out. "I dare say they could have gotten away with killing a few of their victims if they wanted. Most of the deaths they *did* cause were misjudgements, I believe; they simply didn't realise how badly they were injuring their enemies. I wouldn't have expected them to slip into committing genocide."

"I see," Thomas said. "How *do* they fight?"

"Hammer and tongs," Captain Ryman said. Thomas frowned, puzzled. "They'll go all-out to beat you, if they want to fight. The only way to stop them is to hammer the bastards so hard they back off, dazed. It isn't easy for an unenhanced human to inflict enough damage to convince them to submit. And yet, I've never heard of any of them directly defying the Tokomak. I don't know how the Tokomak managed to make them surrender."

He sighed. "Something has changed with them," he added. "Wanting to win at all costs is one thing, but committing genocide is quite another. Maybe they've decided they simply cannot endure the presence of aliens any longer. I honestly don't know."

Thomas considered it for a long moment. "A plague? Or a meme-attack?"

"A plague could have been countered by an autodoc," Captain Ryman said. "A meme-attack...maybe. Their internal politics are something of a mystery. A new religion, perhaps, preaching death to all other races. There's no way to know."

"Do they *have* a religion?"

"If they do, I don't know about it," Captain Ryman said. "They rarely talk about themselves, at least to outsiders. The Tokomak may know more, Ensign, but they're unlikely to respond to a request for information."

"And their borders are over a year away now," Thomas added. "It would be quicker to get answers from Earth."

"The one thing you have to bear in mind," Captain Ryman warned, "is that they are a *very* aggressive race. Show them a hint of weakness and they'll attack. You see this in their trade negotiations too, I'm afraid. I always found it was easier just to set a price and stick to it, because any haggling is seen as either an admission or a charge of weakness."

Thomas frowned. "They don't realise you're setting your first demand too high?"

"They don't understand the concept," Captain Ryman said. "To them, you ask for what the items are worth and stick to it. Dropping your price is an admission you don't have the nerve to hold it and they'll jump on you. And don't play poker or any other game that requires bluffing with them. They always end in naked violence."

"Shit," Thomas said. "The XO is not going to be pleased."

"Of course not," Captain Ryman said. "Nor is anyone else who is likely to encounter them."

SEVEN

The Michigan Free State announced the death by firing squad of a number of criminals charged with crimes against the state, including former federal officials, liberals, radical feminists and a handful of former politicians. It is believed the purge, spearheaded by refugees from federal tyranny, will continue until all remnants of federal authority have been removed.

-Solar News Network, Year 54

It was, Hoshiko had to admit, a common tactical problem - and one that had no satisfactory answer.

The Druavroks, unless they were complete idiots, would be watching for incoming starships and could hardly fail to miss nine heavy cruisers of unknown design. It *was* just plausible that the Druavroks would assume the ships were freighters instead of military vessels, but that would rely on a level of incompetence unmatched since the day newly-minted cadets had been given command of a *simulated* starship to demonstrate just how little they actually knew. No, they'd see her coming, which limited her options. Dropping out of FTL on the edge of the system and sneaking in would take far too long, giving them all the time they needed to prepare for her arrival, while coming in too close ran the risk of running straight into an ambush.

Pity we can't use realspace sensors in FTL, she thought. It *was* possible to track ships moving at FTL speeds, but a starship that dropped out of FTL might as well have vanished somewhere within a vast immensity of space. *There's no way to know what's waiting for us until we arrive.*

She keyed her console thoughtfully, then glanced at the tactical officer. "We'll drop out here," she said. Unless the enemy had supernatural powers, they would find it impossible to *guess* her precise endpoint. "Communicate my intentions to the rest of the squadron. I want to hit maximum velocity and drive straight at the planet as soon as we drop out of FTL."

"Aye, Captain," Biscoe said.

"Prepare to transmit our warning message as soon as we arrive," Hoshiko added, "but hold it until I give the order to send."

Just in case they have a battle squadron we cannot defeat in orbit around Amstar, she thought, sourly. She doubted it, but she didn't dare take the chance. If *that* happened, they would have no choice; they'd have to leave with their tail between their legs. *Uncle Mongo should have given me some goddamned Hammerhead missiles.*

She shook her head, reminding herself not to be an entitled Earther brat. Hammerhead missiles were *expensive*, even for the Solar Union; she didn't blame Admiral Stuart for not assigning any to her command when they were required to protect Sol. But they could smash through a Tokomak battleship as though she were made of paper. One or two Hammerhead missiles might be enough to convince the Druavroks to withdraw without much of a fight.

"Ten minutes to the system line," the helmsman reported. "Twelve minutes to emergence point."

"Red alert," Hoshiko ordered. "I say again, sound red alert. Set condition one throughout the ship. Bring combat datanet to ready position."

"Aye, captain," Biscoe said, as the sirens began to howl. "Red alert; condition one. Combat datanet ready and standing by."

Hoshiko nodded at Wilde, who was watching the live feeds from all over the ship. The XO hadn't complained once, since they'd departed, but she'd been very aware of his concerns about just what they were about to do. Nothing either his officers or the intelligence staff had been able to dig up on the Druavroks sounded good. Hoshiko had the uneasy feeling that nothing, not even the threat of overwhelming force, would be enough to make them submit without a major fight. It rather made her wonder how the Tokomak had kept them under control.

Maybe they just offered the bastards a string of ready targets, she thought, sardonically. *Let them take their malice out on anyone but the masters of the cosmic all.*

She pushed the thought aside as she heard the hatch opening behind her and turned, just in time to see the reporter step into the compartment. Max Kratzok had requested permission to watch from the bridge, after all; Hoshiko nodded to him, then pointed to one of the chairs at the rear of the compartment. She half-expected a fuss - reporters had a tendency to be prima donnas at the best of times - but Kratzok sat down at once. Hoshiko turned back to her display and watched as the seconds slowly ticked down to zero. If everything went according to plan, the Druavroks would expect them to appear much closer to the planet than the emergence point she'd dictated, yet…

They're not gods, she reminded herself. They knew so little about their enemy, but she was sure of *that. The laws of mathematical averages work as well for us as for them.*

"Twenty seconds, captain," the helmsman said. He sounded nervous, although Hoshiko knew he'd been a junior officer during the Battle of Earth. "Realspace drives cycling now."

"Take us out as planned," Hoshiko ordered.

She gritted her teeth as the final few seconds counted down. It was a shame that no one had managed to come up with a genuine long-range FTL communicator - it was hard enough sending messages from one ship to another when they were both in FTL, flying in a loose formation - but at least the enemy wouldn't be able to summon help. They'd have to send a courier boat to their nearest base…unless, of course, they already had enough firepower orbiting Amstar to beat off her squadron. They'd have had to bring it in from another system, though, if Captain Ryman was to be believed. Amstar hadn't had more fixed defences than it needed to fend off pirates.

"Emergence," the helmsman snapped. The ship shook, once, as she plunged out of FTL and lanced towards the planet. "FTL drives recycling now."

Hoshiko leaned forward as the display started to sparkle with red and yellow icons. "Tactical report?"

"Seventeen warships in orbit, nothing larger than a heavy cruiser," Biscoe reported. "The manned fortifications are still present, Captain, but they've been augmented with a number of automated weapons platforms. Assuming standard GalTech, we will enter engagement range within five minutes."

"Stand by all weapons," Hoshiko said. "And send the pre-recorded message."

She sucked in her breath as more icons flashed into existence, little symbols next to them listing known or deduced attributes. At least the Druavroks didn't seem to have any battlecruisers or heavy cruisers... unless they'd cloaked the ships. She doubted anyone would bother, but the Druavroks might have a different view of the matter. Some alien tactics seemed absurd from humanity's perspective. The Tokomak might have crushed the Solar Union if they'd struck at once, rather than waiting for fifty years as humanity made its way into space and started improving on Galactic technology. But then, given how tiny Earth was on a galactic scale, they'd probably found it hard to imagine that any significant threat could come from a backwater of a backwater.

"Message sent," Yeller said. There was a long pause. "No response."

"Their starships are altering position," Biscoe reported. "They're forming an attack formation and angling towards us."

Wilde laughed, harshly. "I think that's the answer, Captain."

"Stand by all weapons," Hoshiko ordered. If Captain Ryman was right, the Druavroks wouldn't hesitate to open fire...which would make it easier to argue, afterwards, that they'd fired first. But if they didn't she'd have no choice but to fire the first shot. "Bring up active sensors and lock weapons onto their hulls."

"Firing range in two minutes, Captain," Biscoe reported. "Enemy formation is sweeping us with active sensors."

"Deploy decoys," Hoshiko ordered. At point-blank range, at least as it applied to starship combat, it was unlikely the decoys would soak up many missiles before the Druavrok sensors burned through the jamming, but it was worth trying. "Can you identify their flagship?"

"It will probably be the heavy cruiser," Wilde commented. "Their commanders won't see any virtue in using a smaller ship."

"Firing range in one minute, Captain," Biscoe reported. "Enemy fleet is advancing directly towards us."

"Order all ships to take evasive action if necessary," Hoshiko ordered. The Druavroks might just be hoping for a chance to ram an ancient warship into one of her shiny new cruisers, even though the impact would destroy both ships. They'd come out ahead if even one suicide attacker succeeded. It wasn't as if she could summon more ships from Sol at the touch of a button. "Concentrate fire on the heavier ships..."

"Enemy vessels are opening fire," Biscoe snapped. "Missiles look to be standard GalTech, Captain, but there's a lot of them."

"Stand by point defence," Wilde ordered.

"Fire at will," Hoshiko said, calmly.

Jackie Fisher shuddered as she unleashed a full spread of missiles towards her targets, then opened fire with her phaser banks. The other ships in the squadron opened fire a second later, their missile warheads automatically forming a tactical net that directed them towards their targets for maximum effect. If the Druavroks were surprised at the speed of humanity's missiles, easily a third faster than standard GalTech, she saw no sign of it. Their point defence started spitting out fire as soon as the missiles came into range.

"Continue firing," she ordered. The Druavroks knew how to fight their ships better than the Hordesmen, she noted; they actually understood how to use their point defence. It didn't *look* as though they'd invented anything new, but merely understanding their own capabilities made them more dangerous foes than the Horde. "Concentrate fire on the heavy cruiser."

"Aye, Captain," Biscoe said. The starship rocked violently as the enemy slammed a hail of phaser bolts into her shields. "They're getting the range on us too."

"Switch missiles to sprint mode and keep firing," Hoshiko ordered, feeling the blood pounding through her veins. The enemy ships were turning slightly to bring more of their phaser banks to bear, although they were still advancing towards her ships. One of their destroyers had dropped out of formation and two more had been destroyed outright, yet they kept fighting. "Ensure they don't come within ramming range of us."

"Aye, Captain," the helmsman said.

Jackie Fisher twisted as one of the enemy destroyers made a run at her, the helmsman neatly evading the suicidal charge as the tactical officer blew the destroyer apart with a pair of missiles and a spray of phaser fire. Hoshiko watched through her implants as the enemy heavy cruiser altered course again, only to find itself being hammered by three human starships in unison. Its shields failed a moment later and a single antimatter missile, slammed into her drive section, blew her into a ball of fire.

"*Harrington* has taken damage," Wilde reported, quietly. "She's still firing though - and regenerating her shields."

"Tell Captain Faison to keep his distance from the enemy," Hoshiko ordered. The Druavroks were still fighting, damn them, even though there was no hope of victory. "Prepare a spread of missiles…"

She broke off as another enemy ship vanished into a glowing fireball. "Cover *Harrington* if necessary," she ordered. "The Druavroks may regard a crippled ship as a sensible target."

"Aye, Captain," Wilde said.

"The automated weapons platforms are coming online," Biscoe reported, sharply. "Captain, they're swinging around to target the planet!"

"Take them out," Hoshiko ordered, sharply. What was *driving* the Druavroks? Turning starship-grade weapons on Amstar would wipe out their own settlements as well as every other race on the planet. "Can you raise the manned platforms?"

"No, Captain," Yeller reported. "They're still spitting missiles at us."

Hoshiko nodded as *something* slammed into *Fisher's* shields. "Target them too," she ordered, as the last enemy ship made a suicide run. It didn't get into ramming range before her phasers burned through its shields and ripped it apart. "Try to avoid targeting anything else unless it's shooting at us."

"Aye, Captain," Yeller said. "What about command and control satellites?"

"If they're helping the Druavroks, take them out," Hoshiko snapped. "If you *think* they're helping the Druavroks, take them out..."

She broke off and watched as a spread of missiles obliterated a handful of platforms, one by one. The platforms were vulnerable - a single burst of phaser fire would be enough to take them out - but there were too many of them to take them all out quickly. She swore under her breath as a couple of platforms started firing towards the ground, then relaxed slightly as the platforms were blown apart.

"Good thing they don't have true AI," Wilde commented. "They could have targeted us as well as the planet at the same time."

"They must have bought the cheap versions," Hoshiko agreed. "Or drew them straight from the Tokomak."

It made sense, she thought, although she'd have to check the records to be sure. The Tokomak hadn't been too keen on the idea of allowing *anyone* to fire on a planet's surface and had modified their technology to make it tricky for the platforms to engage both starships and the planet's surface. It did make a certain kind of sense, she knew; a single missile with an antimatter warhead, or even with a standard nuke, would do one hell of a lot of damage to the planet's surface. *And* the platforms were designed to defend the planet, rather than keep the population a prisoner.

"No active PDCs," Biscoe reported. "I'm picking up a number of military formations on the ground, but nothing that seems capable of posing a threat to anything in orbit."

Hoshiko nodded and interfaced her mind with the computer datanet once again. The final manned platform was spitting missiles in all directions, but it was old and outdated, ill-prepared for a full-scale attack. She had to admit the Druavroks were stubborn; they *knew* they were going to lose and yet they were still fighting. Maybe they thought there was no point in trying to surrender. Wilde had been right. The other races on Amstar wouldn't hesitate to take a brutal revenge for attempted genocide.

The ship shuddered one final time as the orbital battle came to an end. Hoshiko checked the live feed from the other eight ships - three had taken minor damage, including *Harrington* - and then turned her attention to the planet itself. It was definitely an *odd* world; it looked, very much, as though the Tokomak had been more interested in producing full-sized megacities, each one several times the size of the largest city on Earth, rather than settling the planet as a whole. But there were still a large number of military formations on the surface...and hundreds of scorch marks where alien settlements had once been.

"Target their formations from orbit and take them out," she ordered. They weren't too close to non-Druavrok settlements, as far as she could tell. Besides, she had the feeling that giving the aliens a chance to find human shields would be disastrous. Collateral damage was normally unavoidable, particularly when KEWs were dropped on targets from high overhead, but it should be kept as low as possible. "And then try and make contact with the humans on the ground."

She cursed under her breath as Yeller went to work. Captain Ryman had supplied them with a whole list of contacts, humans and non-humans who were involved in fighting the Druavroks, but there was no way to know how valid his list was any longer. It had been two weeks since he'd fled Amstar and the Druavroks were incredibly aggressive. They might well have obliterated the resistance already. She worked her way through the analysis from the tactical staff as the ship settled into orbit and allowed herself a sigh of relief. There were definite signs that the battle was still underway.

"Picking up a response, Captain," Yeller said. "They're demanding Captain Ryman's codes."

"Pass them on," Hoshiko said. "And then order the marines to be ready to drop."

She wanted to go down to the planet herself, but she knew that was impossible. The marines would have to take the lead, accompanied by Captain Ryman - and Max Kratzok, if the reporter still wanted to go. Judging by the reports, the fighting was growing ever more intense, even as her KEWs wiped the visible formations out of existence. The Druavroks simply didn't know how to quit.

And they probably have more weapons than anyone else, she thought, numbly. *Pacifying the planet will take years.*

"They've sent us landing coordinates," Yeller reported. "Captain?"

"Forward them to the marines," Hoshiko ordered. She'd discussed possible steps with her officers during the voyage. Now, they'd find out just how good their planning had actually been. "Mr. Kratzok? Get to the marine boat bay if you wish to join them."

"I do, Captain," Kratzok said. He rose and hurried to the hatch. "Thank you."

Hoshiko smiled. She rather doubted Kratzok knew what was awaiting him. He might have fooled around in simulations, or downloaded a full sensory recording from a marine making the jump into combat, but there was no substitute for the real thing.

"Good luck," she said.

She turned her attention back to the main display. "Do we have any other enemy positions in the system?"

"None as yet," Biscoe reported. "They don't seem to have shown much interest in the industrial nodes."

"Odd," Hoshiko said. Had the Druavroks been so interested in exterminating everyone else that they'd ignored the industrial platforms? "We'll deal with them as soon as we can spare the marines."

"Aye, Captain," Biscoe said. "We're also picking up signals from lunar settlements. They're asking if we're planning to stay."

"Tell them yes," Hoshiko said. The last thing she needed was people, humans or aliens, panicking while her marines dropped into hell. "And ask them for a sit-rep, if possible. I need to know what's going on."

EIGHT

Chinese forces reoccupied Tibet after a bloody uprising. The Chinese Government claims that the Tibetans came to greet their Chinese brothers after the extremists were defeated, but reports on the ground and orbital observations claim that the Chinese destroyed Lhasa and exterminated much of the population.
-Solar News Network, Year 54

Max hadn't been *quite* sure what to expect when he'd run into the boat bay, but he definitely hadn't expected a grim-faced man shoving him into a large armoured suit. He had no time to object before the suit sealed itself, his implants reporting that the control processors were attempting to connect to his neural link. The moment he authorised the link, the suit seemed to fade away to a haze surrounding him, as if he was no longer wearing it. But the icons flashing up in front of his eyes told a different story.

"I understand you've used combat suits before, Max," a female voice said. A stream of information from his implants identified the speaker as Lieutenant Hilde Bergstrom. She was standing far too close to him, wrapped in another armoured suit. "Have you stayed in practice?"

"I haven't used one since my days in the Orbital Guard," Max said. He'd never taken enthusiastically to military service, although it was a requirement for *any* form of advancement on his asteroid. "This suit's a little more advanced than the suits we wore during the war."

"Understood," Hilde said. "I'm slaving your suit to mine, for the moment. I don't want you trying to control your combat jump. If something happens to me" - *if I get blown into atoms*, Max translated silently - "you'll be passed to another marine. You won't have full control over the suit until we land on the ground."

"I understand," Max said. "And once we're down?"

"Follow my lead," Hilde said. "We're not going to try slotting you into our order of battle, but we may need you to plug any holes. If so, your suit will be slaved to us once again and you'll be a helpless bystander until the battle comes to an end."

Max swallowed. In hindsight, he suspected he should have thought more carefully before agreeing to embed with the marines, even though he'd get some great footage of the Battle of Amstar, up close and personal. The idea of being trapped inside the suit as it charged enemy fire on its own was terrifying...but there was no point in trying to change his mind now, not when he'd already committed himself. He hastily set his implants to calming mode as Hilde turned to lead him towards the hatch, then followed her down the corridor. Twenty-two armoured forms were waiting for them. If his suit hadn't automatically supplied names and faces, he wouldn't have been able to tell them apart.

"Slave mode...active," Hilde said. "Sorry."

The suit walked forward. Max tried to send a query into its control processors, but there was no response. He was a helpless passenger now. Gritting his teeth, he braced himself as the hatch opened, revealing the inky darkness of space. Panic flared at the back of his mind as a force field picked up the suit and shoved it hard towards the planet below. More icons flashed up in front of him, warning of incoming fire from the ground, as the suit plunged into formation with the remainder of the marines. Max squeezed his eyes shut as the planet grew larger and larger in front of him, convinced - at a very basic level - that he was going to slam into the ground. He knew it was safe - there were thousands of people who jumped from orbit every year - but his mind refused to believe it. How many of the orbital jumpers jumped straight into the teeth of enemy fire?

"This is fun," Hilde said. If she was trying to be reassuring, she wasn't doing a very good job of it. "Just you wait until we hit the atmosphere!"

Max checked his implants. Only a minute or two had gone by since they'd been launched from the ship, even though it felt like hours. He opened his eyes, then closed them again as he saw the planet looming up in front of him. It was so close he felt as if he could reach out and touch it...

...The suit rocked, violently, as it struck the upper edge of the atmosphere. Max was aware, dimly aware, of the suit reconfiguring itself for a faster descent, even though his mind was screaming for the suit to slow down. He knew it made sense to descend as quickly as possible - the enemy only needed one hit to wipe him and his suit out of existence - and yet it was hard to convince himself that it was true. The suit rocked again and again, striking patches of turbulence in the atmosphere...or, perhaps, dodging bursts of fire from the ground. Max kept his eyes tightly closed as the shaking grew worse. He didn't want to know.

"They're taking pot-shots at us," Hilde commented. "Don't worry. They're not very good shots."

Max hated her in that moment, hated her for her casual dismissal of danger. But then, she would have gone though a thousand simulated combat drops before she'd ever been allowed to take a real suit down to the planet's surface. *He'd* only ever had a handful of lessons. No one had seriously expected the Orbital Guard to have to make a combat drop, not when there were teleporters they could use to get down to Earth or Mars if necessary. But any Galactic world knew to use jammers to prevent people beaming up or down at will.

The suit rocked again, spinning madly through the air. Max opened his eyes and wished, immediately, that he hadn't. There was a city below, wrapped in smoke and fire, coming towards him at terrifying speed. Brilliant flashes of light - his implants identified them as plasma weapons - pulsed in all directions, some of them flashing up towards the marines. It was impossible to tell just what was going on, but it looked like the worst of Stalingrad, of Fallujah, of Paris during the Intifada. The suit's sensors were drawing information from thousands of tactical support drones deployed by the marines, yet it was hard to tell who was on what side. Was there even a united front against the Druavroks or were there hundreds of small groups, fighting as best as they could?

"Prepare for landing," Hilde said, calmly. "Your suit will go free the moment you touch down, Max. Get down and stay down unless you have to fight."

Max nodded wordlessly, then braced himself as the ground came up and hit him, the suit's antigravity compensators coming online bare seconds before he slammed into the surface and died. His head spun; he ducked down as quickly as he could, trying to gather himself as the marines snapped into action. Bolts of plasma fire flashed over his head as the Druavroks tried to muster a counterattack; clearly, they hadn't expected to face a new threat from high overhead. But they had to know their ships and orbiting defences had been defeated, didn't they? Unless their high command believed the groundpounders shouldn't know more than the bare minimum at all times…

He looked up, careful to stay low. The city was strange, a bizarre mixture of styles from a hundred different worlds. A soaring skyscraper, pockmarked with bullet holes, co-existed with a building that looked like an anthill; a blocky building, looking like something built out of brightly-coloured children's bricks, sat next to a black conical building that pointed towards the sky. More and more icons flashed up in front of him as he looked from side to side, warning of everything from possible snipers to heavy weapons emplacements. The drones were building up a picture of the surrounding city, but they were being targeted by enemy countermeasures.

"The enemy are redeploying troops to face us," Hilde told him. She sounded remarkably calm, even though marines were forbidden to use any form of calming software while they were on combat duty. "They're sweeping the sector with drone-killing tech."

Max swallowed. Drones - remote sensors so tiny the human eye couldn't hope to see them - had been the Solar Union's ace in the hole since Steve Stuart had captured the very first Galactic starship. No Earth-based nation could oppose the Solar Union when its leaders, the men who would normally be safe from harm, could be hunted down and targeted by the drones; no secret could be kept when the drones were everywhere, drawing in so much intelligence that the analysts were overloaded. There was no such thing as the Fog of War when GalTech was involved. But the Galactics knew how to counter the drones…

"The Fog of War is drawing in," he mumbled.

"A nice turn of phrase," Hilde said. Her voice was so flat that it was impossible to tell if she was being sarcastic. "I trust you'll put that in the reports?"

"Something like that," Max said. More alerts flickered up in front of him as the enemy formed up, just out of visual range. Smoke and fog was drifting across the battlefield, making it harder to see anything with the suit's visual sensors. Thankfully, the other sensors could peer through the smog as though it wasn't there. "Do you want me to make you sound like Combat Marie or Combat Barbie?"

"That depends," Hilde said. For the first time, she sounded a little irked. Baby-sitting duty wasn't what she'd signed up for. "Would you rather have your testicles cut off with a rusty knife or be force-fed to the ravenous beasts of Scott?"

"I'll just make you sound like a marine," Max said. He wondered, absently, what Hilde had done to be lumbered with the task of riding herd on him. "Will that be safe?"

"As long as you don't make me look like Combat Barbie," Hilde said. "Do you know how many idiots we had trying to pick fights with us after *that* movie came out?"

Max smirked in genuine amusement. Marie and Barbie had been a recruiting movie produced twenty years ago, following the adventures of two female marines: Marie and Barbie. Every marine he'd met had insisted, loudly, that it was either an unfunny comedy or a particularly obnoxious piece of enemy propaganda, intended to damage the reputation of the Solar Marines. They'd certainly made it clear that the movie bore as much resemblance to reality as statements from the governments on Earth. And yet, it still enjoyed a cult following.

Probably because both of them were genuine achievers, he thought. No one cared about beauty in the Solar Union - cosmetic surgery could turn an ugly man into a handsome stud or a fat girl into a goddess - but competence? *That* was a genuine turn-on. *And they didn't take their roles too seriously either.*

He paused as new alerts flashed through the implants, then looked up. The wind was picking up, blowing away the smoke...and revealing a line of enemy soldiers on the far side of the square. They looked like miniature dinosaurs, he thought; their clawed hands gripped weapons as their dark insect-like eyes peered at the human soldiers. Most of them were green, but a handful were yellow or purple. It didn't look as though the colouring served any natural purpose, he thought; it certainly wouldn't be very effective camouflage.

Humans aren't naturally camouflaged either, he thought, morbidly. *We had to invent our own camouflage.*

"Stand at the ready," a marine said. "Let them make the first move."

Max crept forward, bringing the suit's weapons online. It had been years since he'd worn a suit during exercises - he'd never gone to war - but he couldn't just do nothing. Hilde said nothing as he slipped up beside her; Max swallowed nervously as he stared at the aliens, watching the humans with expressionless scaly faces. But then, they were *alien*. For all he knew, they were working themselves up into a frenzy. His implants, for once, had no answers. There was almost nothing on the Druavroks within their files.

And there's no way you can generalise with aliens, he reminded himself. Aliens were *not* human, something he'd been told time and time again. *One race may fart in public as a sign of welcome, but another might take it as a declaration of war.*

The aliens moved, suddenly; they lunged forward, firing as they came. It didn't look as though they were bothering to target the humans, but they were firing so many bursts of plasma fire in the right general direction that they were bound to hit *something*. The Major barked a command and the marines opened fire in return, their plasma cannons tearing great gouts out of the alien formation. Max watched in horror as the alien line staggered, then kept charging forward even as dozens died to a single plasma bolt. How could *anyone* keep coming under such weight of fire? He recoiled, then lifted his own weapons and opened fire himself. And yet the aliens kept coming…

A red icon flared up in front of him. "Horace is down," Hilde said. "Mike is dead."

Max shuddered. The aliens couldn't win, could they? He had no idea how many Druavroks were already dead, but it looked as though thousands had impaled themselves on the human position. More icons flashed up in front of him, warning of incoming fire; his suit snapped off bursts of point defence automatically, even as KEWs slammed down from orbit, obliterating the heavy weapons before they could be repositioned. The Druavroks were piling up their bodies in front of the human position, some smouldering as if they were on the verge of catching fire. And yet they were *still* coming. How many of them *were* there?

He started as a Druavrok hurled himself over the pile of bodies and came right at him. The suit's tactical programs switched to primary mode and lashed out with staggering power, hitting the alien so hard he literally disintegrated. Max felt sick as the marines began to fall back, launching tiny spreads of antipersonnel missiles and mines as they moved. And *still* the enemy kept coming. They were losing hundreds of lives to the minefield alone - they projected forcefields that cut through the enemy like monofilament knives - but they refused to stop.

"Stay low," Hilde warned. "Incoming KEWs."

The ground shook, as though it had been struck with the hammer of God. Max looked up, just in time to see the skyscraper topple and fall to the ground. He stared in horror - how many people had been in the building when it had fallen? A skyscraper could hold thousands of souls. Shockwaves ran through the city - he couldn't help thinking of earthquakes from the disaster movies he'd watched as a child, movies that had taught him how unpredictable life on Earth could be - and, for the first time, the alien charge seemed to falter. The marines held their line, shot down the final set of aliens and waited, grimly, as the fighting came to an end.

"They seem to have lost their momentum," Hilde commented. "Follow me."

Max nodded, not trusting himself to speak, as Hilde dropped to her hands and knees and crawled over to where one of the marines was lying, a nasty scorch-mark covering his chest. Another was lying nearby, his suit so badly damaged that survival seemed impossible; the plasma blast that had stuck him would have burned through the armour and turned the marine into charcoal before he had a chance to bail out. Max shuddered, feeling sick again, then turned to look as Hilde carefully opened the first marine's suit and looked inside. The marine's chest was a blackened ruin...

"The nanites will keep it under control, I think," Hilde said. Her voice was very composed, although she had to know it could have been *her* who'd taken the hit. "They've placed his brain in suspension, but he'll need to have most of his body regrown. I think, for him, the war is over."

"I'm sorry," Max said, unsure what he *should* say. The marine had done his duty, jumping down into the maelstrom surrounding Amstar, and died doing it. His name would be remembered, but for what? "I'll make sure he's mentioned..."

"See that you do," Hilde said. She closed the suit and stood. "There's a shuttle flight being readied now, Max. The reinforcements will set up a base camp here until we know who we can trust. You'll stay here as we secure the perimeter."

"I understand," Max said. The marines wouldn't want a half-trained reporter accompanying them as they poked further out from the LZ.

There was too great a danger of accidentally shooting someone on the same side. "What...is this always what it's like?"

"No," Hilde admitted. "Normally, we're boarding starships or carrying out defence duty on Earth. This" - she waved her hand at the piles of alien bodies - "is something new. The old sweats talked about drug-addled fanatics, but...I never really believed them. What sort of idiot would *do* that to themselves?"

Max nodded. There was no shortage of drugs that could boost a person's combat ability, but they tended to come with nasty downsides. They were addictive and, in the long run, degraded the user's natural reactions. Eventually, they even caused brain damage.

"Maybe they were just desperate," he said, after a moment. The Druavroks had been trying to commit genocide. They'd have to wonder if their former victims would try to return the favour. "They lost control of the high orbitals. Their commanders had to know they'd lose the war."

"Maybe," Hilde agreed. "Or maybe they're just nasty bastards."

NINE

Independent reports from Kurdistan confirm that the Kurdish People's Militia has seized Sunni territory and has been carrying out a program of ethnic cleansing and genocide. All Sunni Muslims have been ordered to leave, taking only what they can carry on their backs, or face death. The KPM stated, in the wake of the engagement, that the Kurds would no longer allow the Sunnis to threaten their existence…

-Solar News Network, Year 54

"They must be mad," Griffin said.

"Not mad," Doctor Carr said. "But *very* angry."

Griffin looked down at the body on the examination table. Perhaps it was latent xenophobia, but he couldn't help feeling that the Druavrok didn't *look* very nice. It was impossible to believe they didn't eat meat - they had the sharp teeth of predators - and their claws suggested they were used to fighting hand-to-hand. *Humanity* hadn't evolved such natural weapons; indeed, even spears and clubs hadn't always been enough to even the odds against tigers or lions. It had been the ability to think, and plan, and *cooperate* that had made humanity the dominant race on Earth.

The Druavrok was a head shorter than him, his mouth crammed with sharp teeth and his skin hard as leather. The dark insect-like eyes looked unpleasant, even in death; it was impossible to read the creature's expression, but he had a feeling it regarded them all as prey. There were faint reddish markings, like tattoos, on its green skin. He had a nasty feeling the creature had used the blood of his victims to paint his scales.

"I've only done a basic scan, but several things are clear," Shari said. "First, on average, the Druavroks are stronger and faster than the average unenhanced human - deadlier too, given that they have those claws. I'm not sure if they're *naturally* as sharp as our friend's claws" - she nodded to the body - "but they can slice though human skin as if it were made of paper, while their scales are tougher than human skin. However, like many other races with tough outer coatings, their ability to heal after their skin *is* cut seems limited. A small cut may mean a long period of healing."

"Or they might bleed to death," Griffin said.

"Maybe," Shari said. "I think they'd understand the value of bandages, though."

She shrugged. "Second, based on my scans, they *do* have a strong reaction when they're frightened or angry," she added. "Their brain releases a chemical into their bloodstream which supercharges their reactions, at - I suspect - the cost of some of their rationality. Human wave charges may be the only way they can function when their blood is up, although it's impossible to be sure without studying a live one. My best guess is that the genocide is fuelled, at least in part, by an *emotional* reaction against other races. They may also be testing their freedom now the Tokomak are gone."

"You make them sound like naughty children," Griffin said.

"The principle is the same," Shari said. "Children grow up under rules set by their parents, not ones they accepted for themselves. They tend to rebel against their parents, as they reach adulthood, or settle into an unhealthy dependency even into their middle-aged years. The Tokomak were the parents, everyone else were the children..."

She shrugged. "The pattern has been seen on Earth, time and time again, long before we knew about non-human life. Giving a state independence without the state having major teething problems afterwards was never easy."

Griffin nodded. "Are they a *rational* race?"

"I would have said they are fairly compatible to us, on the intelligence scale," Shari said, tapping the Druavrok's head. "But then, most races reach a certain level and just *stop*. They don't have any pressing need for more brainpower when they have tools they can use to boost their abilities. I can't tell you anything for certain about their social structure, but I would guess, based on what I've seen here, that they spend a lot of time struggling for dominance over one another. And then perhaps over everyone else."

"Brilliant," Griffin said, sardonically.

"Quite," Shari agreed. "There's a strong possibility that rational negotiations with them will be impossible, Commander. They may not be able to grasp the idea of peaceful co-existence or submission to another power. I have no idea how the Tokomak managed to keep them in line. They must have known the squadron outgunned them and *still* they fought."

Griffin nodded, curtly. It was a worrying sign. On one hand, destroying a chunk of the Druavrok Navy - whatever they called it - without serious losses was not to be dismissed, particularly as he was sure there would be further encounters, but on the other hand it indicated a fanaticism that chilled him to the bone. And then, the brief reports from the marines - he hadn't had the time to access a full sensory - had stated that the Druavroks had launched mass human wave-style attacks against the marines, clearly trying to drown the marines in dead bodies. They'd come too close to overrunning the marines and grinding them into the dust.

He looked back at the body and shivered. "What else can you tell me about this guy?"

"He's definitely a male, I believe," Shari said. "The penis is retractable, sir; it fits between his legs and only emerges when mating begins. I did wonder if they might be functional hermaphrodites, but there's no sign of anything other than a penis and organs that serve the same purpose as our testicles. I'm planning to go through the other bodies that were brought up to the ship in the hopes of finding a female; hopefully, I'll know more about their mating cycle afterwards."

Griffin frowned. "How *do* they mate?"

"It's hard to be sure without a female to compare against the male," Shari said. "My best guess is that they can mate in several different ways, like humans, but I could be wrong. There's just too much sexual variation among the Galactics..."

"Yeah," Griffin said.

The Academy had covered the hundreds of different variations in some detail, the tutors pointing out that sex was one of the easiest ways to get in trouble on an alien world. There were races that mated constantly, races that had mating seasons; races that had intelligent males and unintelligent females or vice versa; races that had elaborate codes that covered every last aspect of the mating rituals, races that thought nothing of doing it wherever and whenever they pleased...like humans, in some ways. The Solar Union didn't give a damn what its citizens did, as long as it was done between consenting adults in private. Adapting the laws to suit aliens with entirely different biological systems had been a major headache when the first immigrants arrived from outside the Sol System.

He shook his head. About the only *real* taboo among the Galactics was interracial sex, although he'd been told there was an underground subculture where different races met and mated in secrecy. He'd never understood why - it wasn't as if a human and a Druavrok could produce a child - but the Tokomak had set the rule. Maybe they'd looked upon the prospect - the impossible prospect - of hybrids and shuddered in horror. Or maybe they'd just been jerks. A race that could deny others the prospect of immortality wouldn't have qualms about banning interracial sex, if only to prevent their subjects from realising they had something in common...

"Let me know what you find, when you find something," he said. "What if their females are unintelligent?"

"I'd argue it was the *males* who were unintelligent, based on this sample," Shari said, mischievously. "But I can't say anything for sure yet, sir."

"I understand," Griffin said. "Do they pose a *biological* threat to us?"

"I doubt it," Shari said. "Their biochemistry isn't *that* different from ours, Commander, but I haven't found anything to suggest their diseases can make the jump into our bodies or vice versa. A couple of the *known* pan-species diseases may pose a threat, but our nanites can handle those before they turn deadly. I'd be surprised if Amstar wasn't already used to handling such threats."

Griffin nodded. Very few diseases could make the jump from humanity to an alien race or vice versa, but those that *could* were incredibly dangerous. The Tokomak, however, had crafted the first set of medical nanites to *prevent* cross-species disease outbreaks. Hell, *disease* was rarely a problem in the Solar Union. Most children had genetic modifications spliced into them from birth that kicked their immune systems into overdrive. The only real danger was a genetically-modified disease configured to defeat an adjusted immune system and spread through the body and *nanites* could handle that.

"They might try for a genetically-modified disease," Shari added, "but they'd be asking for retaliation in kind."

"They're already practicing genocide," Griffin pointed out. "Doesn't *that* ask for retaliation in kind?"

He nodded politely to the doctor, then turned and made his way back to the captain's office, checking his implant's inbox on the way. *Jackie Fisher* had taken very little damage in the conflict, thankfully; the handful of burned-out shield generators had been replaced already, while boarding parties had been dispatched to the industrial nodes before the Druavroks could try to destroy them. The crews, surprisingly, *weren't* Druavroks. They'd been taken prisoner when the Druavroks occupied the system, their families dumped into POW camps and promised safety, as long as the skilled workmen served their new masters. It was odd - the Druavroks seemed to combine a cold-blooded mindset with a hot-blooded desire to exterminate everyone - but *that* hardly mattered. What *did* matter was that Captain Stuart had committed them to an endless war with a savage lizard-like race bent on exterminating everyone else.

The Captain's hatch opened as he approached, revealing Captain Ryman and Ensign Howard, who saluted hastily. Griffin returned the salute - the young officer had a long way to go, but at least he was on the right path - and stepped past him, into the office. Captain Stuart was sitting on her sofa, looking up at the holographic chart of the sector. The boarding parties, thankfully, had been able to recover enough data to fill in the blanks. But almost none of it painted an encouraging picture.

"Captain," he said, as the hatch hissed closed behind him. "The doctor finished her examination of the first alien corpse."

"Very good," Hoshiko said. She sounded as though she was distracted by some greater thought. "I've just appointed Captain Ryman as ambassador-at-large to Amstar, with orders to make connections with as many alien groups as possible."

Griffin blinked in surprise. "Is that legal?"

"It depends how you read the passages in my authorisation," Hoshiko said. She smiled with genuine amusement. "I'm authorised to appoint deputies who can serve in my place, if necessary, although I have to countersign everything they do before it becomes legal. He has the contacts we need to start making connections, so I gave him the authority and a broad range of instructions."

"I think those passages refer to your military subordinates," Griffin sighed. He'd have to go through the authorisations himself, just to see if her interpretation held water. It would probably depend on her success - or lack of it. "*Not* to a random civilian we just happened to encounter."

"He isn't exactly a random civilian," Hoshiko pointed out. She leaned back in her sofa, then indicated the chair facing her. "He does have a roving commission from intelligence as well as a position in the naval reserve."

Griffin sat down. "Do you think he'll make progress?"

"I hope do," Hoshiko said. She cocked her head, sending a command to the room's processor. The holographic star chart vanished, to be replaced by an image of the industrial stations orbiting Amstar or scattered throughout the system. "There's a considerable amount of industrial potential here. The civilian fabbers could start turning out war material within hours, if we crack their limiter codes. *That* shouldn't be too hard."

"No," Griffin agreed. Cracking Tokomak codes was tricky, but humanity had fifty years of experience in outsmarting an unimaginative alien race. "Do you plan to give them human-level missile tech?"

"Among other things," Hoshiko said. She paused. "Not Hammerheads, of course, but everything else."

Griffin stared at her. "I should remind you, Captain, that General Order Number Four clearly states..."

"Which can be overridden by the demands of war," Hoshiko pointed out. "Besides, with the exception of Hammerheads, everything we have can be duplicated relatively easily, now the Galactics have seen them in action. And even Hammerheads are unlikely to remain exclusive for long. The Tokomak *invented* gravity-manipulation technology."

"It won't stop the Druavroks from copying what we pass to Amstar," Griffin objected.

"They'll still need time to duplicate our work," Hoshiko said. "We need to give our prospective allies *something* to prove we're sincere. Weapons technology may serve as a suitable incentive for them to join up."

"Assuming we *do* find allies," Griffin said. A number of ships had taken off from the ground as soon as the blockade had broken, but no one knew who'd been flying them. Druavroks, going to report on the disaster, or other races intent on returning to their homeworlds? "Can we count on anyone here?"

"The industrial workers are willing to assist us, in exchange for protection," Hoshiko said, seriously. "We help them remove the limiters on their fabbers and they can start churning out defences, even if it never goes anywhere else. Give them a few weeks and the Druavroks will find it hard to retake Amstar."

"They'll try," Griffin said. He outlined, briefly, what Shari had told him. "They're a very aggressive race, Captain."

"I saw the recordings," Hoshiko agreed. "At least we managed to bombard most of their formations from orbit."

Griffin shuddered. A *rational* race might have sought terms, but the Druavroks clearly *still* had no intention of surrendering. They'd dug into their enclaves, far too close to the other settlements to allow orbital bombardment, and started preparing for the final fight. The various resistance groups on the surface, had surrounded them, but they were reluctant to actually launch an offensive. Griffin found it hard to blame them. A month of occupation had killed over a *billion* people, from hundreds of different races. Amstar would never be the same, even if the Druavroks surrendered tomorrow. The entire planet had been traumatised.

They were even eating the dead, he thought. *And they were keeping prisoners alive just so they were fresh when they were butchered.*

He understood the captain's desire to intervene, to take a stand against genocide...against a horror that defied description. But, at the same time, he worried about the future. One of their ships had already been damaged, even though her crews had it firmly under control; what would happen, he asked himself, when another ship was destroyed? It would happen, sooner or later...the Druavroks had already shown themselves willing to throw their own lives away, as long as it gave them a chance to close with the foe. The squadron simply didn't have the resources for a long and bloody war.

"Tell me, captain," he said. "Tell me how this ends?"

"With us finding new allies and defeating the threat," Hoshiko said, bluntly. "Do you want these monsters getting anywhere near Earth?"

"They're six months away, Captain," Griffin insisted. "Even sending a handful of ships to Sol would be difficult, if they are at war in this sector."

"The Tokomak ruled a much larger empire," Hoshiko reminded him. "They put together a staggeringly powerful force to hit Sol, even though they must have believed they were going well over what would have been required for *overkill*. The Druavroks might keep going until they run into us."

Griffin had his doubts. He'd studied the Tokomak extensively - it was a required course at the Academy - and their empire had always been more flimsy than they'd realised, dependent on both the FTL drive and their command of high technology. Keeping their subjects ignorant had helped, but there had been plenty of cracks in the system before the Horde had stumbled across Earth. He doubted the Druavroks had the skill to set up other races as bully-boys and enforcers, not when they wanted to purge everyone else...

And they'd unite everyone against them, he thought. *Even races that fear and hate one another will combine their might against an overwhelmingly powerful foe.*

"More to the point, we can make a difference," Hoshiko added. "If we can win more allies among the other races, humanity benefits, but merely stopping an attempt at genocide will be enough."

"But it won't," Griffin said. He leaned forward, trying to make her understand. "We may have knocked them off one world, Captain, but they have others. Many others. We have to stop them completely before we're withdrawn from the sector or they'll just resume the genocide as soon as we look away."

"We won't look away," Hoshiko said.

Griffin frowned. Hoshiko's family was powerful, but it was nowhere near powerful enough to keep the Solar Union involved in the Martina Sector if the public wanted to pull out and abandon Amstar. The ITA would probably do what it could, yet...it still wouldn't tip the balance. Hoshiko was writing cheques the Solar Union might be unable or unwilling to cash.

"I hope you're right, Captain," he said. Hoshiko was treading a very fine line. Giving human tech to aliens, even allies, was a direct violation of standing orders, tempered only by her interpretation of *other* standing orders. "Because, if you're wrong, we may only be creating more trouble for ourselves."

"I understand the risks, Commander," Hoshiko said. "But some risks just have to be borne."

TEN

Reports from Texas, unconfirmed as yet, state that Mexican tanks are reportedly attempting to cross the Rio Grande into Texas after the Governor declared a flat ban on any further Mexican and South American immigration into the state. A unit of the Texas National Guard engaged the Mexicans with antitank weapons and successfully fought a delaying action until helicopters and armoured units could respond.
-Solar News Network, Year 54

"There's no ground fire," the shuttle pilot called back, "but there are reports of rogue enemy units, so we're going down quickly."

Thomas nodded, bracing himself as the shuttle dropped like a stone. His implants compensated as best as they could, but he couldn't help feeling scared as the shuttle swung from side to side, before hitting the ground with a loud *BANG*. The hatch swung open a second later, revealing a trio of armoured marines, their faces hidden within their suits. He scrambled to his feet as they beckoned him forward and ran out onto an alien world. The smell, a strange combination of smoke, blood and something he couldn't identify, caught his nostrils at once. It was hard, very hard, to resist the temptation to gag.

"The locale is reasonably safe, Ensign," one of the marines said, as Captain Ryman followed him out of the shuttle. "However, we would recommend not going beyond the spaceport without an armed escort."

"We may have to leave," Captain Ryman said. "The spaceport is normally neutral territory, but things might well have changed."

Thomas barely heard him. He was staring at the skyline. Hundreds of buildings - some towering up into the sky, others smaller and blockier - studded the city, all marred in some way by the bitter conflict. One skyscraper looked to have taken a direct hit from a missile: the framework had survived, if barely, but the interior had been completely destroyed. He couldn't help wondering why the upper layers hadn't collapsed onto the lower layers, although he guessed the upper interior had collapsed moments after the blast. A number of aliens were dragging dead bodies out onto the spaceport and dumping them on the runaway... he gagged in horror when he realised just how *many* humans and aliens had been killed during the fighting.

"The command tower was destroyed in the fighting," the marine was saying. Thomas forced himself to pay attention as they started to walk towards a smaller building. "We've converted one of the Pan-Gal Hotels into a temporary meeting place, as you suggested. I'm afraid the staff has buggered off sometime during the fighting."

"It will do," Captain Ryman said. "Most of the facilities are robotic, anyway."

Thomas looked up at the older man as the marines escorted them towards the hotel. "A Pan-Gal Hotel?"

"They cater for every known race," Captain Ryman commented. His lips twisted, as if he were torn between amusement and disdain. "Book a room in advance, send them your racial details, and everything will be prepared for you. The food will be edible, the entertainment will be suitable and, if you should be meeting with other Galactics, the hotel will prepare a meeting room that will keep you all from being uncomfortable. All at a cost, of course."

Thomas frowned. "They don't use holograms?"

"Not if it can be avoided," Captain Ryman said. "Sending someone a hologram when you could meet them in person is considered rude, unless there's a very good excuse. No one will blame you for a virtual presence if you were meeting a Tas-pok, but a human? You need to speak face to face."

"I see," Thomas said. "Is it safe?"

"Probably," Captain Ryman said. "It isn't as if we didn't just save them from being killed and eaten."

He said nothing else as they entered the Pan-Gal and looked around. The lobby was curiously dark and empty, Thomas noted; it took him several minutes to realise it was a VR holographic chamber that, for whatever reason, had been deactivated. He'd seen AI-run games and simulations before, but he rather doubted the restricted AIs permitted by the Tokomak could actually handle so many different VR perceptual realities at the same time.

"The main computer network needs to be booted up," Captain Ryman commented. He walked behind the counter and peered underneath it, then produced a small computer node and placed it on the desk. "Let me see…"

Thomas gave him an odd look as he poked at the node with a processor he must have taken from the ship. There was a long moment, then the lights came on; Thomas covered his eyes, then opened them carefully as his implants adapted. The lobby was suddenly washed in soothing colours that made him want to relax and let the world go by. It was definitely a program optimised for human visitors.

"We'll need to recover the staff if we want to put the hotel back into shape," Captain Ryman said, as he flicked through the control systems, "but we can get a meeting room without any problems. It may be a little uncomfortable, but they'll understand."

"I thought diplomats spent weeks arguing over the shape of the table," Thomas said. He hadn't been given any classes on diplomacy at the Academy. "Is that really true?"

"Only if one side is stalling and the other, for whatever reason, is willing to let it," Captain Ryman said. He led the way through a large door, easily big enough to handle five or six humans walking abreast, then paused. "Have you ever attended a multiracial meeting before?"

"No, sir," Thomas said.

"Some basic rules, then," Captain Ryman said. "You're my aide, so you stand behind me and say nothing, unless I specifically ask for your comments. If anyone other than myself tries to speak to you, say nothing unless I tell you to answer. I assume you speak Gal-Standard One?"

"One and Three," Thomas said, speaking in Gal-Standard One. "My accent is a little poor, but I speak the language."

"Poor, yes," Captain Ryman agreed. "Speak *only* in Gal-Standard One. If you can't express yourself properly without switching to English, inform me first. Speaking in a non-standard language is considered rude. Don't even *swear* in English."

He sighed. "I'd bet good money that one of the *reasons* the Galactics are so unchanging is because of Gal-Standard languages," he added. "English steals words from other languages with impunity. Gal-Standard One is so precise that it admits of no flexibility or imprecision, let alone innovation. The Tokomak knew Big Brother before George Orwell was a gleam in his great-great-grandfather's eye."

"Yes, sir," Thomas said. "We studied it at the Academy."

It was nearly an hour before the first set of alien representatives arrived at the Pen-Gal Hotel, followed by several more. Thomas watched as Captain Ryman greeted them, displayed his new authority to his old contacts and introduced himself to new ones, then escorted the guests down to the meeting room. A couple had brought their own servitors, he noted; the marines had to be told to leave the guests armed, despite their concerns. It had taken two days of arguing, over what remained of the planet's communications grid, to convince the guests to attend. After the Druavroks had started to slaughter everyone else, Thomas was mildly surprised that so many had shown up at all.

He studied them as Captain Ryman walked to the head of the table. The human delegate was a tall man, his face badly scarred by...*something*. Thomas couldn't help feeling a little uneasy at how it was impossible to draw anything from the man's implants - assuming he had any - or from the surrounding datanet. The man had been introduced as John Septum, but that meant nothing to Thomas. He didn't even have a datanet social page!

He wouldn't, he reminded himself. *The Tokomak didn't hold with using the datanet for fun.*

The first alien - Captain Ryman called her Sissle - was weird, a strange cross between an orange humanoid and an octopus. Her race had apparently been spacefarers before the Tokomak had contacted them and they'd been swift to spread through the sector, mainly as traders. Beside her, a more humanoid representative sat, his face covered in dark hair that was braided into thorns. His race preferred to farm; the Tokomak had used them to terraform a hundred Mars-like worlds until they could support life, then turned them into the first population. He was introduced as Todd.

Finally, a six-legged spider-like alien inched its way up to the table and, disdaining the seat, stood in its place. Thomas felt a chill run down his spine, even though he'd been exposed to images of hundreds of different races at the Academy. The creature was just too close to a spider for him to be completely comfortable, even though his implants assured him that the aliens were very civilised. Their names were completely unpronounceable, but after a brief discussion Captain Ryman introduced the spider-like alien as Ambassador One of Six. The alien seemed satisfied with that designation.

Unless he doesn't really understand, Thomas thought. The spider - he mentally dubbed the unpronounceable aliens spiders - spoke Gal-Standard One, but did they really understand? It was hard to imagine what such a creature could have in common with humanity. *We could come to an agreement with them and then discover they thought they were agreeing to something else.*

"Fellow Sentients, I greet you," Captain Ryman said. One thing to say for the Tokomak version of Robert's Rules of Order, at least, was that they didn't allow for small talk. "I have called you here to discuss our mutual enemies."

"The Druavroks have gone mad," Sissle exclaimed. "They have attacked dozens of worlds and settlements over the last month. Their fleets are advancing in all directions. Many worlds are under siege."

And I hope to hell that's an exaggeration, Thomas thought. *We might have bitten off far more than we can chew.*

Captain Ryman didn't seem daunted. "When I left, I told you I intended to seek help," he said, calmly. Gal-Standard One encouraged calmness. "I succeeded - I brought a fleet of warships to lift the siege and stop the Druavroks before it was too late."

"For which we thank you," One of Six rattled. It didn't seem to be using a voder to speak, but there was something about its voice that chilled Thomas to the bone. "The Druavroks are not yet defeated."

"No, they are not," Captain Ryman said.

"We will pull our people away from their settlements," John Septum said. "You can take them out from orbit. The problem will be solved."

"The problem is greater than that," Captain Ryman said. If the thought of committing genocide bothered him, he kept it to himself. "This is not a small outbreak of violence on a single world, but a threat to the entire sector. The Druavroks will be back. Next time, they may just scorch every last settlement from orbit and then land ground troops to hunt down any survivors."

There was a long pause. It was broken, finally, by Sissle.

"Are your ships going to remain here to defend us?"

"My commander is unwilling to remain a passive defender," Captain Ryman said. "She wishes to wage war on the Druavroks."

"Amstar is not a warlike world," Sissle objected.

"We have no choice," John Septum said. "The Druavroks *will* be back."

"We have few weapons," Sissle said.

"My commander is prepared to assist you in unlocking the fabber codes," Captain Ryman said. "In addition, she is willing to offer you advanced weapons and defence systems that will even the odds against the Druavroks."

The spider rattled two of its legs together. "And the price?"

"Two things," Captain Ryman said. "First, you join us in war until the Druavrok threat is removed. Call every ship you can, everything from full-fledged warships to garbage scows, so we can outfit them with weapons and turn them against the enemy. Second, that you attempt to convince your homeworlds to join us too. The Druavroks threaten us all."

"My people are reluctant warriors," Sissle said.

"Your people will end up dead," John Septum snapped. "I do not speak for all of my people, Captain, but I believe most of us will join the resistance. There are plenty of humans on trading ships within this sector."

The spider made another rattling noise. "How can we trust you to keep your word?"

"The weapons data will be handed over as soon as you agree to join us," Captain Ryman said, calmly. "We *would* ask you to be careful with it, as the Druavroks will want it too, but we will give it to you without restriction. And afterwards..."

He paused, marshalling his thoughts. "As a very great man from our homeworld once said, Fellow Sentients, we must all hang together or hang separately. The Druavroks threaten us all."

"That makes no sense," Sissle protested.

"It's a play on words, in the language of the time," Captain Ryman said. "*Hang* refers to both staying with one's allies and the standard method of executing people, which was to wrap a rope around their necks and strangle them to death, then leave their bodies hanging from the ropes."

Thomas had a feeling, as the discussion raged backwards and forwards, that the Galactics *didn't* really understand. How could they? Benjamin Franklin's pun made no sense in Gal-Standard One, which used precise terms for working together and had a single technical term for execution. But then, it had a single pronoun for sentients too. There was no attempt to draw a line between male and female, let alone anything else, on the basic level. How could there be when there were so many different races, some of which had only one gender and others which had five or six?

"We will send word to our homeworlds," Sissle said. "Who is to be in command?"

"My commander is the one who took action against the Druavroks," Captain Ryman said, carefully. "We believe *she* should have tactical command, but there will be a council of war to decide matters of grand strategy."

The spider clapped four of its legs together. "And why," it demanded, "should we place overall command in your hands?"

"First, we beat the Tokomak," Captain Ryman said. "And we have no long-term interest in this sector. Our sole concern is eliminating the threat posed by the Druavroks."

But there are humans in this sector, Thomas thought. *Don't we have an interest in them?*

He pushed the thought to one side as the discussion finally came to an end. Captain Ryman remained seated as the representatives rose, then walked out of the door. Thomas watched them go, wondering if they were truly convinced. The agreement to join the growing resistance seemed awfully fragile to him.

"I trust you were keeping a recording," Captain Ryman said. "Your commander will want to see it."

"Yes, sir," Thomas said. The XO had told him, in no uncertain terms, to record *everything*. "A full sensory…"

He paused. "Sir?"

"Spit it out," Captain Ryman said.

Thomas looked at him. "Can you trust them?"

"A word of advice for the future," Captain Ryman said, standing up. "The vast majority of sentients - human or alien - are not selfish, but they *are* self-interested. Appeal to their self-interest and you'll catch their attention. You want them to ask the question 'what's in it for me?' and come up with a satisfactory answer."

He smiled. "In this case, there are three things in it for them. First, they get protection from the Druavroks. Second, they join an alliance of races that will ensure they are not standing, facing the Druavroks, on their own. Third, and perhaps most importantly, they won't be excluded from that alliance."

"Because the Druavroks would target anyone who was excluded," Thomas said.

"That's part of it," Captain Ryman agreed. "Like I said, hang together or hang separately."

He smirked at the pun, then leaned forward. "But it's more than that," he added. "The races that work together, as part of the alliance, will have access to human-level technology, which will make them stronger, individually and collectively, than anyone else in the sector. We're the race that stopped the Tokomak dead in their tracks! If we build the alliance up, if we treat the members as equals, we'll gain a *lot* of respect. But everyone who doesn't join *now*, when the price for joining is relatively low, will find it harder to join later."

Thomas frowned. "Because...because they didn't do any of the heavy lifting?"

"Precisely," Captain Ryman agreed. "The first set of members will demand a high price from anyone who wants to join after the war. We won't need to lift a finger to get more races and worlds trying to join up before the fighting truly starts, not after we showed the sector that the Druavroks could be beaten. *That's* what they needed to see.

"Todd's race will join us - he would have objected if he'd disagreed with anything I'd said. That will probably bring Sissle in as well, as she and Todd are old rivals, while John...well, he's human and we're human and he's not stupid enough to believe the Druavroks will leave Amstar alone just because they got their asses kicked. And they're not the only ones who are going to be sending messages to their homeworlds, begging for them to join."

He smiled. "Take a break, Ensign," he added. "The *next* set of meetings will begin three hours from now."

"Yes, sir," Thomas said. He wasn't sure where he could have a quick nap - the marines had probably set up cots somewhere on the spaceport - but he'd find somewhere. "And thank you, sir."

"Make sure you stream your full recording to the ship beforehand," Captain Ryman warned, as he walked towards the door. "Your commanding officer will want to see it."

ELEVEN

There was a riot at a Solar Union immigrant processing centre in England after forces loyal to the new government threatened to push through the fences and arrest the prospective immigrants, who are fleeing the government's tightening grip on their country. Solar Marines have been deployed and a final warning has been issued to the government.
-Solar News Network, Year 54

"I wasn't expecting it to come together so quickly," Max Kratzok commented, as they stood together in the observation blister. "It's really quite something."

"It's been two weeks," Hoshiko said. "I'm surprised more ships haven't shown up."

She smiled as she saw the sidelong glance the reporter threw her. There were over two thousand ships currently orbiting Amstar, being outfitted with weapons, sensors and human-grade defence systems. Only two hundred were actual *warships*, admittedly, but it was still an immensely formidable force. The only downside was patching up disputes between the various alien races involved in the coalition and trying to arrange matters so that races that disliked one another weren't forced to work *too* closely together. Her crew was being run ragged just trying to keep up with everything.

"The fleet has its limitations," she said. "A single warship could take out the freighters without breaking a sweat, no matter how many weapons and defence systems we cram into their hulls. Tokomak freighters aren't really designed for speedy conversion into warships, unlike our ships. But in sheer numbers we should be able to give any rational foe pause."

"But our enemies aren't rational," Kratzok commented. "They threw mass wave attacks at the marines rather than standing off or trying to surrender. There's still fighting going on down on the ground."

"That's the problem," Hoshiko conceded. "You have to hit them hard enough to make them pay attention."

She'd done more than just summon as many starships and spacers to her banner in the last two weeks. She'd had her intelligence staff collect every last scrap of information they could, putting together a map of the sector that was more than just a list of stellar locations and a handful of planetary names. They now knew more about the Druavroks than she'd ever wanted to know, including the vital piece of information about how the Tokomak had made them behave in the first place. Apparently, they'd hammered the Druavroks so hard that the survivors had practically worshipped the Tokomak. They hadn't rebelled in the years since, not once. Somehow, Hoshiko couldn't imagine *humanity* being so submissive if the Solar Union had lost the war.

"Which leads to a simple question," Kratzok said. "*Can* we hit them hard enough to make them pay attention?"

"I think we're going to find out," Hoshiko said. "We should be getting more starships soon, I hope. But they're unlikely to leave us in peace for long. Word is already spreading through the sector."

She closed her eyes, recalling the star chart. Assuming the Druavroks had managed to get a message out, their forward bases would be hearing about the fall of Amstar about now. Even if they hadn't, the Druavroks had plenty of contacts across the sector. Hoshiko's most optimistic calculations suggested the Druavroks would discover what had happened in two more weeks, although she wasn't banking on it. She'd been trained to hope for the best, but assume the worst until she *knew* it hadn't come to pass.

And it will take them at least two weeks to dispatch a response, assuming they have a quick-reaction force on standby, she thought. They knew very little about enemy fleet dispositions; there was no way to know if the Druavroks had a fleet of battleships orbiting a nearby star or if their heavy warships were further away. *But we can't sit here waiting to be hit.*

She turned to look at him. "Did you enjoy your time on the surface?"

"It was...hair-raising," Kratzok said. "I wasn't counting on being dropped straight into the war."

"Think of the recordings you made," Hoshiko said, wryly. "The entire Solar Union will be accessing them. Or is that a bad idea?"

"I didn't run off screaming," Kratzok said, reddening. "But I think the public would prefer a sensory from one of the marines."

"Which isn't an option, at the moment," Hoshiko said. She gave him a smile. "I did read your report, Max. It was very...dramatic."

"It should be," Kratzok said. "But it's also accurate."

Hoshiko nodded. There was always a difficult balancing act between freedom of the press, subject to the limitations laid down in the Solar Constitution, and preventing the accidental release of information that would be used against the military. Here, she suspected, it wouldn't matter. By the time anyone in the Solar Union saw the reports they'd be six months out of date. Still, she'd insisted on reviewing the full report before authorising its transfer to a courier boat.

"They'll like it, back home," she said. "Where do you want to go now?"

"Unless we're leaving within the next couple of days, I'd like to go from ship to ship, recording the crews at work," Kratzok said. "Is that acceptable?"

"Check with the alien captains first," Hoshiko said. "Some of them may object to being recorded, even for propaganda purposes. And make sure you don't get in their way."

"Understood," Kratzok said.

Hoshiko silently gave him points for being so understanding. Aliens weren't *human*. The triggers that offended them, that started fights, were often different to human triggers. She knew a race that had sex everywhere, as casually as a human might take a breath of air, but regarded eating in public as an unbearably offensive act. And another that was so obsessed with personal privacy that recording a conversation, with or without permission, was essentially a declaration of war. It was unlikely Kratzok would encounter any aliens who weren't experienced in interracial communications, but it was something to bear in mind.

"I'm authorising the release of your recordings," she added. "Do you have anything you want to add?"

"No, Captain," Kratzok said. "I may do a follow-up, after checking the alien ships, but nothing as yet."

"The courier boat will leave this afternoon," Hoshiko told him. "You have until then to change your mind."

She smiled, although she couldn't help feeling a little nervous. Kratzok's report would be accompanied by *her* report, reports from her captains and XO and personal messages from the crews to their friends and relatives back home. God alone knew which way the Solar Union would choose to jump, once they heard what she was doing. Everything she'd done so far could be technically justified, under their standing orders, but…

The hatch opened behind her. She turned to see Commander Wilde, looking tired. Like the rest of her crew, he'd been worked to the bone over the last two weeks, struggling to build up a defence force that would give any attackers pause. And he had every reason to be annoyed with her, for more than just politics and disagreements over their orders. *He* hadn't been assigned one of the alien warships to command. She needed him on *Jackie Fisher*.

"Captain," Wilde said.

"I'll go arrange transport now," Kratzok said. "Thank you, Captain."

Hoshiko nodded and watched him go, then looked at Wilde. "Success?"

"The final fabber has been unlocked," Wilde said. "There are some programming hiccups to be evened out, but we should be on the way to producing another fabber within the month."

Hoshiko nodded as she turned back to the transparent bulkhead, seeking a particular point of light orbiting Amstar. The commercial-grade fabber was a five-kilometre long structure, a gigantic orbital factory that took raw materials in at one end and churned out everything from starship components to farming tools at the other. It was, in many ways, proof that high technology liberated men and women from endless drudgery, and yet…there were some curious limitations worked into the design. A commercial-grade fabber needed to be given the right instructions before it could produce weapons - the Tokomak hadn't been keen on the idea of their subjects using fabbers to churn out defences - and duplicating itself…*that* had been right off the menu without some intensive reprogramming. But humanity had solved that problem too…

"As long as we keep supplying the raw materials," she said. "In a month, we'll have two fabbers; in two months, we'll have four. And so on."

"We've passed instructions on to the other races," Wilde reminded her. "They'll *all* start churning out new fabbers of their own."

"That should give us a great deal of additional firepower," Hoshiko said. She stared into the darkness, towards where she knew the fleet to be massing. "And everything else we need to turn this hodgepodge into a real navy."

"It will also have effects on the sector's economy," Wilde warned. "And create potential new threats."

Hoshiko smiled, remembering the history lessons she'd been forced to endure as a young girl. The Stuarts had *always* been soldiers, she'd been told; they'd donned their armour and picked up their weapons when the call came, then marched off to war to defend their wives and children from the threat. It was practically bred into them from a very early age, along with a ruthless pragmatism. Sure, the methods used to solve *one* problem might easily create the *next* problem, but that didn't mean the first problem should be allowed to fester.

But we were never leaders, she thought, ruefully. *Grandfather was the only one of us who held any real political office. It was never a Stuart making the decisions.*

"We have to deal with the current issue," she said, gently. "If our current crop of allies turn into the next generation of threats...well, we'll deal with it when the time comes."

"There's an awesome amount of untapped industrial potential in this sector," Wilde pointed out. "Giving them the bypass hacks might turn several different races into major powers in their own right."

"They wouldn't have so much *need* for war," Hoshiko said. She shook her head in disbelief as she looked towards the distant fabber. "Why didn't they ever *use* their technology?"

It was a galling thought. The Tokomaks could do so *much*. They had practically-infinite energy at their disposal, they could literally teleport someone from place to place, they could put together automated factories that could build almost anything, given time and raw materials, yet they hadn't created a paradise. It hadn't taken more than ten years for the Solar Union to build enough productive capability to feed and support itself indefinitely, then absorb hundreds of thousands of immigrants every year. Surely, with a head start of thousands of years, the Tokomak could have done the same. They could have built an interstellar civilisation that made the Solar Union look like a handful of primitive islands in the middle of an endless desert.

And all they did was build an empire that kept everyone else firmly under their thumb and slowed scientific progress to a crawl, she thought. *What would have happened to them if even one of their subject races made a major breakthrough and turned it against them?*

Wilde stepped up next to her. "I think they were *scared*."

Hoshiko turned to look at him. "Scared of *what*?"

"Scared of the potential of their own technology," Wilde said. "And the prospects for good and ill."

Hoshiko shook her head, dismissively. "Idiots," she said. "They could have built themselves a heaven and instead they built a hell for everyone else."

Wilde frowned. "Permission to speak freely, Captain?"

Hoshiko nodded, curtly.

"You're too young to understand," Wilde said.

"You're a babe in arms compared to ninety percent of the Tokomak," Hoshiko pointed out, tartly. She wasn't *that* young. "The youngest prisoner we took during the battle was over a thousand years old."

"Bear with me a little," Wilde said. "When I was a child, computers were gigantic calculators and very few people imagined the world would need more than a handful of them, while spaceflight consisted of rockets and a much-overrated space shuttle. The world was changing even before Contact. Suddenly, there was a computer in every home; suddenly, one could be exposed to all manner of material on the internet; suddenly, the world was no longer a certain place. Every new development brought dangers as well as benefits."

He shrugged. "There were people who predicted nanotech would eventually free us from the curse of having to work," he noted, "and people who predicted that one terrorist would eventually release a strain of grey goo that would melt the entire world like a sugar cube dropped into a mug of tea. There were people who predicted that the internet, the precursor to the datanet, would destroy social morals once and for all...and people who predicted that the internet would unleash a wave of innovation and social reform."

"It did," Hoshiko said.

"It did both," Wilde said. "You know what put the first pornographers out of business?"

Hoshiko shrugged. She didn't see the point.

"The internet," Wilde said. "Why would someone pay for a filthy magazine or a video tape when they can just download porn from the internet? But because it was harder to keep pornographic materials from teenagers, even *children*, it started to cause other social problems. On one hand, teenagers were being corrupted by what they saw online; on the other, they were withdrawing from normal society because it didn't match up to their expectations."

"I'm not sure that makes any kind of sense," Hoshiko said.

"Every little technological change has unexpected side effects," Wilde explained. "For example, the internet broke the information stranglehold held by old media - what we used to call the mainstream media. But, at the same time, it made everything *now*. There was no longer any sense of perspective, no longer any time to come to a measured judgement. The slightest mishap, during a war, would instantly become a defeat on an unprecedented scale.

"Reliable birth control technology liberated women from the tyranny of their bodies, from the social structures that controlled their sexuality. That was a net gain because the former social structure had perpetrated countless injustices to keep women under control. But it also destroyed marriage. Young men were no longer committing themselves to marriage, because they could get sex without it, while on the other hand marriage was no longer regarded as sacred.

He shrugged. "If you happen to be old, and a little set in your ways, you find the pace of change disconcerting," he added. "I imagine the Tokomak felt the same way too.

"You grew up on an asteroid. You worked with mature technology and learned to embrace it, for good or ill. Your ancestors, however, didn't have that option. For them, technology was a curse as much as a blessing."

"But technology made their lives better," Hoshiko objected.

"Not always," Wilde said. He waved a hand at the bulkhead. "We already have AIs that can think and react faster than any biological life form. What happens when they start putting AIs in ships permanently, as the sole commander? It isn't as though it's beyond us. An AI core could handle everything from combat operations to repairs while under fire. They might even do a better job. What would you say when they came to you and said that your captaincy is no longer necessary?

"That's what happened on Earth. Every advancement brought gains to some and woes to others. Spinning machines ruined the livelihoods of thousands of people; robotic cash machines and library counters cost the jobs of thousands more. Captain, the *Solar Union* bears some responsibility for the crisis on Earth because we sucked away hundreds of thousands of people who might otherwise have saved civilisation!

"If your job was under threat by some newfangled piece of technology, wouldn't you object?"

He shrugged. "And there's a more cynical point," he concluded. "For the Solar Union, making sure that everyone has enough to eat and drink - the bare minimum - isn't anything more than a tiny percentage of our GNP. But if you expand the fabbers, if you cut the price of everything until giving someone a starship made of gold becomes nothing more than an exercise in logistics, you don't *need* a system to control the distribution of resources any longer. Why would you even need a *government?*"

"So their people were scared of reaching for a prosperous future," Hoshiko said. "That makes no sense."

"Not to you," Wilde said. "To them...I imagine it must have been terrifying."

He smiled, rather tightly. "Right now, putting together a genetically-engineered disease and unleashing it on Earth would be easy," he warned. "There's no shortage of biological labs in the Solar Union that could do it. Or building an antimatter production plant...a single lone maniac with a murderous grudge against society could do *real* damage. The more technology advances, the more risks as well as benefits.

"And it wasn't *us* who created the fabbers in the first place," he concluded. "Or FTL. Or antigravity. We stole the technology and reverse-engineered it, then started to make improvements. The Tokomak might well have had good reasons to be scared."

"I don't believe that," Hoshiko said. "I *can't*."

"I know," Wilde said. "Back when I was young, there was a book about a race of super-Nazis, a twisted society that eventually split into two genetically-modified races: masters and slaves. The slaves were genetically programmed to submit to the masters. Their free will could be overridden at any time, if their masters commanded it."

"It sounds horrific," Hoshiko said. "How did it even *work?*"

"The hell of it is that their society seems ideal, at first," Wilde added. "You have to look below the surface to realise just how twisted it is, just what an offense it is against everything we hold dear…

"And we could make it real, using our technology. And if *that* happens, freedom will become a distant memory. Advanced technology could bring servitude instead of freedom."

"My grandfather said the same," Hoshiko said.

"And he was right," Wilde finished.

TWELVE

Reports of a disease that targets only white or mixed-race individuals have been coming in from Africa over the last two days. Sources on the ground suggest that the disease is genetically-engineered to target those with European ancestry. The Solar Union Health Commission has dispatched a team to Africa to investigate the threat, but notes that - so far - there is no evidence the disease can infect or kill anyone with even basic immune system biomods.

-Solar News Network, Year 54

Griffin Wilde had wondered just what the Captain had made of his little speech, but by the time the senior officers - and a handful of alien representatives - gathered via hologram to discuss their next move, the Captain had said nothing to him about it. Perhaps she hadn't had the time to consider his words - or, perhaps, she'd simply dismissed them out of hand. Finding the balance between advancing technology and protecting society wasn't easy and, over the years, far too much damage had been done in the name of the latter. The stagnancy that bedevilled the Tokomak and the social exclusion that had urged so many to flee to the Solar Union had their root cases in conservatives who'd been afraid of the future.

Afraid of losing what they had, he thought, as he took his seat. The aliens, somewhat to his surprise, had enthusiastically agreed to attend via hologram, once the first set of face-to-face meetings had been concluded. *And afraid of being rendered irrelevant by the future.*

He sighed inwardly at the thought. Unlike Hoshiko, he felt a certain regard for Earth, the homeworld of the human race. The thought of a collapse of civilisation, a fallback into barbarism, was horrifying. And yet, he doubted the Solar Union could truly save Earth from itself, not without a major commitment that would turn the Solar Marines into an occupation force and open the gateways to a moral and ethical corruption that would risk everything the Solar Union had built.

But at least we should try to support the civilised men, he told himself. *And perhaps, through them, Earth could be saved.*

"Welcome, Fellow Sentients," Hoshiko said. She'd clearly downloaded a Gal-Standard One interface module for her implants, although she would have learned Gal-Standard One at the Academy like everyone else. "It is time to decide how to proceed."

She leaned back in her chair, looking calm and composed. It would be wasted on the aliens, Griffin thought; their ability to read human expressions and postures was as limited as humanity's ability to read theirs. Social etiquette in the Tokomak Empire was designed to limit friction and misunderstandings, but it couldn't eliminate them completely. Unless, of course, the aliens had obtained a human interaction file from the squadron. Griffin was fairly sure that at least one of them would have been included with the data packets they'd simply been giving away.

Their implants aren't as advanced as ours, he reminded himself. *They'd have problems keeping the file in primary mode.*

"The Druavroks on the surface have been contained," Hoshiko continued, "and the ones in the system itself have been eliminated. There is no prospect of them successfully regaining the initiative, at least until reinforcements arrive from their forward bases. Should they attempt to launch a second offensive, we will hammer them from orbit and exterminate their remaining enclaves. Furthermore, the defences of Amstar are growing stronger all the time."

She paused for effect. Griffin frowned, inwardly. Exterminating the Druavroks on the surface was a breach of standing orders, no matter what sort of threat they posed to everyone else on the surface. The Solar Union's regulations flatly prohibited genocide. But it had been the only way to compromise between the planet's understandable desire to rid themselves of the threat, once and for all, and humanity's moral qualms. He hoped - prayed—that the Druavroks had enough sense to remain in their enclaves and not come out.

And that our friends on the surface don't take control of the orbital platforms and bombard the enclaves themselves, he thought. *What do we do if they succeed in committing genocide?*

It wasn't a pleasant thought. The reports from the surface had made it clear that local militias and individual vigilantes were patrolling the edge of the Druavrok enclaves, while hunting down and slaughtering any Druavroks caught outside the enclaves. Sniper fire from the enclaves was so intense, the marines had noted, that the other enclaves had been evacuated and the entire area was largely deserted. If nothing else, it would make life easier if the Druavroks ever *did* come screaming out to restart their crusade. The KEWs could be dropped without worrying about civilian casualties.

"We now need to decide how best to proceed to take the war to them," Hoshiko said. "As you can see, we have several options."

Griffin dragged his attention back to her as she activated a large star chart, projecting it in front of them. Red stars marked worlds known to be held by the Druavroks, green stars marked allies; green and red icons represented worlds that were currently disputed. In most cases, the Druavroks had already been settled there in large numbers before the Tokomak had retreated from the sector. They'd promptly declared war on everyone else and attacked.

And there are a lot of red worlds, he thought. The Druavroks had held over twenty systems before the war had begun; now, they held thirty-two and seventeen other systems were battlegrounds. *They're well on their way to becoming a major threat.*

He cursed inwardly as Hoshiko talked her audience through the map. The bypasses and hacks humanity had developed for the fabbers would spread, of course. Griffin would have happily bet half his yearly salary that the Druavroks would have their own hacks within a couple of months, no matter how careful the allies were to protect the data. *Someone* could always be bribed, of course, or the information could simply be stolen. And then the Druavroks would start turning out human-grade weapons and technology of their own.

"The obvious course of action is to attempt to relieve one of the disputed worlds," Hoshiko said, once she'd finished explaining the map. "However, that has its problems; the enemy will be in strength, expecting an attack. They may not realise that we are forming a coalition, but they do know that some of their targets have allies. Therefore, I intend to attack Malachi, here. The Druavroks have been running supplies through the system ever since they captured it, turning the system into a base camp. Hitting it and destroying their supply lines - stealing their fabbers and smashing their warehouses - would put a crimp in their operations."

There was another reason, Griffin knew. The massive fleet simply wasn't very agile at the best of times - and getting thousands of ships from seventeen different races to work together was sheer hell. Hoshiko had freed up too many of her crew to serve as 'liaison officers' for Griffin's comfort. *Jackie Fisher* could, in theory, be operated by only twenty officers and men, but it wasn't something Griffin wanted to try in practice. Cutting the crew to fifty was a major gamble.

But we need them on the ships, Griffin thought. *And we need to blood the crews against a target that can't fight back effectively.*

He scowled at the thought. The coalition was fragile; humanity might have beaten the Tokomak and chased the Druavroks off Amstar, but the other members feared the Druavroks and worried for the safety of their homeworlds. They needed to *believe* they could win, they needed to *believe* they could beat the Druavroks, or humanity would be stuck doing the heavy lifting for the rest of time. And, with only nine cruisers and a handful of smaller ships, Hoshiko simply *couldn't* fight the Druavroks alone.

"We will spend the next three days working through tactical simulations, culminating with a live-fire exercise that will allow the crews a chance to get to grips with human-level technology," Hoshiko continued. "The planning staff is currently working on ways to get a peek into the enemy system without alerting them to our approach. In the unlikely event of us running into more firepower than we can reasonably handle, we'll divert the fleet to a secondary target. This will also give us a chance to further expand the fixed defences surrounding Amstar."

And make sure the system remains secure, Griffin thought. He had to admit that capturing the fabbers had been a lucky break, despite the long-term risks. Their steady output would eventually make Amstar impregnable. *But we don't want to become too dependent on a single source of supply.*

"Once we have completed the operation, we will consider our next set of targets," Hoshiko concluded. "I ask all of you to request as many courier boats as possible, as we will need to move within our enemy's decision-making loop as much as we can. We also need hundreds of additional warships and freighters, both to add fighting power to our forces and to supply our ships as we strike into enemy territory. This is warfare on an unprecedented scale and we need to be ready."

And hope the enemy hasn't done as much planning as we have, Griffin thought. The Tokomaks rarely bothered with serious planning, not when they enjoyed such a vast advantage over any conceivable foes. They just gathered an overwhelmingly powerful force, pointed it at the enemy ship and stomped it into rubble. *The enemy might have taken lessons from their former masters.*

"I thank you for your time," Hoshiko said. "The floor is now open for discussions."

Griffin listened, feeling a twinge of sympathy for his commander - and for some of his former superiors, back in the days of the wet navy. Coalition warfare was never easy, not when each allied nation had its own agenda. Some of them had sought political advantage, some had wanted a formal *quid pro quo* and some hadn't been particularly invested in the war at all. Indeed, he recalled a handful of allies who had been playing both sides of the field and slipping information to the enemies of freedom. The only real difference between coalition warfare on Earth and the growing alliance against the Druavroks was that the aliens understood that they were targets, no matter what they did.

Good thing the Druavroks never learned how to be diplomatic, Griffin thought, as the discussion raged on. *They could split the coalition in two just by making the right promises to the right people.*

"But getting into the system without being detected is impossible," one alien insisted, loudly. "They will see you coming!"

"Yes, they will," Hoshiko agreed. "But the fleet can actually get within a few hours of the system without being detected. We hold position and send a single spy ship on ahead."

Griffin sighed inwardly as the discussion finally came to an end. Hoshiko had been more patient than he'd expected, but it had been easy for him to tell she was growing tired and ragged before finally calling a halt. The argument had begun to go in circles, after all; too many alien races were afraid that their rivals would take advantage of their weaknesses and strike at their homeworlds while they were diverted. Hoshiko had finally promised human retribution against anyone who broke their word, but Griffin was all too aware that she might not be able to *keep* that promise. The Solar Union would certainly object to strikes against allied worlds.

"We will start the first formal exercise tomorrow," Hoshiko said. "And then the main body of the fleet will depart in three days."

She sat back in her chair, looking tired and wan, as the holographic images vanished from the chamber. Griffin watched her, feeling a sudden flicker of concern. It was his job, as XO, to watch his commander's health as well as her mental state and he had a nasty feeling that Hoshiko was pushing herself to the limits. She might have been heavily enhanced - the Solarians had no compunctions about loading their bodies with technology - but she was still human.

"Captain," he said. "I'd suggest a long nap."

"There's too much to do," Hoshiko said. She rubbed her forehead as she sat upright. "It's never that bad when we have our regular meetings."

"Your commanding officers share the same general background and understanding of the universe," Griffin said. "They may be your subordinates, but they expect you to treat them as *people* and not to discard them without *very* good cause. Even if they don't like you, they know you have nothing to gain by throwing their lives away. Pulling a Uriah Gambit would get you flung out an airlock after the inevitable court-martial."

"Sending one of my commanding officers to die because I desired his partner would be shitty," Hoshiko said.

"There are races involved in your coalition that have disputes," Griffin reminded her. "If you were to send one race's battleships to their doom, their rivals will grow relatively stronger and perhaps turn on their enemies once the war against the Druavroks is over. Therefore, even while they fight beside us, they guard their backs against their rivals and prospective future enemies. The only reason they trust us, I think, is because humanity isn't a particularly significant race in this sector - and I don't expect it to last."

Hoshiko raised her eyebrows. "Why?"

"Because there *are* large settlements of humans here," Griffin reminded her. "We might end up using them as an excuse for *Anschluss*."

"I wouldn't want to," Hoshiko said. "We're not interested in annexing worlds."

"They don't understand our society," Griffin said. "And why should they? The concept of a society that is primarily based on asteroids and small moons is alien to them."

"Because the Tokomak were obsessed with worlds themselves," Hoshiko said. "They never made the transition to a spacefaring society."

"And we only did for political reasons," Griffin said. He shrugged. "Captain, if I may make a suggestion, get some sleep."

"Soon," Hoshiko said.

Griffin felt another stab of sympathy, despite his worries. Hoshiko effectively wore three hats now: commanding officer of *Jackie Fisher*, commanding officer of the squadron and commanding officer of the coalition fleet. She had placed dozens of people in positions where they could handle the immense problems facing them, but the buck still stopped with her. And if the Solar Union chose to object to her approach to the problems facing the sector, she'd pay for it with her life...

...*And there's no one she can truly confide in*, he thought. It wasn't uncommon for junior officers or crewmen to form relationships - it wasn't against regulations, as long as they were at roughly the same rank - but there was literally no one who was either an equal or a civilian, not to Hoshiko. *There's no one she can relax around and just be herself.*

Hoshiko cleared her throat. "I want to make some special preparations," she said, leaning forward. "First, I intend to command the exercises - and our first deployment - from the CIC, leaving you in command of the ship. It's *technically* a dereliction of duty, but I see no way around it."

"Nor do I," Griffin said. The regulations that forbade captains from leaving their bridge during a combat situation hadn't been written to cover these circumstances. Normally, there would be a captain on the bridge and an admiral in the CIC. "How do you intend to set up a chain of command?"

"That will be tricky," Hoshiko acknowledged. "Captain Ryman is the most experienced person we have, when it comes to dealing with aliens, but his military experience is somewhat outdated. If something happens to *Jackie Fisher*, Captain Macpherson will assume command of the fleet. We can't risk appointing an alien because everyone who wasn't appointed will complain."

"If this alliance turns into a permanent structure," Griffin said, "we're going to need to get around that somehow."

"Maybe set up a joint space force," Hoshiko said. "It isn't as though we couldn't have multiracial ships."

"The logistics would be a pain," Griffin said. "Even if we insisted on only allowing humanoid races to join, Captain, it would still be a major headache."

Hoshiko smirked. "Wasn't that what they said about allowing women on combat ships back in the wet navy?"

"The problems would be an order of magnitude worse," Griffin said, irked. The wet navy had had problems integrating female crewmembers, but at least the women had been *human* and could use human facilities. He tried to imagine a Hordesman using a human toilet and shuddered. "Even for a bigger ship, even with modern technology, it would still be a struggle."

"Perhaps," Hoshiko said. "But the only way to overcome distrust is to have officers serve together before they take roles in high command."

She sighed. "There's one other thing I've been considering," she added. "I want you to prepare a couple of ships for a small crew. A freighter, for preference, and a courier boat."

Griffin frowned. "Can I ask why?"

"The problem with approaching Malachi is that they'll see us coming," Hoshiko said. "I think there's a way to limit what they can see before it's too late."

She outlined what she wanted, piece by piece. "It should be doable," she concluded. "And I will be commanding the ship myself."

"You shouldn't," Griffin said. The commander should not put herself in extra danger during wartime. "You're the glue holding this hodgepodge together."

"That's precisely why I have to take the risk, Commander," Hoshiko said. "Our allies may be nervous about being knifed in the back by our *other* allies, but they have to be worried about us too. I need to prove to them that we're going to be sharing the risks."

"That's…not a smart choice," Griffin objected.

"I know," Hoshiko said. "But I don't think we *have* a choice."

THIRTEEN

A radioactive 'dirty bomb' was triggered in Delhi yesterday, creating a cloud of radioactive particles that poisoned thousands of civilians. The Indian Government declared it the work of Islamist terrorists and announced a major round-up of Islamists and everyone even remotely connected to them.

-Solar News Network, Year 54

Jackie Fisher, Hoshiko had discovered when she'd first boarded her command, hadn't really been *designed* as a command vessel. The Solar Union had been designing the *Admiral*-class heavy cruisers back when there had been little interest in mounting operations well away from Sol, where there were ample command vessels of other classes available. Her CIC therefore doubled as her secondary bridge, while her flag deck was relatively small and there were only a handful of compartments for an admiral's command staff. But as long as it did the job, Hoshiko found it hard to care. Her uncle had worked hard on reducing personal staffs in any case.

"It's bad for an admiral to be surrounded by ass-kissers," he'd said, back when Hoshiko had been preparing for the Academy. "They tell him what they think he wants to hear and never tell him what he *needs* to hear."

She pushed the thought out of her mind as she looked up at the holographic display, silently replaying the single live-fire exercise they'd completed. Thankfully, they'd carried out a number of simulated exercises first or the Grand Alliance - as she'd dubbed it - would have come to a crashing halt there and then. Accidentally shooting up their own ships was quite bad enough, but it was unlikely that half the races involved would have accepted it *was* an accident. Commander Wilde's assertion that some of the members would take advantage of the alliance to address their own concerns, even at the expense of the other members, was starting to look *very* well founded indeed.

At least we're getting to the point where we can fly in rough formation, she told herself, as the exercise came to an end. The combat datanet had taken a week to set up, then another week of hard practice to operate, but they could fly and fight as a unit now. And they'd worked so many redundancies into the system that it would be hard for the enemy to take it down. *As long as everyone cooperates, at least...*

"Record," she ordered, sending a command to her implants. "Personal for Admiral Stuart, Fleet Command. Admiral. Live fire exercises have proved a success, but there is considerable room for improvement. I intend to keep testing the crews during our flight to Malachi and hold a final set of exercises when we reach the RV point. Unfortunately, there are limits to how much fire our modified freighters can take..."

She droned on, carefully explaining her decisions and the rationale behind them. Uncle Mongo would understand, she suspected, her decision to place her own life at risk, although it wouldn't stop him chewing her out afterwards - if she survived. She was a Stuart, after all, and flinching from the sound of the guns was not in her blood. Even Uncle Kevin, the spy her little brother had thought was impossibly cool during his early years, had never inched away from getting his hands dirty. Some of the stories he'd told about his days in the service on Earth had fascinated her, even though she was sure they weren't entirely true. How could one man have stopped a war by kidnapping a terrorist from his tent?

"I have weighed up the advantages as well as the disadvantages of my chosen course of action," she concluded. "There is a considerable risk in putting my life at stake. However, for diplomatic reasons, I believe I have no choice."

She stopped the recording and uploaded it to the datacore, along with copies of their records and personal messages from the crew to their loved ones. They'd be on their way to Earth before the fleet left Amstar, the last testaments of her crew if something happened to *Jackie Fisher.* Hoshiko knew there was a prospect of death - Stuarts had fallen in battle before over the years - but she feared losing the war more than she feared losing her life. Building the Grand Alliance was important, yet stopping the Druavroks was rather more so. The evil they represented could not be let loose on the galaxy.

Which means we have to pound the living daylights out of them, she thought. The doctor had finally found a female corpse to dissect, but any hopes Hoshiko might have had about Druavrok females being more rational had swiftly been lost. They were just as bloody-minded as the males. *We have to thump them until they're begging for mercy.*

She pushed the thought aside as the recording of the exercise began to repeat itself. The fleet was already working on correcting its weaknesses, although the crews would need real combat experience before they truly understood what they were doing. But then, part of the reason she'd picked their target was that it shouldn't pose too great a challenge, allowing her ships to gain experience without any action risk. Or so she hoped. She knew, better than most, just what could happen when Murphy got a look-in. Whatever could go wrong probably would, at the worst possible time.

The hatch opened with a hiss. Hoshiko turned, just in time to see Ensign Howard peeking into the CIC. "Captain?"

"Ensign," Hoshiko said. She'd left Howard with Captain Ryman as an aide, gofer and quiet supervisor. The young man would have to grow up very quickly now the squadron was going to war. "What can I do for you?"

Howard looked embarrassed. "Captain, umm...*Commodore* Ryman would like to speak with you, if it isn't too much trouble."

"It's not," Hoshiko said, concealing her amusement with some effort. "Send him to my office. I'll be along in a few minutes."

She took one final look around the CIC as the ensign vanished and then walked through the hatch, back to her office. Captain Ryman was waiting outside, looking surprisingly composed; Ensign Howard looked about as nervous as a schoolboy who'd been summoned to meet the principal. Hoshiko kept her amusement under strict control as she opened the hatch - etiquette forbade anyone to enter without her - and led the way into her office. Her steward materialised out of his compartment and shot her an inquiring look.

"Coffee for me and Commodore Ryman," Hoshiko said. She turned to look at Ensign Howard. Keeping him in the cabin would be torture. "You're dismissed for the moment, ensign. Go to the galley and request something to eat."

"Aye, Captain," Ensign Howard said, too young to hide his relief. "I'll remain there until summoned."

He hurried out of the hatch before she could change her mind. Hoshiko shook her head with genuine amusement - she'd probably been just as gauche as a young officer herself - and then looked at Captain Ryman, who shrugged. The merchant spacers were less formal than the Solar Navy. They had to be.

"Please, take a seat," she said, as the steward returned with two mugs of coffee and a tray of sticky buns. Someone, probably Commander Wilde or Doctor Carr, had told him to make sure Hoshiko ate over the last few days. "I trust the recent courier boats brought good news?"

"The Gloudathua and the Tradresh signed up at once," Captain Ryman said, taking one of the mugs of coffee and lifting it to his mouth. "They're deadly rivals, Captain, so neither of them would want to take the risk of allowing the other to gain an advantage. The weapons tech and bypass codes we gave them only sweetened the deal. They'd agreed to earmark a couple of battle squadrons for us apiece if we show them that we can win battles."

"Understood," Hoshiko said. "And the Qluyt'yrti?"

"Still unsure what we can do for them," Captain Ryman told her. "Their representative here is convinced, but her homeworld is rather less concerned about Amstar than you might expect. I suspect they will probably change their minds within the next couple of weeks, Captain, once they see what we've done for the others."

He sighed. "It will be at least another couple of weeks before we hear back from a handful of other homeworlds and races," he added. "I'm seriously thinking about setting up a permanent headquarters on Amstar. It's a multiracial world without a single dominate race, so it would serve as a sensible place to set up our base. Martina might serve as a secondary base if necessary, but their ruling council is still arguing over the best course of action."

"They'll be in the firing line sooner or later," Hoshiko pointed out.

"Amstar forced its inhabitants to work together," Captain Ryman said. "Martina doesn't have a real authority in control of the system. I'm hoping that will change, but it will take time, time they may not have."

Hoshiko nodded. "Are you planning to remain behind on Amstar?"

"Unless you have someone else lined up to do the diplomatic work," Captain Ryman said, bluntly. "It also gives me a chance to expand the network of spies. Just asking questions of merchant spacers as they come into port will tell us a great deal more about the enemy, Captain, and the rest of the sector."

"And let you recruit more spacers," Hoshiko agreed. "Manpower is going to be a pain in the ass for a long time to come."

"I'm afraid so," Captain Ryman said. "We can expand the trade schools now, if you like, even establish new ones, but it will be years before we see a major increase in engineers and other trained experts. Much of what passed for engineering while the Tokomak were in power basically consisted of removing one item from the drives and replacing it with another drawn from spares. If they lacked a spare part…tough shit."

"Crazy," Hoshiko said.

Captain Ryman shrugged. "How many of your officers know how to tear down and rebuild an FTL drive?"

"My engineers do," Hoshiko said. The Solar Navy paid a higher salary to anyone with a genuine working knowledge of GalTech, which didn't stop them being poached by merchant shippers and commercial concerns. Someone who could modify a Galactic FTL drive, to say nothing of a fabber or orbital defence array, was worth his or her weight in just about anything, if not more. "I've always been more interested in the tactical side of space combat, myself."

"And without the engineers, your ships wouldn't function for long," Captain Ryman said. "I think the Tokomak didn't want their subjects actually repairing their ships. They may even have been playing silly buggers with the fabbers."

Hoshiko nodded, remembering one intelligence briefing. There had been a suspicion - never confirmed - that the fabbers included programming to hardwire override codes into everything they produced, allowing the Tokomak to take over the systems at will. The thought of having her command network suddenly stolen from under her was terrifying, given just how dependent she was on the computers. But no amount of investigation had managed to find proof the codes actually existed. Solar Intelligence had eventually concluded the suspicion was little more than a rumour, one intended to keep the subject races from rebelling. What was the point of trying to launch an uprising when one's ships could simply be deactivated at will?

"We can change that," she said, simply. Given time, who knew what alien minds would produce? "And we will."

"There are a number of other issues," Captain Ryman said, "but all of them are only really important if we manage to defeat the Druavroks. They want some trade deals, either with us or with the ITA, yet…"

"There's no point in worrying about that at the moment," Hoshiko said. They had a war to fight. "Keep the Grand Alliance focused on military matters."

"I shall certainly try," Captain Ryman said. He finished his coffee and returned the mug to the tray. "I should tell you, Captain, that I'm very pleased with young Ensign Howard. He handled himself very well in the endless series of meetings down on the planet."

"I'm glad to hear that," Hoshiko said. She hadn't had time to do more than glance at the reports, but no one had exploded with rage or demanded that the poor ensign be declared *persona non grata*. "Do you wish him to remain with you or return to the ship for combat duty?"

"I have a small staff now," Captain Ryman said. "The Pan-Gal had a number of human employees who were willing to work for me. If you want Thomas back, I won't fight to keep him."

Hoshiko considered the matter, briefly. She needed every officer she could get on *Jackie Fisher*, even someone who'd been fresh out of the Academy when the squadron had been dispatched to Martina. Ensign Howard showed promise, at least; a few months of combat duty would give him the practical experience he lacked. But then, diplomatic experience would also be helpful, if he wanted to go into command or diplomatic tracks.

"Unless you have an urgent need for Howard, I'll take him back for the moment," she said. It was possible that the ensign would view the transfer as a punishment, although it wasn't really anything of the sort. Detached duty wouldn't be counted in his favour when the promotions board met. "In any case, we have to defeat the Druavroks at Malachi or the Grand Alliance will come apart before it's even fairly begun."

"Agreed," Captain Ryman said. He glanced at his watch, an old clockwork model that looked old enough to predate Contact. "With your permission, Captain, I'll beam down to the planet now. My reports - to you and to the ITA - have already been filed. Should the Druavroks return…well, we can at least give a good account of ourselves this time."

"Try and keep the locals from bombarding the enclaves," Hoshiko said, as she rose. "And good luck."

"I'll do my best," Captain Ryman said. He took her hand and kissed it, lightly. "And thank you for everything."

Hoshiko watched him go, then sat down and closed her eyes as she accessed his reports through her implants. They weren't particularly detailed, but they touched on everything of importance; she smiled, in genuine amusement, when she read the details about what *else* several races wanted the Grand Alliance to do. A trade deal was one thing, but a semi-united federation of planets was quite another. The idea was attractive, she had to admit, yet it was a far cry from her original plan. Perhaps, once the Druavroks were defeated, they could consider a long-term alliance.

She rose and walked to the bridge, taking her command chair as the starship prepared for departure. The aliens, thankfully, didn't seem to have a problem with being punctual; the fleet status display was showing an endless wall of green icons, with only a handful marked out as yellow for unready and red for disabled. She checked one of them and discovered that an FTL drive had burned out and repair crews were struggling to get the freighter ready to depart on time. It looked unlikely they'd be remotely ready to go, but she decided to see if they made it. The more enthusiastic they were about taking the offensive, the better.

"Captain," Commander Wilde said, an hour later. "The fleet is ready to depart."

Hoshiko nodded, studying the display. The alien repair crews *had* made it, after all, and the freighter was ready to leave with the rest of the fleet. She was a heavy freighter, crammed with missile launchers, but Hoshiko had no illusions. She'd die very quickly if a warship decided to kill her.

But they won't die for nothing, she promised herself. *We're going to face a genocidal foe.*

"General signal to all ships," she ordered, coolly. "Set FTL drives to the correct coordinates, then prepare to jump to FTL. All ships acknowledge."

She waited, as patiently as she could, until the final ship had reported in. The formation would horrify her superiors, let alone the Tokomak, but it would have to do. Flying so many ships in close formation at FTL speeds would be asking for trouble. And the gravitational eddies would be so powerful that they couldn't risk getting too close to the target system before they knew what they were facing. The Druavroks would see them coming and prepare a surprise of their own.

"All ships have acknowledged, Captain," Wilde said, formally. "The fleet is ready to depart on your command."

Hoshiko hesitated. For better or worse, her every action was being recorded and whatever she said or did would serve as an example to her successors, either as an example of moral judgement or what *not* to do under any circumstances. She wanted to say something that would resonate down the ages, but she couldn't think of anything that might pass muster.

"Take us into FTL," she ordered, instead.

"Aye, Captain," the helmsman said. The starship shuddered slightly as she slipped into FTL, followed by the remainder of the fleet. "We're on our way."

"Good," Hoshiko said. She glanced at the XO. "Give the crew a day of reduced duty, then return to the simulations and disaster drills."

"Aye, Captain," Wilde said. He had doubts - she *knew* he had doubts - but he wouldn't let them interfere with his duty. And as long as he didn't, she'd ignore his doubts. His advice was always good, even if she didn't take it. "I'll see to it personally."

"You have the bridge," Hoshiko said. She *needed* a break, if nothing else. Her XO could handle the ship long enough for her to have a long nap. "Inform me if anything happens."

"Aye, Captain," the XO said.

FOURTEEN

Investigative teams in South Africa have confirmed that the white-killing disease is almost certainly man-made and, worse, is very likely to mutate and target non-white/mixed individuals. It is strongly advised that all people within the danger zone be vaccinated against the virus and, if they wish, take immune boosters. This virus threatens to spread rapidly.
-Solar News Network, Year 54

"Well," Ensign Sandra Higgs said, as she rolled off him. "I needed that, Tom."

Thomas smiled, taking a moment to bask in the glow of simple contentment. Sandra had caught him as he finished his duty shift and invited him, in line with the simple etiquette governing onboard relationships, into the privacy tubes. Thomas hadn't needed to think before accepting. It had been too long for him too.

"So did I," he said. "You were great."

Sandra gave him an affectionate look. "You're new to shipboard duty, aren't you?"

Thomas nodded. There was no point in trying to hide it. He'd been the baby ensign, the lowest commissioned officer on the ship, ever since he'd boarded *Jackie Fisher* before she departed Sol. It was uncommon to be the baby for longer than a few months, when the next graduating class left the academy, but no one had given him a hard time over it. There'd just been too much to do for more than a little good-natured hazing.

"Don't make more of this than it is," Sandra warned, as she stood. Her breasts glimmered with sweat as the lights grew brighter. "I just wanted a little relief and so did you. We're too young for a formal romance."

Thomas smiled, although he felt oddly hurt. She was right - they were both too young to attempt to start a courtship that would lead to marriage - but it still bothered him. And yet, in the normal run of things, most shipboard relationships lasted only a few months. One of the lovers would be transferred or the relationship would simply run its course. It was absurd to think that Sandra and he would be any different. She simply wasn't interested in anything other than spending the night with a willing partner.

"I'm not looking to settle down yet," he said. Most Solarians married formally in their forties and settled on one of the asteroids to raise children, before going back to work or seeking something completely new. "I'm not even sure where I want to go."

Sandra gave him a smile as she stepped into the sonic shower. "Amstar? I hear you did well there?"

Thomas considered it. He'd never thought about a career as a diplomat, although he had to admit that diplomats got to travel from place to place. It had struck him as boring…and yet, juggling requirements for a dozen different races had been fun, if complex. He'd seriously wondered about trying to find a job with the Pan-Gal, if he didn't stay in the navy. Running a multiracial hotel was one hell of a challenge.

"I'm not sure," he said, finally. "I got sent back up here when the squadron left."

"Detached duty isn't counted as shipboard duty," Sandra said, her voice echoing oddly as she turned on the shower and washed the sweat from her body. "You need at least twelve months as an ensign before you can be considered for promotion, in the normal run of things, but a month or two on detached duty wouldn't count. And then the promotion board would start asking pointed questions, if you stayed in grade long enough to be considered for an automatic promotion."

"That's not fair," Thomas protested, when he worked it out. "I could have twelve months of service, but only ten of them would count!"

"Life isn't fair," Sandra said. She stuck her head out of the shower and smirked. "Only a baby ensign would think it *was*. Would you like me to kiss your ego better?"

"No, thank you," Thomas said, biting down the rude suggestion he'd wanted to make. She would probably have refused to have sex with him again. "But you could tell me how best to outsmart the promotions board."

"Do something heroic and get promoted," Sandra said. She stepped out of the shower, picked up her shipsuit and started to pull it on. "But I doubt there's much hope of getting anything other than a provisional promotion before we return home, Tom. And if you did..."

Thomas sighed as he sat upright and stood. They'd been told that, in certain cases, a commanding officer could hand out a provisional promotion, if there was a reason the officer needed the authority of a higher rank. But such cases were always carefully scrutinised when the starship returned home, just in case favouritism - or worse - had been involved. The Academy staff had been careful to note, more than once, that provisional promotions were rarely confirmed, let alone counted as time in grade. It hadn't struck him as fair either, but there had to be limitations on a commander's authority when the ship was far from home.

"I need to nip down to my cabin for four hours of sleep before I go back on duty," Sandra said. She leaned forward, kissed him on the lips and then stepped back, all professional once again. "Try not to grin *too* broadly as you walk back to your cabin."

Thomas flushed, then hurried into the shower and washed himself clean. When he stepped back outside, Sandra was gone and the automatics were already cleaning the bed and readying it for the next users. He shook his head, pulled his shipsuit on as fast as he could and checked his implants. He had seven hours before his next duty shift, which would be well spent sleeping or eating something before he reported to the bridge. His stomach rumbled as he stepped out of the privacy tube, urging him to head down to the mess to get something to eat. And then a new icon popped up in front of his eyes, demanding his immediate attention. The XO wanted a word.

Shit, Thomas thought. The message's time-stamp indicated that it had been sent thirty minutes ago, but - because it hadn't been tagged urgent - it hadn't reached him while he'd been in the privacy tube. Unless he invented a time machine in the next ninety seconds, he would have to explain to the XO why he was over thirty minutes late. *I'm dead.*

Thomas tried to come up with an explanation as he hurried to the XO's office, but nothing came to mind. He'd just have to tell the truth and hope the XO didn't do more than assign him a thoroughly unpleasant duty for several weeks. He should have removed the filters, he told himself angrily, but he hadn't expected to be dragged into the privacy tube. There hadn't been any sign Sandra was interested in him...

He pushed his hand against the buzzer, feeling as if he were going to his own execution. The hatch hissed open a second later, revealing the XO sitting at his desk. Thomas braced himself, then strode forward and into the compartment. The hatch hissed closed behind him, trapping him. There was no escape.

"You're late," the XO said.

"Yes, sir," Thomas said. "I was in the privacy tubes."

The XO gave him a dark look. "And do you think that's a good excuse?"

"No, sir," Thomas said.

He swallowed, hard. There were all sorts of rumours, nasty rumours, about the old crewmen who'd served in the wet navies before transferring to the Solar Union. All of a sudden, the stories about them ramming red-hot pokers up the backsides of ensigns who displeased them seemed alarmingly plausible. Some of them were so old he was tempted to believe they dated all the way back to the age of sail, even though cold logic told him it was unlikely. The oldest in naval service couldn't have been born long before 1950.

"For the record, I *strongly* suggest you don't put any filters on your messages, even while you're in the tubes," the XO said, dryly. "Had the meeting been urgent, young man, you would have been in deep shit."

"Yes, sir," Thomas said.

"As it happens, you may be in deep shit anyway," the XO said. "I understand from your Academy records that you know how to fly a Galactic courier boat?"

"Yes, sir," Thomas said. "They were trying to attract couriers to transport messages from star to star."

The XO nodded. "And why didn't you take a post on one of the boats?"

"Too claustrophobic, sir," Thomas said. "The idea of being cooped up with two or three other couriers was too much to handle, even with VR sims and other entertainments. I didn't think the incentives made up for it."

"And promotion would be very slow," the XO said. "But you know how to handle a courier boat?"

"As long as it's in working order, sir," Thomas said. "An emergency on a courier boat in FTL would be very difficult to handle."

"It probably would be," the XO agreed. He cleared his throat. "We have a mission for you, Ensign. You're not the only person who can fly a courier boat, but you're the only *expendable* person at our disposal."

"Yes, sir," Thomas said. He had to admit that the baby ensign was certainly the least important member of the crew. Indeed, he'd been so unimportant that he hadn't been offered a billet on one of the alien ships. "You want me to fly a courier boat?"

"In a manner of speaking," the XO said. "We have ten days until we reach our target. If you accept the assignment, you'll be taken off the regular duty rota and put to work in the simulators, testing everything before we commit you to the operation. I should warn you that the prospect for disaster is actually quite high."

Thomas kept his face impassive as he considered it. The assignment made little sense, unless there was something he hadn't been told. The Galactics practically had a *fetish* about protecting courier boats, although the Druavroks might have other ideas. They might break the rules about not firing on courier boats, but few courier boats would fly right into the teeth of their fire in any case. Did the XO intend to turn a courier boat into a spy? It would explain much…

"I accept the mission, sir," he said. If the XO was right, Thomas was the only one who could be spared…and besides, it might look good in his file. Turning down the mission, on the other hand, would look very bad indeed. "What do you want me to do?"

"We're sending a modified bulk freighter into the system," the XO said. He cocked his head, sending a command to the compartment's processors. A holographic image of a Galactic bulk freighter, scarred through centuries of faithful service, appeared in front of them. "The freighter has been slaved to a courier boat that is currently stowed in the lower hold. You will be piloting that courier boat when the Captain decides she wants to abandon the freighter and leave the system."

Thomas stared. "The Captain, sir?"

"She will be in command of the mission," the XO confirmed. It was hard to be sure, but he didn't sound happy about it. "When the time comes, you will abandon the freighter and jump back into FTL."

"Yes, sir," Thomas said. It didn't sound *that* hard or dangerous, which suggested there was a nasty sting in the tail somewhere. "I should be able to do it."

"See that you can," the XO said. "We're giving you the simulation chamber. I want a full report on your progress in eight days. The Captain will be watching with great interest."

"I understand, sir," Thomas said. Inwardly, he was reeling. *He* was expendable, but the Captain? She shouldn't be putting herself on the front line. "I won't let you down."

MAX STOPPED OUTSIDE the hatch and hesitated, feeling oddly reluctant to enter. He'd spent the last two days editing the sensory recordings he'd taken during the landing on Amstar, but now he needed interviews to help flesh out the follow-up stories. None of the marines had responded, save for Hilde, a fact that worried him. Hilde might well have *orders* to allow him to interview her, orders she was unlikely to *like*. And while, on one hand, it didn't matter if she liked her orders or not, he knew it wouldn't make her an easy interview subject.

And allow her a chance to sue, later, he thought, as he pressed the buzzer. There were quite a few precedents that suggested a senior officer couldn't *order* a junior officer to talk to the press, whatever the situation. Hilde could easily claim she'd denied permission to have the recordings made public. *She'd have every chance of winning quite a substantial judgement in her favour later.*

The hatch hissed open, revealing a changing room. Max stepped inside, suddenly feeling a great deal warmer. Sweat started to trickle down his back as the hatch hissed closed behind him, locking closed with an ominous *click*. He hesitated, then stepped forward, looking around with interest. A curtain at the far end of the room concealed a shower. It was brushed aside a second later as Hilde stepped out of the shower, water dripping down her frame and peered at him.

Max couldn't help himself. He stared. Hilde was *huge*, her arms and legs so muscular that he was *sure* they were the results of genetic engineering. Her skin was a golden-brown, but there was something almost *leathery* about it; her breasts were sunk into her skin, the nipples barely even there. He had to fight to keep himself from stumbling backwards as she advanced towards him, trying hard not to stare at her naked body. There wasn't even a *hint* of hair anywhere within view.

Hilde laughed, throatily. "Like what you see?"

She watched him for a long moment, then picked up a towel and began to dry herself. "My father is practically a brain in a machine now," she said. "He lives in an asteroid without air or heat or gravity, without any of the conveniences you take for granted. My combat biomods are less extensive, but I can still survive in space for long periods without a spacesuit. How do I look to you?"

Max watched, unable to speak, as she turned slowly. Muscles rippled across her back and thighs, her bottom was tart, almost mannish. He'd known, of course, that there were cantons where genetic enhancement and biomods had been carried far further than in any of the inner cantons, but it was still a surprise to see one face to face. The sight was terrifyingly intimidating. Hilde could break him across her knee without effort.

"Strange," he said, finally. "Why…?"

"I choose not to be bound by baseline humanity," Hilde said, as she finished drying herself and dumped the towel in a basket. "You're enhanced too, are you not?"

"Not as extensively," Max said, feeling his heart racing as she came forward to loom over him. His feet felt as if they were rooted to the deck. "I never considered the advantages of living in space."

"It takes a lot to kill me," Hilde said, without heat. She motioned to the bench and sat down, her eyes following his every move. "Put me on Earth and I'd be able to survive indefinitely, eating and drinking whatever I could find. My children, assuming I had children, would have the same enhancements."

She smiled. "Getting through the atmosphere without a suit would be a pain, though."

"It would be," Max agreed. But that wasn't entirely true. There *were* people who jumped from orbit down to Mars for fun, he recalled. It wouldn't be *hard* to make a primitive space capsule to allow an enhanced human to get down to the surface. Getting back to orbit, on the other hand, would be a real problem. "Can you…can you have children?"

"Of course," Hilde said. "My womb and menstrual cycle is currently in suspension, thanks to the biomods, but it wouldn't be hard to reactive it. The dominants in my genetic code would assert themselves against baseline humans, though. I wouldn't want children who didn't have the advantages I have."

"I can understand that," Max said. She motioned for him to sit beside her, again, but he remained standing. Being so close to her was...*difficult*. "Do you plan to go to Earth one day?"

"Probably not," Hilde said. "I *am* a Solarian. But the corps may be deployed there one day."

Max cleared his throat. "I do have a number of questions to ask you," he said. Had Hilde walked out naked to intimidate him - or to make it harder for him to use any of his recordings in his work? He'd look like an ass if he complained to her superiors too. "Before we start, do you want to put something on or do you mind me recording you in the buff?"

"It might stop young idiots wandering into marine bars and trying to pick up marines," Hilde said. Her voice was so deadpan that Max couldn't tell if she was teasing him or not. "It's really quite annoying being chatted up by youngsters who haven't done anything like as much as I have. Or bastards who only ask me out on a dare. They'd freak out if they knew just what I did for a living."

"I suppose they would," Max agreed. He'd nearly freaked out when he'd seen the Druavroks charging their position. "So I can record you?"

"Go wild," Hilde said. She stretched back nonchalantly and smirked, like a cat. "What's your first question?"

Max swallowed. It was hard to keep his eyes off her.

"Down on the planet," he said. "How did the Druavroks make you *feel?*"

FIFTEEN

Turkey imploded into chaos yesterday as an Islamist coup took out the government and declared the foundation of an Islamic state. Greece, already shivering under endless economic problems and domestic unrest, has sealed the borders, but fears it will be unable to handle the expected tidal wave of refugees. Thousands of other refugees have already requested asylum in the Solar Union and millions more are expected to make the trip into space.

-Solar News Network, Year 54

"That's our target star," the helmsman said. "Malachi Primary."

Hoshiko nodded. From nine light months, Malachi Primary was barely more than a dot of light against the endless darkness of interstellar space. Long-range passive sensors picked up bursts of radio emissions coming from the planets orbiting the star, but it was impossible to collect any current data at such a distance. Even if a telescope existed that would allow her to see starships and orbital defence platforms, the information would be nine months out of date and completely useless. She'd have to take the ship a great deal closer to pick up any *useful* intelligence.

Which is the plan, she reminded herself as she rose. *In a manner of speaking, that is.*

"Mr. XO," she said, formally. "You have the bridge."

"I have the bridge," Wilde confirmed. He took a breath. They'd gone through a thousand different simulations of what they could expect to fight at Malachi and not all of them had ended well. He'd tried, several times, to talk her out of going, even offering to go in her place. But Hoshiko had always refused. "Good luck, Captain."

Hoshiko nodded, took one last look around the bridge and then headed for the hatch, stepping through and down towards the teleport chamber. Wilde and she had gone over so many contingency plans that she doubted there was any room for mistakes, unless the enemy came up with something new. The Druavroks *might* have a picket far enough from the primary star to pick up her fleet, they might launch an immediate strike of their own…and, if they did, her officers knew what to do.

But I have to remember that they might innovate too, she reminded herself as she stepped into the teleport chamber. *Just because the Tokomak deliberately kept them ignorant doesn't mean they're stupid.*

"Captain," the operator said. "Teleport to the *Eyesore?*"

"Yes, please," Hoshiko said. She stepped up onto the teleport platform and turned to face him. "Energise."

The old immigrants - her grandfather's generation - had never quite gotten used to teleporting, she recalled, as she felt her body dissolve into light. Her grandfather had agonised for years over just *what* teleporting did to the human soul, as if every time he stepped into a teleporter he committed suicide and was then replaced by a copy so perfect that it literally didn't know it *was* a copy. Hoshiko and her generation - and the Tokomak, for that matter - had far fewer doubts. The teleporter simply *couldn't* produce a copy, because duplicating something as complex as a human mind was impossible. There was no way she was anything other than herself, even if she *had* been teleported more times than she cared to count. She smiled to herself, again, as the courier boat materialised around her and the sensation of being light and energy faded away. The tiny bridge held one other occupant.

"Captain," Ensign Howard said. He sounded nervous, even though he'd done well on the simulations. "Welcome onboard."

"Thank you, Ensign," Hoshiko said. She took her chair in front of the sensor console and examined it, briefly. The poor ensign had to be terrified. He was trapped in a confined space with his senior officer. On the other hand, assuming they survived, the whole stunt would look very good when the promotions board came calling. "Are we ready to depart?"

"Yes, Captain," Ensign Howard said. The freighter had been heavily automated before the human engineers had gone to work. Now, it was *completely* automated, slaved to the courier boat, as long as nothing went wrong. There was no way they could carry out repairs while they were in flight. "FTL drive is online, ready to jump; sensors and jammers are online, ready to pulse."

"Very good," Hoshiko said. She wanted to say something reassuring, but she had a feeling the ensign might faint. "Inform *Jackie Fisher* that we will be departing on schedule."

She clicked the display back and studied the fleet for a long moment. A handful of ships had dropped out along the way - the order of battle stated that several freighters had left the formation - but none of their allies had deserted as a body. The flurry of updates exchanged between ships indicated, more than anything else, that the Grand Alliance was still a going concern, although that might be about to change. If they were defeated...she pushed the thought aside, irritated. They were not about to be defeated.

But retreating in the face of superior firepower would also be bad, she thought, as the ensign ran down the departure checklist. She'd picked what she thought would be an easy target, just to make sure the alliance got a morale boost, but if she was wrong and called the attack off...they'd wonder just how committed she truly was. *We have to prove to them that we can win battles.*

"Captain," Ensign Howard said, formally. "We are ready to depart."

"Then take us out," Hoshiko ordered.

She sat back in her chair as the display blanked out, the darkness of FTL enveloping the freighter like a shroud. It was hard to avoid doubts, now they were on their way; it was a great deal easier to be brave when one was standing on the bridge of an *Admiral*-class heavy cruiser, one of the finest ships in the galaxy. She had no illusions about how much firepower the freighter could soak up before it was blown to atoms, if the Druavroks realised they were being probed. They'd have to cut themselves loose from the hulk and flee into FTL, cutting their losses. And *that* would be far too revealing.

They'll know we're coming, she reminded herself. *But they won't see us as anything other than a freighter.*

"Five minutes to emergence point," Ensign Howard said. His voice was starting to rise, nervously. "The faked drive failure pattern is uploaded and ready for transmission."

"Very good, Ensign," Hoshiko said. "Just take us out of FTL as planned and everything should be fine."

She sighed, inwardly. It would have been preferable, infinitely preferable, to have a more experienced officer accompanying her, but none could be spared. The handful of other officers she had who knew how to handle a courier boat were needed elsewhere, while there wasn't time to train up someone new. Indeed, if the Solar Navy hadn't been desperately keen to recruit more couriers, she wouldn't even have Ensign Howard. Courier boat crews were simply weird.

The thought made her smile. *She* wouldn't have cared to spend more than a day or two on the courier boat...and couriers spent their entire *careers* on the tiny ships. There was barely room on the bridge to swing a cat, while there were only two tiny cabins and a single washroom at the rear. She'd heard that most courier crews wrote novels, played games or spent their time seeking sexual release...assuming, of course, they could stand each other after being cooped up for several weeks in the same ship. She couldn't help feeling sorry for the crews taking her messages from Amstar to Sol. They'd be trapped in the ships for nearly seven *months*.

It's what they signed up for, she thought. *And it isn't as though they're not compensated for their role.*

She pushed the thought out of her head as the timer ticked down to zero. The freighter shuddered violently as the drive failed, creating a flare of energy that would be visible halfway across the system. Very few freighter crews would willingly put so much wear and tear on their FTL drives; even the military, knowing that FTL drives were expensive, would hesitate. The Druavroks would be unlikely to suspect trouble if the approaching freighter had clearly had a major drive failure.

"Give it two minutes, then send the planned distress call," she ordered, as the display began to fill with icons. The system had been industrialised for centuries, unlike Sol, and it showed; there were mining ships everywhere, a giant cloudscoop orbiting the gas giant and a number of fabbers near the planet itself. "We don't want them to think our arrival was planned."

She watched the display grimly, silently calculating the odds in her head. If a freighter had crashed out of FTL in the Sol System, the Solar Navy would have instantly dispatched a couple of ships to investigate. Who knew what sort of trouble it portended? And even if it *was* a genuine accident, assisting the crew and finding out what had happened might come in handy. A decent reputation might convince other races to assist humanity, when the Tokomak finally launched a second major offensive against Sol.

But what would the Druavroks do? There was no way to know.

"Send the signal," she ordered, after two minutes had passed. "Inform me the moment we get any response."

"Aye, Captain," Howard said. "The signal has been sent."

"Keep us limping towards the planet," Hoshiko ordered. "We don't want them to think we're *completely* crippled."

She smiled, inwardly. Her engineering crews had worked overtime to come up with a plausible disaster that would leave them locked out of FTL, but allow them to make their way towards the planet without help. The message they'd recorded would acknowledge the problem, yet make it clear the freighter didn't need immediate help. There should be no need for the Druavroks to dispatch a welcoming committee…but if they were suspicious or merely paranoid, they probably would. She'd just have to wait and see.

"Launch the long-range recon probes," she ordered, after a moment. "Send them out as planned."

"Aye, Captain," Howard said.

Hoshiko watched as he worked his console, then turned her attention back to the ever-swelling display. It struck her, once again, just how long the Galactics had been in space…and just how rapidly humanity had jumped ahead, once it had stolen technology from a race that didn't know how it worked, let alone how to use it. Sol had considerably more industrial activity than the system before her and humanity had only *really* been in space for the last fifty years.

She shook her head in amused disbelief. Malachi had, according to the records, only been settled for three hundred years. There was little to like about the world, either; the Tokomak had considered it barely suitable for settlement and dropped a terraforming package on the surface before passing the job of turning the world into a habitable place to live. The Druavroks were the majority population, so vastly outnumbering the other races that taking control of the surface couldn't have been particularly hard. And yet, with three hundred years of settlement, she would have expected something more.

The Tokomak screwed the economy deliberately, she reminded herself. *They really didn't want their subjects taking control of their lives.*

Her eyes narrowed as new icons popped up on the display. The system had three massive battlestations orbiting the planet, as well as a number of remote weapons platforms and automated defences, but there didn't seem to be many starships in residence. *She* would have preferred at least a single squadron of heavy cruisers to give the defenders some mobile firepower, yet the largest ship her sensors could detect was a light cruiser that might only have been passing through. There certainly didn't seem to be anything attached to the system bigger than a single squadron of destroyers.

They may well be concentrating their efforts on expanding their space as quickly as possible, she thought. *They may know it won't take long before the other races start to unite against them.*

"Picking up a signal," Ensign Howard said. "They're ordering us to hold position at the edge of the planetary defence sphere until they can get an inspection crew up to us. *And* they want our manifest."

"Send it to them," Hoshiko ordered. The freighter manifest was nothing more than a tissue of lies, but she'd composed it with malice aforethought. If the Druavroks believed the freighter was carrying spare parts for starships, they'd be less willing to blow her out of space. Given the speed of their advance, she'd bet money their logistics were barely superior to hers. "And let me know what they say."

They'll want to seize the cargo, she told herself. The Galactics had some very strict rules on how freighter in distress were to be treated, but she doubted the Druavroks would honour them. At best, they'd insist the freighter's cargo would be forfeit in exchange for repairs and whatever other charges they could cram onto the bill; at worst, they'd simply take the cargo, the ship and enslave the crews. *That should help them decide to keep us alive.*

She allowed herself a tight smile as the probes slipped closer to their target. The Druavroks presumably didn't have any better sensors than the ones their former masters had invented and passed on to them, because they didn't seem to have any inkling the probes were slowly slipping into engagement range. Given thirty years or so, she told herself, and humanity's warships would be able to tear through a Galactic fleet with no losses at all, unless the Galactics themselves started innovating. And if they did, the status quo the Tokomak had created would be destroyed.

Enough data to target our attack precisely, she thought. *And enough to program the missiles to overwhelm their targets by sheer weight of fire.*

"There doesn't seem to be anything on the planet worth having," she muttered to herself, darkly. "And hitting their settlements would be bad."

Hoshiko sighed, inwardly. She doubted many of the races that had joined up with the Grand Alliance would feel the same way.

Ensign Howard glanced at her, very briefly. "Captain?"

"Never mind," Hoshiko said. "Has there been any response?"

"None as yet," Ensign Howard said. "They haven't sent anything to us..."

He paused. "Captain, two of their destroyers are breaking orbit and heading towards our position," he warned. "Estimated ETA, nineteen minutes unless they go FTL."

"I see," Hoshiko said. The last thing she wanted was to abandon the freighter with two destroyers in firing range. "Watch carefully for a Picard Manoeuvre."

"Aye, Captain," Ensign Howard said.

Hoshiko nodded. It was hard to believe that Jean-Luc Picard was fictional when he'd given his name to a well-known Galactic tactic. Jumping into FTL would allow the destroyers to reach her position before she knew they'd moved, before the emissions from their realspace drives reached her sensors. If they did, she was in deep trouble. She'd have to risk deploying ECM systems to confuse them while the courier boat separated from the freighter.

We're not close enough to the planet for certain success, she thought, darkly. *And to think it was going so well too.*

Don't be stupid, her own thoughts answered her. They sounded very much like her uncle in a cranky mood. *War is a democracy. The enemy, that dirty dog, gets a vote too.*

"Prepare to separate from the freighter," she ordered. "I..."

An alarm sounded. "*Contact*," Ensign Howard snapped. "They just dropped out of FTL, right on top of us."

Hoshiko sucked in her breath. The enemy destroyers were closing in, far too quickly. She mentally saluted their commanders - they'd pulled off a *perfect* Picard Manoeuvre - as she hastily re-evaluated the situation. It was time to cut their losses and leave.

"Rotate the freighter," she ordered. Thankfully, the enemy hadn't tried to come in on two separate vectors. "Make it look like we're panicking, but kept the hulk between us and them."

"Aye, Captain," Ensign Howard said. He paused. "They're sending us a message, Captain; they want us to prepare to be boarded."

"Cut our ties to the freighter," Hoshiko ordered. There was no longer any time to waste. "As soon as we're free, send the scuttle code to the ship and bring the FTL drive online."

"Aye, Captain," Ensign Howard said. He sounded perfectly in control, now there were only seconds between life and death. A shudder ran through the courier boat as she broke free of the freighter and moved into open space. "We're free."

The display turned red. "Enemy ships are targeting us, Captain!"

"Evasive manoeuvres," Hoshiko ordered, curtly. If they were lucky, the Druavroks would still be reluctant to blow up the freighter, but she dared not count on it. "Send the final code to the freighter, then jump us out."

"Aye, Captain," Ensign Howard said. "FTL in three...two...one... *now*!"

Hoshiko smirked as the Druavroks launched missiles, far too late to be any good. It no longer mattered if they were trying to take out the courier boat or the freighter, not now the former was in FTL. The final device she'd had loaded onto the freighter would not only explode with staggering force - it was just possible the destroyers would be crippled or destroyed if they didn't back off quickly enough - but blind gravimetric sensors right across the system. If she was *very* lucky, the Druavroks would have no idea the fleet was on the way until it was *far* too late.

And even if the plan fails, she thought, *we already have the intelligence we need*.

"Take us straight back to the fleet," she ordered. Either the plan had worked or it hadn't; it no longer mattered. "And drop the teleport jammers as soon as we arrive."

"Aye, Captain," Howard said.

SIXTEEN

Desertion rates in the United States Army have skyrocketed over the past two months, according to a highly-classified report, in the wake of the military coup, fighting along the borders and ethnic cleansing in a number of US cities and states. The current military commander, however, insists that the restoration of order is only a matter of time - and that deserters will receive the death sentence when they are caught.
-Solar News Network, Year 54

If there was one lesson Druavrok history had taught the Druavroks, it was that the universe was divided into two different subsets: predators and prey. Their evolution on a harsh world had shaped them for war, first for bare survival against the other creatures their homeworld had birthed, then against the strange aliens who'd arrived on their world with gifts and demands for submission. The Druavroks had fought, of course, because it wasn't in their nature to submit, but they'd been crushed so badly that the survivors and their descendents were still reeling. Resistance to the Tokomaks had moved, in their heads, from *necessary* to *inconceivable.* The idea of lifting a clawed hand to slash at a Tokomak face was beyond them. They had become slaves.

It hadn't taken the surviving Druavroks long to discover that the Tokomaks were masters of far more than merely the half-savage

Druavroks. Indeed, they were masters of hundreds of races of prey, each one strange and appalling to Druavrok eyes. None of them had any right to exist, not when they had never imposed themselves on the Druavroks. The Druavroks could not see them as anything other than prey. And, when the Tokomaks had started turning the Druavroks into soldiers and enforcers, the Druavroks had taken to the role like ducks to water. What better role was there, they asked themselves, than serving the only race that had defeated them decisively in battle?

And then the Tokomaks had retreated, abandoning the sector.

The Druavroks hadn't been able to understand it, not at first. A minor defeat that had cost a bare handful of starships was hardly enough to break the Tokomaks. And yet, the Tokomaks had simply abandoned the Martina Sector. The Druavroks puzzled over it for months, trying to determine what their masters wanted them to do. Eventually, one of their leaders had realised the truth. The Tokomak had given the Druavroks the sector as a reward for good service, as a master might pet his slave on the head. And all the prey in the sector was theirs to do with as they willed. Why *not* build an empire of their own?

And so the Great Conquest, Warlord Junju thought, had begun.

It was a frustrating thought. He should be out among the stars, winning glory with his clan-brothers, rather than stuck defending a worthless planet. The Great Lords might argue that Malachi had to be defended, but Junju knew better. There was no way the prey could or would muster the nerve to attack a world of their betters. They were *prey*! The forces that had shaped them hadn't given them the killer instincts his people had needed to survive their homeworld, let alone their work for the Tokomak. No, he was trapped because the Great Lords feared what he would do, if he were given his freedom. He would win such great victories that they would no longer be able to turn their backs on him.

"Warlord," a voice said. Warlord Junju turned to see a junior officer prostrating himself on the deck. "The destroyers are intercepting the prey freighter."

Warlord Junju hissed his amusement as he turned to examine the giant system display, his eyes flickering over his subordinates. The prey had *no* idea how much things had changed, now the Tokomak were gone. Their ship would be confiscated, their cargo would be put to use supporting the Great Conquest and, if the prey submitted quickly enough, they would be put to work as labourers of war. Or, if they didn't submit, they would be dumped into the hunting pastures for his soldiers to hunt. They needed practice, after all; the Great Conquest needed experienced soldiers. Maybe he'd take a few hours off and go hunting himself. Some of the prey were almost intelligent in how they fought back against their betters.

"The destroyers..."

The speaker broke off as the display turned into a haze of static. Warlord Junju bared his teeth, fighting down the reflex that would have turned the CIC into a bloody combat zone, and waited until his officers calmed down. In that, so much as anything else, they took their cue from their betters. Warlord Junju had *earned* his post and he never let any of them forget it.

"Report," he ordered, calmly.

"The freighter released a courier boat, which jumped into FTL seconds before the freighter exploded," one of the officers said. She sounded terrified, knowing her superior could execute her on the spot if he held her responsible for failure. "The explosion released a wave of charged gravity particles. Damage to the system's long-range sensors has been extensive."

Warlord Junju flexed his claws. If it had been the officer's fault, he would have cut her throat and drunk her blood without a second thought. The weak and foolish died so that the strong could survive and prosper. But there was no point in punishing her merely for giving him an accurate report.

"Get the repair crews out there," he ordered, keeping his bloodlust under tight control. The freighter crew must have sensed their fate and panicked, like some of the more challenging forms of prey. But why had they been carrying a courier boat? "I want those sensors back up within the hour!"

— —

HOSHIKO SUCKED IN her breath the moment she materialised in the CIC, then keyed the intercom as she sat down in front of the big display. "Do you have the data download from the courier boat?"

"Aye, Captain," Wilde said. "We're passing it to the remainder of the fleet now."

"Inform them we're going with Attack Plan Alpha-Three," Hoshiko said. She'd composed nine separate plans, but Alpha-Three fitted the situation best. "Order them to bring up their drives and be ready to jump within five minutes."

She leaned back in her chair, then looked at Lieutenant Brown. "Is the CIC ready to take over as fleet command?"

"Aye, Captain," Brown said. He was a competent officer, although his file claimed he was a little unimaginative for his role. "We're ready."

Hoshiko sat back in her chair. They'd practiced, endlessly, but now they were about to undergo the *real* test. If something went wrong...

At least we can break off and escape those battlestations, she told herself. *A handful of destroyers and a light cruiser won't pose a major threat if we have to leave.*

"Then take command," she ordered. "Signal to all ships. Go to condition one, then jump on my command."

"Aye, Captain," Brown said. "All ships report ready."

"Jump," Hoshiko ordered.

She sucked in a breath. If everything had gone according to plan...

Stop worrying, she told herself firmly, as the timer ticked down to zero. *You're about to find out the hard way*.

"Emergence in two minutes, fifteen seconds, Captain," Brown reported. "Fleet control systems, up and ready; fleet datanet sub-networks, up and ready."

"Good," Hoshiko said. "Pass the word. If any enemy ships are within engagement range as soon as we arrive, they are to be attacked with maximum force."

"Aye, Captain," Brown said.

Hoshiko sat back in her chair as the timer ticked down the final few seconds. No one, apart from the Tokomak, had ever deployed so many ships in a single battle - and *no one* had deployed quite so many different *types* of ships. Command and control was going to be a major headache, even if everyone cooperated perfectly; her simulations had shown her, in far too much detail, just what could go wrong. But there was no longer any time to rehearse...

"Emergence, Captain," Brown reported, as the display began to fill with red lights. "No enemy ships within engagement range; I say again, no enemy ships within engagement range."

Pity, Hoshiko thought. She looked at the display towards where the freighter had been before she'd abandoned the vessel to her fate. One enemy destroyer was nearby, clearly crippled; there was no sign of the other. *Let us hope it was destroyed in the blast.*

She turned her attention back to Malachi itself. "Order the fleet to shake down and advance towards the closest battlestation," she ordered. The enemy was already sweeping the fleet with tactical sensors, looking for targets. They'd have to be blind to *miss* the fleet, although human-grade ECM was already making life difficult for their tactical staffs. "Task Force 2.1 and Task Force 2.2 are to engage with missiles as soon as they enter engagement range; the remainder of the fleet is to hold back and ready itself for a successive engagement."

"Aye, Captain," Brown said.

"And once they have expended their missiles, they are to retreat to the RV point," Hoshiko added. The alien crews already knew, of course, but the desire for revenge burned strong in their breasts. "They'll be nothing more than targets once they've shot themselves dry."

She forced herself to watch calmly as the giant fleet slowly closed in on its target. For once, the Druavroks didn't seem inclined to launch suicide attacks, although she had a nasty feeling they suspected such attacks would be useless. But then, if they took out a handful of genuine warships, her fleet's ability to fight would be sharply reduced. Thankfully, the ECM would make it harder for them to pick out the targets they should be hitting. Instead, their handful of starships were slowly settling into a defensive formation. If they'd been human, one or more ships would already have been dispatched to raise the alarm.

"Twenty seconds to engagement range," Brown reported. "Task Force 2.1's CO requests permission to launch a wide spread of missiles."

"Denied," Hoshiko said, sharply. A wide spread, under normal circumstances, would force the defenders to concentrate on preventing missiles from striking the planet's surface, but she had a feeling the Druavroks wouldn't give a damn for their own civilians, let alone anyone else's. "Missiles are to be targeted on the battlestation and its remote platforms alone."

And the battlestation mounts plenty of point defence, she thought, grimly. *We need such a high density of missiles to be sure of scoring a kill.*

"Ten seconds to engagement range," Brown said.

"The missile-slingers are to open fire as soon as they enter engagement range," Hoshiko reminded him. "They're not to wait for orders."

Because the bastards will start opening fire as soon as we enter their engagement range, she thought, grimly. Task Force 2.1 and Task Force 2.2 carried Galactic missiles, not human. It was a calculated risk, but Malachi was a fairly soft target. Besides, it gave the fabbers time to produce hundreds of additional human-grade missiles. *They'll try to give as good as they get.*

"Five seconds," Brown said.

"Stand by point defence," Hoshiko ordered.

WARLORD JUNJU'S FIRST inclination had been to demand the head of whoever had started a training simulation without giving the command crew sufficient warning, as laid down in the regulations they'd copied from the Tokomak. His second had been to refuse to believe in the invading fleet. It couldn't exist. It simply couldn't exist…and yet, the more his sensors reported on its composition and steady approach, the harder it became to deny reality. The freighter hadn't been an accident, or a panicking crew; the freighter had been the first shot in the Battle of Malachi.

"Keep the ships back," he ordered. Their commanders wanted to charge into the teeth of enemy fire, weapons blazing in their contempt for the prey, but these were clearly very dangerous prey indeed. And yet, three-quarters of their giant fleet was composed of freighters, rather than warships. "They are to hold position until I give the order to move."

He hissed in agitation as the enemy fleet moved closer. Some prey were cunning, almost *intelligent* in their cunning, others…were inclined to panic the moment they encountered true predators. *These* prey looked to be the former, except there were so many ships in their formation that it was hard to tell who was crewing them, let alone who was in command. He couldn't tell if sending freighters against his battlestations was a desperation move, intended to soak up his missiles, or if they truly had no conception of the difference between warships and freighters.

"We shall not fall for such simplistic trickery," he hissed. "Our missiles are to be targeted on the warships - and the warships alone."

"Yes, Warlord," his subordinates chorused.

Warlord Junju ignored them as the sensor readings started to fuzz. He was familiar with ECM, of course, but *this* was a great deal more advanced than anything he'd seen in his long career. It was suddenly a great deal harder to target the warships, although it wouldn't matter as much as the prey presumably thought. His sensors would have no difficulty locating and tracking the warships when they opened fire. And then…the warships would no longer be able to hide.

"Enemy ships are entering engagement range," one of his subordinates warned. "Enemy ships are opening fire…*impossible*!"

"BURN, YOU BASTARDS," Hoshiko muttered.

The engineers had done her proud, as always. They'd crammed hundreds of missile launchers and thousands of missiles into the freighters that made up Task Force 2.1 and Task Force 2.2. The Druavroks could not possibly have expected to see so many missiles from only a hundred ships...and, if they had a moment to think about it, they'd have good reason to worry about what the remainder of her fleet might be carrying. A solid wall of nuclear firepower was making its unstoppable way towards the enemy battlestation.

"The enemy are opening fire," Brown reported, as the battlestation began to spit fire towards her fleet. It was pathetic, utterly pathetic, compared to the single giant volley she'd hurled at the battlestation. "They're targeting Task Force 2.1 and Task Force 2.2."

"Order them both to jump out, as planned," Hoshiko said.

Her eyes narrowed as the solid wall of icons roared towards its target. The Druavroks had made a mistake in trying to hit her freighters, the ones that had already shot themselves dry...why? Had they thought they were shooting at warships? She hoped, inwardly, that the enemy wouldn't be able to adjust their missiles to engage new targets, but she doubted they'd be that lucky. The Druavroks weren't the Horde.

"Forty seconds to impact," Brown reported. "Enemy missiles are retargeting themselves on Task Force 3.1 and 4.1."

"Order point defence to cover them," Hoshiko said. She'd feared the enemy would try to use their missiles as makeshift point defence weapons - they could, if they were carrying antimatter warheads - but it seemed as though the Druavroks hadn't had time to think of it before it was too late. "And ready a second barrage, just in case."

"Aye, Captain," Brown said. A new set of icons flashed to life. "Enemy ships are altering position."

"Order Task Force 1.2 to engage," Hoshiko ordered. The chance to smash a handful of ships at little risk could not be disregarded. Their allies would like a crack at the bastards before they were destroyed. "And move Task Force 1.3 up in support."

— —

"Order all point defence to engage as soon as the enemy missiles come into range," Warlord Junju hissed. "We will not be beaten by *prey*!"

He glowered at two of his subordinates until they got the message and went to work. Their brains had practically shut down the moment the enemy ships - a tenth of their force, no less - had begun spewing out missiles, as if they couldn't accept the sudden shift in reality. It was hard to blame them, he knew; he'd never suspected the presence of battleships in the enemy fleet, despite their ECM. And yet, the battleships were jumping out. It made no sense. How much of the fleet looming over the battlestation was actually *real*?

"Monitor their formation to determine who engages the missiles," he ordered, grimly. If he'd had long-range probes, he would have launched them. No ECM could hide *everything* from a prowling probe. "Once you know, reassign the missiles to target them."

He hissed again as the wall of missiles swept towards his command. *They* had to be real…and there were just too many of them to stop. His subordinates hadn't realised it yet, but the battlestation was doomed. The *prey* had turned into *predators*. Indeed, they'd shown tactical brilliance by positioning their fleet so the other two battlestations couldn't *hope* to engage them, while the defending ships couldn't hope to match their firepower. Warlord Junju and his subordinates were on their own.

"Order the ships to retreat," he said. It would get him in trouble, when word reached the Great Lords, but he doubted he'd survive long enough to face their rage. And he was beyond caring what the commanders thought. "They're to jump out and alert the Great Lords to a new and dangerous species of *prey*."

The point defence opened fire as soon as the missiles came into view, but for every incoming missile they killed there were ten more that made it through the defences and rammed into the shields. Warlord Junju clung on to his command chair for dear life as the battlestation rocked, time and time again, before the shields finally failed and the missiles started slamming into the hull. Damage reports mounted so rapidly that he could barely keep track of them before they were superseded by something new, enemy warheads exploding within his hull…

…And then the universe went away in a blaze of white-hot light.

SEVENTEEN

Mobs stormed the palaces of the rich and powerful in Brasilia after the economy, looted beyond repair, collapsed into chaos. Reports from sources within the Brazilian military suggest that the soldiers flatly refused to intervene, when ordered, as their families are among the hundreds of thousand starving to death…

-Solar News Network, Year 54

"Commander," Biscoe reported. "The first battlestation has been destroyed."

Griffin nodded. The Druavroks had fought desperately, but even a human-built battlestation would have found it impossible to stop more than a fraction of the missiles fired at it. He had to admit the station had lasted longer than he'd expected, yet the outcome had been inevitable.

Score one for the captain, he thought, although cold fear was coiling through his gut. Amstar was one thing, but *this* was a direct attack on a world that undisputedly belonged to the Druavroks. They wouldn't find it so easy to write off the attack, when - if - the diplomats met to settle the war. *And they'll feel obliged to hit back.*

"ORDER TASK FORCE 4.1 to target Battlestation Two," Hoshiko ordered. "Task Force 4.2 is to target Battlestation Three."

"Aye, Captain," Brown said. He worked his console for a long moment as icons moved over the display. "Orders have been sent, Captain."

"All other ships are to target the automated platforms," Hoshiko ordered. The handful of remaining Druavrok starships had either mounted suicide charges or jumped into FTL, fleeing the system as fast as they could. She had a nasty feeling they were only going as far as the nearest enemy squadron. "I want the skies cleared of everything hostile."

She sucked in her breath as the remainder of the fleet opened fire, targeting the automated platforms and blowing them out of space. Like the missiles she'd hurled at the battlestation, it was overkill, but she needed everyone in her fleet to think they'd made a contribution. She rather doubted any of the spacers would be fooled - they'd understand the realities of interstellar combat as well as her crews - yet if the alien media outlets were anything like their human counterparts, the news could be spun to make it appear that their contribution had been decisive. Assuming, of course, the aliens *had* media outlets. The Tokomak had never been big on distributing information to the peons.

And they didn't share movies either, she thought, ruefully. A number of human movies had been quite popular among humanity's closest neighbours, although not quite the ones she would have expected. The aliens looked at pre-Contact movies about aliens and laughed themselves silly. *I wonder how long it will be until they start their own media services.*

"The second battlestation is under heavy attack, but it's fighting back," Brown reported. "A number of freighters have been destroyed."

"Move Task Force 4.3 up in support," Hoshiko ordered. The Druavroks were doomed, but they didn't seem to care. She would have been impressed if they hadn't been her enemies, the bastards she had to kill. "And angle Task Force 1.2 over in that general direction, just in case they need additional point defence."

"Aye, Captain," Brown said.

Hoshiko nodded and turned her attention back to the display. Battlestation Three hadn't been anything like as lucky as Battlestation Two, although there was no way to know *why*. Her shields were flickering desperately as missiles pounded them into scrap, shimmering in and out of existence as her shield generators burned out. A handful of missiles made it through gaps in the shields, slamming into her hull and blasting their way into her interior. The end could not be long delayed.

"Picking up multiple drive signatures on the surface," Brown snapped. "They're launching small craft."

"Odd," Hoshiko muttered, tearing her attention away from the doomed battlestation. The Druavroks on the ground had nothing to gain by launching shuttles…or did they? Her sensors hadn't been able to detect any large planetary defence centres, but that didn't mean they didn't exist. "Keep an eye on them…"

The display flared with red icons as hundreds of shuttles took off and clawed their way into space. Hoshiko cursed under her breath, remembering her great-great-uncle's stories about Imperial Japan and how it had died in fire. The Druavroks thought nothing of kamikaze attacks, even with starships. Why *wouldn't* they turn shuttles into suicide craft?

"The shuttles intend to launch suicide attacks," she said, keeping her voice calm. It was unlikely that any of the craft carried weapons that could hurt her warships, but there were far too many soft targets amongst her fleet. "They are to be targeted and destroyed as soon as they enter engagement range."

"Aye, Captain," Brown said.

The Druavroks showed no hesitation as their formation bunched up and roared towards its targets. She noted, coolly, that they seemed to be more interested in targeting the warships, even though hammering the converted freighters would probably score them more kills. A highly macho culture like Imperial Japan might well have encouraged its flyers to target warships, despite the mass of firepower surrounding them. The Druavroks clearly thought along the same lines.

And they have nerve, she thought, as the shuttles ducked and weaved their way through a barrage of firepower. No one had managed to make a genuine starfighter, despite plenty of research in the Solar Union, but the Druavroks were flying the next best thing. Perhaps there was something to be said for missile-armed gunboats, after all. *But they can't hide from my sensors*.

She drew back her lips into a snarl as red icons began to vanish from the display, one by one, even as their comrades pressed closer. The Druavroks couldn't hide, nor could they react in time to escape point defence fire. And yet they were closing in...a destroyer, part of Task Force 1.4, staggered as a shuttle rammed into its shields, followed rapidly by another. A frigate, passed down through so many owners that only the hull could be said to be original, exploded as four shuttles slammed home in quick succession. And then the last of the shuttles was blown apart, leaving local space clear.

"Battlestation Two has been destroyed," Brown confirmed. "Battlestation Three is a powerless wreck."

"Take it out completely," Hoshiko ordered. It was unlikely the Druavroks would be able to repair it in time to matter - it might well be cheaper to build a whole new battlestation - but there was no point in taking chances. "I want it smashed to rubble."

"Aye, Captain," Brown said.

"Take the warships into orbit," Hoshiko added. If the Druavroks had a PDC concealed somewhere on the surface, which was still possible, they would have to open fire or throw away their sole remaining opportunity to inflict harm on her ships. "Is the bombardment plan complete?"

"Yes, Captain," Brown said. "Tactical has located and tagged everything in the first and second list of ground targets."

Hoshiko sucked in her breath. A modern planet had dozens of spaceports, military bases, communications hubs and power centres. Taking them all out in a single blow was unprecedented, even on Earth. But then, the Solar Union had had the technology to go directly after the leaders of rogue states. It had never needed to rain down death indiscriminately from the safety of high orbit.

We're not bombarding civilian targets, she told herself, firmly. She honestly wasn't sure there *was* such a thing as a civilian Druavrok. But all that really mattered was ensuring the planet was unable to support the enemy war effort for the foreseeable future. Once it was stripped of everything that might be useful, it could be left to wither on the vine. *And there aren't many non-Druavroks on the surface to put at risk.*

She frowned as the holographic display changed, showing the targets on the ground. The Druavroks had more spaceports than she'd expected, each one including a warehouse complex that was easily three or four times the size of anything she'd seen on Amstar, Martina or Earth. They were surrounded by ground-based weapons systems, but there didn't seem to be anything capable of reaching up and striking her ships in orbit. Unless they had something concealed, of course. The Druavroks hadn't really had time to prepare an ambush, but *she* would have kept half her defences concealed if *she'd* been in command.

And some of them are far too close to civilian targets, she thought, grimly. The Solar Union was not foolish enough to believe that civilian casualties could be avoided completely, unlike some of the more absurd nations on Earth, but hard questions would be asked. Her detractors wouldn't care that preventing her allies from committing outright genocide was hard enough, not when they'd be trying to score political advantage at her family's expense. *But they're the ones who put them there.*

"Targets locked, Captain," Brown reported. "KEW firing patterns are locked and the tubes are loaded."

"Fire at will," Hoshiko ordered. "I say again, fire at will."

She smiled to herself as the first KEWs fell from her starships. The Druavrok defences tried to engage the projectiles as they fell through the atmosphere, but her ships had no shortage of ammunition. KEWs really were nothing more than rocks dropped on a ballistic trajectory, aimed at a target on the ground. One by one, her targets began to die...

"There was a major explosion after Target #362 was struck," Brown commented. "I think it must have been an ammunition dump."

Hoshiko shrugged, unconcerned. An ammunition dump was a legitimate target, as far as the Solar Union's ROE were concerned. It might not pose an immediate danger to her ships, but it was definitely supporting the enemy war effort. And if the enemy *had* put it in the midst of civilian settlements, trying to use their own civilians as 'human' shields, the Solar Union's ROE agreed it was their fault. But the Druavroks didn't seem to realise they could use intelligent beings as shields. They cared so little for their own lives, she suspected, that they couldn't grasp that others cared more.

The Tokomak must have been harsh masters, she thought, as the final targets vanished from the display. *And the Druavroks just treated them as gods.*

"All targets destroyed, Captain," Brown reported. "Their ground-based communications network appears to have gone down."

"Maybe," Hoshiko said.

She studied the display for a long moment. It was easy to forget that the neat little icons, flickering and vanishing off the display, represented an immensely destructive KEW strike that had smashed buildings, cratered runways and killed hundreds, perhaps thousands, of enemy personnel. From high overhead, warfare was so clean and tidy; on the ground, it was devastating. The enemy had been dealt a blow it would take them years to recover from...

...And yet, she knew better than to take it for granted. Her grandfather, in one of his rants about the military on Old Earth, had talked about how easily the air force had been fooled into believing its bombardments, with smart precision weapons no less, had been devastatingly effective. It was quite possible that the Druavroks had a hardened communications network based around wires, rather than signals, and that their command and control system was still intact. She certainly had no way to know if she'd killed off the high commander on the planet or not. A human commander would have been on one of the battlestations, sharing the hazards facing his men, but would a Druavrok commander feel the same way?

"As long as their ability to hit the fleet has been crippled, it shouldn't matter," she added, grimly. "Are there any enemy vessels remaining in the system?"

"Not as far as long-range sensors can tell," Brown said. "If they're cloaked and watching from a safe distance..."

Hoshiko nodded. If *she'd* been in command, she would have left a single ship in the system, under cloak, to keep an eye on the invaders while the rest of the squadron went for help. A relief force could drop out of FTL near the watcher and get an update before either proceeding to counterattack or harassing her pickets, depending on the exact situation.

Not that it matters, she reminded herself. *We're not going to remain in the system for long.*

"Inform the fleet that we will now proceed to Phase Two," she said. "The starships attached to the out-orbit task forces are to separate themselves from the fleet and proceed as planned."

She gritted her teeth. The allies wanted *blood* - and they'd be reluctant to follow her standing orders, if they ran into superior firepower. Hoshiko saw no reason to throw her ships away for nothing, but aliens who wanted revenge - and also to show up their allies - wouldn't be so careful. But there was nothing she could do about it, but hope the liaison officers she'd provided would be enough to keep tempers cool.

Win the war first, she told herself. *Revenge can come afterwards.*

"Confirm," she ordered. "The industrial nodes and fabbers didn't attempt to engage the ships."

"Confirmed," Brown said. "They did not attempt to engage our fleet."

The Tokomak never thought to outfit their industrial nodes with weapons, Hoshiko thought, grimly. *But their former slaves might have different ideas.*

"Order the marines to board and storm, if the workers refuse to surrender," she ordered, tightly. Taking the fabbers intact would be a considerable coup, adding their industrial capabilities to her forces. But if the Druavroks were lying in wait, ready to either fight to bleed her forces or simply blow up the fabbers as soon as the marines boarded, it was going to be costly. "If they meet significant resistance, they are to withdraw and the fabbers will be destroyed."

"Aye, Captain," Brown said.

Hoshiko winced, inwardly. The Galactics would be shocked at the thought of someone blowing up a fabber, even though it was a legitimate tactic of war. They were just too important, after all. The Tokomak might just have left their fabbers unharmed to ensure that attacking forces had no *reason* to open fire on the giant orbital factories. They would probably have assumed the attackers would have no time to turn the fabbers against them, if they could hack their way through the security codes, before reinforcements arrived from deeper within the empire.

Which is what happens, she thought savagely, *when you have so much power you can organise reality to suit yourself and to hell with everyone else.*

She shook her head in droll amusement as the fleet closed in on the fabbers, readying the marines for launch. The Tokomak had been knocked back by the Battle of Earth, shocked and terrified by the outcome of what should have been a walkover. How long would it take them to put together a second fleet, far larger than the first? And how long would it take humanity to invent something that would turn their entire fleet, hundreds of thousands of giant battlecruisers, into so much scrap metal? The Tokomak had been stagnant for so long that they probably couldn't innovate, even if they tried. Given enough time, humanity would steamroller over the Tokomak and claim their place in the universe.

"The marines are ready to launch," Brown reported. "And they have that reporter tagging along."

"Understood," Hoshiko said. "Tell them to jump once we're in range."

"THE MARINES ARE ready to launch, sir," Biscoe said. "Captain Stuart has cleared them to jump as soon as we enter range."

"Understood," Griffin Wilde said.

He looked down at the near-space display, trusting the bridge crew to alert him if the situation suddenly changed for the worse. The remains of three battlestations and countless automated platforms were drifting in orbit, a sizable percentage slowly drifting into the planet's gravity well. Griffin wouldn't have cared to be under the pieces of debris when they finally entered the planet's atmosphere and plunged to the surface, even though only a small percentage of them would survive the fall. There were so many large pieces of debris that they would be almost certain to hit *something*...

And even if they don't, he thought, *adding so many atoms to the atmosphere is bound to cause a great deal of damage.*

He cursed under his breath as he accessed the live feed from the drones hovering high over the planet, peering down at the aliens far below. The KEW bombardment had done immense damage to the planet's facilities, almost certainly making it impossible for the authorities to ship food around the settlements or keep the planet under control. God alone knew how the Druavroks organised themselves - Griffin didn't care to know - but a human planet that had been bombarded so badly would probably fragment.

Like Earth, he thought. *Only worse, perhaps.*

It wasn't a pleasant thought. Griffin knew what *he'd* like to do to a race that had done so much damage to humanity - and he had to assume the Druavroks agreed. Tit for tat was rarely a workable rule in the real world...and, in any case, the Solar Union hadn't been attacked. The Druavroks would find it harder to give up the war, assuming they wanted to in the first place. Nothing the doctor or the intelligence officers had dug up suggested the Druavroks could be talked into a truce.

And they will come for revenge, he thought, bitterly. *What choice do they have?*

"Commander," Biscoe said. "The marines are launching now."

"Understood," Griffin said. It was a distraction from his worries, but he knew it wouldn't last. "Keep me informed."

He understood Hoshiko's desire to intervene, both to protect fellow humans and to ensure the Druavroks never had a chance to threaten the Solar Union. But the price...humanity might wind up embroiled in a war at the end of a very long supply chain...

...And facing a long war with an alien race that wouldn't hesitate to commit genocide if it won.

EIGHTEEN

Federal American troops encircled Dearborn, Michigan, after an Islamist vigilante group came out of the shadows and declared an Islamic state. Reports from the ground are confused, but videos and statements uploaded to the datanet suggest that the group has already begun ethnic cleansing the city. However, there are strong suspicions that the federal government allowed the group to take power to provide a convenient rallying cry to restore federal power. The Governor of Texas has already declared the uprising nothing more than a fraud.
-Solar News Network, Year 54

Max felt…claustrophobic.

He'd been in the suits before, during his military service and the landing on Amstar, but this was different. He was trapped in the darkness, unable to move, unable even to take control of the suit while it rested in the launch tube. If he'd *known* they wouldn't be making a formal combat drop, or taking a shuttle, he might have had other ideas. But he hadn't checked before it was far too late.

He felt the urge to scratch his nose as he wondered just how long he'd actually been in the tube. His implants insisted that it had only been five minutes since Hilde had shown him to the tube, helped him to get inside and then slammed the hatch closed; his mind was sure it had to be longer, far longer. He'd never felt so isolated in a combat suit before, even though he knew objectively he was wrapped in a suit of armour that would protect him from hundreds of threats. But then, the combination of implants and VR projectors made him *feel* as though he wasn't trapped, even though he knew he was. The tube, on the other hand, left him feeling as though he'd been locked in the darkness to die.

"Do not speak unless you're spoken to," Hilde had told him. "We're operating under strict radio silence."

Max shuddered in the confines of the suit. He had to fight the urge to contact one of the other marines, even though he knew it would have cost him his chance to be embedded with them in the future. In hindsight, he should have loaded a game or two into his implants, running a program that would have distracted him from his confinement. Or he could run a program that would keep him calm, despite the risk of accidentally putting himself to sleep. Brain-modification programs weren't forbidden in the Solar Union, but they were considered dangerous in a combat zone. And to think he'd *volunteered* for the assignment!

Hilde wouldn't be impressed if you backed out, he told himself. He'd spent a great deal of time with Hilde over the last few days, growing more impressed with her every time they spoke. There was a bluntness about her character that appealed to him. *But then, she wouldn't be impressed with you anyway.*

He jumped as a voice echoed through the suit. "Five seconds to launch," it said. "Five seconds to launch..."

There was a sudden wave of pressure as the suit was ejected from the starship and hurled towards their target, a fabber hanging against a blue-green orb. Max let out a sigh of relief, then cursed inwardly as the suit's automatic systems slaved him to Hilde. He tried to follow the icons as the fabber grew larger, a five kilometre-long structure, but rapidly found it impossible. The suit was jerking from side to side, in anticipation of defensive fire, as it closed in on the fabber. He closed his eyes as his perspective shifted, knowing better than to risk allowing the sudden change to disorientate him, then opened them again as a new timer appeared in front of him. Ten seconds until landing…

"Watch yourselves, but only fire if fired upon," the major said. A dull *thump* echoed through the suit as it touched down on the fabber. "The enemy may just throw in the towel."

Max doubted it very much, but he kept that thought to himself. He'd *seen* the Druavroks hurling themselves forward, trying to bury the marines under their dead bodies…and they'd kept coming until every last one of them was dead. The idea they'd just *surrender* the fabber was absurd, not when even a civilian-grade fabber would be a prize well worth the lives of a dozen marines. And if they knew the Tokomak codes could be bypassed, they'd have *very* good reason to keep it out of human hands.

And they'll try to find a way to copy those codes for themselves, he thought, as he fell back and allowed the marines to take the lead. *They may not think much of any other races, but they won't be able to deny the advantage it gives us.*

He kept his eyes wide open as the marines placed disintegrator charges on the giant hatch, where completed products were released into space, then stepped back as the field turned the metal into dust. The marines plunged forwards, weapons at the ready, but no one greeted them with a hail of fire. Max followed them, peering into the darkened chamber as tiny sensor drones raced ahead, sending their live feed back to the suits. It was crammed with boxes of produced goods - there was no way to tell what they were, without opening them up for inspection - but there was still no sign of the enemy. The marines advanced carefully forward, one of them - a young woman who'd flatly refused to talk to him - opening up an access hatch and inserting a modified hacker core into the fabber network.

"They've locked their system, Major," she reported. "It's going to take the hackers some time to crack their codes, unless someone has an AI hidden up their sleeves."

"Let the intelligence staff handle it," the Major ordered. "Fall back into position."

Max felt the tension rising as the marines reached the far end of the chamber and began to work on the hatch leading into the crew quarters. Unless the Druavroks had changed the original design, the vast majority of the crew would live in a separate - and somewhat isolated - compartment, allowing them to be rounded up without delay. He rather suspected they would have scattered themselves throughout the fabber, if they were intent on delaying the inevitable, but the major had his reasons for wanting to secure the crew compartment first. The hatch clicked open…

…And a horde of Druavroks emerged, firing madly.

"Take them out," the Major ordered.

Max stared in horror. The aliens were wearing masks, rather than suits; didn't they *know* they were charging right into a depressurised bay? They *had* to have known, he told himself, even if they'd cut though all the safety precautions. Bypassing the hatch would have set off all kinds of alarms; hatches would be slamming closed further into the fabber, just to prevent the rest of the structure from depressurising. His suit jerked as it was slaved to Hilde's suit, his weapons coming up and opening fire of their own accord. One by one, the aliens were blasted to the deck before they could do any damage. None of the marines were injured.

"Move forward," the Major ordered. "Quickly!"

Max followed, knowing that Hilde could override his commands and take control of his suit any time she wanted. Inside, the crew compartment was a mess. He couldn't help thinking of a water bird's nest, although - with the temperature dropping rapidly - ice was forming everywhere. The Druavroks liked it hot, according to the briefing; lowering the temperature, even for a short period of time, would be enough to make them miserable.

"Maybe they liked playing in the mud," one of the marines commented. "Those showers look better than ours."

The Major led the way forward, picking his way through a second set of hatches. This time, the airlock had been left intact; inside, the atmosphere was suitable for most humanoid races, although the suit reported traces of a number of dangerous elements. The marines sealed the hatch behind them, just to make sure the fabber didn't depressurise further, then kept moving forward. There was no sign of anyone else until they turned a corner and ran into an ambush.

"Sniper," Hilde snapped, as a plasma burst shot down the corridor. "Only one, but in a good position."

She launched a grenade down the corridor, then ran forward as soon as it exploded. Max followed her carefully, barely noticing the remains of the Druavrok plastered against the bulkhead. Several more snipers popped up, each one slowing the marines for a few brief moments, but inflicting almost no damage at all. The only minor casualty was a marine whose suit was damaged, forcing him to return to the first chamber and wait for pickup. And then they punched their way through a set of sealed doors..."

"Max," Hilde said. She sounded genuinely angry. "You'll want to come see this."

Max hesitated, then slipped forward and peered through the doors. The compartment was crammed with bodies, hundreds of bodies. None of them were Druavroks, he noted dispassionately, using his implants to keep his emotions under control. He didn't recognise half the races gathered in the compartment, but all of them were dead. His suit flashed up a warning as he stepped forward, identifying a deadly nerve toxin that would be lethal to almost every carbon-based race.

"Keep your suit sealed," Hilde warned. "You could have the full spectrum of combat biomods and nanites and you'd still have problems if that toxin touched your bare skin."

"I understand," Max said, feeling sick. He'd known the Druavroks had no problems committing genocide, but this...? The workers had been slaves, worked to death and then gassed when there had been a prospect of rescue. "What sort of monsters are we fighting?"

"A race that cares nothing for anyone, even themselves," Hilde said. "Keep that in mind when you write your report."

"Major, this is Locke in Intelligence," a new voice said. "I've isolated the hacking protocol that should let me take control of the fabber. Permission to proceed?"

"Granted," the Major said. "Download the live feed from any internal sensors into the combat network."

Max followed Hilde back out of the compartment and into combat position as the gravity and lights flickered, briefly.

"I have direct control," Locke reported. "It looks as though the Druavroks were attempting to blow the reactors, but civilian-grade units aren't designed for rapid destruction. I'd prefer to power them down, sir. The engineers can bring them back up after you've finished sweeping the fabber."

"Understood," the Major said. "Can you open all the hatches and vent the atmosphere?"

There was a pause. "I can, Major," Locke said, finally. "But that would kill the remaining Druavroks..."

The Major snorted. "Are there any non-Druavroks left on the station? If not, vent the fabber and save us the task of hunting them down and killing the bastards."

"Understood, Major," Locke said. Max couldn't help thinking that he sounded oddly reluctant to kill the last Druavroks, even though he *knew* what they'd done. "There aren't any other races on the station, save for you and the bad guys. I'm overriding the safety protocols and opening the hatches now."

Max smiled, rather coldly, as red icons flashed up in front of his eyes, warning him that the atmosphere was steadily draining into the vacuum of space. The fabber was vast - it would take some time for the atmosphere to vent completely - but the Druavroks would have no time to muster further resistance or get into suits before the cold overcame them. He wondered, absently, if he should feel guilt, then reminded himself that the Druavroks had casually massacred their slaves just to keep them from being rescued. There was no way to know what drove the monsters, but they *were* monsters.

And some bastard in the future will probably say they weren't that *bad*, he thought, as he hastily reviewed his recordings. One of Old Earth's many problems was an upswing in revisionist history, including attempts to suggest that the great men of the past should have been guided by the morals and ethics of the present. *And that we were the ones who introduced the toxin, not them.*

He scowled at the thought, then followed the marines as they carefully swept their way through the remainder of the structure. The Druavroks had set up a handful of traps, but none of them were particularly lethal. They simply hadn't had the time to turn the entire fabber into a battleground.

"Interesting," Locke said, through the communications network. "It looks as though they were attempting to circumvent the Tokomak security codes."

The Major snorted. "You mean they were attempting to produce weapons?"

"No...well, yes, but not in the way you think," Locke said. "They weren't actually producing *weapons*, they were producing components that could be made *into* weapons and then assembling them elsewhere. The Tokomak didn't install an AI on the fabber, so there was nothing intelligent enough to realise that everything the Druavroks were fabricating could easily be misused."

"How unusually cunning of them," the Major commented.

"Someone else could have come up with the idea," Max offered, before he could stop himself. "One of their slaves, perhaps. He might have thought it would buy him his freedom."

"Or they copied the idea from the Tokomak themselves," Hilde suggested. "We know the Tokomak had plenty of time to study the chinks in their own defences."

Max shrugged. He didn't see why the Tokomak would build the fabbers, carefully programming them so they were only useful for civilian purposes, and then leave a deliberate loophole for their subjects to exploit. Unless it was an intelligence test, with the race that successfully passed it marked for extermination. The Tokomak wouldn't be interested in raising up potential rivals.

"Not that it matters," the Major said. "How much did they manage to produce?"

"I'm not sure," Locke confessed. "I've got a team of analysts studying the specs and trying to work out what the Druavroks could have produced, but it will take some time. They could certainly have put together plasma cannons or antimatter containment fields with a little effort; I think they might have been able to construct mines, although missiles would be beyond the components they could produce here."

"Antimatter mines would be a major headache," Max commented.

"True," Hilde said.

"Time to go back to work," the Major said, loudly. "Once the station has been swept, we'll hand the fabber over to the engineers and return to the ship."

Max kept his amusement to himself as they completed the sweep and then headed back to where they'd broken into the fabber. A handful of crates had been opened, revealing a number of civilian-grade components. Hilde speculated, out loud, that they were designed to serve as magnetic containment fields, either for superhot plasma or antimatter. Either one, Max knew, would allow for any number of makeshift weapons. The Druavroks might not have been able to crack the command codes for the fabber, but they'd certainly done the next best thing.

"Good luck," the Major said, as the engineers teleported into the chamber. "The fabber is all yours."

Hilde caught Max's attention. "We'll be teleporting directly into the quarantine chamber until the suits have been scrubbed," she said, as the marines assembled for teleport. "Do *not* crack your suit until we are sure there's no biological hazard. That toxin was *deadly*."

"I understand," Max said.

He said nothing as the teleport field picked them up and deposited them in a large white room, where the suits were scanned *thoroughly* for prospective threats. The idea of a toxin getting loose on a Solar Union starship was alien - and, on the face of it, absurd - but it was wise to take precautions. Hilde was right. Whatever the Druavroks had used to kill their slaves, it had clearly been nasty enough to slaughter the poor bastards *despite* whatever medical nanites and genetic modifications they'd had. By the time the suits were declared free of contamination, he had almost completed the first draft of his report.

The first report, he corrected himself. He'd watched enough of the battle though the ship's sensors to have a fair idea of how everything had gone, although he'd check before sending the report off on the next courier boat. *The folks back home will have to understand that these monsters will need to be fought.*

"You can open your suit now," Hilde said, dryly. Max started, shocked out of his silent musings. "We'll make sure it gets back to the rack."

Max frowned, disapprovingly. He'd been taught, back when he'd been in the service, that the wearer of the suit was the person responsible for taking care of it. His former CO would have blown a gasket if he'd seen Max handing the duty over to anyone, even a marine. But Hilde had flatly refused to allow him to do it for himself. He didn't have the years of intensive training the marines had had before they donned their suits and took them into combat.

He opened his suit and clambered out. Hilde stood in front of him, wearing a dark overall that showed off her muscles and the shape of her body. He couldn't help feeling small in front of her, even though he was slightly taller than average. She checked the suit, nodded to him and started to key commands into the onboard processors. The suit turned and clanked towards the hatch on its own.

"I'll catch up with you later, if you want a few more interviews," she said, glancing back at him. "Unless I managed to put you off last time."

"You didn't," Max assured her. "But I need to get the first report ready to go before the courier boat leaves."

NINETEEN

Texan forces, according to a news bulletin released by Austin, have trapped and annihilated a Mexican armoured column that successfully forced its way across the Rio Grande. The Governor reportedly issued orders to refrain from taking prisoners after Mexican troops looted, raped and murdered their way through a number of settlements along the border. As yet, there has been no word from the Mexican Government…

-Solar News Network, Year 54

"All things considered," Hoshiko said, "it was a successful operation."

She looked up at the display and studied it for a long moment, then looked back at her XO, who was seated at the far side of the cabin. He hadn't been too keen on the whole offensive, but even *he* had to admit that it had been a success. They'd smashed three battlestations, seven starships and an uncertain number of shuttles and automated platforms in exchange for a handful of converted freighters. By any reasonable standard, she knew, it had been the most one-sided victory since the Horde had tried to attack Earth in Year 10.

"And something they cannot ignore," Wilde said, curtly. "How many of them did we kill?"

Hoshiko shrugged. It was hard to care after they'd found out what had happened to the slaves on the fabbers…or, for that matter, when the drones had made it clear that very few members of the planet's population were anything but Druavroks. They might have been the majority population before the Tokomak withdrew, yet they hadn't been the *only* settlers. They'd slaughtered the other settlers almost as soon as they'd found themselves independent and abandoned.

"We now have three more fabbers," she added. "As we have no intention of keeping the system, we'll tow them out into interstellar space and make use of them there. The remainder of the out-system infrastructure can be destroyed."

"Clever," the XO said. He didn't sound pleased. "And supplying them is going to be a pain."

"The only other alternative is destroying them," Hoshiko reminded him. "I'd prefer to at least *try* to get some use out of the fabbers."

She glanced down at the manifest the intelligence staff had pulled from the fabber. The Druavroks had been producing all sorts of components, some of which were giving her ideas for later tricks. Putting together an entire antimatter production station out of spare parts was mildly impressive, she had to admit; they'd neatly bypassed the security protocols without ever hacking into the computer cores. It was a shame she hadn't been able to capture the station intact, but the Druavroks had turned off the containment fields as soon as her shuttles approached, blowing the structure into atoms. They'd just been lucky the bastards hadn't turned the *moons* into antimatter storage facilities.

Although theirs was the only planet at risk, she thought, wryly. *Maybe that was a step too far even for them.*

"I want to load the antimatter storage pods and everything else onto the freighters, then ship them back to Amstar," she said. "They're useless without antimatter, but I think I've had an idea about what we can do with them."

"There's an antimatter production station at Amstar," the XO said.

"And a fabber capable of producing a few more surprises," Hoshiko agreed. She gave him a devilish smile. It was his *job* to serve as the Doubting Thomas, it was his job to question her decisions…but she half-wished he could open himself up to the idea. "We may have turned the Grand Alliance into a reality, Griffin, but we still have a long way to go."

She sent a command to the room's processor, replacing the in-system display with a holographic starchart. "I'm going to be sending a report and most of the supplies to Amstar, but I think we should be going elsewhere," she added, slowly. "I want to take advantage of their surprise and launch an attack on Dab-yam."

"Which is under siege," Wilde said, sharply. "The Druavroks will have a major force present in the system, Captain."

"But not an overpowering one, not if they haven't already taken the system," Hoshiko pointed out. "I believe we could give them a nasty shock. At the very least, we might open up a channel to run more supplies to the defenders. They only have a single military-grade fabber and they have to be running short of supplies."

"True," the XO agreed. "But taking our rather ragged force up against a full-sized fleet of enemy warships is asking for trouble, Captain."

"I know," Hoshiko said. She picked up a datapad and passed it to him. "That's why I intend to ask Amstar to put together one of these for me."

The XO's eyes narrowed. "Captain, with the greatest of respect…"

"The secret is already out," Hoshiko said. She'd anticipated his objections. "The Tokomak know what happened to them, Commander. Our allies near Sol also know. I doubt it will be long before they start producing gravity-well generators of their own. This is probably the one chance we have to use one to score a complete surprise."

The XO met her eyes. "And if you're wrong?"

Hoshiko shrugged, keeping her concern off her face. The Tokomak might well have won the Battle of Earth, even if their ships had been old and primitive, if they hadn't run straight into an artificial gravity field. And Hammerhead missiles…*they*, at least, *were* a secret she had no intention of sharing with her allies. The principles wouldn't be hard to deduce, but she'd be lucky to escape execution if she came home and admitted she'd given away one of the Solar Union's most closely-held secrets.

"Then I will likely be court-martialled and marched out an airlock," she said. "But we need to use our handful of advances to best possible effect, Griffin, while we still have them."

She looked back at the starchart. "We don't have enough starships to make a real difference," she added. "All we can really do is use our technology to assist our allies, build up their fighting power and support them where necessary. And, if we can keep the Druavroks off balance, we can eventually build up a fleet that will stop them in open battle and take the offensive to their homeworld."

"I hope you're right," Wilde said. He looked down at the deck for a long moment. "But I would still like to register my objections in your log."

Hoshiko kept her face blank with an effort. A recorded objection almost certainly meant a Board of Inquiry when the squadron returned home and Fleet Command started parsing its way through their records. It could mean the end of Commander Wilde's career, if Fleet Command thought he'd overstepped himself, and the end of hers if they didn't. And they'd be judging everything she did with the benefit of hindsight.

Posterity can take care of itself, she told herself, sharply. *All I can do is make what seems the best decisions at the time.*

"If that is your decision, I won't try to stop you," she said, finally. She couldn't help feeling as if he'd knifed her in the back. "I will, of course, record the reasons for my command decisions in the log too."

"Understood," Wilde said.

Hoshiko cleared her throat, changing the subject. "The main body of the fleet will head to the Paradox System," she said. "It's a bare two light years from Dab-yam, which will give us a chance to send a spying mission into the target system and confirm the presence of enemy warships. We can also alert the defenders, if we can make contact, that we're going to try to slip supplies through the blockade."

"I would be surprised if we had a hope in hell of defeating them," Wilde said. "They must have a hard core of battleships there."

"I'm not planning a conventional engagement," Hoshiko said. Wilde was right. A conventional battle with enemy warships could only have one outcome. "I intend to bait a trap."

She keyed the datapad. "I want a few more supplies from Amstar," she added. "Assuming there are no unexpected delays, Commander, they should reach us at Phoenix at least a day or two before the planned offensive. Then, with a little careful preparation, we should have a chance to bait a trap."

Commander Wilde took the datapad. "They may hesitate to hand all of these over, Captain," he warned. "The antimatter alone...they're going to be churning it out as fast as they can for missile warheads."

"I know it's a risk, Commander," Hoshiko said. "But if the operation succeeds, we'll give them one hell of a bloody nose.

"And there's another point," she added. "It's time to start sending raiding ships into their space, just to keep them off balance. The more we can force them to react to us, the better."

"Or goad them into launching an all-out attack on us," Wilde pointed out.

Hoshiko smirked. "Where will they go? Sol's six months away at best possible speed, Commander, and the Solar Union will have plenty of warning."

"Amstar," Wilde said. "Or Martina."

"Perhaps," Hoshiko said. "But the longer they wait, the tougher the defences will be."

"If Martina manages to put together a shared defence force," Wilde said. "The last report said they were still stalling."

"True," Hoshiko agreed. "But we have time to convince them to work with us."

She looked back at the display. "I want Ensign Howard and his courier boat to take the message to Amstar," she added. "Captain Ryman will need to be briefed and he may as well get the briefing from someone he already knows. Then the ensign can head to the RV point at Phoenix and pass on his response."

"He'll need at least one other person assigned to the courier boat," Wilde pointed out. "He may be able to handle the ship completely on his own, in theory, but he'll be alone for ten days. *Not* a good idea."

"Not if he refused courier service," Hoshiko agreed.

It wasn't a pleasant thought. Couriers were paid well over the odds, far more than anyone below the rank of commander, but it was still hard to attract new recruits. She'd heard, through the grapevine, that Fleet Command was seriously considering trying to find other rewards for couriers. It said something about the sheer unpleasantness of the job that hardly anyone bitched about the couriers being favoured by their superiors.

"See to it," she ordered. "He can depart in" - she glanced at the display - "five hours. The fleet itself will leave in two days. We should be at Phoenix for at least a week before he joins us, with the supplies following after."

"If they do," Wilde said.

"They will," Hoshiko said, seriously. "After what we did here, in this system, the Grand Alliance is very definitely a going concern."

— —

"WELL," HILDE SAID, as she stepped into his cabin. "You did manage to write a decent report, after all."

Max looked up from his desk. The cabin was small, although any inclination he might have had to complain about it had been stifled by the realisation that only Captain Stuart and Commander Wilde had bigger compartments to themselves. But it suddenly seemed a great deal smaller as Hilde made her way into the compartment, the hatch hissing closed behind her. She seemed to take up a great deal of room, merely by being here.

"Thank you," he said.

"I was particularly fond of some of the more descriptive phrases you used for our dead enemies," Hilde added. She sat down on the deck, crossing her legs. Her muscles strained against her overalls. "I'm sure some humourless bastard will make a fuss about it."

"It's hard to show sensitivity to aliens who are responsible for billions of deaths," Max commented. *That* sort of stupidity was mercifully absent from the Solar Union, for the most part. Needing to maintain the environment with great care tended against it. "What one does in private is one's own business, but what one does in public is the public's business."

"The Druavroks feel differently, of course," Hilde observed.

"I don't think they do," Max said. "They haven't done anything to attempt to *hide* the genocide. Rumours are spreading through the sector as fast as courier boats can fly. I think they're either proud of slaughtering so many innocent people or they just don't give a damn about outside opinions."

"Probably the latter," Hilde suggested. "They don't seem to be shouting their work to the skies either. They're just…*doing it*."

Max nodded, slowly. "Are you here for another interview?"

Hilde gave him a sharp look. "Did you somehow call me here to attend an interview with the power of your mind?"

"No," Max said, feeling his face heat. "But I would have called you here sooner or later."

"I just came to congratulate you," Hilde said. "Your recordings are not only going to Earth, but right across the sector. You'll be the most famous reporter in the galaxy by the time this is through."

"Because telling the sector the Druavroks can be defeated is important," Max said. He wasn't sure if he believed her. Hilde was the last person on the ship he'd have chosen as a messenger girl. "Do *you* feel they can be defeated?"

"Everyone can be defeated," Hilde said. "It's just a matter of knowing how to do it and actually *doing* it."

Max smiled. "Even the Solar Marines?"

"We like to think not," Hilde said. She shrugged. "But we do need to understand our own limits too."

She gave him a mischievous smile. "Thinking of joining up?"

"I'm tiny compared to you - and the others," Max protested.

"*That* wouldn't be a problem," Hilde countered. "There's no reason why you couldn't have a body like the major's - or mine - through a long session in the bodyshop. You'd have to keep it in shape, of course, but you could do that if you wanted. It's all about mental toughness, not physical toughness. You have to have the urge to keep going no matter how much gets dumped on you from high above. Even among the Solar Union, Max, that sort of urge is rare."

She shrugged. "For every marine who graduates, Max, there's fifty who don't make it through the final exercises and a hundred who quit during Hell Week."

"I'm not sure what I'd do with a body like the major's," Max said.

Hilde winked. "I can tell you what *he* does with it," she said. "Captain Sharpe was pissed at me for some reason and sent me to take a message to the major, while he was technically off duty. Turned out I interrupted him in the middle of an orgy with three girls and he was not best pleased."

"He wouldn't be," Max said. He'd spent plenty of time testing out the limits of sexual expression during his own adolescence, but the major had to be at least fifty. "*Three* girls?"

"We know, every time we go out, that we might be the unlucky ones who buy the farm," Hilde said, gently. "*We* don't have a million-ton starship wrapped around us and the suits, while tough, are not invulnerable. A single lucky shot could wipe one of us from existence before we know we're under fire...and a rigged demolition charge could wipe out a whole platoon. So yeah, we work hard and we play harder because the next mission could easily be our last."

Max shuddered. There was something about the marine lifestyle that was tempting to him, a sense of...*camaraderie* he'd never felt in the Orbital Guard, but he doubted he'd be able to cope with the training. Did he have it in him not to cut and run when the shit got too hot? He'd managed to stay embedded with the marines, but he knew he could pull out at any moment before zero hour. Hilde and her comrades didn't have that option.

He looked at her. "And do you play hard too?"

Hilde met his eyes. "Do you really want to find out?"

Max's throat was suddenly very dry. "Is it safe?"

"Life is rarely safe," Hilde pointed out. She rose, slowly. Max was suddenly very aware of the sheer power of her body. His heartbeat started to race as she took a step forward. "Do you want to back out now?"

"...No," Max said. He was nervous, but he knew he'd hate himself afterwards if he turned her down. "I don't."

He raised a hand as she came closer, one hand removing her overalls with practiced ease, and gently pressed it against her skin. It was warmer than he'd expected, despite the leathery feel; he lifted his head to meet her lips as she bent down and kissed him, her arms wrapping around him and holding him gently. Resistance, he realised suddenly, was futile. Her grip was too strong for him to fight. If she'd wanted to hold him down and have her way with him, he couldn't have stopped her. The thought was both terrifying and exciting.

She broke the kiss and smiled down at him. "Still want to find out?"

Max allowed his hands to trail over her chest. Her breasts felt strange to his touch, warmer than the rest of her chest and yet practically non-existent. She made no move to stop him, but he was very aware of her muscled arms holding him. He heard her sigh, deep in her throat, as his finger traced her nipple. Her hand moved down and started to unbutton his pants. A sudden surge of excitement ran through him as she kissed him again, firmly. She was very definitely in control.

He gathered himself. "Are you going to carry me into the bedroom or are we going to do it here?"

Hilde grinned, then picked him up almost effortlessly and carried him towards the bedroom door.

TWENTY

The price of food over the former United States of America has skyrocketed as farmers refuse to sell crops at affordable prices or simply walk off the land, in the wake of new demands by the federal government. Insurgent activity - termed bandit activity - has trebled as the government attempts to enforce its control, while rogue states like Texas have flatly refused to accept the government's orders.

-Solar News Network, Year 54

"The Grand Alliance is delighted, young man."

"Thank you, sir," Thomas said. He hadn't enjoyed the flight from Malachi to Amstar, but he had to admit he was still the only real candidate to fly the courier boat. The only upside was that he'd had time to review a number of manuals, catch up on some sleep and play games while the courier had been in FTL. "I believe the Captain is delighted too."

Captain Ryman smiled. He'd greeted Thomas in person, when he'd teleported down to the Pan-Gal, then told Thomas to go into one of the human-compatible suites and have a few hours of sleep. Thomas had been astonished at just how compatible the suites actually were, now most of the staff had been put back to work. They'd even offered to find him a girl for the night, which he'd declined hastily. The mere *concept* was embarrassing, even though he'd been raised in the Solar Union.

"I'm sure she has good reason to be pleased," Captain Ryman said, peering down at the datapad. "Did she...do you know what she's requested?"

"I wasn't made privy to her private message, sir," Thomas said. The idea of the captain confiding in *him* was ludicrous. "I'm just the messenger boy."

"We can get her most of what she wants, particularly if we tell everyone what she wants it *for*," Captain Ryman said. "Giving up so much antimatter will worry people, though. They think they need it to defend Amstar."

Thomas frowned. It had only been twenty days since the fleet had left Amstar, but it had been clear, the moment he arrived, that the planet's defenders hadn't wasted their time. A ring of new-built orbital weapons platforms surrounded the planet, backed up by shoals of mines and remote single-shot buoys. Behind them, dozens of freighters and a handful of warships were waiting, ready to give the Druavroks a bloody nose if they came back to Amstar. But even Thomas's limited experience was enough to tell him the Druavroks probably *could* retake Amstar, if they were willing to soak up the casualties.

"I can't speak for the Captain," he said, carefully, "but surely keeping the Druavroks reeling is a good idea."

"I think so, too," Captain Ryman said. "But everyone here is terrified of the Druavroks coming *back*."

He scowled. "And a couple of the items she requested will take at least ten days to produce," he added. "The engineers she left here are great, but they say they'll have to reprogram one of the fabbers to produce the components and then put it together themselves."

"I believe the Captain is prepared to wait," Thomas said. He hoped he was right. "But we do need to go on the offensive again as soon as possible."

"So we do," Captain Ryman agreed.

He put the datapad down on the desk and looked up at Thomas. "Are you recording a sensory for your commander?"

"Yes, sir," Thomas said. He'd taken the earlier orders to heart. "A full sensory."

"Very good," Captain Ryman said. He cleared his throat. "Production of missiles and orbital defence weaponry proceeds as planned, Captain. Full figures will be sent along with your" - his lips twitched - "messenger boy, but I have no doubt that the Druavroks will get an unpleasant surprise when they come calling. In addition, we've received reports from several Grand Alliance members that they have successfully unlocked their fabbers. Production rates should skyrocket over the whole sector.

"Several other races and worlds have also signed up with the Grand Alliance, including two that have volunteered to dispatch warships to take part in the offensive. I've asked them to send the ships to Amstar first, where they will be given Grand Alliance communications and datanet protocols before being forwarded to the fleet. News of your success will, I'm sure, increase the willingness of the rest of the sector to join us, although many of the more developed worlds are nervous about their own defences. We've also recruited several thousand additional private freighters, all of whom will be outfitted with modern weapons and defences.

"We've also been recruiting additional spacers from Amstar and nearby worlds," he concluded. "Training is something of a mixed bag, Captain, as they only had to pass the Tokomak exams to qualify for service in space. I've started work on assembling a training facility on Amstar, but that's pretty much a long-term project. Mercenaries, on the other hand, we have in abundance, if we can pay them. Amstar's provisional government is willing to offer military-grade spare parts, as there's a shortage of ready cash, but they have to look to their own defences first. The only upside to this is that the Druavroks don't seem to be interested in recruiting mercenaries."

He paused, smiling thinly. "Is there anything I've missed?"

"Martina," Thomas said, after a moment. "Have they signed up with us?"

"They're still haggling over a planetary government, according to the last message," Captain Ryman said. His lips quirked. "Just because there's a horde of genocidal monsters moving through the sector is no excuse for not following the proper procedures for establishing a federal government. I expect they'll come to an agreement sooner rather than later, but they were kept divided by the Tokomak for a reason and old habits die hard."

Thomas nodded. There were so many gravity points in the Martina System that whoever controlled it would be in a position to influence and control economic development all over the sector. The Tokomak might not have put the system under their direct control, but they'd definitely done the next best thing. And yet now, with the Druavroks advancing steadily towards Martina, the planetary governments could hardly afford to ignore the threat.

"We have helped them to unlock their fabbers too, so the planet's defences will be boosted," Captain Ryman added. "Putting additional defences around the gravity points, however, will be politically unacceptable."

"Because the Tokomak banned it," Thomas said.

He'd wondered, back when he'd been at the Academy, why there were so few fixed defences orbiting the gravity points. The opportunity of catching the enemy ships as they came through one by one should have been irresistible. But the Tokomak, when they'd cracked the secret of FTL and bypassed the gravity points, had banned all further fortifications. Given how desperately they relied on the gravity points to move forces around their empire, it made a certain amount of sense. They just hadn't bargained on losing a war and control of hundreds of sectors.

"And because it would give the planet a stranglehold on economics," Captain Ryman added, dryly. "I suspect there will be complaints from the systems on the other side of the gravity points if Martina starts establishing fortifications. They'd see it as the first step towards levying higher transit tolls."

"Politics," Thomas said, in disgust.

"Economics," Captain Ryman said. He smirked. "For nine out of ten Galactic races, Ensign, money talks and politics walk."

"It doesn't talk to the Druavroks," Thomas muttered.

"No, it doesn't," Captain Ryman agreed. "There's always someone who refuses to come to terms with you, if they can understand the concept of coming to terms in the first place. They need to be fought because there's no alternative. Far too many of our problems stem from refusing to grasp that some people are simply unwilling to compromise."

"Yes, sir," Thomas said. "I was taught about the history of Earth at the Academy."

"Now you have a chance to put some of it into practice," Captain Ryman said. "Of course, as my old history teacher was fond of saying, those who don't study history are doomed to repeat it, while those who *do* study history are doomed to watch helplessly as *others* repeat it."

"Yes, sir," Thomas said. He'd been told the same thing. "Why does no one ever *learn*?"

Captain Ryman snorted. "Remind me to tell you, sometimes, about the trading missions to Tatton. Rich world, very xenophobic; greets incoming aliens with hails of fire…and at least one or two traders, every year, will attempt to make contact with the locals and get holes blown in their hulls. They never learn."

He shrugged. "I'll have the freighters loaded with the first set of supplies over the next two days and send them off to Phoenix with a handful of warships as escort," he said, changing the subject. "Do you have specific orders for yourself?"

"I'm to take your response back to Captain Stuart," Thomas said. "If you have any reports or messages you'd like to forward, I can take those too."

"No messages from Sol yet, of course," Captain Ryman said. "There are a handful of messages marked for her attention, mainly from governments trying to seek out a better deal or one that can be twisted to their advantage. I'll forward those to her, but I'd be surprised if they weren't sent straight back to me."

Thomas nodded in understanding. *He* wouldn't have cared to open the Captain's private mail either. "I'll probably be coming back soon too."

"We *are* working to set up an improved courier network," Captain Ryman offered. "We're just short of courier boats we can feed into a rota."

"And pilots," Thomas guessed. *He'd* already decided he'd been quite right to turn down the offer of a permanent post to courier service, even if it *did* entail generous pay and fantastic retirement bonuses. There was no prospect of anything, but remaining trapped on the ship for days on end. "There's no way you can recruit more?"

"We can probably pass the task on to some of the spacers we've recruited," Captain Ryman said. "Actually, setting up a better postal service, one that replaces the Tokomak system, might help to put the Grand Alliance on a more solid footing. But again, it will take some time to set up, even without the war."

"Yes, sir," Thomas said.

"I'm going to try to copy the system the Solar Union developed, but there would be a great deal of duplication," Captain Ryman added. "And we'd really need more developed shipping lines."

He shrugged. "But that's a problem for another time."

"Yes, sir," Thomas said.

"I'd suggest you spent some time on the surface, while I prepare the messages for Captain Stuart," Captain Ryman suggested, "but that's really up to you. Do you want to just teleport back to the courier? Or grab something to eat in the Pan-Gal? Or even go exploring the remains of the city?"

Thomas frowned. "Is it safe?"

"It should be, as long as you don't go near the Druavrok enclaves," Captain Ryman said. "I think we've rounded up most of the rogues now; most of them expended themselves in suicide attacks, rather than going to ground or creeping back to their fellows. They're probably just biding their time."

"Yes, sir," Thomas said.

He considered it for a long moment. There was nothing to be gained by teleporting back to the courier boat, not when he'd see far too much of its bulkheads during the flight from Amstar to Phoenix. And he was curious to see more of Amstar…but he doubted he had time to explore anything outside the city itself.

"I'll go to the Pan-Gal," he said. "I could do with something good to eat."

"It's all on our tab," Captain Ryman assured him. "Just make sure they know you're human when you order food."

"Yes, sir," Thomas said.

He concealed his amusement as he walked out of the office and back towards the Pan-Gal. It wasn't actually bad advice, even though it sounded absurd. The workers at the hotel, used to serving guests from hundreds of different races, needed to be *sure* of his race before they fed him something that an alien race considered a delicacy and another considered deadly poison, something his implants and nanites wouldn't be able to handle. A pair of armed guards at the doors checked his ID, then waved him through into the lobby. This time, with the projectors in full working order, it looked like a fancy hotel from Earth.

Someone must have downloaded a perceptual reality, he thought, as he strode through the lobby and into the restaurant. *I wonder what it looks like to other races*.

He pushed the thought aside as he stopped in front of the counter, where a human waitress in a long black gown checked his ID for the second time, then led him towards a table in the corner. There was something odd about the way she moved, something that made him wonder if her humanity was as illusionary as the lobby, although he couldn't quite put his finger on it. Maybe she'd just spent so long on Amstar, among aliens, that she'd forgotten how to relate to her fellow humans. He'd read an article, while he'd been at the Academy, that talked about humans raised on alien worlds, even if they hadn't been adopted by alien parents. They'd tended to be different, in many ways, to either Solarians or Earthers.

But they grew up in a different environment, he thought. He'd seen plenty of differences between Solarians and Earthers too. *Surely, they'd have a different mindset from the rest of us.*

He shook his head, dismissing the thought, and looked around the giant room. It was a strange mixture of open and closed dining compartments, some sealed closed so no one could see their occupants. A large alien resembling a giant spider was sitting in one of the open compartments, casually devouring an animal than looked like a dog. Thomas couldn't help feeling sick when he realised it was still alive. The spider sat next to another alien, a creature that reminded Thomas of a tree. It didn't look to be eating, but it was sitting in a flower pot...

"The human-compatible menu is here," the waitress said briskly, tapping a switch to bring up a hologram. "If you wish to stick with human dishes, they're listed in set one. Non-human dishes are listed in set two."

Thomas nodded, watched the waitress walk away and then turned his attention to the menu as it flickered in front of him. Set one was surprisingly long, although with fabbers and food processors it probably wouldn't be hard to produce almost anything quickly; set two was longer, but included hundreds of dishes that sounded disgusting or looked inedible. He was tempted to try something new, yet he had no idea what he could eat. It was considered bad manners to order food and then reject it.

"I'd try the Glazed Topsham Beast, myself," a voice said, in oddly-accented Gal-Standard One. "You're human, are you not?"

"Yes," Thomas said, looking up. The speaker was human, a tall girl with black skin, long red hair and a face that bore a number of scars. "And you?"

"Human too," the girl said. She sat down facing him. "Most non-human dishes are inedible, for all sorts of reasons, but Glazed Topsham Beast is reasonably tasty."

Thomas nodded, feeling awkward. "My name is Thomas," he said, as he placed his order and banished the hologram. "And you are?"

"Marie," the girl said. "My ancestors were taken from Earth centuries ago. Some of us genuinely believed our homeworld to be a legend before we heard of you."

"We're real," Thomas said.

"So I hear," Marie said. "I was actually hoping to ask you about Earth. What's it like?"

Thomas hesitated. On one hand, strange girls *didn't* just come up to him and make random conversion, not in the Solar Union. Marie wanted something, but what? It wasn't as if they were the only two humans on the surface. But, on the other hand, all she seemed to want to do was talk. He ordered his implants to record the entire conversation, then tried to answer her question.

"Right now, it's a nightmare," he said. He had no interest in discussing the dispute between Solarians and Earthers, but he didn't really want to lie. "The smart people are fleeing the planet, while the dumbasses are fighting a civil war over lots of little nothings."

Marie looked stricken. "Is that true?"

"More or less," Thomas said. "But those of us who live in space are doing very well."

He looked up as a waiter arrived, carrying two plates of food. His eyes narrowed - he hadn't seen Marie order anything - as the plate was placed in front of him. The Glazed Topsham Beast didn't smell like *anything* he'd smelled before, but he took a bite and decided it tasted like a combination of chicken and ham. He made a mental note to try and get the pattern for the autochef and tucked in, fielding Marie's questions as he ate.

"Some of us would like to go to Earth," she confessed, as they finished. "Just to see what it's like."

"The Solar Union would take you in," Thomas said. "What's life like *here* for humans?"

"We're…homeless," Marie said, after a moment. "Very few races are interested in looking out for us, or anyone who isn't one of them. Finding Earth…it seems like a dream come true."

"You would be welcome in the Solar Union," Thomas said. "But Earth itself is a nightmare."

Marie thanked him, paid for the dinner and left the restaurant before he could ask for her contact code or anything else. Thomas watched her go, suspecting that he was missing something, then carefully saved a copy of the whole discussion in his implants. The intelligence staff would need to see it…

…And perhaps they could tell him what it meant.

TWENTY-ONE

The Lieutenant Governor of Texas was reported dead yesterday in an explosion that destroyed his residence. Sources in Texas are uncertain what precisely happened, but the datanet is filling with speculation that the explosion was caused by a missile fired from a stealth drone, either from Mexico or the Federal Government. The Governor has promised a full investigation and retaliation.
-Solar News Network, Year 54

"More warships," Hoshiko said. "*They'll* be very useful."

"And more supplies," Commander Wilde agreed. "They'll be *more* useful."

Hoshiko nodded in agreement as she stared at the display. The new warships didn't show the polish of the older ships - she'd been drilling the fleet ever since it had arrived at Phoenix - but they represented a significant addition to both her fighting power and the Grand Alliance itself. Convincing the rest of the sector that the Druavroks could and *would* be stopped would, in the long run, be worth more than *just* a handful of warships. She was still dependent - far too dependent - on the converted freighters, but the fleet was growing stronger all the time.

"We got almost everything we asked for," she said. The gravity-wave generators, in particular, would allow her to give the Druavroks a *real* surprise. "And we should be ready to take the offensive in a couple more days."

"Assuming they take the bait," Wilde noted. "Are you sure they will?"

"I think I'm starting to get an idea of how these creatures think," Hoshiko said, after a moment. "They *don't* think very highly of anyone, perhaps even themselves. A challenge has to be accepted, not ignored. We'll be throwing down a gauntlet they'd be hard-pressed to ignore."

She shrugged. In truth, she had contingency plans. It might not be possible to drive the Druavroks away from Dab-yam, but she could give them a bloody nose. Given the fleet reported to be laying siege to the system, no one seriously expected her to challenge the Druavroks to a straight fight. The Grand Alliance would be lost along with the fleet.

"I need you to take command of Task Force 6.1," she said, instead. Task Force 6.1 was a small formation, but it had a vitally important task. "You'll be covering the ambush."

"Understood," Wilde said. "I assume Biscoe will be taking command of the ship?"

Hoshiko nodded, reluctantly. She would have preferred to keep Wilde with her and place another officer in command of Task Force 6.1, but she needed someone completely reliable in place to spring the trap. Besides, it was *important* to show she was prepared to put humans - Solarians - on the front lines. Wilde could handle the mission and, at the same time, serve as a symbol of her resolve. But it meant putting a largely-untried officer in command of the ship in a time of war.

"I'll be ready to retake command myself, if necessary," she said. It wasn't a perfect solution, but she'd parcelled out too many of her officers to alien ships for any other solution to be contemplated. "I don't intend to take the fleet *right* into the teeth of enemy fire."

"They'll know about us now," Wilde told her, bluntly. "They have to know we overwhelmed Malachi."

"I know," Hoshiko agreed. The Druavroks should take her fleet seriously, after they'd blown the defences of one of their systems into scrap metal, but they might see the hundreds of converted freighters and dismiss the threat. It wasn't as if she'd risked charging the fleet into the fire of a squadron of enemy battleships. "But as long as they're not abandoning the siege, we have to go to them."

"And they'll know that too," Wilde said.

Hoshiko had her doubts. Nothing she'd seen suggested the Druavroks had a concept of war like humanity's - or the Tokomak, for that matter. They'd just declared war in all directions, as if they were completely contemptuous of their opposition. Perhaps they'd had a point - it had taken her squadron's intervention to forge the Grand Alliance - but she was sure they would have outrun their logistics, sooner rather than later. And yet, if their enemies hadn't managed to get together by then, they might well have overcome the problem and just kept going.

But the more space they need to control, the harder it will be, she thought. *Eventually, their grip will be so light it won't be there at all.*

She shuddered. It wouldn't matter, not with the Druavroks. They intended to *exterminate* every other race in the galaxy, not set up their own empire and enslave the rest of the universe. They'd just wipe the worlds they occupied clear of life and move on. Hell, given how fast they seemed to breed, it wouldn't take them long to build up settlements that would need to be wiped out by their opponents or permanently surrendered to the Druavroks. If they couldn't be beaten quickly, their enemies would find themselves having to make a choice between committing genocide and being the *victims* of genocide.

And if we have to make that choice, she thought, *better to commit genocide than allow it to be committed against us.*

It was a sickening thought. She knew - she'd had it hammered into her head from a very early age - that Stuarts went into the military to *protect* their families, their friends, their nation...not to crush their enemies or commit atrocities. Her grandfather had talked about the need to uphold one's own standards, even as one's enemies gloried in turning empathy and compassion into weapons. *He'd* had to deal with human shields, with shooters and bombers who were still children, with enemy populations that worshipped death and rejected the life offered to them by outsiders…or, perhaps, were too scared to take a stand against the monsters that turned them into slaves and cannon fodder. And *he* had never urged the mass slaughter of enemy combatants and civilians alike…

But if we can't convince the Druavroks to stop, she told herself, *we might have to kill them all.*

"Captain?"

She blinked, coming back to herself. "Yes, Commander?"

"I can teleport over to the task force later this afternoon," Wilde said. It took Hoshiko a moment to remember what he'd been saying. "Biscoe should be properly briefed on his duties and the attack plan."

"Understood," Hoshiko said. "Patrick will remain as my second, just in case something happens to *Fisher*."

"They'll certainly *try* to target her first," Wilde agreed.

Hoshiko shrugged. A *human* commander would almost certainly target the warships first, knowing they represented the only long-term threat. But the Druavroks? She wasn't so sure *what* they'd do. They might not be capable of judging the correct level of threat posed by each and every one of her ships, not if they were all spewing out missiles. She shook her head, dismissing the thought. She'd find out soon enough.

"We'll be well-protected by the datanet, if push comes to shove," she said. "But the idea is not to enter missile range if it can be avoided."

"It might not be avoidable," Wilde said. He looked back at the display. "The latest reports, Captain, make it clear that the planet is under heavy attack."

"All the more reason to move quickly," Hoshiko said. "Brief Biscoe, if you please. I'll speak to him myself before we enter FTL."

"Aye, Captain," Wilde said. "The task force will also need practice in deploying the mines, I think. Time will not be on our side."

Hoshiko nodded. "Start running through the exercises as soon as you board the freighter," she ordered, curtly. "And let me know if you need more time."

"Ask me for anything but time," Wilde quoted, as he rose. "I'll let you know what happens."

He left the cabin, the hatch hissing closed behind him. Hoshiko ordered more coffee, then picked up the datapad and started to read through Captain Ryman's latest reports. Martina, it seemed, had *finally* patched together a government of sorts, although the local sub-governments were quick to explain that it *only* represented the planet to the rest of the Grand Alliance and had very little authority on the surface. Hoshiko had to smile at how *human* it sounded, then read the final sections with growing relief. Martina's fabbers had been unlocked, as she'd hoped, and the planet was building up its defences as fast as possible, with some help from the naval base. Given time, it would even start producing warships of its own.

Pity we can't just replicate warships, she thought. A fleet composed of thousands of warships like *Jackie Fisher* would make humanity the dominant power in the galaxy. *That would make life so much simpler.*

She shook her head, dismissing the thought. It was theoretically possible, with AIs to handle the calculations, but the power requirements were staggeringly high. She'd read studies where engineers had proposed using zero-width wormholes to tap a local star, yet they were years away from any kind of workable hardware. Besides, even the Solar Union would hesitate at the thought of tampering with Sol. A large flare - or a supernova - would wipe out seventy percent of the Solar Union and *all* of Earth.

And that hasn't stopped us from working on ways to trigger flares or supernovas, she thought. A chill ran down her spine as she considered what the Druavroks would do with such technology. *They could wipe out trillions of lives in a heartbeat.*

The doorbell rang. "Come in!"

She looked up as the hatch opened, revealing Max Kratzok. The reporter was wearing a standard shipsuit, rather than the suit he normally wore; he walked forward as if his arms and legs were aching, although it didn't look as though he were in pain. Hoshiko's eyes narrowed, but she knew she couldn't ask. Respecting the privacy of a fellow Solarian - too - had been drummed into her from a very early age.

Because there were too many busybodies on Earth, she thought, as Kratzok took a seat facing her. *They thought they had the right to poke their noses into everyone's business.*

"Captain," Kratzok said. There didn't seem to be anything wrong with his voice, at least. "I completed the second set of interviews and features and uploaded them into the datanet. I think they will be a hit back home."

Hoshiko smiled. She had a private subroutine running in her implants, counting down the days until her first reports reached Sol. And, of course, until the first response could come back from her superiors. No matter what she said in public, she knew fleet command could jump either way, when it came to deciding how to react to her actions. They could approve them uncritically or order her back home to face a court martial…or anything in-between.

"I certainly hope so," she said. "Did you get anything from Malachi itself?"

"They ignored my requests for interviews," Kratzok said. He smiled. "I don't think they were interested in explaining themselves to our media."

"I suppose not," Hoshiko said. Her grandfather had gone on and on, at length, about media-savvy enemies and reporters who practically *worked* for the bad guys. The Solar Union, at least, didn't have that problem. "I don't even think they *have* a media."

"Probably not," Kratzok said. He shifted, uncomfortably. "I believe you promised me an interview, Captain."

Hoshiko groaned inwardly, but there was no point in trying to deny it. "I have an hour, roughly, before I have to go on duty," she said, after checking her implants in the hopes an urgent message was waiting in her inbox. "Is that enough time?"

"It depends on how you answer my questions," Kratzok admitted. "I have a list, Captain, but I will probably also want to ask follow-up questions."

"Very well," Hoshiko said. She was tempted to ask just why he was uncomfortable - and to hell with politeness - but as long as he wasn't complaining, there was nothing she could do about it. And yet, she was curious and a little concerned. "If you don't mind me asking…"

"I was having sex," Kratzok said, before she could finish the question. "Hilde and I were breaking furniture when she was off-duty."

It took Hoshiko a moment to place the name, but when she did she nodded in amused understanding. Marines were reputed to be wild in the sack, although she'd never bedded one herself. She *was* surprised that Kratzok hadn't used his nanites to smooth out the aches and pains, but it was his choice.

"I see," she said. "Now, what was your first question?"

— —

"Welcome onboard, Commander," a dark-skinned man said, as soon as the teleport field shimmered into nothingness. "I'm Captain Markham."

"Commander Wilde, Griffin Wilde," Griffin said. The freighter's bridge was cramped, even though half the crew had been pulled out and reassigned to other ships. "Thank you for volunteering for Task Force 6.1."

"If I'd known what we'd be doing, I would have insisted on volunteering for one of the other task forces instead," Markham said. He clasped Griffin's hand briefly, then nodded towards a console that had clearly been installed only a day or two ago. "There won't be much fame in this part of the operation, sir."

"There will be, if it works," Wilde said. He tried to keep his doubts out of his voice. The Captain's plan, on paper, looked sound…but there were too many moving parts for him to be completely happy with it. "Is everything installed?"

"The hold is loaded, sir," Markham confirmed. "We were told not to even *look* at the devices for fear they might explode."

"They might," Griffin confirmed. Markham was exaggerating, but not by much. "Don't even touch them until we're ready to leave."

"Of course, sir," Markham said. "Do you want to test the console?"

Griffin nodded as they walked over to the console. "Did you have any problems installing it?"

"None," Markham said. "It's basically separate from everything, but the fusion core; we didn't have to worry about linking it into the ship's computer. The downside is that it will be fairly clear to the enemy that *we're* the flagship."

"It shouldn't matter," Griffin said. "Task Force 6.1 isn't intended to come to grips with the enemy, not directly."

"Let us hope so," Markham said. "A single warship would be able to wipe the entire task force out without trouble."

They might get a nasty surprise, Griffin thought, as he keyed the console and activated the datalink. There were forty freighters in Task Force 6.1, each crammed to the gunwales with mines and improvised weapons. *Hit one of the ships and it'll go up with one hell of a bang.*

He studied the datalink for a long moment, then nodded. "We'll start practicing the deployment pattern in an hour," he said. "And then we will be ready to depart with the rest of the fleet."

"Of course, sir," Markham said.

Griffin gave him a sharp look. "Are you so keen to hurt the enemy, Captain?"

Markham nodded. "I had family on Amstar, Commander," he said. "There aren't many humans who've managed to amass the cash to put a deposit on a freighter, not there. I was away for months at a time, just trying to build up a reserve of cash, and every time I came home it was a great party. My wives and children were proud of me - I used to promise my eldest son a place on the ship when he was old enough…"

His voice darkened. "And then the Druavroks took over and my family vanished in the chaos," he added. "I wasn't there at the time. I don't know what happened to them, if they were killed or eaten or simply lost somewhere in all the madness, but the Druavroks either killed them or are responsible for their deaths. So yes, I *do* want to hurt them. I want to hurt them so badly they'll *scream*."

Griffin studied him for a long moment, then nodded. "You'll have your chance," he said, quietly. Markham's determination to hurt the Druavroks was worrying - in his experience, a desire for revenge led to indiscipline - but it could be used. "Now, if you don't mind, we have to start drilling."

"THE FLEET REPORTS that it is ready to depart, Captain," Lieutenant Bryon Yeller said. "All units have acknowledged their orders."

Hoshiko nodded. Two days of intensive drilling, two days of trying to prepare for every possible eventuality…soon, she'd see just how well it worked in practice. They were only three days from Dab-yam. She thought - she hoped - that the exercises had smoothed out the kinks in their formation, but she knew just how much could still go wrong. There were too many different races and planets represented in her fleet.

"Alert the fleet," she ordered, coolly. "They are to jump to FTL on my mark."

And hope to hell we don't screw up the timing, she added, mentally. The Druavroks shouldn't be able to see Task Force 6.1 when it broke away from the remainder of the fleet, but if she was wrong…well, she'd just have to improvise. *And, if nothing else, we'll win the defenders of the planet some time.*

"The fleet has acknowledged, Captain," Yeller said. He sounded confident, at least, although he'd been spared detached duty. Hoshiko had needed to keep most of her communications officers on her original ships. "All ships are standing by."

"Take us into FTL," Hoshiko ordered.

She settled back in her command chair as the fleet rocketed into FTL, keeping her expression under control. Wilde would play his part, she was sure, but would the Druavroks? If she was wrong about them, the plan was going to end in an expensive failure…

…And the Grand Alliance might just come apart at the seams.

TWENTY-TWO

The Japanese Government has ordered compulsory pregnancy for every woman between 16 and 40 in order to cope with the country's growing population crisis, in which over 70% of Japanese civilians are over 70. However, as analysts have noted, they have done nothing about either the economic crisis or the democratic deficit that have forced Japanese youngsters to flee the country.

-Solar News Network, Year 54

"They're launching another attack, Matriarch."

Matriarch Yah-Sin would have snarled a curse if she thought it would have done any good, even though it would have set a bad example for the hatchlings. Dab-yam's government had thrown billions upon billions of interstellar credits at the planetary defence network, but constant attacks were steadily wearing it down. The first attack had failed badly, so badly that even the Druavroks had thought better of trying it again, yet their current strategy was far more effective. Depowered missile strikes, redirected asteroids…even a single one, getting through the defences and into the atmosphere, would do a great deal of damage. It could not be allowed.

"Order the Orbital Guard to intercept," she ordered. "And ready back-up forces if they're required."

She watched the display, grimly, as red icons roared down to meet green. Her forces were growing tired and making mistakes, the constant tempo wearing them down until they could no longer muster the awareness to fight. If the government had built warships instead things might be different, but her people had always been reluctant to get involved in galactic affairs. Better to have a strong defence, the government had argued, and mind their own business. But the Druavroks couldn't be dissuaded by solid walls, let alone a network of orbital battlestations, automated weapons platforms and a handful of refurbished warships.

There's definitely something to be said for taking the battle to them, she thought, as more red icons flared into life on the display. The Druavrok missiles didn't seem to be any better than hers, thankfully, but there were a lot of them. *This way, they just keep wearing us down until we collapse.*

"Matriarch, five of their missiles are targeted on Fabber One," the hatchling warned. She was young for her role, but the more experienced officers had been farmed out to other positions in the defence grid. Half of them were dead now. "They're trying to cripple the defences."

"Order the automated platforms to prioritise defending the fabbers," Yah-Sin ordered, ignoring the hatchling's shock. "Nothing else, even the planet itself, is to have a higher priority. The fabbers must be preserved."

She rubbed her feathers in irritation. There was no choice. Without the fabbers, the defenders would be unable to resupply their missile launchers and keep the enemy from hammering the grid at will. But the Druavroks *had* effectively cut them off from all sources of raw materials. Her people were working hard to shove debris from the endless battle into their insatiable maws, yet it wasn't enough. The most optimistic projections suggested the planet's defences would collapse in less than two weeks at most.

And if that happens, we are doomed, she thought. Her people had never been happy on other worlds, even when the Tokomak had introduced them to FTL and showed them the greater universe beyond their atmosphere. There were only a handful of her kind off-world, nowhere near enough to serve as a breeding population. *When Dab-Yam dies, we will die with her.*

"They're launching a second set of projectiles," the hatchling added. "The mass drivers are spitting buckets of rock at us."

Yah-Sin clacked her beak in acknowledgement. She had to give the Druavroks credit; they weren't known for being imaginative, but they'd come up with a cheap way to keep her defences on their toes. Bombarding the planet with mass drives seemed like an exercise in futility when pitted against modern defences, yet they forced her to keep her crews on their toes, blasting the projectiles - which were little more than scaled-up rocky KEWs - into vapour. And a single failure would mean planetary devastation on a terrifying scale.

"Keep the defences online and engage them as soon as they come into range," she ordered, tiredly. *She* needed to sleep too. "And alert me when they bring their fleet back into engagement range."

— —

"WE'RE READING POINT Tsushima, Commander," Markham said. "FTL drive is ready to disengage."

Griffin nodded. The fleet - over two thousand starships - was flying in such close formation that the Druavroks shouldn't be able to notice when a relative handful of ships dropped out of FTL, while the remainder continued to blaze towards the planet. Or, at least, that was the plan. It was the least of his quibbles with the whole operation that Task Force 6.1 would be completely out of touch with the rest of the fleet, leaving them to carry out their orders without knowing what had happened to Captain Stuart. If something went wrong…

"Disengage on the mark," he ordered. "And then prepare to start deploying the mines."

"Aye, Commander," Markham said. The freighter shuddered, violently, as she dropped back into realspace. "FTL disengagement, complete."

Griffin tapped his console, hastily. The remainder of the Task Force had made it out of FTL without incidents...but then, he'd taken care to select the most reliable freighters after the first battle. Markham wasn't the only one who wanted a little revenge. He established the datanet, checked for emergency messages, then smiled coldly to himself.

"Start deploying the minefield," he said. "And once the mines are in place, ready the gravity-wave projector."

And hope to hell the Captain is right, he added, mentally. *Because this could easily go very wrong.*

"Task Force 6.1 separated successfully," Brown reported. "Twenty minutes to designated emergence point."

Hoshiko nodded, allowing herself a moment of relief. Even a tiny misjudgement could have scattered Task Force 6.1 over hundreds of thousands of kilometres, ensuring that setting up the ambush would be worse than useless. No one, not even Mongo Stuart himself, could have retrieved the situation. But Wilde was now in place to kick some enemy ass, once she lured them into position.

"Take us out when we reach the designated emergence point," she ordered. She glanced at the reporter, sitting at the rear of the compartment, and shot him a reassuring smile before turning back to the display. "Give me a countdown when we reach two minutes to emergence."

She studied the display for a long moment, silently calculating possible enemy responses and wishing, again, that someone had invented an FTL sensor. The Druavroks would see them coming, of course, but what would they do? Assemble their fleet to fight off the threat, assume it was too powerful and retreat, or...what? Wait and see what arrived? They'd be fairly sure her fleet was mostly freighters...

Which won't matter, she reminded herself. *They'll have good reason to know there's a fleet attacking them that includes thousands of freighters.*

"Five minutes, Captain," Brown said. "Countdown starting...now."

"Sound Red Alert," Hoshiko ordered. "All hands to Condition One. I say again, all hands to Condition One."

The final seconds counted down and the fleet burst back into realspace. Hoshiko leaned forward as the display began to fill up with icons: red for the Druavroks, yellow for the Dab-Yam…she hoped - prayed - that the Dab-Yam recognised them as friendly. She had no intention of taking her ships anywhere near the planet's defences until they'd opened communications, but the risk of friendly fire was dangerously high.

And they may not be too keen on aliens these days, she thought, as she took in the defences as they appeared on the display. Dab-Yam had nine battlestations and hundreds of automated weapons platforms, although the analysts thought they were slowly being ground down by the Druavroks. *They might just mistake us for a second predatory alien race.*

"Long-range sensors are detecting over fifty battleships and four hundred smaller warships," Brown reported. "They also have mass driver installations on the moons and smaller starships in the asteroid belt."

"Order Task Force 4.1 to cloak, as per Deployment Plan Beta," Hoshiko said, as the Druavroks hastily assembled a formation. They didn't seem to have been moving before her fleet actually arrived, something that puzzled her until she realised they'd probably expected her to drop out of FTL closer to the planet. "The remainder of the fleet is to prepare to engage the enemy."

Let them think we intend to fight a conventional engagement, she reminded herself. She had no idea if the Druavroks had ever heard of Napoleon, but they would certainly have read Tokomak tactical manuals. *They'll be happy to sit back and let us make a mistake.*

"Aye, Captain," Brown said. "They're sweeping us with long-range sensors."

"Spoof their ECM as much as possible," Hoshiko said. She doubted the Druavroks would be intimidated, even if she pretended her entire fleet was composed of battleships, but at least she could keep them guessing. Besides, if they thought they held an unbeatable edge, they'd be less likely to do something unpredictable. "And launch probes towards their formation."

She glanced at the display, then keyed her console. "Have you managed to get through to the planet?"

"Negative, Captain," Yeller said. "The Druavroks aren't using jamming, as far as I can tell, but we're not getting any response, even using the Tokomak protocols. It's possible the command and control network has been altered or disrupted by the fighting."

"Or that they're not interested in talking," Hoshiko said. Everything she'd read about the Dab-Yam race had made it clear that they weren't particularly sociable. *She* certainly hadn't been able to avoid thinking that they looked like giant chickens, complete with feathers and eggs. "Keep trying to get through to them."

"Aye, Captain," Yeller said.

Hoshiko watched grimly as the seconds ticked away. Allowing the Druavroks a chance to mass their forces was a gamble, although she knew she couldn't have destroyed a smaller enemy force before its allies arrived to even the odds. The Druavroks certainly didn't seem inclined to give her an incentive to move faster…she smiled, rather thinly. Napoleon had been quite right, after all. Why interrupt the enemy when he was in the process of making a mistake?

She studied the long-range readings grimly. Dab-Yam itself might be largely intact, but the Druavroks had ravaged the rest of the system badly. There had been colonies on the outer worlds, according to the files, that no longer existed. Her probes revealed craters on the surface where the colonies had been. A number of asteroid settlements were gone - she hoped they hadn't been directed at the planet to force the defenders to waste their firepower - and the cloudscoop the Tokomak had established, centuries ago, was nothing but debris. The Druavroks must have been frustrated, she decided. They certainly hadn't tried to put the cloudscoop to use.

And the planet must be running short of HE3 too, she thought, morbidly. She'd heard stories of energy shortages from her grandfather and the other old sweats, but she'd never really believed them. Energy in the Solar Union was cheap, clean and limitless. And yet, it all depended on a supply of HE3 that could be easily interrupted. Dab-Yam was completely dependent on the cloudscoop, unless the locals could find another source. *They must be refining it from seawater, if they can.*

"The enemy fleet has formed up, Captain," Brown reported. "We will be entering our missile range in seven minutes; enemy missile range in nine minutes."

Hoshiko smiled, coldly. The Druavroks, like everyone else, had copied the Tokomak missiles, but humanity - and now its allies - had improved upon the original designs. She doubted her first barrage would do *that* much damage, not when pitted against a colossal fleet of battleships, yet it would give the enemy a nasty shock.

"Prepare to engage," she ordered.

— —

"THEY'RE CLAIMING TO be part of a…a Grand Alliance," the hatchling said. "They say they're here to fight the Druavroks."

"We shall see," Matriarch Yah-Sin said.

The awe in the hatchling's voice was understandable, but she couldn't allow herself to share in his delight - and hope. The newcomers had an impressive fleet, yet only a tiny percentage of it was composed of actual *warships*. She had a feeling the Druavroks would tear the fleet apart, if it came down to a real fight, and then resume their attack on her homeworld. The only advantage she could glean from the whole affair was a chance to reload some of the automated weapons platforms.

"We could fire missiles into their position," the hatchling suggested eagerly. "Make them deal with two threats at once."

"No," Yah-Sin ordered. She understood the impulse, but she couldn't allow it to rule her thoughts. "We hold our fire."

She ignored his squawk of indignation. She wanted to help, but what could they do? There was no way her forces could make a difference, not when the Druavroks were careful not to come too close to her missile-armed battlestations. It was possible, she supposed, that they would be distracted if she attacked, but she dared not waste the missiles trying to tip the balance. All she could do was watch, wait and take what advantage of the pause she could.

"Scramble the commando teams," she ordered. The Druavroks had been prowling space too closely for her to risk sending commandoes to the lunar bases, but now…now she could take the chance of dispatching them. It would win the planet some more time. "The enemy are distracted and now we hunt."

She clacked her beak, then looked at the display. There was no way to help the newcomers, whatever they claimed to represent. She just hoped - prayed - that they had a few tricks hidden in their feathers…

…Because, as far as she could see, they were dangerously outgunned.

"ENTERING MISSILE RANGE, Captain," Brown reported. His voice was very flat, a sure sign he was trying hard to keep it under control. "Weapons locked on targets; combat datanet up and running."

"Fire," Hoshiko ordered. "I say again, fire at will."

She watched, feeling a cold exultation, as her ships began to fire. It hadn't been hard to mount missile launchers on freighter hulls, even though reloading them during a battle would be next to impossible. The display fuzzed for a long moment as the missiles were launched, so many missiles appearing on the sensors that it looked like she'd hurled an entire *wall* at the Druavroks, then reset itself, silently informing her that over nine *thousand* missiles were roaring towards their targets. There were so many missiles that the command network was having trouble organising them into squadrons and pointing them towards their targets. It was probably a trick of her mind, but she could have sworn she saw the enemy ships *flinch*.

"The enemy are deploying ECM drones," Brown reported. "And they're charging forward."

Hoshiko nodded, irked. The enemy CO was no fool - and clearly not inclined to panic, either. Advancing *towards* her wall of missiles looked stupid, on the face of it, but it was his wisest course of action. It would give him a chance to bring her ships into *his* missile range before he started losing ships to her missiles. She mentally saluted her foe, then looked at Brown.

"We will proceed to Deployment Pattern Beta," she said. "All ships are to reverse course and head out along the pre-planned route; I say again, all ships are to reverse course and head out along the pre-planned route."

"Aye, Captain," Brown said. New icons flared to life on the display. "Enemy ships are firing missiles."

"Clever bastard," Hoshiko muttered. Using antimatter shipkiller missiles - even straight nuclear warheads - would allow them to take out bunches of her missiles. It would be costly, but missiles were cheaper than warships and took much less time to build. "Order the missile command network to compensate."

"Aye, Captain," Brown said. "The network is already altering targeting patterns."

But there are limits to just how much they can alter course, Hoshiko reminded herself. She'd assumed as much, when she'd been drawing up her plans, but it was still galling to watch it happen. *The enemy are going to kill a lot of missiles.*

Brown looked up, alarmed. "Enemy missiles are detonating now."

Hoshiko watched, grimly, as hundreds of missiles died, but there were thousands left to close in on their targets. The Druavroks had clearly been drilling hard - if she'd wanted confirmation they knew what had happened to Malachi, it was right there in front of her - and yet it still wasn't enough. Their ECM was no match for human-grade sensors. They might as well not have bothered launching decoy drones. She sucked in her breath with savage glee as nineteen battleships and over a hundred smaller ships were blown into flaming plasma, dozens of other ships staggering out of formation as they were badly damaged. One ship even exploded, two minutes after the last missile slammed into its hull.

Must have skimped on antimatter safety, Hoshiko thought, vindictively. It was odd - no one would ever accuse the Tokomak of not taking every last precaution they could - but she couldn't think of another explanation. A nuke, detonating inside a battleship hull, wouldn't destroy the ship, merely do a great deal of damage. *Or maybe it was just a lucky shot.*

"The enemy fleet is picking up speed," Brown reported. He sounded torn between relief and fear. "They're launching probes and targeting missile locks on us."

"Let them follow us," Hoshiko ordered. The Druavroks had to be *mad*. She had no idea what their superiors would say to a CO who'd lost a dozen battleships to an inferior fleet, but she doubted it would be pleasant. "And prepare to drop back into FTL."

TWENTY-THREE

A number of senior government officials and their families fled California today, flying directly to Texas. Texan forces sealed off the airport where they landed and took them into custody. Further details have not yet been released by the Texan authorities, but sources in California suggest that the provisional government has collapsed into chaos in the wake of the latest water shortage.

-Solar News Network, Year 54

Warlord Tomas was *furious*.

Being assigned to Dab-Yam should have been the pinnacle of his career. The Dab-Yam were holding the line with grim determination, but - like all prey - they didn't have the killer instincts that would turn them into a real threat. Crushing their defences was only a matter of time, then their world would lie in front of his forces, ready for the taking. It wasn't as if anyone was going to come to their rescue. Prey never saw the value in fighting back before it was too late.

But someone *had* come to the rescue.

Tomas hadn't believed the first reports, when a handful of messages had reached Dab-Yam from Malachi. A fleet largely composed of freighters couldn't hope to crush the planet's defences, he was sure; he'd suspected, when he'd finished reading through them, that the planetary commander was lying to cover up gross incompetence and corruption. *Some* prey could be dangerous, some *could* see the moment to strike...and losing to prey was just embarrassing. The planetary commander would be lucky, assuming he'd survived, if his eggs weren't cracked and his penis burned off as proof that such stupidity wouldn't be allowed to breed. Execution might seem a preferable punishment.

He hissed in anger as he glared at the display, silently assessing the fleet that had dropped out of FTL and confronted him, smashing more of his ships than he cared to admit. It *was* mainly composed of freighters - the reports hadn't lied - and it was armed with missiles that had a longer range than anything at *his* disposal. Perhaps, just perhaps, the defenders of Malachi had been badly outmatched. If the prey could hammer more than a dozen battleships into scrap metal and superhot plasma, they could take out a planet's defences too.

"Continue course," he ordered. "Take us in pursuit."

He kept a wary eye on his crewmembers as the battleship slowly picked up speed. There was no way to disguise the fact that he'd just taken a beating, that his position had been fatally weakened. The Great Lords would probably congratulate anyone who managed to assassinate him, particularly if the new commander went on to exterminate the attacking fleet. He could only rebuild his position by taking out the enemy fleet completely and branding it a victory, even though most of his targets were civilian freighters rather than warships. And he would have bet his scales that the freighters had fired off *all* their missiles in a single overwhelming salvo.

The enemy ships were reversing course, moving with an ungainly precision that mocked him, even though the calculating part of his mind suggested the enemy were simply having problems coordinating so many ships. It was impossible to be *certain*, naturally, but he suspected that the enemy forces included ships from several different species of prey, each one probably looking to its own advantage rather than uniting against the common foe. There was nothing to be gained by making promises - promises to prey had no validity - but the prospect of splitting their alliance rose up in front of his eyes. Maybe, just maybe, if he was careful which ships he destroyed, the prey would suspect he'd made a deal with one of their members and turn on one another.

"Target the warships," he ordered, as the fleet started to close on its enemies. "Prepare to fire on my command."

He bared his teeth and snarled at the display. The enemy warships were nimble, certainly capable of outracing his battleships, but their freighters were lumbering monstrosities. They had neither the speed to outrun him nor the defences to beat off his attacks. And, as long as the enemy were willing to keep their warships within weapons range, he could put the freighters to one side and deal with them later. The chance to take out a number of warships could not be denied.

"Weapons locked," the tactical officer said.

"Fire," Warlord Tomas ordered.

— —

The plan, Hoshiko thought ruefully as the enemy ships belched missiles, *may not have been quite as brilliant as it sounded.*

It had been simple enough. Sting the enemy, make them mad, make them give chase when she swung her fleet away from the planet. But her ships hadn't quite managed to build up the speed they needed, leaving them exposed as the enemy opened fire. And she needed to buy time before the fleet dropped into FTL.

"Deploy decoy drones, then fire a second salvo of missiles," she ordered, coolly. "And start the FTL clock ticking down."

"Aye, Captain," Brown said.

Hoshiko nodded, then watched as the enemy missiles closed in on her formation. There were only four thousand, compared to the *nine* thousand she'd hurled into the teeth of their defences, but there were quite enough of them to do some real damage. Thankfully, the Druavroks didn't seem to have improved their firing patterns, let alone modify their seeker heads. A number of missiles would be drawn off and tricked into wasting themselves harmlessly against her decoys.

"The majority of the missiles appear to be targeted on the warships, Captain," Brown noted, grimly. "Almost none of them are aimed at the freighters."

Someone over there has a working brain, Hoshiko thought. From a tactical, if cold-blooded, point of view, allowing the enemy to expend their missiles on the freighters made a great deal of sense. But the Druavroks hadn't made *that* particular mistake. *They've fired too many missiles for us to stop them all.*

"Inform the fleet," she ordered. "We are to jump to FTL along the pre-planned course as soon as the drives are ready."

"Aye, Captain," Brown said.

WARLORD TOMAS WATCHED, his long tongue licking his teeth, as the missiles plunged right into the teeth of the enemy point defence. The newcomers, like all prey, had plunged resources into self-preservation, cramming their ships with point defence weapons, but they hadn't anything like enough firepower to stop *all* his missiles. He had to admit the skill they'd used to craft their network - hundreds of missiles were picked off as they crossed the threshold and closed in on their targets, even though it wasn't something he could ever say out loud. The concept of *defending* a starship was alien to his people.

The prey starships fought desperately, but it wasn't enough. Four warships vanished in quick succession as his missiles struck home, two more fell out of formation as their drives were battered into uselessness. Their crews had no time to make repairs before a hail of missiles from his ships wiped them out of existence. But hundreds of other missiles were lured away by the decoys, expended uselessly against cheap drones. He kept his frustration to himself, even though he was starting to wonder if the prey might have a point. Their cowardly tactics had preserved the vast majority of their fleet.

"Continue firing," he ordered. The prey were belching out missiles themselves, but their rate of fire was much reduced. He'd been right. Their missile-armed freighters were one-shot weapons, only good for a single barrage. "Do not give them a moment to recover."

He leaned forward, flexing his claws. The prey would be battered into helplessness and any prisoners they took would be eaten. Or maybe not, maybe they'd be given the honour of being killed out of hand. They might have been prey - he was *sure* they were prey - but they were unusually dangerous prey. The challenge of facing them almost made up for the losses he'd taken in the opening round.

It won't be long now, he told himself firmly. *And then we can go back to Dab-Yam.*

— —

"Task Force 2.1 has lost two ships," Brown reported. "Task Force 2.3 has lost one ship, but two more are badly damaged."

Hoshiko nodded. "Time to FTL?"

"Two minutes," Brown said.

"Take us into FTL the moment the drives are ready," Hoshiko ordered.

She leaned back in her command chair, forcing herself to relax. The enemy was belching wave after wave of missiles, steadily wearing down her point defence. Their own point defence was pathetic, compared to hers, and their datanet had been knocked down almost at once, but each of their ships had enough firepower to almost make up for the loss of coordination. A straight fight would be disastrous, if they had to fight one. If the enemy didn't take her bait, she would have to abandon Dab-Yam until she built up a far more powerful fighting force.

"Captain," Brown said. "FTL in ten seconds."

And hope to hell this works, Hoshiko thought. *Let them take the bait.*

She watched, grimly, as the seconds ticked down to zero. *Jackie Fisher* shuddered violently as she dropped into FTL, gravity waves striking her hull as the remainder of the fleet followed her. Normally, a fleet flying in formation could compensate, but her formation was terrifyingly ragged. It didn't matter, she knew, as long as they reached their destination, yet it was quite possible that one or more of her ships would be accidentally knocked back *out* of FTL. The irony would be chilling…

"FTL engaged, Captain," Brown said. "We're *en route* to the rendezvous point."

— —

"THE ENEMY HAS jumped into FTL," the sensor officer reported. His tail dropped, as if he expected to be ripped apart merely for giving the report. "They're gone, Warlord."

And they will come back to harass us, Warlord Tomas thought. *Except… they jumped out far too close to our position…*

"Take us in pursuit," he ordered. "FTL…*now*!"

He allowed his mouth to drop open in amusement as the fleet dropped into FTL. It was never *easy* to chase ships though FTL, but they were close enough to the prey to shadow them…assuming, of course, the enemy fleet didn't try to scatter. Once the prey dropped out of FTL, his ships would follow and smash them before they could rebuild their formation. He would hit them so hard the Great Lords would never question his success, or punish him for losing so many warships to their first attack.

"We are in pursuit," the helmsman reported.

"It's not easy to track them," the sensor officer cringed. "They're flying in such close formation that it's hard to locate individual ships."

"Just keep us following the mass," Tomas ordered, irked. Maybe he *would* kill the sensor officer after all. Bringing bad news wasn't a crime, at least not in his book, but failing to do the obvious definitely was. "And take us out of FTL as soon as they drop out themselves."

— —

"SENSORS CONFIRM, CAPTAIN," Brown reported. "They're in pursuit."

Because we made them mad, Hoshiko thought. *And because they think they won't have a better chance to hit us right where it hurts.*

"Continue along the planned course," she ordered. The timing was everything, of course; a second or two might make the difference between success or failure. And if the plan failed, the fleet would have to scatter and hope for the best. "How long until we cross the line?"

"Seven minutes," Captain," Brown said. "It's going to be close."

"I know," Hoshiko said. Sweat trickled down her back as she leaned forward. "Hold us steady."

— —

"THEY'RE COMING AT us like…some very angry things," Markham said.

Griffin smiled, never taking his eyes off the display. "A swarm of hornets, mad at you because you were throwing rocks at their nest?"

"Or a swarm of Needle Bugs," Markham commented. "You wouldn't want to be *caught* by a swarm of flying monsters that could strip the skin off your bones."

"I've had exes like that," Griffin said. "And the Druavroks are likely to be madder than an ex-wife who thinks she has a right to half your salary."

He smiled again, then checked the timer. It was easy enough to separate the two swarms of starships, but there was so much gravimetric interference that it was difficult to get the timing absolutely perfect. Starting the gravity-wave generator too late would be a dangerous move, yet starting it too early would be absolutely disastrous.

"It was much simpler," he muttered, "when we did the same thing at the Battle of Earth. And we brought more firepower to the party too."

So did they, he reminded himself, as the seconds ticked down to zero. He would have sold his soul for a third of the Solar Navy, enough firepower to kick the Druavroks out of the sector without having to rely on alien allies. *The Tokomak brought thousands of ships to the party.*

The final seconds ticked away as the Grand Alliance ships rocketed past his position. Griffin watched, bracing himself, as the gravity wave generator went to work, broadcasting a stream of artificial gravity into space. If everything worked as planned...

He sighed in relief as the display lit up with red lights. It had worked.

THERE WAS NO warning at all before the deck heaved as the battleship crashed back into normal space. Warlord Tomas found himself hurled across the bridge as the artificial gravity fluctuated wildly, slamming into the far bulkhead so hard he broke one of his legs before he fell to the deck. The helmsman had been thrown into the ceiling, banging his head so hard he was either stunned or dead; the other officers looked to be injured or stunned. Tomas pulled himself upright, despite the growing pain, and stared at the display. It showed realspace.

He gathered himself, somehow. "What happened?"

"The drive must have failed," the sensor officer stammered. He sounded shocked, but alive and breathing. "I..."

He hesitated as new icons appeared on the display. "The entire *fleet* suffered a drive failure at the same moment?"

Tomas crawled towards the console, cursing savagely. The entire fleet suffering the *same* failure at the *same* time? It was unthinkable. His engineers might not be as capable as those of the Tokomak, but they weren't *incompetent*! He pulled himself up onto his knees and reset the console. The command network was filling with cries of alarm and demands for answers, answers he couldn't give them...

"Warlord," the sensor officer said. "There's a number of...*objects* nearby."

"Show me," Tomas ordered.

The display flickered and changed. Now, the fleet was surrounded - no, infiltrated - by hundreds of tiny objects, each one no larger than a shuttle. They were clearly designed to be stealthy, as the sensors were having problems tracking them. And they looked oddly familiar…

His scales shivered with sudden horror. He *knew* what they were.

But it was already far too late.

— —

"Blow the mines," Griffin ordered.

The display went white as the antimatter containment chambers switched themselves off, allowing the antimatter to meet matter for the first time since it had been produced. He mentally saluted the Captain for putting the enemy components to good use, even though he'd thought the plan was unlikely to work. Mining interstellar space was normally a waste of time, but the Captain had lured the enemy right into the minefield she'd created, knowing the enemy wouldn't expect to be yanked out of FTL. And the plan had worked perfectly.

And we used a lot of antimatter, he thought, as the display began to clear. The Druavroks wouldn't appreciate the irony - they'd used civilian fabbers to construct both production plants *and* containment chambers - but even battleships couldn't hope to survive the furies he'd unleashed. *Even if some of them survive, their self-confidence won't.*

"Most of the enemy fleet is gone," Markham said. "There's only a handful of survivors and they're badly damaged."

"Looks that way," Griffin ordered. Half of the surviving ships were streaming oxygen, which didn't bode well for the crews if they failed to seal the hatches. "Do any of them look to have working FTL drives?"

"Unknown," Markham said. "The shock of being yanked out of FTL might have disabled them."

Griffin nodded in agreement. The Galactics - until recently - had assumed that starships in FTL were invulnerable, at least until humanity had taught them differently. They certainly hadn't bothered to take precautions against the drive blowing, when the ship ran into an unexpected gravity field. Chances were the remaining ships didn't have a hope in hell of jumping into FTL. It was, he supposed, vaguely possible that the Druavroks would manage to limp back to Dab-Yam. The Galactics had plenty of legends about starships that had lost FTL drives, but somehow managed to survive the long journey to safety.

And yet, if they do, it will still take them months at best, he thought. *Years, if they want to go somewhere - anywhere - other than Dab-Yam.*

He looked at Markham. "Are you avenged?"

"Hell, no," Markham said. He skinned back his teeth in a savage snarl. "But at least I've made the bastards pay."

Griffin nodded in agreement. By any standards, they'd just won a battle they should have lost - and lost badly. They'd been so badly outgunned that it wasn't remotely funny - and yet they'd prevailed. The Captain and the Grand Alliance would have good reason to be pleased, while the Druavroks...if they ever worked out what had happened to their fleet...would be furious. It was, he knew, a good sign, a sign the Druavroks could be beaten, a sign they could use to line up more alien allies...

...And yet, he couldn't help feeling nervous. Who knew *what* the Druavroks would do in response?

TWENTY-FOUR

New Mexico and Arizona became the second and third states to sign up to the Texas-led Alliance for the Preservation of the United States, following a tidal wave of refugees from California into Arizona. Both states have instituted draconian measures against illegal immigrants, terrorists and federal agents, arresting and expelling as many of the first two as they can catch. (Federal agents are rarely taken alive.) Washington has so far said nothing, but sources close to the President suggest that the government is currently looking at its options.

-Solar News Network, Year 54

They do look like oversized chickens, Hoshiko thought, as she bowed politely to Matriarch Yah-Sin. The Dab-Yam looked *very* much like a chicken, complete with feathers and beady eyes, although she had hands that, judging by the shape, might well have been wings, on her distant ancestors. *But they did a very good job of defending themselves.*

She studied the Matriarch with interest. The Dab-Yam, according to the files, were a female-dominated race, the males generally being smaller and weaker than the females. Who knew what they'd make of nanotechnology that could change a person's gender overnight, if they wanted, or give one person equal strength to another? She pushed the thought aside - the Dab-Yam could make use of such technology or not, as they pleased - and bowed for the second time, as the protocol files insisted. The Dab-Yam did not shake hands with anyone.

And their station is very hot, she thought, feeling sweat prickling down her back. The air was hot and smelled, faintly, of something unpleasant. *Their world must be an uncomfortable place for humans.*

"We greet you to our world," the Matriarch said, through a translator voder. Her beak couldn't pronounce human words. "But we ask you to speak bluntly."

"I shall," Hoshiko said. "You may speak your mind."

She would have preferred to send Captain Ryman, but who knew how the Dab-Yam would react to a *male* ambassador? They might not be able to tell the difference between human males and females - human gender dimorphism was nowhere near as obvious as theirs - yet there was no point in taking chances. Besides, he was fourteen days away by courier boat *and* very tied up in turning the Grand Alliance into a functional unit.

"We have little interest in the outside universe," Matriarch Yah-Sin said. Her voice was flat, the voder being unable to convoy emotion. Hoshiko's implants told her that the Dab-Yam had almost no expressions; the only way to read them was to listen to their voices, which were so high-pitched that they were hard for humans to hear. "We do not understand why you wish us to join your Grand Alliance."

Because I sacrificed over a thousand crewmen for your world, Hoshiko thought, although she kept it to herself. The Dab-Yam hadn't *asked* her to come to their rescue. Their world had just been the closest target to Malachi. *And because we need you.*

"The Druavroks are unlikely to leave you alone, Your Ladyship," she said. Her implants insisted that was the correct title for a Matriarch. "They may have been knocked back, their fleet crushed, but they have many more fleets. You joining us will make us stronger and more able to take the fight to them."

"We have few warships, Lady Captain," Matriarch Yah-Sin said. "Those we did have are badly damaged."

"Then allow us to use your world as a base and supply us with weapons," Hoshiko said, seriously. "Your world is closer to the enemy homeworlds than Amstar."

"Our warriors will not fight outside our system," Matriarch Yah-Sin insisted. "You would have to do the fighting yourself."

That, Hoshiko had to admit, was a puzzling attitude. Almost every other race known to exist had liked the idea of settling up colonies and enclaves, if only to make sure that all of their eggs were not kept in one basket. The Dab-Yam didn't seem aware of the dangers their race faced, even without the Druavroks threatening their homeworld. A supernova or asteroid strike could exterminate almost all of their race. But they didn't seem inclined to set up colonies away from their homeworld.

"We have enough warriors," she said, curtly. "But we do need basing rights, weapons and supplies."

There was a long pause. Hoshiko waited, suspecting that Matriarch Yah-Sin was communing with her fellow nest-mothers. The Dab-Yam would not be remotely pleased with the request for basing rights, but they had to admit they *needed* a powerful fleet presence based within their system, unless they *wanted* the Druavroks to return and resume grinding their defences to powder. Assuming they had a month or two of grace, they could rebuild some of the fortifications orbiting their planet, but it wouldn't alter the final outcome. Dab-Yam was doomed unless she joined the Grand Alliance and went on the offensive.

"We can supply you with weapons and other supplies, once we tend to our own defences," Matriarch Yah-Sin said, finally. "And while we *can* grant you basing rights, we must insist that your warriors do not set foot on our planet. They will frighten the men."

Or give them ideas? Hoshiko thought, cynically. *Are you scared of us convincing them they can do more than stay home and look after the kids?*

She pushed the thought aside. The Solar Union had been founded by a man who was a strong believer in voting with one's feet. If the residents of a canton found it unbearable, they had the right to move away…and if they chose not to make use of it, it was their own stupid fault. Given time, the spread of technology - unlocked fabbers, unlocked medical nanites - would bring change to Dab-Yam too. Who knew where *that* would lead?

"That is acceptable," she said. "We would be willing to base the fleet on one of your moons, once we established a naval base."

"We would prefer you to place the base in orbit around the gas giant so you could protect the new cloudscoop," Matriarch Yah-Sin said. "Our world is running short of fuel."

"We are willing to offer improved fusion reactors as part of the deal," Hoshiko offered, seriously. "They're considerably more efficient than the Tokomak designs."

"We would accept those gratefully," Matriarch Yah-Sin said. "We would also accept assistance in securing raw materials for the fabbers."

"We would be happy to provide it, as long as the fleet remains here," Hoshiko said. It wouldn't be *hard* to steer a couple of asteroids towards the planet, provided no one was shooting at them. "However, the vast majority of our ships need to be rearmed."

"That is understandable," Matriarch Yah-Sin said. She stood a little stiffer. "And we thank you for your assistance."

Hoshiko suspected she understood. The Dab-Yam had never been a very sociable race, not even once they'd discovered the vast universe just beyond their atmosphere. Matriarch Yah-Sin didn't seem to be uneasy, in her presence, but even *she* had to find contact with aliens difficult. Humans had had similar problems, just after Contact…and *humans* were more sociable than the Dab-Yam. There would be time to break down the barriers later.

"I thank you too," she said. "With your permission, I will return to my ship."

Matriarch Yah-Sin bowed. Hoshiko bowed back, then keyed her wristcom and called for teleport. The teleport field enveloped her a moment later and then faded away, revealing the teleport chamber. Commander Wilde was standing there, waiting for her. He looked tired, but pleased with himself. And, as he'd destroyed a considerable amount of tonnage in a single ambush, he had good reason to be.

"Captain," he said. "Welcome back."

"It was an interesting meeting," Hoshiko said. She returned the teleport officer's salute, then allowed Wilde to lead her back towards her cabin. "They're grateful, but also concerned about the future."

"They're a profoundly conservative race, according to the files," Wilde commented. "I honestly wonder how they managed to invent the wheel."

Hoshiko shrugged. The Dab-Yam had a history that stretched back over millions of years, almost all of it profoundly boring. Unlike humans, they didn't seem to pick many fights with their own kind; the only real wars they'd had in their history had been small skirmishes over resources and occasional mating rights. It was almost as if they didn't have much of an aggressive instinct at all, unlike humanity - or the Druavroks. They'd been lucky they'd managed to get into space when the Tokomak arrived. That, at least, had won them some respect.

"I think our history was driven by war," she said, although she wasn't entirely sure if that were true. "Once we developed the concept of steadily improving our technology, we just kept trying to find new ways to do things."

"When we didn't stagnate," Wilde pointed out. "How many of our cultures simply stopped innovating because they were satisfied, technologically speaking?"

Hoshiko shrugged. "Neither Imperial China nor Imperial Rome had access to the kind of communications systems we enjoy," she said, tartly. "And neither of them dominated the world."

"They were destroyed by outside forces," Wilde said. "The Dab-Yam could easily have gone the same way - still could, if they don't build a more effective defence."

"True," Hoshiko agreed. "And we will be helping them with that, as we prepare to take the war into their territory."

"If they accept our help," Wilde said, pessimistically. "They're not too keen on having us here."

Hoshiko shrugged. She'd requested copies of Matriarch Yah-Sin's records when she'd returned to the system and, somewhat reluctantly, the Dab-Yam had provided. Their defences had been formidable, *and* they'd stopped the first enemy attack so decisively that the Druavroks had chosen to wear down the defences rather than risk another major attack, but choosing to go permanently on the defensive had doomed them to defeat before her fleet had arrived. The Dab-Yam *needed* her help if they wanted to survive the next few years.

She opened the hatch to her cabin and stepped inside, using her implants to send a request for coffee to her steward. Her clothes felt sweaty, despite the cool air; she wondered, suddenly, just what else lurked in the planet's atmosphere. Nothing dangerous, she was sure - her implants would have taken care of it - but she couldn't help feeling uncomfortable. She made a mental note to shower once the meeting was finished, then catch up on her sleep as soon as they returned to FTL.

"On other news, we shot all of the freighters dry," Wilde added, as the steward appeared with a tray of coffee and biscuits. Hoshiko took her mug and a chocolate chip cookie, then sat down on her sofa. "We expended much of our stockpile of missiles in a single barrage."

"At least it took out a number of their ships," Hoshiko said. "We'd have killed more if we'd taken down their datanet quicker."

"Perhaps," Wilde said. "But we're going to have to replenish our supplies before we can take the offensive once again."

He paused. "And there's another problem."

Hoshiko took a sip of her coffee, then lifted her eyebrows. "There is?"

"Yes, Captain," Wilde said. "We cheated. We lured the enemy into a trap, one set using a device they had no reason to anticipate."

"They should have been paying more attention to the reports from Earth," Hoshiko said, dipping her cookie in the coffee. "It isn't as if we stopped a handful of Horde starships, is it?"

"They probably didn't know the details," Wilde said. "We didn't share much and I doubt the Tokomak wanted to talk about their defeat. Still...

"Captain, we hit them with an outside context problem," he said. "But as far as much of the Grand Alliance is concerned, we kicked their ass with a handful of warships and a few dozen freighters. They might start thinking the bastards are really nothing more than paper tigers."

"We lost seven ships in the engagement," Hoshiko said. "And it would have been a great deal more if they'd targeted the freighters instead."

"And if they'd managed to take down our datanet," Wilde agreed.

Hoshiko rather doubted they *could*. The Tokomak might insist on having a single command ship, ensuring a great deal of confusion when - if - the flagship was blown into atoms, but human datanets were decentralised. If *Jackie Fisher* was destroyed, one of the other warships would pick up the slack instantly. It would be a little harder if one of the alien ships were to be taken out, as they used the Tokomak-designed system, yet they'd practiced rebooting the datanet with a new command ship during their first exercises.

Better to hope for the best and prepare for the worst, she reminded herself. *They might get lucky or come up with an ingenious way of disabling our command net...or simply throw enough missiles at us that even we can't stop more than a small fraction of them.*

"The point is," Wilde said, "that the Grand Alliance might start fragmenting if they think beating the Druavroks will be easy, instead of a long hard slog."

"That's something we will have to watch," Hoshiko said, after a moment. She didn't think it was particularly likely, not after the Druavroks had ransacked Amstar and a dozen other worlds, but the prospect had to be borne in mind. "We did lose a number of freighters in the attack on Malachi."

"By any reasonable standard, Captain, that victory was bought cheaply," Wilde reminded her, calmly. "But we won against an enemy who was unprepared for us. Word is spreading. The *next* enemy force we face will be tougher."

Hoshiko nodded. There was no way to be *sure*, but the Druavroks she'd faced at Dab-Yam had definitely been more competent than the defenders of Malachi. They'd done all the right things and only lost because they'd run into an outside context trap. What would they do, if they realised the truth? In their place, she would have mounted another attack on Amstar - or Martina. Occupying Martina would give them both the gravity points *and* cut Hoshiko off from her superiors...

Not that that's a bad thing, part of her mind noted. *If Uncle Mongo wants to relieve me of command, sending the orders will take years without the gravity points*.

She pushed the thought aside. "We'll also be getting tougher," she said. Dab-Yam might or might not provide enough supplies to make saving the planet worthwhile, from a long-term point of view, but giving the enemy a bloody nose would help recruit more allies. "And the more allies we make, the more ships we will have at our disposal."

"We really ought to be considering deep-strike missions," Griffin pointed out. "But that would run the risk of leaving Amstar and the other threatened worlds uncovered."

Hoshiko nodded. Leaving the naval base at Martina uncovered was a risk, but the Grand Alliance could produce everything she needed if something happened to the multiracial world. She could trade space for time if necessary, yet her allies couldn't make the same calculation. Their homeworlds were under threat. Indeed, the Druavroks might manage to split the alliance if they grabbed everything within reach and launched an all-out attack on a major homeworld.

But there are powerful defences there already, she thought. *And they will get stronger as human technology and unlocked fabbers spread through the sector.*

"We can send a handful of smaller ships deeper into enemy territory," she said, after a moment. The Grand Alliance couldn't operate as a single fleet indefinitely. "We can spare the crews to handle them."

"Maybe," Wilde said. "We are cutting our margins of safety alarmingly thin."

"I know," Hoshiko said. *Jackie Fisher* now had a permanent crew of fifty, the remaining crewmembers spread over a hundred alien warships. The other cruisers in her squadron had the same problem. She simply didn't have the manpower to ensure everyone spoke the same language, let alone operated as a team. "We're going to be putting junior officers in command of raiding parties."

"Well, Ensign Howard *did* manage to command the courier boat," Wilde said, with a flicker of amusement. "He might *just* be qualified for something larger."

"With *one* crewman under his command," Hoshiko said. The idea of a courier boat having a standard chain of command was ridiculous. Barriers that were easy to maintain on warships wouldn't last a day on a courier boat. "But you're right - he might have to take command of a refurbished warship, if we can't find the officers and crew elsewhere."

She shook her head. "We'll leave a squadron of warships and a pair of officers here," she said, as she rose. "The remainder of the fleet will head back to Amstar tonight. We'll use the journey to plot out our next move."

"And hope the enemy doesn't come up with a plan of his own," Wilde said, warningly. He rose too. "They're bound to be fuming with rage."

"I'm not worried about them fuming with rage," Hoshiko said. She'd provoked the Druavroks deliberately to lure them into a trap. "Massive wave attacks are alarming, but easy to handle. I'm worried about them thinking their next step through carefully before launching their attack."

She watched him go, then walked into the washroom and undressed before peering into the mirror. Her body looked as healthy as always, but her eyes were tired. She hadn't slept well since the battle, despite her implants. There had just been too much else to do. She turned on the water, stepped into the shower and sighed in relief as the warm water washed her clean.

Have a nap afterwards, then take the fleet back to Amstar, she thought, as she scrubbed herself clean, then used a force field to dry herself. Her body tingled under its touch. *And pray that the enemy doesn't come up with something clever.*

TWENTY-FIVE

Water riots have torn the richer parts of California apart, following the collapse of the provisional government and media stories about the rich using water to wash their dogs while the poor are on strict rationing. The news has helped encourage thousands more to flee into the countryside or cross the border into Arizona, which has proven safer. A number of militia groups have actually been firing on civilians entering their territory.
-Solar News Network, Year 54

"There are thousands of humans who wish to sign up with us," Captain Ryman said, as he sat down in Hoshiko's office. "But they want something in exchange."

Hoshiko leaned forward. "What?"

"Either a largely-human colony within the sector or permission to immigrate into the Solar Union," Captain Ryman said. "The Druavroks haven't done much for diversity in the sector."

"I imagine the Tokomak didn't do much either," Hoshiko said. Humans - the descendents of humans who had been taken from Earth centuries before Contact - were regarded as second-class citizens, like many other races that hadn't developed space travel before the Tokomak arrived. "They can certainly have permission to immigrate to the Solar Union. It isn't as if we could stop them, as long as they obey the rules."

Captain Ryman nodded. "But some of them also want a human colony within the sector," he said. "Finding a suitable world isn't going to be easy."

"Impossible, I would have said," Hoshiko said. *She* would have preferred an asteroid colony, maybe a large cluster of asteroids that could be reshaped at will. "Much of the good real estate within this sector has already been taken."

"That's the problem," Captain Ryman agreed. "They're actually talking about exterminating the Druavroks on Malachi and claiming the planet for humanity."

"I won't commit genocide," Hoshiko said, flatly. "There's nothing stopping us from establishing an asteroid settlement, something that can grow into a canton, but we're not going to wipe a world clean just so humans can settle on it. That would make us no better than the Druavroks."

"Proving the Druavroks can be beaten, which you have done, has only fuelled demands for indiscriminate revenge," Captain Ryman said. "The Grand Alliance is already wondering about putting out peace feelers to the Druavroks."

"If I thought they'd honour them, I'd support making the attempt," Hoshiko said. "But if they even agree to talk to us, Captain, they'll break the agreement as soon as they think they can get away with it."

"I don't disagree with you," Captain Ryman said. "The problem is that not everyone thinks along the same lines. It isn't a problem, at the moment, but it could easily become worse."

"I'm planning to start dispatching smaller raiding missions into enemy territory, now we have more warships at our disposal," Hoshiko said. "How are we doing for weapons production?"

"Still crawling upwards," Captain Ryman said. "You expended a great many missiles at Dab-Yam."

"And we killed a great many enemy ships," Hoshiko countered. "They won't be able to replace those losses in a hurry."

"But they will, given time," Captain Ryman said. "Do you intend to hit their shipyards?"

"Eventually," Hoshiko said. "We also need to target their fabbers."

She ignored his frown. Targeting fabbers, even enemy fabbers, would incur the disapproval of the entire sector, but stripping the enemy of their capability to produce war material was a great deal more important. If the Druavroks truly preferred to concentrate on the offensive, rather than the defensive, targeting their homeworlds might be more effective than anyone had a right to expect. And if they lost the ability to produce missiles, they'd lose the war itself soon afterwards.

"The Grand Alliance will not approve," Captain Ryman said.

"I wasn't planning to tell them," Hoshiko said. It was odd to realise that her allies had limits, when she knew that war was always total. "But those fabbers are the lifeblood of their war machine."

"I won't tell them either," Captain Ryman said. "But be careful, please."

"I will," Hoshiko said. "Has there been any more actionable intelligence?"

"I've already forwarded everything my people collected to your staff," Captain Ryman said, leaning forward. "The only interesting piece of data was that the Druavroks abandoned the siege of Treehouse."

Hoshiko blinked. "Treehouse?"

"It's a rough translation of the world's name, rotated through two separate Gal-Standards," Captain Ryman said. "The inhabitants look like giant trees; they have, I believe, an empathic link to their world. There have been rumours that they have a long-range telepathic capability ever since they entered the Galactic mainstream, but nothing was ever proven. The Tokomak wouldn't have hesitated to exploit them if they actually *could* beam messages over light years."

"I imagine so," Hoshiko agreed. The concept of telepaths gave her the chills. "Is their world important?"

"They had a formidable network of defences," Captain Ryman said. "They're quite an industrious race, Captain. Treehouse isn't the production capital of the sector, but it's definitely in the top five or six. I doubt they will hesitate to join the Grand Alliance and add their productive capabilities to ours."

"You already have ambassadors on the way," Hoshiko guessed.

"I do," Captain Ryman confirmed. "But I have no explanation for why the Druavroks abandoned the siege."

Hoshiko nodded, slowly. The Druavroks had been convinced not to charge into the defences of Dab-Yam - at least, not *twice* - but they hadn't simply given up. She'd had to lure them into a trap to end the threat they presented to the alien world. There was no reason for them to abandon another siege, particularly if they knew Treehouse would join their enemies as soon as it could.

"They have a use for the ships elsewhere," she said, finally. "Here, perhaps?"

"It's a possibility," Captain Ryman said. "If, of course, they take the Grand Alliance seriously."

"We smashed one of their fleets and crushed the defences of one of their worlds," Hoshiko said. "They really *should* take us seriously."

She sighed, inwardly. The Tokomak hadn't *just* been overwhelmingly superior, when they'd met the Druavroks; they'd beaten the living daylights out of them. Hoshiko knew *she'd* hurt the Druavroks, but it wasn't anything like on the same scale. And, for maximum effect, she had to hurt them badly in a single battle.

"We'll mind our defences here, but concentrate on reloading the fleet," she said. "Do we have additional warships?"

"Several," Captain Ryman confirmed. "Along with a number of ancient starships we're refurbishing and a Tokomak battlecruiser."

Hoshiko frowned. "A *Tokomak* battlecruiser?"

"It was apparently in storage near Glenda," Captain Ryman said, "along with a number of other outdated ships. Why, I don't know. They sent them along in the hopes we could put them to use."

"Interesting," Hoshiko said. "Is she flyable?"

"With a little effort," Captain Ryman said. "Half of her weapons and defences were stripped out at some point, and her computer cores were removed, but we can replace them."

"Then I may have a use for her," Hoshiko said. The Druavroks revered the Tokomak. That had to be good for something, if she could find a way to exploit it. "Have her brought back into fighting trim, as best as we can."

"The problem is rigging up a control system," Captain Ryman said. "She doesn't have anything like the automaton of other, more modern ships. I think she actually predates the Tokomak expansion into the Sol Sector. Controlling her in a battle would be tricky without a very large crew."

"See what you can do," Hoshiko ordered. The idea wasn't gelled yet, but it would come in time. "And let me know if there's anything I can do on the diplomatic front."

"Just keep winning battles," Captain Ryman said. "As long as it looks like we can turn the tide, the Grand Alliance will stay together."

Hoshiko smiled. "We'll do our best."

THOMAS PAUSED OUTSIDE the XO's office, feeling a worried sensation growing in his gut even though - this time - he wasn't remotely late. Indeed, the XO had given him a time instead of merely ordering him to report immediately, which suggested he wasn't in trouble. And yet...he reminded himself, impatiently, that spacers were brave and tapped the buzzer. The hatch hissed open a moment later, allowing him to step inside.

"Ensign Howard," the XO said. He didn't sound pleased, although Thomas was sure it wasn't directed at him. "Did you enjoy your courier service?"

Thomas tried, for a moment, to think of the correct answer. The truth was he hadn't enjoyed it, although it *had* given him a chance to catch up on his reading. But was that the answer the XO wanted? His tutors at the Academy had been fond of sneaky questions that doubled as secret tests of character, when he'd never been entirely certain what was being tested, let alone the purpose of the tests. Speaking honestly might get him in trouble.

"It had its moments, sir," he said, finally. The chance to take a break on Amstar would have meant more to him if he'd had a chance to explore the city. "Do you want me to take another set of messages?"

"Not this time," the XO said. He studied Thomas for a long time, leaving him feeling worried and antsy. This was going to be bad. "I understand that you applied for command track?"

"Yes, sir," Thomas said. *Everyone* wanted command - and, with the fleet constantly expanding, there was a good chance of winning a command within ten years. The Captain was in her thirties, according to her file, and she had command of a whole squadron. "I applied for command track after my first year at the Academy."

"You're also a commissioned officer," the XO said. "There's a...task that needs doing, one that needs a commissioned officer. I should tell you, before I go any further, that the task is volunteers only. If you turn it down, Ensign, it will not be noted in your file."

And that might not be actually true, Thomas thought. The old sweats had warned him that refusing a mission would be held against him, even if nothing was *officially* written down. It would certainly suggest he didn't have the nerve to be a starship officer, let alone hold independent command. *What does he want?*

"There are a number of small warships - patrol boats and frigates, mainly - that we're currently outfitting for deployment as raiders," the XO informed him. "The crews will largely consist of humans recruited from the sector's population as auxiliaries, but we're short of local officers to command them. Your role, if you choose to accept it, will be to command one of those ships."

Thomas felt his mouth fall open. Technically, he *could* wind up in command of *Jackie Fisher*, but any accident that wiped out every higher-ranking officer would almost certainly destroy the entire ship. He hadn't expected to stand watch outside FTL, let alone take command of the ship in a potential combat zone. There were just too many officers ranked above him.

"Sir?"

The XO smiled, although there was a hint of rueful annoyance in the expression. "You will have command of a small vessel, with orders to raid enemy shipping," he said, bluntly. "If you don't feel you're up to the task, say so now and nothing more will be said about it."

Thomas swallowed, caught between a desire to grab the opportunity with both hands and a sudden urge to flee. He had no illusions about his ability to command men, not when he had only four months in active service. His tutors had talked about positional authority and personal authority and he had very little of the former, let alone the latter. The thought of being in a courier boat was bad enough, when he was alone or only with a couple of others; being commander of a ship, at the age of nineteen, was worse.

And yet, he thought, *it would look very good on my record.*

His mouth was suddenly very dry. "I would be honoured," he stammered. He had the feeling he wouldn't see promotion again, if he showed a lack of self-confidence. The old sweats had warned him that Fleet Command would enthusiastically agree with any officer who declared himself unready for command. "If…if you feel I can be of service."

"You have the training," the XO said. His voice hardened. "What you lack is the experience, but we're short of officers and men right now. You won't have anyone from the ship backing you up - I'd hoped to give you a handful of marines, but they can't be spared."

Thomas nodded, almost gratefully. The marines had always scared him, just a little. He'd had the standard unarmed combat course at the Academy, and he had combat programs loaded into his implants, but he was no match for any of the groundpounders. They did things he couldn't imagine doing himself. And yet, he knew he should have prayed for a handful of marines to escort him. He might need their help.

"The ship should be ready for crewing tomorrow, if the latest update is to be believed," the XO said. "I have never assigned an officer as junior as you to a role like this, Ensign, nor have I put one on such an exposed limb. If you want to back out, say so by the end of the duty shift and it won't be held against you."

"I'd hate myself forever if I refused, sir," Thomas said, fighting down an insane urge to giggle. When he'd been younger, growing up on sensory programs about spacers blazing a path into the unknown, he wouldn't have needed longer than a second to make up his mind to accept the post. "I accept the task."

"Good," the XO said. Thomas's implants bleeped up an alert, informing him that the XO was sending him a datapacket. "You're off the duty roster from now, Ensign. I want you to spend the rest of the day reviewing that packet - if you have any questions, forward them to me - and then get some rest. And I mean rest. Tomorrow, you take command of your ship."

"Yes, sir," Thomas said. A patrol boat or a frigate...either one would be tiny, and probably not designed for humans. Somehow, he doubted the XO would put a heavy cruiser in his hands. "And thank you."

The XO gave him a sharp look. "Thank me when you come home," he said. "And not a moment before."

"Yes, sir," Thomas said. He smiled as a thought struck him. He could tell Sandra! "Can I...can I tell others?"

"It might not be a good idea," the XO said. "You're not the only one being given a command, but not everyone is getting one. Wait."

Thomas sobered. "Yes, sir."

"Report back to my cabin at 1000 tomorrow, unless I call you earlier," the XO added, looking back down at the paperwork on his desk. "Dismissed."

"Yes, sir," Thomas said.

GRIFFIN WILDE WATCHED the painfully young - had *he* ever been that young? - Ensign leave his office, then cursed under his breath. He was experienced enough to read Ensign Howard perfectly, no matter how carefully the younger man tried to hide his emotions. Howard was excited and scared and willing and reluctant…a complex tangle of emotion that reminded Griffin, as if he'd had any doubt, that Howard was still a *young* man. Too young to feel truly confident in himself, too old to accept failure as a possibility.

And it wasn't helped by the fear he would never be offered a second chance, Griffin thought, darkly. *It isn't as if we make a habit of offering young officers command billets.*

He cursed again, savagely. The Captain's war demanded that a young and inexperienced officer be sent out on a mission that might well be suicidal, in command of a tiny number of largely inexperienced crewmen. Griffin had never sent someone out before, fully expecting him to die, but now…now he wondered if he'd crossed that line. And yet, no matter how he worked the problem, he couldn't see any other solution. They *needed* to keep the Druavroks off balance, but there was no time to recruit more locals and train them for shipboard duty.

All of those training programs are long-term, he thought. It took months to train even a basic engineer - and a full engineer took years. *Let us hope the war doesn't go on that long.*

Picking up a datapad, he glanced at the report from the chief engineer. *Jackie Fisher* had an onboard machine shop, complete with a miniaturised fabber, but even so…they were pushing their ability to repair their cruisers to the limits. The Captain might discover that her squadron needed to be refitted at the worst possible time, if she was lucky. If she was unlucky, something would break at the worst possible time. And she knew the dangers…

She's choosing to run a risk, he thought. Hoshiko had been completely unconcerned about risk, right from the start. *And she could easily lose the whole squadron if something goes wrong.*

It was a bitter thought. He would have admired her determination if it hadn't been so dangerous. As it was...he hoped - prayed - that they would have the time to do some proper maintenance before they faced the Druavroks once again. He'd told her about the problem, as a good XO should, but half the ship's engineering crew had been assigned to other vessels. It would be ironic, if they lost a battle because something failed, yet he had to concede it was a possibility.

He shook his head. It was his duty to support her and yet...

...What should he do, he asked himself, if her quest led to disaster?

TWENTY-SIX

In a speech that has gone viral on the datanet, the leader of the largest militia in California blamed the city-folk for the water shortage and flatly refused to let the refugees into his territory. "If you sheeple hadn't voted for dumb-o-crats and cuckservitives," he said, "you wouldn't be dying of thirst now." His words are a reference to California's democratic deficit, a problem made worse by increased immigration from Mexico and emigration to the Solar Union.

-Solar News Network, Year 54

"It's time to get up," Hilde said, pulling Max out of bed. "You have an appointment on a patrol boat."

Max opened his eyes, groggily. Sex with Hilde was exhausting, despite his enhancements; she always left him feeling tender and sore. She could be strong at one moment, rolling over to pin him beneath her body and having her way with him, and vulnerable the next, as if she expected him to reject her at any moment. Max honestly wasn't sure why she had chosen him, unless she couldn't risk sleeping with one of the crew, but he wasn't really inclined to care. He had a suspicion she didn't have any strong feelings for him at all, merely a desire not to go to bed alone.

"I don't," he said, as she put him down on the deck. "My day is free..."

"It just popped up on the datanet," Hilde told him. "You're ordered to board an unnamed patrol boat and interview the crew."

"Oh," Max said. He checked his implants and discovered the message. *Someone*, probably the captain, was determined to make sure he carried out a few interviews while the squadron was at Amstar. "I'll just shower before I teleport over."

"Good idea," Hilde said, sniffing the air mischievously. "You stink of sweat. And a few other things."

Max shrugged. "Do you want to shower first?"

"I'm due in the gym in thirty minutes," Hilde said, reaching for her shipsuit. "I'll shower there, I think. See you tonight?"

"If I'm back by then, sure," Max said. Hilde couldn't fit in the shower with him or he would have suggested sharing the water. "Have a good day."

Hilde smirked. "There are no good days when the major decided we haven't been tested enough," she said, ruefully. "We haven't seen enough action out here."

Max frowned, remembering the marine deployments since the squadron had left Martina, then decided not to comment on it. Instead, he picked up his towel and walked into the shower, washing the sweat from his body. There was no sign of Hilde when he stepped back out and started to dress; he wondered, absently, what her comrades thought of her affair before deciding it was probably none of their business. It wasn't interfering with her duties - or his - and therefore it was outside regulations. He finished dressing, grabbed a ration bar from the drawer and headed down to the teleport chamber. The codes he'd been given, with the message ordering him to the patrol boat, opened the hatch and allowed him entry.

"You're going to Boat #34," the operator said, looking up from his console. "I'll just verify access permissions with them."

"Please do," Max said. "I don't want to end up merged with a fly."

He shuddered at the thought. Beaming a bomb onboard was such an obvious ploy that even the Tokomak, notoriously unimaginative, had built jammers into their starships to prevent uninvited guests. Anyone who tried to beam onboard without permission would wind up scattered across the solar system, if they were lucky - and, if they were unlucky, they'd be the subject of countless horror movies. He'd had nightmares after watching the one where a small boy was tossed into a defective teleporter and turned into a monster.

"Ah, we've got filters to keep that from happening," the operator said. He grinned as he looked back down at his console. "You know they were messing about with teleport transmutation? Some egghead had the bright idea of adjusting the particle stream in flight, allowing for bodily adjustments?"

"Sounds awful," Max said. "What happened?"

"None of the animal subjects survived," the operator said. "The experiments were shut down long before they moved on to human testing."

"Oh," Max said. He vaguely recalled reading a news report about the experiments, although it hadn't stuck in his mind. "Why did they fail?"

The operator shrugged. "Even the smallest change in the matter pattern can cause instant death," he said. "That's why we have so many filters built into the teleporter."

He looked up and gave Max a wintery smile. "You're cleared to board the patrol boat," he added. "Step up onto the pad."

Max swallowed, realising that the operator had intended to rattle him, then stepped up onto the pad and turned to face him. The operator nodded and tapped a switch. A low hum echoed through the chamber as the world dematerialised into shimmering white light and reformed into a tiny bridge. Max stumbled forward as the teleport field released him. He would have fallen if a uniformed officer, standing beside the pad, hadn't caught him with one hand.

"Thank you," he said.

"Think nothing of it," the officer said. Max looked up and recognised Ensign Howard, now wearing a pair of captain's stars. "The gravity is a little lighter than Earth-normal."

Max nodded, making a mental note to walk carefully until his body adjusted properly. Living on Luna was fun - a human could fly with a pair of wings - but newcomers always lost control of themselves and bumped their heads against the ceilings. His enhanced body would adapt quickly, of course, yet it wouldn't spare him from embarrassment. He looked around as he took a step forward, testing the gravity, and blinked in surprise as he realised just how tiny the bridge actually *was*.

"This is a patrol boat that has been passed down through at least a dozen owners," Ensign Howard said. "Someone actually removed the flight records box years ago, leaving us without a clue to her history."

Max smiled. "I thought that was against Galactic Law?"

"It is," Howard said. "Judging from the number of different components that have been crammed into her hull, I have a strong feeling she was a pirate before being captured and placed into storage."

"I see," Max said. He looked around, taking note of the different models of console that had been crammed into the bridge and the handful of human crew. "Is she a reliable ship?"

"I certainly *hope* so," Howard said. "The real test will be just what happens when we light up the drives."

Max felt a stab of sympathy for the younger man. Human engineers were *very* well trained, capable of fixing everything from the plumbing to the FTL drive; human *starships* were designed to allow the engineers to go to work without needing to return to a shipyard. But Galactic ships were not...and if anything went wrong on the patrol boat, Ensign Howard and his makeshift crew were doomed. Unless, of course, they managed to limp to safe harbour...

He's more worried than he lets on, he thought, grimly. *Very few officers would admit to hoping for anything.*

"I hope she works like a dream," he said, instead. "And what do you intend to do once you're on the way?"

"Hunt enemy shipping," Ensign Howard said, immediately. "We have a hunting ground inside enemy space, where we will prowl around and watch for enemy ships. If we find something we can take out, we'll hit it and then vanish into FTL."

Max nodded. The Druavroks would probably expect pirates, either *genuine* pirates or the remnants of the navies they'd already overcome and destroyed. But interstellar piracy was only cost-effective if the targeted ships were captured, looted, renamed and then sold onwards to unscrupulous buyers. They'd be surprised when the 'pirates' blew freighters out of space instead of trying to take them as prizes.

He frowned. "Isn't it worth trying to capture the ships?"

"We don't have the manpower to attempt to board them, not against fanatical resistance," Ensign Howard said. He didn't sound too pleased by his own words. "If we had a reason to believe the ships would surrender, we might try - but, so far, the Druavroks don't seem to allow other races to crew their ships."

"Not an unwise decision on their part," Max agreed. A single bulk freighter would make one hell of a mess if it rammed into a planet; indeed, there had been whispered rumours of genocidal war long before humanity had encountered the Druavroks. "You don't think we could use the ships?"

"I'm sure we could," Ensign Howard agreed. "But trying to capture even a single freighter introduces random elements into the equation."

He shrugged and led Max on a tour of the patrol boat. She really was a small ship, Max noted. Most of her bulk was nothing but drives, sensors and weapons; the crew had a handful of tiny compartments at the front of the vessel. A single antimatter warhead - or a nuke, perhaps - would be enough to inflict crippling damage. The Tokomak clearly hadn't intended the patrol boats to be anything more than a tripwire, if war actually threatened their domains. Ensign Howard's ship couldn't hope to stop a destroyer or a frigate, let alone a capital warship.

"I meant to ask," he said, as they returned to the bridge. "Does the ship have a *name?*"

"Not as yet," Ensign Howard said. "She has an ID code from the last set of owners, but no actual name. I'm planning to choose a name just before we depart."

Max wondered what Hilde would say, if he proposed naming the patrol boat after her, then decided it was probably better not to find out. Instead, he spoke briefly to the remainder of the crew, all of whom were humans who'd been born on Amstar. Their Gal-Standard One was far better than his, but their English was non-existent. The Tokomak hadn't bothered to allow their human captives and their descendents to remember their original tongue.

"I'm surprised the crew is only human," he said, finally. "Aren't you going to have aliens on the crew?"

"It's tricky to provide life support for more than one race at a time, at least on a small ship," Ensign Howard said. "Even the most *human*-like races have differences that make it hard for them to work alongside humans. In the long term…I think we're going to have to work on a handful of multiracial ships, but for the moment single-race crews may be the only way forward."

"Particularly if the Solar Union starts taking in more non-human citizens," Max commented, dryly. "They'll want to serve in the military too."

Ensign Howard considered it for a long moment. "I knew a Hordesman at the Academy," he said, thoughtfully. "We had to make a number of allowances for him - he wasn't stupid, by any means, but he was shaped differently from us and it caused problems. He couldn't climb a ladder, for example. It might not be practical to build a starship that allows all known races to serve without problems."

"I see," Max said. "And what is that going to mean for the Grand Alliance?"

"I think Captain Stuart will have to answer that question," Ensign Howard said. "But, for the moment, we need to finish our preparations and depart."

Max nodded, recognising the polite dismissal. "If you'll teleport me back to *Fisher*, I'll get on with my latest story," he said. "Did you see my earlier one?"

"I saw your description of the Battle of Dab-Yam," Ensign Howard said. "It was very…*dramatic*."

"I hope so," Max said. He'd put the story together carefully, detailing the resistance to the Druavroks, the fate of those unlucky enough to be caught outside the planet's colossal defences, the steady enemy attacks… and, finally, the Grand Alliance arriving, like the 5th Cavalry, to save the innocent Dab-Yam from being eaten alive - literally. "The story is on its way to Sol."

"They'll love it," Ensign Howard said.

Max smiled as he turned and walked towards the teleport pad, barely large enough to accommodate a grown man. It would be at least three months before Sol heard *anything* of their adventures, let alone sent out other reporters to cover the story. By then, he would be firmly established in the public's mind as the *only* reporter with access - to the squadron, to Captain Stuart, to the growing Grand Alliance…he'd be unbeatable. His reputation would be made once and for all.

He silently checked his implants, counting down the days. Nine months before *any* rival could hope to appear, unless - of course - the Grand Alliance managed to produce a proper media machine of its own. And even then…

"Good luck," he said, as he turned to face Ensign Howard. "Bring back another story for me?"

"I'll try," Ensign Howard said. He checked the teleport settings carefully, then keyed a switch. "Goodbye."

— —

THOMAS WATCHED, UNSURE if he should be concerned, as the figure of the reporter dissolved into blinding white light before fading from view. He had no illusions about the task before him, or the odds against a safe return. The XO hadn't minced words - and, if he'd been inclined to believe it would be easy, four days fixing the patrol boat would have been quite enough to convince him otherwise. His ship was on the verge of falling apart at the seams.

It's not quite that bad, he told himself, as he walked back to his console and sat down. Even uniting the different control linkages had been a major headache, despite the Galactic fetish for standardisation. Whoever had worked on the patrol boat before losing her to the previous owners would have gone far, if they'd had a proper education. *It could be a great deal worse.*

He sat in the command chair - although it was also the tactical station - and studied the readings from the rest of the ship. A single hit might not be enough to destroy the vessel, but it sure as hell would be enough to disable them. He'd done what he could, before the engineering crews had been withdrawn to patch up another ancient ship, to build as many redundancies into the system as possible, yet he knew - all too well - that there were limits to what they could do. Anything that knocked out the main control network would probably knock out the backup network as well.

But it's your first command, he told himself. He could be addressed, legally, as *Captain*. He was master of the ship, commander of the crew... and almost certainly doomed, if the ship was disabled. There would be no hope of escape. *And when this is finished, you'll go right back to being an ensign.*

He scowled down at his console as he ran through the final checks, then told himself - firmly - not to be silly. Command experience at such a young age, even of a patrol boat that had entered service at roughly the same time as King Richard was fighting in the Crusades, would look *very* good on his record...assuming, of course, that he made it back alive. The odds were not in their favour. He shook his head, irritated, then checked the latest intelligence reports. He'd been warned, time and time again, that they were out of date, but they *were* the only things he had to go on until they actually reached their patrol area. They'd find out for sure what was facing them shortly afterwards.

The communications console chimed. "Captain, we are being hailed by the flagship."

Thomas nodded. The handful of crewmen under his command were *all* newcomers to the Solar Union, all born on Amstar, all offered citizenship in exchange for enlisting in the squadron. They all had experience on freighters - and some of the ships Amstar had used to patrol its territory before the Druavroks arrived - but they lacked the discipline of Solarian crewmen. And yet, they were all he had. He was mildly surprised Captain Stuart had seen fit to assign *him* to the crew.

"Put it through," he ordered.

"Mr. Howard," Commander Wilde said. Thomas wasn't particularly surprised that the older man didn't address him as *Captain*. "Are you ready to depart?"

"Just about, sir," Thomas said. They'd loaded antimatter missiles - Galactic missiles, unfortunately - early in the morning, then checked the handful of weapons the ship had carried when she'd been passed to the Grand Alliance. "We should make our departure time as planned."

"Very good," Commander Wilde said. "And have you chosen a name?"

Thomas hesitated. The Solar Union wasn't *particularly* superstitious - although there were cantons that practiced one form or another of religion exclusively - but very few spacers would choose to serve on a ship without a name. It was supposed to be bad luck.

"Yes, sir," he said, taking the plunge. Thankfully, there was no requirement for a dignified name, not for a tiny and expendable patrol boat. "She's the *Rustbucket*."

"A very fitting name," Commander Wilde said. He didn't sound either pleased or horrified. But then, choosing the name - by long tradition - was Thomas's right, as the ship's first human commander. "And the crew?"

"We've drilled as much as possible, sir," Thomas said. He tried to keep his doubts out of his voice, although he was sure the vastly more experienced officer could hear them. "And we'll be drilling more on the way."

"Very good, Mr. Howard," Commander Wilde said. "You are cleared to depart, as planned."

"Thank you, sir," Thomas said. "We'll come back with an enemy ship painted on our hull."

"I hope you are right," Commander Wilde said. "But remember, you're not flying a human ship. Don't assume you can fix anything that goes wrong."

"Yes, sir," Thomas said. He felt a shiver running down his spine. "I won't forget."

TWENTY-SEVEN

President Garrison - formerly General Garrison - blasted the Texan-led Alliance for the Preservation of the United States in a speech today, in which he asserted that the Texans, far from preserving the Union, are intent on destroying it. He made particular reference to the flat ban on illegal immigration put into law by Texas, noting that the law is a civil war waiting to happen. Outside observers have noted that the civil war is already happening.

-Solar News Network, Year 54

"The Grand Alliance has offered to cede the Polychrome System to us, as partial payment for our operations," Captain Ryman said.

Commander Wilde snorted. "You mean - keep us active within the sector," he said. He eyed the starchart doubtfully. "This is another Guantánamo Bay."

Hoshiko gave him a sharp look. "How so?"

"Guantánamo Bay kept the United States involved in Cuba, even though there were some solid reasons to withdraw," Commander Wilde said. "Turning the Polychrome System into a Solar Union settlement will keep us involved *here*, no matter what happens."

Captain Ryman shrugged. "Is that a bad thing?"

Hoshiko studied the display, thinking hard. The Polychrome System had been the subject of several disputes in the sector, mainly between the Gloudathua and the Tradresh. It had no life-bearing world, but it did have a gas giant and a *mammoth* asteroid field that - by some freak chance - had never become a planet. The Tokomak had never bothered to assign it to one of the races in the sector, leaving it up for grabs…and several races had tried, very hard, to grab it.

"It would make a convenient place to establish a permanent settlement," she mused. "Even if there isn't a great deal of long-term investment, the combination of fabbers and a human population keen on establishing a home of its own would certainly make the system viable."

"They'd make a very large canton," Wilde noted. "And they'd be a *very* long way from Earth. They'd have a great deal of autonomy whatever political system they adopted."

"That would be true in any case," Hoshiko said. "*We're* six months from Earth."

She tapped the display. "We don't have the resources to start work on the system now, but we can certainly lay the groundwork," she added. "Once we have a few dozen habitats up and running, the population can start to flow into the system."

"Not *everyone* likes the idea of living on an asteroid," Wilde pointed out. "They may push for a *real* homeworld."

"Then they can go back to Earth," Hoshiko said, bluntly. "A fight over land rights here, in this sector, will be a great deal worse than anything back home."

She shook her head in tired disbelief. Why would *anyone* sane want to live on a planet's surface? There was limited room for expansion, there was a shortage of natural resources and too many idiots were allowed to breed. Space, at least, killed off the morons who forgot the four basic rules of airlock safety before they managed to threaten others. She had no doubt, once a fabber or two was established in the Polychrome System, the system would start becoming habitable very quickly. And then it could start churning out starships of its own.

"Captain," Wilde said. "I should..."

He broke off as the intercom bleeped. "Captain," Lieutenant-Commander Biscoe said. "Our long-range sensors are picking up a small flight of enemy warships in FTL, heading directly towards Amstar."

Hoshiko sat upright, her tiredness forgotten. "Do you have an accurate count?"

"They're flying in close formation, Captain," Biscoe said. "The FTL gravity waves are overlapping. Battle Comp thinks they have somewhere between nine and fourteen ships, but it's impossible to be sure."

"I see," Hoshiko said. She exchanged glances with Wilde. "ETA?"

"Two hours, unless they pick up speed," Biscoe said. "They're making a very leisurely approach."

"Odd," Hoshiko said.

She keyed a switch, activating the tactical display. The Druavroks were either being very stupid or they had something up their sleeves - and she dared not assume it was the former. There was no way to prevent the defenders from getting at least *some* warning of their approach, but it wouldn't have been hard for them to ensure the defenders had much *less* warning. They seemed determined to make sure she had all the time she needed to prepare a hot reception.

"It's a trick of some kind," Wilde said. "It has to be."

"Probably," Hoshiko said. She cleared her throat. "Commander Biscoe, bring the fleet and planetary defenders to yellow alert. Order civilian ships within the system to slip into FTL or get under the planetary defences. We'll go to red alert ten minutes before the enemy are due to arrive."

"Aye, Captain," Biscoe said.

"I'll return to the surface," Captain Ryman said, standing. "The Grand Alliance needs to know we'll be sharing the danger with them."

Hoshiko watched him stride out of the cabin, then looked at her XO. "It's a trick of some kind," she agreed. "But what?"

"I wish I knew," Wilde said. He studied the display thoughtfully. "Those are cruisers, at a guess. But even if they were battleships they'd still be massively outgunned."

Hoshiko couldn't disagree. The Grand Alliance had responded to the success at Dab-Yam by sending dozens of additional warships to her fleet. If the enemy had counterattacked at once, she thought, they *might* have had a chance to do some real damage, but not now. Her freighters had been reloaded and she'd absorbed more refitted ships into her ranks. The only real downside was that she'd sent a hundred raiders into enemy space...

But those ships didn't add much firepower to our forces, she reminded herself, firmly. *I wouldn't have sent them away from the fleet if they did.*

"Maybe it's a suicide run," she said. A handful of cruisers flying right at the planet - and slamming into it at a fair percentage of the speed of light - would be enough to depopulate Amstar and render it uninhabitable once and for all. She certainly wouldn't put it past the Druavroks to *try*. "But we have plenty of firepower assembled to defend the planet."

She scowled at the display. The fabbers had been working non-stop, turning out everything from automated weapons platforms to mines and missile launchers. There were no battlestations covering the planet - those took months to construct, even in the Solar Union - but she could practically *walk* across the orbital defences now. Amstar could give a good account of itself even without the Grand Fleet to back up its own defenders. The Druavroks could charge the planet if they wished, yet they didn't have a hope of reaching the surface.

"I'll be in the CIC," she said. "You take command on the bridge."

"Aye, Captain," Wilde said.

Hoshiko sucked in a breath as he left, then walked through the hatch herself and strolled down to the CIC. A new mood of urgency was spreading through the ship, but the tense awareness that they were in a battle had yet to materialise. Yellow alert, after all, merely called the crew to *prepare* for a possible engagement. She walked through the hatch, checked the display quickly to make sure nothing had changed, then settled down in her chair to wait. There was nothing else she could do.

At least the planet's defenders are taking the threat seriously, these days, she thought. It had been hard, very hard, to convince the provisional government that the success at Dab-Yam did *not* give them an excuse to commit genocide themselves. The Druavroks in the enclaves were doing nothing, save for the occasional burst of sniper fire. *They're certainly more aware of what will happen if we lose.*

She forced herself to watch, grimly, as the timer slowly ticked down to zero. She'd ensured her subordinates knew what to do, if the Druavroks came calling. There was nothing to be gained by micromanaging them, let alone peering over their shoulders as they struggled to do their work. But she wanted - she needed - to be doing something. Grimly, she pulled up the latest set of intelligence reports and started to work her way through them. The reports were out of date - of course - but they agreed that the Druavroks had abandoned two sieges and withdrawn a number of squadrons from the others. They were clearly planning *something*...

It was a frustrating thought. The Druavroks had to know - now - that they were meeting heavier resistance and counterattacks. It wouldn't be long, either, before they knew that starships were raiding their supply lines, even reaching their homeworld itself. But what would they do in response? Attack Amstar? Attack Martina? Or send a fleet on the long voyage to Sol? She doubted they'd take the risk, but still...it was a thought that nagged at the back of her mind, when she was having trouble sleeping late at night.

They have to know the fleet they're sending here isn't enough to wipe the system, she thought, darkly. *Which means...what?*

"Captain," Brown said. "The enemy fleet has entered the system limits."

"Sound red alert," Hoshiko ordered. "Bring the fleet to condition one."

She leaned forward as the squadron girded itself for war. The Druavroks were *still* making their frustratingly slow approach, although *slow* was an odd term when applied to FTL starships. It would be at least fifteen minutes before they reached the planet, before she knew just what she was facing. She glanced at the network of human-grade stealthed recon platforms she'd scattered around the system, bound together by a web of laser beams that were impossible to detect, save by sheer luck. If the enemy intended to try to sneak something through the defences under cloak, it was unlikely to escape detection.

New icons flashed into life on the display. "Contact," Brown snapped. "Twelve cruisers; I say again, twelve cruisers. Holding position!"

Interesting, Hoshiko thought. The Druavroks weren't *trying to* hide; they weren't trying to do anything, save announcing their presence. She doubted there was anyone in the system who *wasn't* aware of their arrival, thanks to their casual advance towards the planet. *Are they trying to make us look away from something else?*

She studied the display for a long moment, as if she could wrinkle answers out purely through mental effort. But there was nothing. No freighters were moving in a suspicious pattern that might have warned of suicidal attackers, no cloaked warships were attempting to make their way through her defences...it was odd, yet, as far as she could tell, the enemy were doing *nothing*.

Wilde's voice echoed in her ear. "If they're trying to intimate us," he said, "they didn't send anything like enough ships."

"True," Hoshiko agreed. She looked at Brown. "Signal Task Forces 5.3 through 5.6. Order them to proceed towards the enemy and obliterate them."

"Aye, Captain," Brown said.

Hoshiko forced herself to relax as the alien warships moved out of formation, advancing on the Druavroks with casual grace. It would, if nothing else, give the newcomers a chance to draw some blood...and, if it *was* a trap, her most valuable ships would not be at the epicentre. But what could it be? She racked her brain, tossing ideas around as she tested and rejected each one...surely, they couldn't have loaded the cruisers with antimatter? Even *they* would hesitate just to throw away so many ships.

And it wouldn't cost us much, she thought. *Unless losing forty or so warships proves to be enough to convince some of our allies to back off.*

"Captain," Brown said. "The Druavroks are moving."

"I see," Hoshiko said, as the display updated. "They're *retreating*?"

"Confirmed," Brown said. He sounded as puzzled as Hoshiko felt. "They're withdrawing from the planet."

Hoshiko's eyes narrowed. The Druavroks were actually pulling *back*, declining the offer of battle. *That* was unprecedented. Had she ever *seen* a Druavrok fleet refusing to offer battle, even against massively overwhelming firepower? Were they launching stealth missiles on ballistic trajectories? Or were they merely trying to put her on edge? Or…had she inflicted so much damage that they had become more sensitive to losses? There was no way to know, but she rather doubted it. The Druavroks had thousands of warships under their command.

"Launch a spread of tactical probes," she ordered. Cold suspicion washed through her mind as she turned her attention to the overall display. It *had* to be a trick of some kind. "I want every last atom of space dust within one AU of the planet noted and logged."

"Aye, Captain," Brown said.

Hoshiko thought, quickly. Could the Druavroks have come up with a way to fool gravimetric sensors? Could they have sneaked an entire fleet into the system without setting off alarms, allowing them to mount a surprise attack? But if they had, why send the first squadron into the system, giving her all the warning she could possibly need? Besides, if neither the human race nor the Tokomak had been able to figure out a way to hide their FTL emissions from long-range sensors, she rather doubted the Druavroks had managed. It just made no sense.

Unless they're just carrying out a reconnaissance in force, she thought. Twelve cruisers, even with Galactic-grade sensors, would be able to chart out most of her defences without problems. And then they'd go home and whistle up the battleships. *That might make a certain kind of sense.*

She scowled as she recalled the intelligence reports. None of her allies had any real idea just how many battleships the Druavroks actually *had*, but they were certainly supposed to have well over nine hundred. *Thousands*, if one report was to be believed. If they threw all of those ships at Amstar, against her fleet and the planet's defences, they might well win...but it would cost them dearly. They'd never be able to rebuild before their enemies punched their way into their systems, blew through the defences and bombarded their worlds into radioactive ash. And, irony of ironies, if they did take out the defences of Amstar, they'd kill the only people interested in saving the Druavroks from becoming the victims of yet another genocide.

"Task Force 5.5's commander reports that the Druavroks are evading contact," Brown said, curtly. "He requests the dispatch of additional units to help him run the prey to ground."

"Denied," Hoshiko said, shortly. She understood the impulse, but there was no point in risking uncovering Amstar. And yet, what *was* the enemy trying to do? "Inform him that we need to keep the remainder of the fleet at Amstar."

"Aye, Captain," Brown said.

The display flickered and changed, the red icons popping out of existence. "They jumped back into FTL, Captain," Brown reported. "They're heading away from the system at maximum speed."

Hoshiko blinked. That was *it*? The enemy just retreated, as if they were humans? Or another more rational race? Could it be that the Druavroks had gained control of their blood lust? Or, perhaps, that they had a battle fleet lurking somewhere nearby, just out of sensor range? Why not? It was a common tactic, one older than the entire human race. She'd done the same at Malachi.

"Order the fleet to alter position in line with contingency plan beta-three," she ordered. If the Druavroks were counting on her ships being in a particular formation, or occupying a particular location, they were going to be disappointed. "And then contact the planetary defences and suggest, very strongly, that they reposition some of their mobile defence platforms."

"Aye, Captain," Brown said.

"Keep the remainder of the fleet at alert status, for the moment," she added. Assuming the Druavroks had brought a fleet as close as they could, without being detected, they'd be less than half an hour away at maximum speed. "We have to proceed on the assumption we're about to face a much more powerful attack."

She closed her eyes in contemplation. "And order Task Forces 5.3 through 5.6 to return to the fold. We may need their firepower."

"An interesting turn of events, Captain," Wilde said, through the command network. "The precursor to a far greater invasion?"

"It certainly seems that way," Hoshiko agreed. She narrowed her eyes as she contemplated other possibilities. Nothing came to mind. "But they may have something else up their sleeves."

She settled back to wait, expecting to see the enemy fleet appear on the scanners at any moment. But nothing materialised, not even a handful of freighters running supplies in and out of the system. The Druavroks had apparently come, seen and retreated without bothering to fire a handful of shots for the honour of the flag. And it made no sense at all.

Maybe they decided our defences were too strong to risk tangling with, she thought, as the minutes turned into hours. But Dab-Yam's defences had been stronger, at least on paper, and the Druavroks hadn't hesitated to try to wear them down. *And we had a powerful mobile fleet to back them up.*

"Order the alpha crews to go off duty, catch something to eat and get a little sleep," she said, grimly. Her crews had been at red alert for over three hours, leaving them tired and strained - and ready to jump at shadows. It wouldn't be long before there was an accident, perhaps with tragic consequences. "The beta crews are to remain at alert."

"Aye, Captain," Wilde said. "It doesn't look as if they have any intention of returning to the system. They may have just wanted to test the waters and force us to go on the alert."

"It certainly looks that way," Hoshiko agreed. She scowled at the blank display as if it had personally offended her. "Our enemies are suddenly acting like rational men and it worries me."

TWENTY-EIGHT

Texas - and the other states of the Alliance for the Preservation of the United States - began a mass round-up of illegal immigrants today, following the victory over Mexican troops in the Battle of El Paso. All immigrants are being taken to concentration camps where they will be held, pending the end of the Texan-Mexican War. The Governor's office, citing the precedent of the round-up of Japanese-Americans during World War Two, has refused to consider halting the program, despite legal challenges. Indeed, a number of lawyers who did challenge the program were arrested on charges of sedition and aiding and abetting criminal acts.
-Solar News Network, Year 54

"Captain, I think we have something here," Lieutenant Octavo said.

Thomas leaned forward as a new icon blinked to life on the display. It had taken three weeks to reach the Druavrok-held system, shadowing an enemy convoy so closely as to be lost in the convoy's gravimetric backwash, then another week to establish the fact that most of the freighter convoys making their way in and out of the system were heavily escorted by enemy warships. Attempting an attack would be nothing more than suicide. He'd been on the verge of seriously considering moving on to another system when Octavo had called for his attention.

"I see," he said. Thankfully, three weeks of constant drilling had improved his Gal-Standard One to the point they could communicate without any problems. "What *is* it?"

"It's a mass driver," Octavo said. "Or, rather, it's a mass-driven piece of rock, spewed out from one of the asteroid mining stations and spat towards the fabber."

Thomas studied it in some puzzlement. He couldn't help being reminded of some of the early Solar Union settlements, back when GalTech had been in short supply and human technology had been all there was for the vast majority of founding citizens. The concept was simple enough - raw materials mined from an asteroid were fired towards a fabber, where they were caught and fed into the gaping maw - but the Druavroks should have had no need for such a primitive construction. They'd copied the Tokomak, after all, and the Tokomak had always dragged the asteroids to the fabber and carved them up there, rather than hacking the asteroid to pieces where it was found.

"Maybe they're running short of GalTech," he mused.

It made a certain kind of sense, he thought. The Druavroks would have a handful of military-grade fabbers, but they'd want to keep them focused on supporting the war, rather than maintaining their economy. Someone with a far less advanced tech base - even pre-Contact Earth - could build and maintain the mass driver without any need for GalTech. He wondered, absently, just how advanced the Druavroks had been before the Tokomaks arrived, then dismissed the thought. By now, they were as capable with GalTech as any of the other Galactic races.

He smiled as a nasty thought occurred to him. "How many of those projectiles are they tossing at the fabber?"

"I think there's one every ten minutes," Octavo said. He'd been a merchant spacer before transferring to the Solar Union's auxiliary forces and had plenty of experience with passive sensors. "They're hard to detect, but I'm picking up an electromagnetic spike from the direction of the asteroid belt at ten minute intervals."

Thomas tapped his console, running a calculation. The projectiles would take four days to reach the fabber, assuming nothing went wrong along the way. And what *could* go wrong?

Us, he thought. *Time to do something nasty*.

He glanced at Octavo. "Are there any sensors mounted on the projectiles?"

"I don't *think* so," Octavo said. "They're just pieces of rock, as far as I can tell."

And passive sensors would be impossible to detect, Thomas thought. But really, why *would* the Druavroks bother to rig the projectiles with passive sensors? *They'd have to strip them off at the far end before they shove the projectile into the fabber*.

He rose. "Match our course and speed with the projectile," he ordered. "And then order Roxy and Tarquinii to suit up and meet me at the airlock."

"Of course, sir," Octavo said. He sounded puzzled. "Do you mind if I ask *why?*"

"We're going to unlock one of the missiles from the hull, then fix it to the projectile," Thomas said. "I want to give the bastards a *very* nasty surprise."

He grinned at Octavo, then nodded. "You have command," he added. "In the unlikely event of them coming to investigate, take the ship out of range and we'll go doggo."

"Understood," Octavo said. "Good luck, sir."

Thomas nodded, then turned and walked back to the airlock hatch. Roxy and Tarquinii were already waiting for him, wearing everything apart from their helmets. Thomas had a private suspicion the two girls had actually been pirates, judging from some of the things they'd said when he'd been trying to get to know them, but he'd kept that thought to himself. As long as they did as they were told, when the chips were down, he didn't give a damn about their past lives, Besides, they *were* hellishly competent.

Roxy leaned forward. She'd dyed her hair purple, for reasons Thomas couldn't begin to fathom. "What's the plan, boss?

"We're taking an antimatter warhead to the projectile, fixing it to the rock and then leaving it there for the enemy to find," Thomas said, as he reached for his suit. Thankfully, like so much else, Galactic suits were standardised. "Any more questions?"

Roxy and Tarquinii exchanged glances. "No, sir," Roxy finally said. "Are you sure the warhead is *safe*?"

"Antimatter is *never* safe," Thomas said. He finished pulling his suit on, buckled an EVA pack to his back and then picked up his helmet. "But it's a lot safer to rig one of their projectiles than it is to try to attack the fabber ourselves."

He smiled at the thought as he clicked the helmet into place, then checked Roxy and Tarquinii's suits and allowed them to do the same for him. The enemy fabber was heavily defended, surrounded by a network of automated weapons platforms which were backed up by the planet's mobile defenders. He'd hoped to find a way to get into attack range, but one look at the defences had told him it would prove futile. They'd be blown out of space a long time before they managed to launch a missile at the fabber. But this way…they might *just* get a warhead into contact range before the enemy noticed it was there.

"Check radios," he said. "Sound off."

"Here and hear, sir," Roxy said.

"Confirmed," Tarquinii said. Her voice was lighter than Roxy's. Thomas thought she was younger, but neither girl had been forthcoming about their age when they signed up. "Here and hear, sir."

"Good," Thomas said. The low-power radio wasn't *passive*, but it would be next to impossible to detect unless the enemy had a stroke of amazingly good luck. "Let's move."

He stepped through the airlock, silently grateful they weren't anywhere near a planet. He'd grown up on an asteroid, of course, and he'd made his first EVA almost as soon as he could walk, but being in orbit around a planet had often struck him as disconcerting. It was an illusion, he knew, that the planet was either falling on him or he was falling on *it*, yet the knowledge wasn't enough to keep him from feeling antsy. In deep space, by contrast, he was actually *swimming* through the inky darkness...smiling, he climbed out onto the hull and headed towards the missile launchers. The spare missiles were bolted to the hull behind them. Reloading was going to be a right pain.

And if we get hit, the containment fields fail and we die, he thought. It was something he'd overlooked until the drills had brought it to his attention. Antimatter warheads *could* be a major problem, but most missile storage compartments were heavily shielded. *One hit and we're dead.*

He pushed the thought aside as the first missile loomed over him. It was *huge*, easily twice the size of a shuttle; he recalled, with a flicker of gallows humour, just what missiles had been called back at the Academy, when the prospect of a violent death had been somewhere in the future. He muttered orders to Roxy and Tarquinii, then carefully deactivated the control systems, released the missile from its bolts and pushed it away from the ship. There was no point in keeping it - it *was* GalTech, after all - once they removed the warhead. He keyed the EVA controls on his wrist and thrust away from the ship and out towards the missile. Thankfully, landing on the missile's hull would not be enough to trigger the warhead.

"We need to remove the warhead," he said. His skin felt cold, very cold, as he peered down at the sealed hatch. "Get ready to catch it when I remove it from the casing."

Praying silently under his breath, he opened an access hatch, linked into the system with his implants and shot a handful of codes into the processor. It bleeped once, then opened the latches, allowing him to remove the antimatter containment system from the missile and push it out into space. Roxy caught it a moment later and checked the processor herself, making sure the antimatter was secure. A mistake now would destroy the ship.

"It's secure," she said.

"It doesn't look very big," Tarquinii commented. "You sure you got the right warhead?"

"Antimatter doesn't have to be any bigger than my fist," Thomas reminded her.

His skin crawled as he took the warhead, then pulled it towards the projectile. Up close, the projectile was colossal, easily twice the size of *Rustbucket*. He landed on the rocky surface and waited as Roxy and Tarquinii landed beside him, then used cutters to burn their way into the projectile. No one would notice, he was sure, as they carved out a chamber large enough to take the warhead. The surface was already scarred and pitted where the Druavroks had burned it free of an asteroid and carved it into a shape they could load into a mass driver and shoot towards the fabber. He placed the warhead within the chamber, set a proximity alarm just in case the Druavroks *did* discover it, then watched as the chamber was sealed again. It was almost unnoticeable when the girls had finished.

"Back to the ship," Thomas said, once they were done. He checked his timer, then led the way back to the airlock. "They're in for a *very* nasty surprise when they melt the projectile down for raw materials."

The two girls were grinning from ear to ear when they removed their helmets, once they were back on the ship. Thomas left them to return to their duties and headed forward to the bridge, where he checked the tactical console to be sure his calculations were correct. It would be two days before the rigged projectile reached the fabber...until then, *Rustbucket* could carry out a tactical survey of the system and look for other prospective targets. Who knew? The information might be very useful if - when - Captain Stuart went on the offensive.

"Keep an eye on the projectile," he ordered, when his shift came to an end. "We'll sneak closer to the fabber just before it reaches its destination."

"Yes, sir," Octavo said. He sounded impressed, although - unlike a Solar Union officer - he hadn't raised any objection to Thomas taking personal command of the away team. "Have a good night, sir."

Thomas couldn't wait until they were in position to watch the fireworks, but there was no way to speed the process up. He slept, commanded the ship as they surveyed the handful of asteroid mining stations - all built with technology that would have been outdated on pre-Contact Earth - and slept again, as they slowly curved back to the planet and into position to observe the effects of their sabotage. It was hard to be *entirely* sure - there was no way to track the projectile using passive sensors, unless they were at very close range - but the projectile had been fired on a ballistic trajectory. Thomas found himself leaning forward as the seconds ticked away to zero...

They'll have to melt the rock down once she's inside the maw, he thought. *And that would destroy the containment system...*

The fabber exploded with stunning force, a chain of explosions ripping the giant structure apart and leaving nothing apart from tiny pieces of debris drifting down towards the planet's atmosphere. A small explosion might have been contained, even by GalTech, but nothing - not even a human force field - could have hoped to save the fabber, once the containment field failed. Thomas watched, smiling coldly, as the Druavroks went on alert, hunting for an enemy attacker that was nowhere to be found. They didn't have a hope of detecting *his* ship, not unless they got very lucky.

"How long will it take them," he asked out loud, "before they deduce the truth?"

"Unknown, sir," Octavo said. "The force of the explosion will certainly tell them that *antimatter* was involved, but they may feel the projectile was rigged at the mining station."

"Then sneak us out of the system," Thomas ordered. He hesitated, then shook his head. "No, belay that order. Take us towards the asteroid station."

"Aye, sir," Octavo said. He sounded puzzled, but obedient. "We'll be nearby in forty minutes."

Thomas leaned back in his chair, thinking hard. What would *he* do if he thought the asteroid's crew had deliberately rigged the projectile? *He'd* send a ship to arrest the crew, then subject the poor bastards to a merciless interrogation. Or, for that matter, maybe just shout questions at them. GalTech was perfectly capable of producing perfect lie detectors for humans, after all. There was no reason to assume it couldn't do the same for Druavroks. No, the crew would be interrogated, found innocent and then released, while the Druavroks started a hunt for a mystery starship.

And if they think they are facing dissent in the ranks, he thought, as he watched the Druavroks flurry around the system, locking the barn door long after the horse had bolted, *they may spend too much time watching their backs*.

"Launch a probe at the asteroid," he ordered. "And route the results direct to my console."

"Aye, sir," Octavo said.

Thomas watched, grimly, as two enemy warships left the planet, heading directly for the asteroid mining complex, then turned his attention to the live feed from the probe. The complex *definitely* reminded him of some of the early Solar Union structures, a handful of tunnels carved into the rock and sealed to provide a habitat barely worthy of the name. He smiled, remembering some of the stories from the old sweats, about how they'd spent five or six months at a time digging for ore, then heading home to spend their bonuses in the brothels on Luna City. His grandfather had been an asteroid miner and he'd had some *very* interesting stories to tell.

"I'm reprogramming a missile," he said, keying his console. He'd never reprogrammed a missile outside simulations, but he knew the basic theory. Normally, a missile would race to its target as fast as possible, trying to outrace or outsmart any counterbattery fire. Now, though, he wanted the missile to be almost unnoticeable. "Stand by to fire one."

"Aye, sir," Octavo said.

Thomas finished his task, then hesitated. He had no compunction over killing the enemies of humanity - and the Druavroks were the enemies of *everyone* - but did the asteroid miners deserve to die? The fabber crews had *needed* to die - even if there had been some way to get them off the fabber before it had been too late, they would have been moved to another fabber - yet was that true of the miners? For all he knew, they were just attempting to make a living by shipping rock ore home. Did they need to die?

He stared down at the console. If the miners survived, the Druavroks would deduce the truth, once they eliminated the miners as possible suspects. There would be literally no other alternative, not since natural antimatter was rarer than hen's teeth. The odds of a pocket of antimatter surviving at the heart of an asteroid were beyond calculation, so much so that it simply *didn't* happen outside children's sims designed to teach them about the nature of the universe. No, the miners had to die so they could take the blame. There was no other outcome...

Unless we want them to know we're on the prowl, he thought. Part of the reason so many ships had been sent to slip into enemy-held systems was to keep the enemy on the alert. *It would make them worry about their rear-area security*.

He sighed. *What would Captain Stuart do?*

The asteroid mining station was hardly an important target, not in its own right. There was nothing stopping the Druavroks from establishing another, or just using a starship to tow an asteroid to the fabber and have it sliced up there. The fabber would take years to replace, certainly without the codes that permitted the fabber to duplicate itself; the station wouldn't take long to replace at all, even without a fabber...

"Pull us back," he ordered, hoping desperately that he'd made the right call. It would have been a great deal easier if the miners had been shooting at him. "We'll find another ship leaving the system and shadow her out."

"Aye, sir," Octavo said.

There was no condemnation - or agreement - in his voice. Octavo probably had an opinion - everyone had opinions - but he wouldn't voice it. And yet, Thomas knew he'd always be haunted by his choice. All he could was hope, in the end, that he'd made the right one.

And that it doesn't come back to haunt me, he thought, silently. *And that Captain Stuart understands why I did what I did.*

TWENTY-NINE

The Alliance for the Preservation of the United States carried out a number of air strikes against targets within California, followed by an air drop of weapons and supplies to various militia forces currently struggling to defend their territory against gangbangers and irregular forces from the cities. Reports from the cities report that the average civilian no longer has enough to eat or drink, while the streets are completely unsafe…
-Solar News Network, Year 54

"We need to go back on the offensive, of course," Hoshiko said.

Griffin kept his face impassive with an effort. It had been two weeks since the probe - or the reconnaissance in force, if that was what it had been - and the Captain was growing antsy, eager to resume the offensive. Amstar hadn't been attacked, the Druavroks remained suspiciously quiet and the Grand Alliance was growing stronger. He couldn't help wondering if the Druavroks were looking for another angle of attack, hoping their enemies would let down their guard if months passed without a further offensive, or if they were merely gathering their forces for a major attack. Either way, the Captain had no intention of just *giving* them the time to prepare their forces.

"Amstar is strongly held, at the moment," Hoshiko continued. "And they haven't launched an attack."

"Yet," Griffin said. "They *could* have a major force lurking just outside detection range, hoping we'd uncover Amstar for them."

"It's a possibility," Hoshiko conceded, reluctantly. "But even *they* would have problems keeping a fleet on standby for so long, so far from their bases."

She eyed the display. "*And* we've pushed recon ships out several light months from the planet," she added. "If there *is* an enemy fleet lurking in the interstellar depths, they're not sending courier boats back to their homeworld."

"They could just be waiting," Griffin pointed out. "Those cruisers might well have concealed the arrival of another ship, one watching us from a distance. Or they might have slipped a spying mission into the system, under the guise of a freighter passing though."

"Assuming they can get someone willing to work for them," Hoshiko countered. She gave him a mischievous smile. "It isn't as though we're allowing Druavrok ships to enter the system to trade."

"It would be easy," Griffin said. "You just hold a spacer's family hostage until he returns with the intelligence you need. They may not think *quite* like us, Captain, but they do have working brains."

"We can't stay here either," Hoshiko said. She nodded towards the display. "The enemy have, according to the intelligence reports, been running supplies into the Palsies System and tightening their blockade. And it's only a two-week flight from Amstar."

"Two weeks is a long time in interstellar warfare," Griffin said. "If they *are* bracing themselves for an attack on Amstar..."

"We can still hold the planet," Hoshiko insisted. "They'd bleed themselves white trying to retake it, now the defences are stronger than they ever were. And every day they refrain from launching an attack the stronger the defences *get*. The main body of the Grand Fleet can leave, Commander, while the defences and support fleet hold the line."

She altered the display, drawing out flight vectors. "We'll depart on a course that suggests we're heading deep into their territory," she said.

Griffin knew she'd been considering a deep-strike operation, but there was just too much chance of the enemy launching a major counter-offensive once they noticed the Grand Fleet was gone. "We'll drop out of FTL *here*, two light years from Amstar, and wait. If the Druavroks *do* have a fleet lurking somewhere nearby, just waiting for us to uncover Amstar, we'll be in position to get back to the system and take them by surprise."

"They may see us coming," Griffin said.

"It can't be helped," Hoshiko pointed out. "There's no way we can sneak an entire fleet back into the system without being detected.

"If no enemy fleet materialises, we'll alter course and head straight for Palsies. Once there, we trap the enemy ships against the planet's defences and smash them before pulling out and heading straight for Amstar. If nothing goes wrong, we can then reload the ships and head to the next world under siege. The Druavroks will have to respond to us, which will give the rest of the Grand Alliance more time to prepare their defences."

"And build more warships," Griffin said. He had a great deal of respect for the spacers who would take freighters up against capital ships, but he was too experienced an officer to believe they had a chance in a straight fight. "We're going to need them. And more trained officers and crew."

He sighed. Training crewmen up to Solar Navy standards would take at least two years, assuming the infrastructure was put together at astonishing speed and the training officers were found from somewhere. Ideally, he would have sent the recruits back to Sol to attend the Academy, but that was obviously impossible. All he could really do was pull the training simulators out of the ships, assign a handful of crewmen to supervise and make sure the newly-minted crewmen received a *lot* of supervision on the job.

Not that they'll be having it on the squadron, he thought, grimly. *Even Captain Stuart hasn't overridden the prohibition on allowing non-Solarian crewmen to serve on our ships.*

"We'll overcome the problems," Hoshiko assured him. "Did you imagine we'd get this far?"

Griffin shook his head. He had no illusions. The squadron had accomplished miracles, simply by taking the enemy by surprise, but the Druavroks were ready for them now and they *still* had hundreds of warships. Perhaps more, if they were throwing all of their resources into building up their fleet. They *were* a highly aggressive race, after all. The *real* question was if the Grand Alliance could out-produce the Druavroks before the Druavroks pushed forward and smashed it flat.

But we took the limiters off the fabbers, he reminded himself. *Our industrial base will grow more powerful - much more powerful - over time.*

"I'm merely worried about the future," he said. "We *still* have no word from Sol."

"We won't for at least another eight months," Hoshiko reminded him. "And even then, they'll only know we set off to liberate Amstar and stop a genocide."

Griffin shook his head slowly. Everything they'd done...it might look very good, when they got back home, but that wouldn't be enough to keep them from an inquiry. His career - her career - might come to a screeching halt. Assuming, of course, that the human race didn't have too many other concerns. The Druavroks might win the war, snatch control of the fabbers and the unlocking codes and then start advancing towards Sol. They'd certainly have a murderous grudge against the Solar Union.

"We'll be fine," Hoshiko said.

She cleared her throat. "Inform the fleet that we will be departing in two days," she ordered, looking back at the display. "That should be *just* enough time to recall the crew from the fleshpots of Amstar, correct?"

"*Just* enough," Griffin agreed, gravely. The humans on the planet had been more than *merely* welcoming. They'd taken the spacers into their homes...hell, a string of romances had already broken out. In the long-term, he had a feeling that some of them would lead to marriage. "Captain, if they *do* have someone watching the system..."

"Put the system into lockdown as soon as we issue the recall order," Hoshiko said. "It won't be enough to make *certain* the enemy can't slip a message out, but at least we can detect any ship leaving the system."

"Aye, Captain," Griffin said. He rose. "I'll get started at once."

— —

"TAKE US OUT of FTL," Hoshiko ordered, quietly.

She leaned back in her command chair as the display rapidly filled with stars - and the endless wastes of interstellar space. It was rare, even for spacers, to gaze on the emptiness of interstellar space, light years from the light and warmth of a star. She'd heard stories of aliens who refused, for incomprehensible reasons, to use FTL and insisted on flying between the stars at sublight speed, but surely even they were reluctant to stare into the darkness. It made her feel small.

Pushing the thought aside, she watched the display as the sensors probed for flickers of gravimetric pulses that might announce the presence of an enemy fleet. There was nothing, but that was meaningless. The Druavroks might not have noticed - yet - that the fleet had departed...or they might be on the other side of Amstar, well out of detection range. Or, for that matter, they might have tracked the fleet itself and guessed it was a trap. Assuming, of course, there *was* an enemy fleet lurking near the system.

But the more complex a tactical plan, she reminded herself, *the greater the chance of something going wrong.*

She scowled at the thought. She'd studied the Tokomak tactical manuals at the Academy, but they'd struck her as unimaginative, if not stupid. The Tokomak hadn't bothered to come up with fancy tactics, not when they wielded the biggest stick in the known universe. *Their* favoured tactic was merely to locate the enemy homeworld, launch an overwhelmingly powerful fleet towards it and force the defenders to stand in defence of their world, absorbing whatever losses were necessary to crush all resistance. They certainly didn't try to come up with clever tactics to knock a stronger foe off balance or avoid casualties as much as possible...

We came up with more ideas than them before we even made it into space, she thought, crossly. *Surely they had more ideas before they came up with the FTL drive.*

The thought chilled her to the bone. Admiral Stuart - Uncle Mongo - was *still* in overall command of the Solar Navy, a post he'd held since Year 1. Admittedly, he'd built the Solar Navy up from a handful of outdated Galactic starships to a force that could take on the Tokomak and win, but he was *still* in command. What would happen, in the long run, if he *never* left command? It was possible, in theory; human-grade genetic enhancements and nanites conferred effective immortality, barring accidents. And what would happen when young and ambitious officers discovered that the pathway to the top was permanently blocked?

She scowled. The younger Tokomak had certainly become inured to waiting their turn, even though they had to know their turn might never come. But humans? Humans were aggressive, scheming bastards. How long would it be before junior officers were literally plotting to murder their senior officers? The Solar Union trained its officers to be aggressive, competent and determined, not to give up at the first hitch. What would happen when the Solar Navy stopped its steady expansion and there were fewer billets for experienced officers and crewmen? Human history suggested it wouldn't be pleasant.

"Captain," Brown said. "I have not detected any ships leaving Amstar."

Hoshiko nodded. The lockdown - a ban on all ships departing the system without permission - should have made it impossible for any prowling spy ship to use an innocent freighter as cover for a daring escape. They'd have to leave on their own, ensuring their detection. But it nothing showed up...

You can't prove a negative, she thought, crossly. *There's no way to know there isn't an enemy fleet lurking near the system.*

She ground her teeth in irritation. She understood why Commander Wilde and the other doubters wanted to be careful, but - in many ways - an enemy attack on Amstar would be a dream come true. The Druavroks might break through to high orbit and regain the planet, yet the victory would come at staggering cost. They'd be crushed the moment she returned with the Grand Fleet. And besides, she *wanted* - she *needed* - to go back on the offensive. Giving up the initiative was nothing less than accepting eventual defeat. She had space to trade for time, but the Grand Alliance might not feel the same way.

"Hold position here," she ordered, coldly. "We will wait."

She forced herself to concentrate, thinking through the list of possible alternatives for future operations. Taking the offensive into enemy space risked bruising encounters with fixed defences, although her preliminary recon reports suggested that the Druavroks had concentrated on building up their fleet at the expense of their planetary defences. The Solar Union had done the same, although - in their case - it had proved impossible to build fixed defences on Earth. But she could raid enemy ships, hack away at their industry and eventually wear down their defences and invade their homeworld.

But landing a military force on their homeworld might lead to a long and bloody conflict, she thought. *It won't be easy to force them to surrender.*

"Captain," Wilde said, an hour later. "There has been no sign of movement."

"No, there hasn't," Hoshiko said. The enemy didn't have a fleet, then...unless, of course, the enemy was being *very* cagey. Or they'd seen her fleet drop *out* of FTL and thought it was a trap. "I believe we can proceed to our destination."

"Yes, Captain," Wilde said. He didn't sound pleased, but he offered no argument. "I'll order the fleet to proceed along the planned course."

Hoshiko nodded. Unless they were *very* unlucky, which was possible, the enemy would lose track of the fleet long before it altered course and headed to Palsies. They'd *have* to assume she was heading straight into their territory, perhaps all the way to their homeworld. And then...what would they do? If they understood the true nature of the alliance she'd built, they'd have no choice but to give chase. There was no target in her alliance that could make up for the loss of their homeworld.

"Take us back into FTL," she ordered. There was no longer anything to be gained by waiting for the enemy. "And make sure the crew gets plenty of rest. They're going to need it."

"Aye, Captain," Wilde said. "I'll make sure the alpha and beta crews go straight to sleep."

Hoshiko winced, inwardly. There was a hint of disapproval in his voice, despite his best attempts to keep it muted. The crew was pushed to the limits because she'd sent a third of her personnel to the Grand Fleet and they both knew it. She hadn't *quite* broken the regulations concerning minimal numbers of personnel, but it was only a matter of time before something snapped. When it did, she knew it was going to be bad.

But there's no choice, she told herself, as the fleet slipped back into FTL. Her evasive course would ensure plenty of downtime for the crew, but it wouldn't be enough. *We have to keep pushing at the enemy or they'll have a chance to take the offensive themselves.*

She rose, then ordered Brown to shut down the CIC and strode back to her cabin. The only advantage to the fleet's rag-tag nature was a shortage of paperwork, even though she had to trust alien captains to tell her if there was anything wrong with their ships. In the long term, something would have to be done to put everyone on a common standard... assuming, of course, that the Grand Alliance survived. Thankfully, the Tokomak had already standardised as much as they could, from war material to operational protocols.

"Record a message," she ordered, once she was back in her cabin and the steward had brought her a cup of coffee. She couldn't go to sleep, not when her crew was badly overworked. It would set a very bad example. "Admiral Stuart. In line with my overall objective to keep the Druavroks from launching a counterattack against the Grand Alliance, I have ordered a major attack on..."

She spoke calmly, running through the entire report. Technically, she should have sent it while they'd been orbiting Amstar, but she hadn't seen any real point. No matter *what* she did, any response would be a year out of date by the time it reached her. It was good, in many ways, that she was free of interference by people who had no idea just what it was like on the ground, but it was also frustrating. There was no hope of getting support from the rest of the navy.

Not that they'd send it to us even if they did have instant FTL communications, she thought, amused. *This sector is far too far from Sol for them to be comfortable dispatching half of Home Fleet to back us up.*

She smiled wistfully at the thought. She'd no longer be in command, if half of Home Fleet arrived in the Martina Sector, but it wouldn't matter. All that would matter would be the simple fact they'd have enough firepower to carve though the Druavroks and march all the way to their homeworld. The war would be over in less than a month.

But I don't have half of Home Fleet heading out here to support me, she reminded herself, as she finished her coffee. *All I have is nine cruisers and a handful of support ships. The rest of the firepower has to come from the alien warships.*

Pushing the thought aside, she rose to her feet and headed for the bridge. Commander Wilde needed rest too, before problems started to crop up with the crew. She'd relieve him and let him get some sleep, along with the alpha and beta crews. And then, finally, she could get some rest herself.

At least we're on the move again, she thought, as she stepped through the hatch. The bridge, at least, was fully-manned, even though it felt more like Commander Wilde's territory these days. *The enemy won't have time to take the offensive themselves.*

THIRTY

Federal troops are reported to be heading to Texas, following the air strikes launched by the Texan-led Alliance for the Preservation of the United States against California. However, the remains of the USAF have not attempted to intercept the Alliance aircraft or mount counter-strikes against Texas or any of the other states. Anonymous reports on the datanet suggest that USAF pilots are walking off the job in large numbers - or, in at least two cases, deserting to Texas.
-Solar News Network, Year 54

Warlord Joist sat in the command perch, waiting.

Patience was not something that came naturally to the Druavroks. Their evolutionary history, to say nothing of their experience since they'd been welcomed into galactic society, told them to spring on the prey as soon as possible, before it could get away. The concept of prey that fought back was hard for them to grasp, let alone one that might prove dangerously intelligent and vindictive. Hadn't every other race in the galaxy, all prey, taken their technology from the god-like Tokomak? It boded ill for their intelligence, Warlord Joist had often considered, that none of the prey had ever improved on the technology of the gods. But then, it *was* created by the gods. If the Druavroks couldn't improve on it, how could any of their prey?

He kept his face impassive as he eyed his crew, all crouching forward in their perches as they maintained the siege. They were impatient, he knew; he'd already seen off three challenges from younger officers who thought they were serving under a coward. *That*, at least, wouldn't have been a problem, but they'd allowed their bloodlust to drive them forward, overriding prudence and caution. They hadn't realised, of course, that *no one* survived being promoted to warlord without plenty of experience and skill, as well as the willingness to use it. He'd licked their blood from his claws, knowing it would dissuade future challengers for a few weeks. The siege would be maintained without a bloody attack on the planet that would leave his fleet in ruins.

And besides, he reminded himself, *there is a plan*.

He wasn't too surprised that his forces hadn't already been attacked, despite their proximity to Amstar. Prey, even dangerous prey, simply didn't know how to fight. But even prey would eventually cast their eyes on his force and rate it a suitable target. This new species of prey - these *humans* - were strange, but there was no denying the damage they'd inflicted on the forces laying siege to Dab-Yam. Only a handful of warships had survived the holocaust the humans had unleashed. Charging madly into the teeth of their fire was a good way to get oneself impaled on the horns of a maddened animal.

"Warlord," an officer said, approaching and baring her neck before him. Her scent indicated it wouldn't be too long before she entered mating season, sparking off a frenzy among her male crewmembers for the right to mate with her. "The picket ship has been detected returning to the planet."

"They are coming," Warlord Joist said, thoughtfully. He'd put a handful of ships out on picket duty, extending his sensor range far enough to get some additional warning of the prey's approach. "Inform the fleet to prepare for the engagement as planned, then dispatch the courier boat to the homeworld."

He allowed his mouth to loll open, showing his teeth. It was possible, even probably, that the system was under covert observation. His forces had been running convoys in and out of the system, as planned. The enemy had had plenty of opportunity to sneak a ship into the system and set up a network of stealthed recon platforms, as called for by all the good tactical manuals. But, if everything had gone according to plan, it wouldn't matter. And if it hadn't...well, they were only prey, after all, even if they *were* dangerously *capable* prey. He wouldn't bet against his own forces in an even fight.

The crewwoman drew back. "Yes, Warlord," she said. "It is my pleasure to serve."

She backed off, never turning her back on him. Warlord Joist watched her go, then turned his attention to the display. The return of the picket ship was all the warning he needed, really; it told him that the enemy were approaching *and* their rough vector. He would have all the time in the world to set up his side of the operation. It had been frustrating, even for him, to hold back when he *knew* he could have taken the planet, but it *was* the bait in a trap. Afterwards, he promised himself, his crews would feast on the planet's inhabitants. He might even secure the world as his family's demesne.

And the prey will break before us, he promised himself. *And order will return to the universe.*

— —

"We will be dropping out of FTL in thirty minutes, Captain," Brown said. "The fleet has moved to condition two."

"Take the fleet to condition one in twenty minutes," Hoshiko ordered, curtly. "I want to be ready for anything."

She sucked in her breath as the timer continued its long countdown to zero. Palsies, according to the last set of reports, was only surrounded by two squadrons of enemy battleships and a handful of smaller vessels, but she refused to allow overconfidence to blind her. The enemy battleships *should* be easy targets, particularly if they were handled poorly, yet the enemy *had* been acting oddly. She was tempted to believe that they'd learned a few harsh lessons from her attacks, but she dared not take it for granted. All she could do was handle her ships with confidence and brace herself for any surprises.

"The fleet signals that it is at full readiness," Brown continued. "I believe the beta and delta command networks are operational, ready to take over if necessary."

"Good," Hoshiko said. "Run a final operational test at fifteen minutes, then keep both redundant command networks at standby. They can take over if the shit hits the fan."

She closed her eyes, hoping - praying - that wouldn't be necessary. The aliens seemed willing to accept orders from human commanders, because humans weren't involved in their pre-war power struggles, but they were less willing to accept commands from their former rivals. Somehow, she wasn't too surprised to discover that the Grand Alliance couldn't really do anything more than paper over the cracks as it struggled to keep the aliens going in the same direction. But then, her grandfather's stories of wars in the Crazy Years, as he'd called them, had made it clear she was far from the first commander to face the same problem.

Wilde's face appeared in front of her. "Captain," he said. "The squadron is fully at your command."

"Very good," Hoshiko said. She sucked in a breath as the timer reached ten minutes to their destination. "Sound red alert, Commander; set condition one throughout the fleet."

Brown turned to face her as the display shifted to red. "The fleet has checked in, Captain," he said. "They're at red alert."

Or whatever they use to signify condition one, Hoshiko thought. There were races that considered red to be a light, *friendly* colour and races that were completely colour-blind, unable to understand why other races made such a fuss about them. Without AIs, keeping track of each race's preferences was a minor nightmare. *And even with it, we may find it harder to operate a much larger force.*

"The reporter would like to join us," Brown added. "Captain?"

"Tell him he can enter the compartment, as long as he stays quiet," Hoshiko ordered. No doubt the reporter had realised that the observation blister wouldn't provide much of a view, let alone an awareness of what was actually going on. "And then prepare for combat."

She turned her attention back to the timer and watched as the final minutes faded away and the fleet dropped back into the normal universe. Palsies appeared in front of her, a blue-green world surrounded by orbital battlestations and makeshift defences...and nearly a hundred red icons, each one representing an enemy warship. Oddly, the Druavroks didn't seem to have set up mass drivers or anything else that would wear the enemy down. They were just sniping at the defences from just beyond their effective range.

Not that that won't prove effective, she reminded herself. *They only need to get lucky once to score a hit on the planet, slaughtering thousands of natives. The defenders need to be lucky all the time to keep them from committing genocide.*

"No enemy ships within engagement range," Brown reported. He frowned. "Captain, the enemy fleet has not assumed a defensive posture."

Hoshiko's eyes narrowed as she stared at the display. The Druavroks were badly outnumbered - and they had to know it - but their fleet was scattered, instead of hurrying to form up into a formation that allowed for mutual support. Could they have missed her fleet as it approached the system? That wasn't possible, surely? Every starship carried gravimetric sensors, even freighters that weren't supposed to be anywhere near the front lines. No, the aliens *had* to have known she was on the way. And yet they hadn't taken even basic precautions.

She studied the display, thinking fast. It was tempting - very tempting - to simply lunge forward and obliterate the enemy ships before they had a chance to correct their blunder. A battleship was a powerful vessel, but she could smother them in missiles if she wanted, overwhelming their defences in a single blow. And yet, the enemy *had* to have something up their sleeves. What? Surely it was a trap of some kind...

They didn't move reinforcements into the system, she thought. *We had it under observation for weeks. They shipped in hundreds of freighters, presumably crammed with supplies, but no additional warships.*

"Task Forces 2.1 through 2.5 are to advance forward," she ordered, slowly. Had the enemy mined space, intending to dare her to impale herself on the mines? "Launch probes - I want every last atom drifting through space noted and logged before we enter weapons range."

"Aye, Captain," Brown said.

Hoshiko sat back in her command chair, considering. If it *was* a trap, how was it to be sprung? And if it *wasn't* a trap, why weren't the enemy attacking? Or jumping into FTL and fleeing for their lives? What were they *thinking*?

— —

"WARLORD," THE SENSOR officer said. "The prey are sending a smaller force forward to engage us."

Interesting, Warlord Joist thought.

He stroked his teeth in consideration. The more aggressive species on his homeworld were inclined to take advantage of weakness - or perceived weakness. Leaving his ships strung out, like goats to lure the tiger, had seemed *certain* to lure the enemy into the trap. But instead, the prey were hesitating, as if they could *see* the jaws starting to spring shut. And there was no time to let them overcome their doubts. The longer they took, the greater the danger they'd see the trap while there was still time to make their escape.

"Order the fleet to assume defensive formation," he ordered. "And to launch probes towards the attacking fleet."

The display updated slowly, very slowly. There were so many enemy ships that it was impossible, even with the most advanced sensors, to count them all, but it was clear that only three hundred or so were actual *warships*. *That*, at least, tallied with the earlier reports that the prey were dependent on freighters. And everyone *knew* that freighters, no matter how many missiles or energy weapons were crammed into their hull, were not warships. They'd be easy prey once the warships were gone.

They won't have a better opportunity to kill my ships, he thought. Prey were dangerously unpredictable when they saw danger; some would move fast, hoping to defeat the danger before it could grow stronger, others merely retreated to safety. *I have to offer them the chance to take my ships out before they form a defensive formation.*

He glanced at the timer, baring his teeth. Whatever else happened, the prey were in for a very nasty surprise.

"THE ENEMY FLEET has begun to assume defensive formation," Brown reported. "They're launching probes towards us."

Hoshiko frowned. "Are they powering up their FTL drives?"

"I think so," Brown said. His voice was doubtful. "It's impossible to be sure, Captain. Their drives are heavily shielded."

"I see," Hoshiko said.

She cursed under her breath. Two squadrons of enemy battleships were a worthwhile target by anyone's standards, not least because they were scattered rather than concentrated into a single formation. She *knew* she should follow in the footsteps of her ancestors - both sides of her family - and strike them before they had a chance to escape. She'd only have to face them again, perhaps in a far larger and deadlier formation. And yet...the more she looked at it, the less sense it *made*. Something was definitely very wrong.

Task Forces 2.1 through 2.5 cannot handle an enemy defensive formation, she thought, grimly. By now, the Druavroks would have a good idea of just how capable her missiles were...and reprogrammed their point defence systems to cope with them. A hundred freighters firing missiles *might* be enough to smash the enemy formation before it could escape - or it might not. *But if I order the rest of the fleet forward, we may spring a trap.*

She studied the display. Humanity's probes, active or passive, were among the most capable in the known galaxy. There was *nothing* between her fleet and the enemy ships, apart from dozens of pieces of debris from the first set of battles for the system. And her probes had taken a look at the debris and concluded it was harmless. There was nothing lying in wait for her…

"Captain," Brown said. "The enemy fleet is definitely powering up its FTL drives."

"Understood," Hoshiko said. *That* changed matters. The enemy fleet had to be smashed before it had a chance to escape - or summon reinforcements. "General signal to the fleet, Lieutenant. The battle line will advance to engage the enemy."

"Aye, Captain," Brown said.

— —

"WARLORD, THE PREY are advancing forward," the sensor officer reported.

"Excellent," Warlord Joist said.

His mouth lolled open in silent amusement. By any reasonable standard, three *thousand* ships bearing down on his fleet was anything *but* excellent, yet it made the prey overconfident and worked in his favour. Powering up the FTL drives and keeping them on standby, despite the wear and tear on the drives themselves, had proven to be enough to lure the humans forward.

"Continue assembling the formation," he ordered. The humans wanted to back him against the planet's defences and he would oblige them, for as long as it suited him. "Launch an additional set of long-range probes, then bring up *all* of our targeting sensors and sweep the enemy fleet."

The sensor officer offered no objection, even though it was generally regarded as a tactical misstep. Passive sensors were silent, utterly undetectable, but active sensors could be located by the enemy…often before the active sensors detected the prey themselves. The humans could isolate and track each and every one of his ships, just by their own emissions. They'd find it a great deal easier to target their missiles now…

But you won't have a chance to fire, he told himself, sternly. He didn't understand why the humans, let alone the other prey, were coming to the defence of the weak, but he could take advantage of it. *And even if you do, you'll risk the entire planet when you start firing missiles towards a gravity well.*

— —

"The enemy ships are bringing up targeting sensors, Commander," Biscoe reported. "They are trying to locate our ships."

Griffin stroked his chin in growing concern. The Druavroks were acting uncharacteristically…and that worried him. Were they panicking? Were they torn between the impulse to stand their ground and fight, despite knowing it would mean certain death, and the unfortunate necessity of a tactical retreat? Given what he'd read about them in the reports, he wouldn't have cared to be an enemy officer proposing to refuse battle. He'd probably have his throat slit by his superiors or be assassinated by his juniors.

He glanced down at the sensor feed and swore under his breath. There was nothing. The enemy didn't have anything, apart from a hundred ships in orbit that seemed torn between a futile last stand and a withdrawal from the field of battle. It made no sense to him at all. If *he'd* been in their place, he would have lifted the siege and abandoned the system without a fight. Losing eighteen battleships for nothing would weaken the enemy quite badly.

Which is why the Captain is trying to bring them to battle, he thought. *And, on the face of it, she's right.*

"Continue monitoring the situation," he ordered, finally. It was a useless order and he knew it, but he had to say *something*. The sense that something was badly wrong was growing worse, far worse. "And standby to launch additional probes."

— —

"WARLORD, THE PREY are in position," the sensor officer reported.

"Send the signal," Warlord Joist ordered. The timing wasn't *quite* perfect, but only the gods had ever been *perfect*. All that mattered was that the prey were in the kill box, ready for the slaughter. "And then stand ready to repel attack."

"COMMANDER," BISCOE REPORTED. "I'm picking up..."

Griffin swore as the display lit up with red icons, *behind* the Grand Fleet. Hundreds of icons, spearheaded by seventy battleships and fifty-six battlecruisers. The Druavroks had laid a trap and the Grand Fleet had blundered right into it. He stared in horror, unable to quite comprehend what he was seeing. They'd *known* the system was empty, save for the fleet laying siege to the planet. How the hell had the Druavroks managed to sneak a fleet into the system without being detected?

And they have enough firepower to kick our ass, he thought, numbly. *The Grand Alliance is about to die.*

THIRTY-ONE

The Alliance for the Preservation of the United States has posted an 'enemies list' on the datanet, listing over twenty thousand politicians, newspaper writers, liberal statesmen and other opinion-shapers for crimes against the United States. All of the named 'enemies' have been ordered to report to Texas for internment, pending deportation. A bounty has been placed on the heads of any 'enemies' who refuse to enter the holding camps.
-Solar News Network, Year 54

For a long moment, Hoshiko could only stare in horror.

The Druavroks had trapped her fleet with a precision she could only admire, combined with a willingness to sacrifice their own people that chilled her to the bone. If the timing had been messed up - and it wasn't *perfect* - she could have obliterated eighteen battleships before the second fleet slammed into her rear. As it was, she was caught between two fires…

…And the time for correcting matters was short, *very* short.

They sneaked a fleet into the system without alerting us, she thought, numbly. *How the hell did they do it?*

A dozen ideas flashed through her mind. The Druavroks had been the local enforcers for the Tokomak and they could have been given a secret weapon. But if there had been a way to travel at FTL speeds without radiating betraying emissions, she thought, the Tokomak would have used it themselves at the Battle of Earth. There was no reason to share it with the Druavroks when it could have proved a decisive advantage…

Understanding clicked. *The freighters*, she thought. *Every freighter that entered this system was towing a battleship under cloak. They released the ties as soon as they dropped out of FTL and hid, well away from the planet. And we didn't have the slightest idea they were there until it was far too late.*

She pushed the thought aside as she studied the display, considering her options at lightning speed. The Grand Fleet could hurt the enemy badly - she hadn't expended her missiles on the first enemy force - but they'd trap her against the planet and tear the fleet apart, piece by piece. No, a straight-up missile duel wasn't in the cards. She needed to extract her fleet from the trap and reconsider, not fight when the enemy held most of the advantages. But there were options…slowly, an idea took shape in her head. It would be costly, immensely so, yet she saw no other way to preserve the Grand Alliance.

"Order the fleet to alter course," she ordered. All hope of raising the siege had to be abandoned, now the second enemy fleet had arrived. "I'm designating a vector now."

"Aye, Captain," Brown said.

"Any ships that kept their FTL drives stepped down are to bring them online," Hoshiko added, grimly. Jumping the fleet out would be easy, but the Druavroks would simply give chase, running down her warships before they could put enough distance between themselves and their pursuers to make pursuit impossible. "All missile-armed freighters are to prepare to fire their missiles in a single barrage."

She sucked in her breath. "Deploy additional probes," she added. "I want every last enemy ship localised."

The Druavroks weren't hesitating now, she noted grimly, as the fleet altered course slowly, far too slowly. They were closing in relentlessly, their targeting sensors sweeping space and locking onto her hulls, firing off probes of their own. They'd have no trouble picking out her warships, she suspected, and simply overloading their point defence by smothering them with missiles. No doubt they'd copied the tactic from her own attacks on enemy fortifications.

This is a reverse, she told herself, coldly. *But we will be back*.

"Signal to Commander Rogers," she said, looking up. His face appeared in front of her, seconds later. "Commander, on my mark, I will be passing tactical control of every non-Solarian ship in the fleet to you. Your orders are to designate a RV point, then jump out as soon as possible and scatter the fleet in all directions to prevent pursuit. If I, Commander Wilde or the other captains fail to make it back, return to Amstar, link up with Captain Ryman and do what you see fit."

Commander Rogers looked pale. "Captain...what about *you*?"

"If I don't make contact, promote yourself to squadron commander," Hoshiko ordered. She didn't bother to point out that if *all* of her captains were dead, there wouldn't *be* a squadron any longer. "At that point, you will be in command of the Grand Fleet."

She closed the channel without bothering to wait for a response. The Druavroks were closing in, their weapons locking onto the warship hulls. Somehow, she wasn't surprised they weren't bothering to target the freighters. They'd *definitely* learned a few things from the earlier encounters, not least the simple fact that the freighters were defenceless - and harmless - once they fired off their missiles. It would be far more effective to target the warships.

"Commander, the squadron is going to show them *precisely* why the Tokomak were so scared to tangle with human warships," she said, keying her console. "I want a full barrage of missiles, ECM drones, gravity mines - the kitchen sink - and then I want the squadron to turn and charge the enemy formation. Let them see our challenge."

There was a long pause. "Understood, Captain," Commander Wilde said. "Enemy ships will enter firing range in ninety-seven seconds."

"We open fire as soon as they enter range," Hoshiko ordered. If nothing else, the barrage would do a great deal of damage. "And then rotate ships and *charge*."

She closed the connection and looked at Max Kratzok. The reporter looked pale. He wasn't a *complete* ignorant when it came to reading the display, after all; he'd *know* just how badly they were in trouble. And charging the enemy formation, even behind a barrage of missiles, gave only slim odds of survival. It was quite possible she and her entire squadron were about to die heroically, covering the retreat.

At least we won't be abandoning the Grand Alliance, she thought, as the timer ticked down to firing range. *They'll watch us die to save alien lives.*

GRIFFIN WAS HONESTLY unsure if Hoshiko was completely brilliant, absolutely insane or some combination of the two. *Charging* the enemy fleet was madness, yet it was the only way to salvage as much as they could from the looming disaster. They had blundered - he had to admit *he* hadn't seen the looming trap either, before it had sprung closed - and now the only way out was to fight. And yet, all of his fears had finally come true. The squadron was facing destruction at the hands of a vastly superior foe.

If we survive, he told himself, *something will have to be done. But not now.*

"Prime all weapons," he ordered. Closing to knife-range, they'd have to put the weapons on automatic or hundreds of tempting opportunities to take a shot would be missed. He cursed - again - the lack of an AI. "Ready everything we have to engage the enemy."

"Aye, Commander," Biscoe said.

"Don't let us fly a predictable flight path for a second," Griffin added. "Pretend you're flying an assault shuttle, because we're heading straight into the teeth of enemy fire. We do *not* want to take a hit."

"Aye, Commander," Lieutenant Sandy Browne said. "Our flight path will be completely random."

"Enemy ships entering firing range," Biscoe reported. "They're opening fire; I say again, they're opening fire."

The command popped up in the display. "Fire," Griffin ordered. "And then take us right into the heart of their formation."

— —

WARLORD JOIST ALLOWED his teeth to show openly as he admired the display, silently congratulating the Great Lords on their plan. The prey were already losing their admirable discipline, turning away from the planet instead of taking the opportunity to obliterate his force before they were obliterated in turn themselves. There was no hope of escape, even if they jumped into FTL. The secondary fleet had enough smaller ships to hunt down the enemy warships and bring them to battle before they had a chance to escape. It would scatter the fleet, but it couldn't be helped. *And* it would be worthwhile.

"The prey have opened fire, targeting the secondary fleet," the sensor officer reported, as the display lit up with a solid mass of red icons advancing towards their targets. "They have fired…they have fired over fifteen *thousand* missiles."

Impressive, Warlord Joist thought. It was a one-shot weapon, it had to be, but even a *single* colossal wall of missiles being launched into space was terrifying. *If they could do that several times in a row, they might win the battle outright.*

"It also shows their weaknesses," he said. "Target their warships and open fire."

— —

"THE ENEMY SHIPS have opened fire," Brown reported. "Their missiles appear to be targeted on our warships."

"As expected," Hoshiko noted. "Rotate ships, then charge!"

She braced herself as the starship altered course, following the wave of missiles she'd launched towards the enemy ships. The decoys and ECM drones would make it harder, far harder, for the enemy to pick out the real ships, although she had no illusions just how long they would remain effective as they closed with the enemy. Hopefully, the Druavroks would be too busy trying to swat as many of the missiles out of space as they could to notice what she was doing.

"Commander Rogers, I hereby transfer command of the remaining ships to you," she said, as the first missiles started to slam into their targets. "You have your orders. Good luck."

She blanked the console, then watched the display as the enemy ships grew closer. She'd reprogrammed the missiles, trying to disable as many enemy ships as possible rather than destroying them, but it was a fiendishly imprecise targeting matrix. An enemy battleship exploded into a ball of fire, another was saved - barely - by an enemy cruiser taking the missile that would have wiped the battleship out of existence. Dozens of other starships fell out of formation, some leaking air into the icy darkness of space, but others were still advancing forward, belching a second salvo of missiles. They *knew* she didn't have a second mammoth salvo in her.

Just surprise, she thought. *And the very best of human tech.*

"Go to rapid fire, then fire at will," she ordered. "I say again, fire at will."

Perhaps it was her imagination, but the Druavroks seemed to flinch as her squadron bore down on them. Charging right into the teeth of enemy fire was suicide, yet *they* had been quite happy to do it in the past. They hadn't thought to expect such behaviour from other races, Hoshiko thought, as the squadron opened fire, spitting out antimatter missiles, phaser bursts and leaving a trail of mines in their wake. Her ships ducked and dodged like shuttles making an opposed landing, forcing the Druavroks to fire wildly in hopes of scoring a hit, their weapons raking holes in the enemy formation. And yet, somehow, they survived...

"*Harrington* has taken heavy damage," Brown reported. "She's out of control!"

Hoshiko had barely a second to switch her display to the stricken cruiser before *Harrington* slammed right *into* an enemy battleship, blowing both ships into vapour. By any reasonable standard, it was a worthwhile trade, but for her it was disastrous. One-ninth of her most advanced ships - along with an irreplaceable crew - was now gone. Even if Sol dispatched reinforcements when they received her first set of messages, it would be at least eight months before anything arrived...

Fisher rocked, violently. "Enemy ships are targeting us," Brown added. "They're hitting us with phasers and particle cannons."

Hoshiko stopped herself - barely - from barking orders. She wasn't on the bridge; she wasn't in command of the ship, even now. It wasn't her place to issue orders to her crew. But she wanted to...

"Pass the word," she ordered, as *Fisher* rocked again. "Continue firing."

"EVASIVE ACTION," GRIFFIN snapped. An enemy gunner, sharper than most, had drawn a bead on the cruiser and was proving incredibly difficult to escape. "Launch decoy drones!"

"Drones away," Biscoe reported. The shaking stopped, long enough for the cruiser to evade another spread of phaser fire. "Enemy targeting locked onto the drones."

"Keep us on an evasive course," Griffin ordered. It wouldn't take the enemy long to realise they'd been tricked, not when their weapons were just burning *though* the images on their display. "Continue firing!"

"Two enemy battlecruisers altering course to block our escape," Biscoe said. "Their formation is coming apart."

"Target them both with antimatter missiles," Griffin said. Thankfully, they were at dangerously short range. He could fire the missiles on sprint mode, knowing the enemy would have bare seconds to retarget their point defence before it was too late. "Fire!"

"Missiles away," Biscoe reported. "Enemy ships are opening fire..."

"Taking evasive action," the helmsman snapped. "They're lousy shots."

"As you were," Griffin said. One of the battlecruisers disintegrated into a fireball; the other fell out of formation, bleeding plasma into space. "Keep firing..."

"Commander, *Jellicoe* is gone," Biscoe said. "She just collided with another enemy battleship."

Griffin winced in pain. Captain Sonja Farrakhan - *Jellicoe's* commanding officer - had been an old flame, back since they'd both served together on *Titan*. The affair had run its course, as shipboard affairs tended to do, when they'd been promoted and assigned to separate vessels, but they'd parted as friends. Hell, she'd been one of the few he could talk to about his doubts, even if they'd been too busy to sit down and have a proper chat. And now she was gone, lost along with her entire ship.

The Captain's war, he thought, bitterly. Another enemy battleship loomed up in front of them, blasting away madly as it tried to score a direct hit. *This war is going to cost us dearly*.

"Continue firing," he ordered. There would be time to mourn the dead later, assuming they survived. "And keep us in line with the rest of the squadron."

"Gravity mines are detonating," Biscoe reported. "The remainder of the fleet is escaping into FTL."

"THE FLEET IS making its escape, Captain," Brown reported. "I highly doubt the enemy can track them."

Hoshiko nodded as the starship shook again, worse this time. She glanced at the status display - a rear shield was weakening, after being hit several times in quick succession - and then put her fears out of her mind. The Grand Fleet was making its escape and, thanks to the gravity bombs, the Druavroks didn't have a hope of being able to run down *any* of the ships while the waves of distortion were spreading through space. Their ambush had been a nasty surprise, and it would be a blow to morale, but it hadn't proved fatal.

"Take us out of their formation as soon as the last ship is gone, then jump us into FTL," she ordered, praying silently that none of her ships had lost their drives. They *were* tough, but *anything* could be disabled or destroyed if it was hammered hard enough. "There's nothing to gain by staying here."

"Aye, Captain," Brown said. "The last ship has jumped out - *now*."

Hoshiko sucked in her breath as the squadron raced through the remainder of the enemy formation, firing off its final missiles as it fled, then jumped into FTL. The Druavroks *might* give chase, but after she'd hammered the enemy fleet so badly it was rather more likely they'd pause to lick their wounds and celebrate their victory. And it *was* a victory, no matter how much she would prefer to deny it. They'd defeated the Grand Fleet, taken out two irreplaceable ships and forced her to run.

"Stand down from red alert," she ordered, once she was reasonably sure the enemy weren't trying to give chase anyway. "I want a tactical analysis as soon as possible."

"Aye, Captain," Brown said. "It will take some time to compile the data - longer, if you want to include data from the rest of the fleet."

"Just concentrate on our data," Hoshiko ordered. "I..."

She frowned as a message popped up in front of her from Commander Wilde, asking for a meeting in her cabin. Rising, she sent back a quick acknowledgement and strode out of the hatch, feeling sweat trickling down her back. She needed a shower, sleep and a fuck, perhaps not in that order, but only the shower would be forthcoming. There was no time to sleep until she knew just how badly the squadron had been pounded. *And* she was reluctant to draw a sexbot out of general supplies just for her own pleasure.

"Captain," Commander Wilde said. He looked...oddly reluctant to enter her cabin. "I need to talk to you."

"Very well," Hoshiko said, feeling her eyes narrow in suspicion. It was unlike Wilde to demand a meeting, particularly just after a battle when they both had a great deal of work to do. "What is it?"

"I'm formally requesting permission to call a Captain's Board," Wilde said. "This matter has gone *far* beyond the intent of our orders."

Hoshiko stared at him, feeling a tidal wave of numb shock mixed with betrayal. He was her XO! How could he betray her? But if he felt that calling a Captain's Board to judge her conduct was the only choice, it was his right - his duty - to call one.

"Very well," she said, fighting to keep her voice level. She'd known Wilde had doubts, but she hadn't expected him to move to actively opposing her. "We'll hold the board as soon as we return to Amstar."

"We can hold it now," Wilde said. "According to regulations..."

"I'm familiar with the regulations," Hoshiko said, coldly. She glanced at her wristcom, then back at him. "We'll hold the board in seven hours. That will give us time to shower, sleep and make repairs."

"Agreed," Wilde said. He looked as if he wanted to say something else, perhaps a pointless apology, but thought better of it. "I'll see you in the conference room."

THIRTY-TWO

Sit-down protesters in Oklahoma were violently dispersed by federal troops as they blocked the interstate leading towards Texas. The Governor of Oklahoma has called out the National Guard and publicly declared that he will not tolerate further federal bullying of his state's inhabitants.
-Solar News Network, Year 54

Griffin Wilde couldn't help feeling like a betrayer.

He understood - he understood perfectly - why Captain Stuart had wanted to intervene. They were under orders to protect humans, after all, and a genocide was something that should be stopped on moral grounds alone. But the mission had blossomed out of control, becoming a multi-racial crusade against an alien race that might pose a clear and present threat to the Solar Union itself...and a promise to the Grand Alliance that the rest of humanity might not be willing or able to keep. Hoshiko had stepped far beyond the limits of her orders.

Because no one ever expected us to be drawn into local politics, he thought, as he stepped into the conference room. *And that was a mistake all along.*

He took a breath as the hatch closed behind him. Hoshiko was sitting at the other end of the chamber, but the other commanding officers were represented by hologram. No doubt they, like Griffin, had spent the last two hours reviewing the regulations covering their current situation - and, perhaps, fretting over how their participation would be seen by Fleet Command. A full Captain's Board had only been called twice in the last fifty years - and one of them had ended with the participants charged with mutiny. It was quite possible, Griffin knew, that *he'd* wind up charged with mutiny himself.

I knew the risks when I made the call, he reminded himself, firmly. He sat down and opened his implants to the room's processors, allowing them to confirm his identity. *And if I am sentenced to death, I will accept it as the price for making the wrong call.*

"Captain Macpherson will assume control of the discussion," Hoshiko said, flatly. Her voice was so atonal that Griffin was *sure* she was using her implants to keep all emotion out of her tone. "Commander Wilde and myself, of course, will abstain when the time comes for a vote, leaving us with six voters. Captain Macpherson will have the deciding vote if the voters are evenly split. I trust that is acceptable?"

Griffin nodded, along with the other participants. A formal Captain's Board was an awkward affair at the best of times - they were generally only authorised when there was no hope of contacting higher authority within a reasonable space of time - but Hoshiko had put forward the best possible solution. He wasn't sure where Captain Macpherson stood, now two irreplaceable ships had been blown to atoms, yet he *was* the senior commanding officer in the squadron. There was no alternative to putting him in control of the discussion.

"I yield the floor to Captain Macpherson," Hoshiko said.

"Thank you, Captain," Macpherson said. He cleared his throat. "It is my duty to remind all of you that a full recording of this discussion, along with our shipboard and private logs, will be presented before Fleet Command when we return home and, perhaps, used in evidence against us. If any of you wish to record a dissent from the decision to hold a formal meeting, speak now or forever hold your tongue."

Griffin didn't - quite - roll his eyes. Macpherson had always had a turn for the dramatic, but there were limits. The meeting was *serious* - even if the assembled captains voted to shut it down immediately, Fleet Command would review everything anyway - and there was no time for levity. But, at the same time, humour would defuse the tension they were all feeling, now they were committed. Their words and deeds would be studied with a fine-toothed comb when the remainder of the squadron returned home.

"No one has spoken," Macpherson said, after a minute had passed in awkward silence. "We have very little in the way of precedent for these meetings, but I believe Commander Wilde should speak first."

Griffin took a breath. "Thank you, sir," he said. "I will be brief.

"Our mission in this sector was to set up a naval base at Martina, nothing more. It was anticipated that the naval base would eventually turn into a full-fledged outpost, staffed with diplomats and traders who would establish links with the worlds and races within the sector and, ideally, seek out new allies and new civilisations. It was not anticipated - it was *never* anticipated - that we would be drawn into a multiracial war.

"I concede that our orders authorised us to take action to protect and defend human settlements throughout the sector, regardless of their origins. Taking the squadron to Amstar and engaging the Druavroks was justifiable, although there was a considerable element of risk. Doing what we could to ensure that the human settlements across the sector were also protected was, depending on how one looks at it, covered by our orders. That far, no serious objection can be raised.

"But since then, our involvement in local politics has skyrocketed. We have forged an alliance between fifteen different races and over two hundred star systems, an alliance directed against the Druavroks. We have invaded one of their systems, sent raiders deeper into their space to make their lives miserable and attacked their ships wherever we found them. Worse, perhaps, we have unlocked fabbers and shared human technology freely, creating a potential new threat to humanity.

"And now, two of our cruisers are gone, after the enemy set a successful ambush. We *cannot* replace those ships! The Druavroks lost more ships - far more ships - and yet they still hold the advantage in firepower.

"We have gone so far beyond our orders that it is just incomprehensible. We have made promises of alliance to alien races that the Solar Union may not choose to ratify. We have built an alliance that commits us to war against the Druavroks, a war that has already spread out of control. And now that we have taken heavy losses of our own, our ability to support our allies has been sharply limited. The Grand Alliance itself may come apart after we were ambushed and defeated.

"This has gone too far. We need to reconsider our position."

"Thank you, Commander," Macpherson said. "Captain Stuart. The floor is yours."

HOSHIKO TOOK A moment to gather herself before speaking, a trick she'd learned at the Academy. Deliberately or otherwise - and she knew Commander Wilde was an experienced officer - she would be addressing a group whose feelings were running high, after losing over two hundred friends and comrades in an ambush. They would be more than human if, at some level, they didn't blame her for falling into the trap, although none of them had seen it coming either. She mentally saluted Commander Wilde - holding the meeting so quickly after the battle gave him the greatest chance of winning - and then leaned forward, choosing her words with care.

"I will not deny the problems we have with supplying the squadron, let alone the entire fleet," she said. "And I will not deny that losing *Harrington* and *Jellicoe* cuts deep into our deployable firepower, although we *did* inflict considerable damage on their forces and bought the Grand Fleet time to withdraw and scatter. But the fact remains that our involvement in the war against the Druavroks is both legal and moral.

"Our orders, as Commander Wilde notes, authorise us to protect humans wherever we find them. The orders do not draw any distinction between Solarians or the descendents of Earthers, taken from the planet by the Tokomak. Indeed, one of our many tasks when we arrived on station was to attempt to forge links with the local humans, in hopes of turning them into allies or Solarians. Going to the rescue, when human settlements were threatened with being exterminated, turned them into allies.

"But it is not enough to merely drive the Druavroks away from Amstar. That world is not the *only* human settlement in the sector. Nor were the Druavroks likely to leave Amstar in peace, if we pulled out the squadron shortly after liberating the planet. How many problems in history became worse, far worse, because they were allowed to fester? The only hope of winning peace and security for the human settlers in this sector is to take the war to the Druavroks and defeat them. There is *nothing* about them that suggests they would be amenable to a negotiated settlement."

She paused, wishing she could gauge their feelings, then pushed on. "We also have orders to take advantage of any opportunity to set up diplomatic links with as many races and worlds in this sector as we can," she continued. "Liberating Amstar gave us a chance to forge an alliance with some of the most powerful races in the sector, a chance to recruit allies to take the war to the Druavroks. Their interests coincide with ours. They want the Druavroks defeated as much as *we* do. Giving them human technology only strengthens the alliance between us. It is the sign of respect, of equality, that they never received from the Tokomak.

"And it has paid off! They have sent thousands of ships to join our fleet! They have committed vast resources to the cause. They have fought beside us and *died* beside us!

"This war is more than just a crusade against a genocidal race. This war is an *opportunity*, an opportunity to build an alliance that will make the human race far more secure in a very hostile galaxy. How long will it be, I ask you, before the Tokomak return to Sol, with hundreds of thousands of warships and blood in their eye? This is an opportunity we cannot let pass, even if it weren't covered by our orders.

"The enemy have proved themselves more artful than we would have preferred," she admitted. "They made no advances in technology, but they used what they had to make a canny ambush and cost us two cruisers. War is, after all, a democracy - the enemy gets a vote. But we have not lost the war. Our allies are turning out more warships, our fabbers are ringing our worlds in orbital defences and we are priming ourselves for taking the offensive further and further into enemy space.

"Losing *Harrington* and *Jellicoe* was a blow," she concluded. "I mourn their loss as much as any of you. But we are all experienced personnel who understand the facts of life. A conflict - any conflict - risks lives, but we cannot allow the fear of losing our people to stop us. If we choose to abandon the conflict, if we choose to pull our ships back to Martina, the Grand Alliance will come apart, the Druavroks will resume the offensive and humanity's name will be mud throughout the cosmos. We will be the race that abandoned its allies when it got a little bloody nose!

"Commander Wilde would have you believe that this war does not involve us. But it does! It involved us the moment the Druavroks started targeting human settlements on a dozen different worlds. Taking the war to the Druavroks is the only way to end the threat once and for all."

"Thank you, Captain," Macpherson said. "Commander Wilde, do you wish to respond?"

"No, sir," Wilde said.

"Then we will debate the matter," Macpherson said. "Please wait."

The holographic images vanished. Hoshiko looked at where they'd been for a long moment, then activated her implants, calling up the latest set of reports from the engineering crews and skimming them rapidly. *Fisher* had taken a beating - there was no doubt about *that* - but she'd be ready for combat once again by the time they returned to Amstar. That, at least, was a relief. Hoshiko had no doubt the Druavroks would seek to reclaim the initiative as soon as possible, perhaps by launching an immediate attack on Amstar. It was what *she* would have done.

But they'll have to reload their missile tubes before they depart, she thought, morbidly. *And we need to reload too.*

She sighed inwardly, then started considering future operations. She'd have to go back on the offensive herself as quickly as possible, if she could find something she could use to give the Druavroks a nasty surprise. The Grand Alliance would become unstable, she suspected, now the Grand Fleet had met its first real defeat. They'd have to do something to prove that the Druavroks hadn't suddenly become invincible. But then, the Druavroks would probably anticipate that too…

— —

GRIFFIN FELT GUILT gnawing at his soul as he watched Hoshiko meditate, waiting for the Captain's Board to decide her fate. There was no way to avoid the fact that her career would take a major blow, no matter the outcome. Fleet Command knew that her subordinates wouldn't have called for a Captain's Board if they hadn't lost faith in their commanding officer and forced her to submit to their judgement. But it had been necessary…

He scowled to himself. Perhaps it had been a mistake calling the board. And yet, the affairs of a sector six months from Sol were none of their concern. Hoshiko had bent their orders into a pretzel. Forging links with alien races was one thing, but forming a full alliance was quite another. And giving up human technology…

There are hundreds of civilian-grade fabbers in this sector, he thought, sourly. *What does it mean for us if they are all switched to producing war material?*

It wasn't a pleasant thought. Human history showed, time and time again, that the solution to yesterday's problem led directly to *tomorrow's* problem. Griffin was old enough to remember arming insurgents against one enemy, only to have the insurgents become the *next* enemy themselves. Forging a balance of power was incredibly difficult, even without ancient hatreds that had become habit by now. The Grand Alliance might not last past the hour the Druavrok homeworld died in antimatter fire…

He looked up as the holograms snapped back into existence, using his implants to covertly check the time. Thirty-two minutes had passed since Macpherson had called for a private discussion. He'd expected longer, somehow. But then, the *real* question was just how far their actions could be justified, under the orders they'd been given.

"We have discussed the matter," Macpherson said. "It took longer than I had expected to come to a decision."

Get on with it," Griffin thought, feeling the tension rise in the chamber. *Please*.

"We voted, four to two, that the mission was justifiable under our orders," Macpherson said, carefully. "Captain-Commodore Stuart remains in command of the squadron."

Griffin kept his face impassive with an effort. Six voters...there had been no need, then, for Macpherson to cast the deciding vote. *He* would get to keep his opinion to himself. The records would be sealed until the squadron returned to Sol, where Fleet Command would go over the entire discussion before assigning blame. God knew which way *they'd* jump when they had the advantage of hindsight.

"Thank you," Hoshiko said, coolly. There was a very definite hint of relief in her voice. If she'd lost the vote, her career would have been beyond salvaging. "The squadron will continue to Amstar, whereupon we will make preparations to take the offensive again as soon as possible. Until then, see to the repairs. We'll hold a formal remembrance ceremony for the dead the day before we drop out of FTL."

Griffin watched, grimly, as the holograms vanished, leaving him alone with an understandably unhappy commanding officer. She had every right, if she wished, to relieve him of duty - or put him on a courier boat and dispatch him to Sol. The trust they'd shared had been broken the moment he'd called for the board. And his career was probably in ruins too.

"Commander," Hoshiko said.

"Captain," Griffin said. He was damned if he were grovelling to her. "Congratulations on your victory."

"I'm sorry you felt the need to call for a formal Captain's Board," Hoshiko said. Her voice was icy cold. "I would like you to assume command of the defences of Martina, Commander. The system is becoming more important to us - and to the Grand Alliance - as both an economic chokepoint and a production node. Defending it against all comers is an important job."

But one that removes me from the chain of command, Griffin thought. On paper, it wasn't much of a punishment; in reality, it was a slap across the face. Maybe it wasn't quite an assignment to a remote asteroid mining station, but it might as well be. *And it lets her still make use of me.*

"Understood, Captain," he said.

"I will be forwarding a formal report, along with the sealed recordings, to Fleet Command," Hoshiko added. "They will, I suspect, call us both on the carpet. Until then..."

She shrugged. "You'll be relieved of duty once we reach Amstar," she added. "Until then, I want you to continue supervising the repairs. We need to be in fighting trim by the time we reach the planet."

"Because the Druavroks might have launched a counterattack," Griffin said. He was surprised he hadn't been told to stay in his cabin until the time came for him to leave the ship, but the Captain *was* short on experienced personnel. "Amstar is heavily defended, but they might be willing to soak up the losses needed to take it."

"Correct," Hoshiko agreed. She shook her head. "The force that mounted a successful ambush, Commander, was clearly more devious than any of the other forces we faced. Who knows what we'll face in the future?"

THIRTY-THREE

Oklahoma became the fifth state to join the Alliance for the Preservation of the United States after the National Guard was attacked by federal troops. Reports from the ground state that the situation is confused, with the federal troops unsure if they should be holding their current positions - despite sniper fire - or withdrawing to safer territory.

-Solar News Network, Year 54

"It's not quite as bad as you might have feared," Captain Ryman said.

"That's a relief," Hoshiko said. The squadron had exited FTL at red alert, all weapons and shields ready for war, only to discover that the predicted attack on Amstar hadn't materialised. They'd entered orbit, allowing her to teleport down to the Grand Alliance's rapidly-expanding headquarters. "Just how bad *is* it?"

"There was some panic at first," Captain Ryman assured her. "But when the council had a good chance to review the records, Captain, they realised just what a powerful and capable ally you were. Putting your own ships at risk to save countless alien vessels made a very good impression on them. They wouldn't have blamed you for ordering the fleet to scatter without fighting a rearguard action."

"I would have blamed myself," Hoshiko said. "I couldn't have just fled for my life."

"It probably saved the alliance," Captain Ryman said. "And it certainly saved the Grand Fleet."

Hoshiko nodded. "I'm going to have to go back on the offensive as soon as possible," she said. "Is the Tokomak ship ready for deployment?"

"As ready as she will ever be," Captain Ryman said. "She really needs a proper refit before we can take her into combat, but..."

"It won't matter," Hoshiko said, cutting him off. "I only want her to carry as many missiles as we can cram onto her hull."

"It shouldn't take more than a week to make any changes," Captain Ryman said. "What do you plan to do with her?"

"The Druavroks worship the Tokomak," Hoshiko said. "I dare say a Tokomak ship, with Tokomak codes, has an excellent chance of sneaking through their defences and opening fire at point-blank range. Even if she doesn't...at least we'll give them a fright."

"Understood," Captain Ryman said. "It will be a suicide mission, Captain."

"I know," Hoshiko said. "We could use a courier boat again, if we can't fly the ship remotely. I think we'll just have to work on the ship and see what becomes practicable."

She sighed. Losing Commander Wilde was going to hurt, even though she couldn't avoid doing *something* to make her displeasure known. If he'd come to her privately...but she wouldn't have changed her mind, no matter what he'd said. Calling the Captain's Board had been his only reasonable option and it had failed. And that failure had come with a cost.

"I've been gathering intelligence over the last couple of weeks," Captain Ryman said. "My officers have prepared a full briefing, but it looks very much as though the Druavroks are readying a force to attack deeper into our space. They may well intend to target Amstar itself."

"I'm surprised they haven't already tried," Hoshiko said. "The longer they leave Amstar alone, the stronger our defences become."

"They may fear the consequences of even a *successful* attack," Captain Ryman said. "It will cost them dearly if they try to plunge though our defences."

Hoshiko nodded. The argument had been rehashed time and time again during her strategy sessions - and deflected, perhaps, with the observation that the Druavroks were not human and might not be bound by human - or Tokomak - logic. They *had* managed to set a quite successful ambush, after all. Clearly, there was more to their conduct than mindless rage and hatred of everything different from themselves.

"Or they're planning to hit elsewhere," she mused. "Where could they go?"

"There's at least seven possible targets within two weeks of flight," Captain Ryman said. "A successful attack on even one of them would cost us dearly, all the more so if they don't land on the planet and just bombard it from space."

"I'll read the full report later," Hoshiko said. Her wristcom bleeped. "One moment."

She keyed the wristcom, then raised it to her mouth. "Stuart."

"Captain," Biscoe said. "*Rustbucket* has just returned to the system. Her commander reports a successful mission."

"Good," Hoshiko said. The small patrol boat would be nothing more than an easy target, if all hell broke loose, but she had her uses elsewhere. "Inform her commanding officer that I wish to see him as soon as he is within teleport range."

"Aye, Captain," Biscoe said.

Hoshiko scowled inwardly as she made her goodbyes to Captain Ryman - declining his offer of lunch or a chance to press the flesh with some of their alien allies - and teleported back to the ship. Losing Griffin was *definitely* going to hurt. Biscoe didn't have the experience to command *Fisher* himself, which meant she had to split the task of commanding the Grand Fleet *and* commanding the cruiser. It was why Admirals normally came with huge staffs of their own, even in the Solar Union. They were meant to be *separate* from the commanding officers of their ships.

But it couldn't be helped, she told herself bitterly. *There was no choice.*

— —

"WELCOME BACK, ENSIGN," Captain Stuart said, as Thomas stepped into her office. "I read your report."

"Thank you, Captain," Thomas said, nervously. He'd expected to meet Commander Wilde, not his ultimate superior. "We took out an alien fabber."

"I also read your report on the decision you made concerning the alien miners," Captain Stuart said. "You do realise they may have been tortured and killed by their own people?"

"Yes, Captain," Thomas said. He *still* wasn't sure if he'd made the right call or not. "I didn't want to kill innocent beings."

"I understand your position," Captain Stuart said, curtly. "However, you *were* under orders to do everything in your power to disrupt the Druavroks. Or was I mistaken when I wrote your orders?"

Thomas swallowed. "I believe the asteroid miners would not have made much difference," he said, finally. He wanted to argue, but he knew it could end badly. "It would not be hard for them to replace the miners, if they didn't just tow an asteroid into orbit and start breaking it down for raw materials there."

"The hell of it is that you will probably never know," Captain Stuart said. She looked down at her desk for a long moment. "Would losing the miners have ensured that the Druavroks lost the war? Or would it just have been a pinprick they'd barely notice?"

She looked up at him. "What do *you* think?"

"I think it would have been a pinprick," Thomas said. "Killing the miners would not have made much difference, certainly nothing on the same scale as destroying a fabber."

"Probably not, no," the Captain agreed. "But you will *never* know."

She leaned back in her command chair. "Is *Rustbucket* ready to depart?"

"She just needs a replacement missile," Thomas said. "We didn't expend our missiles against an enemy target."

"Your crew can have a day of leave, then ready the ship to depart tomorrow," the Captain said. "I have a specific task for you."

"Aye, Captain," Thomas said.

The Captain keyed a switch, projecting a starchart into the air above the desk. "The Druavroks have been gathering forces here, at Tarsus," she said. "At least ninety battleships, according to the last report; they're well within striking range of a dozen possible targets, including both Amstar and Martina. Your mission is to keep an eye on them and report at once the moment they depart."

"Yes, Captain," Thomas said. "We won't be able to shadow them, though."

"Not without being unable to report home," the Captain agreed. "And yes, they *could* change course in midflight. But at least you'll give us *some* warning."

Thomas nodded. *Rustbucket* might be old, but she was fast. If the Druavroks set off for Amstar, there was a very good chance he could out-race them and warn the defenders before the enemy entered long-range detection range. And even if they went somewhere else, there was at least a reasonable chance he could get warning to the Grand Fleet in time to intervene and intercept the enemy before the Druavroks crushed their target.

"Understood, Captain," he said. "My crew will be glad of the leave too."

"They deserve it," the Captain said. She smiled, wryly. "What made you think of sneaking an antimatter warhead through their defences like *that*?"

"I couldn't think of a way to get at the fabber without being blown to atoms," Thomas said, reluctantly. "And then I remembered the freighter we used to approach Malachi."

The Captain's smile grew wider. "Good luck, Ensign," she said. "You were definitely one of the more successful raiders."

Thomas blinked. "How many others have returned?"

"Five, so far," the Captain said. "They all hit freighters or asteroid mining stations. You're the only one who got a fabber."

"But there were nearly a *hundred* ships sent out," Thomas protested.

"Yes," the Captain said. "And, so far, only *six* have returned. Think on that while you're enjoying your leave."

"Aye, Captain," Thomas said.

"I believe the reporter will want to speak to you too," the Captain added. "If you don't want to be interviewed, I suggest you keep out of sight while you're on the planet."

"Yes, Captain," Thomas said.

THE SENSOR RECORDS had been stepped down, Max noted, but he still had more than enough data to put together a comprehensive picture of the running battle that had cost two cruisers and over two hundred human lives. He honestly wasn't sure if the Captain was brave or a complete lunatic, yet he had to admit that her actions had probably saved thousands of ships and hundreds of thousands of lives. The story wasn't *quite* as dramatic as the attack on Malachi or the liberation of Dab-Yam, but it still showcased human ingenuity and determination overcoming treacherous alien ambushes.

But they did manage to ambush us successfully, he thought, remembering the moment the second alien fleet had appeared on the display. *And it would have worked if the Captain hadn't plunged us right into the teeth of their fire.*

It was an odd thought. He'd grown up in a universe where technology was the only thing keeping the human race alive, where a single mistake with a spacesuit could kill someone before they had a chance to realise what had gone wrong. It hadn't taken him and his peers long to understand *why* they had to maintain everything, why they couldn't drop their guard even once. But now, he felt oddly conflicted about remaining on the ship. He'd felt braver when he'd jumped down to Amstar or followed the marines onto the alien fabber.

I suppose I was more in control then, he thought. He was nothing more than a helpless passenger on the ship, even if the ship was far stronger and more durable than even a heavy combat battlesuit. *I could shoot back at the enemy while I was in the suit, if I wanted...*

Max uploaded the completed report to the network, then turned his attention to a list of notes for future reports. Interviews with aliens were inherently less popular in the Solar Union - it was hard to convince watchers and readers that internal alien affairs mattered to Sol - but a set of good interviews would make interesting viewing, particularly if he termed them bonus material. The viewers who wanted more in-depth information would be gratified...he started to key requests for interviews into the command network, only to be interrupted by a message. The Captain wanted to see him.

"I'm on my way," he said, rising. "I'll be there in five minutes."

He shut down his terminal, then walked through the hatch and up to the Captain's cabin, slipping past a number of crewmen working on the ship. *Fisher* hadn't been *badly* damaged, he'd been assured, but the hammering she'd taken had inflicted enough harm to force the crew to spend weeks repairing it. Max had a private suspicion that the damage was worse than he'd been told, although he'd kept that theory to himself. There was no point in adding it to the reports when losing two cruisers was already quite bad enough.

No one would notice the loss of two cruisers back home, he thought. It wasn't *entirely* true, but the Solar Navy operated over two *thousand* heavy cruisers. Hell, they made up the backbone of the fleet! *Here, losing a single cruiser damages our ability to fight.*

The hatch leading into the cabin hissed open when he approached, allowing him to step inside. Captain Stuart was sitting behind her desk, reading yet another report; she looked up, then nodded to the sofa. Max sat down and waited, patiently, until she was finished. He wasn't *quite* sure why the XO had been dispatched to Martina, but reading between the lines of a couple of ambiguous comments, he had a sneaking suspicion that there had been a major clash between them. Why else would Captain Stuart have sent her strong right arm light years from the squadron.

"Max," Captain Stuart said, putting the datapad aside. "I viewed your report. It was as concise and detailed as always."

"Thank you, Captain," Max said. "I try to embed as much data within the reports as possible."

"Thankfully, local morale has not been *too* badly damaged by the bruising encounter," Captain Stuart added. "It would have been worse, I suspect, if they'd lost a great many warships in the fighting, but as it turned out casualties were quite low. However, we still need to retake the offensive as soon as possible."

"Of course, Captain," Max said. "You want to convince the aliens that we're not going to allow the Druavroks to intimidate us."

"More or less," Captain Stuart agreed, with a thin smile. She leaned forward, resting her elbows on the desk. "The Druavroks, I suspect, have started to class us as a more dangerous race than anyone else within the sector, but they don't seem to have learned caution yet. I need to hit them before they start thinking we're not so dangerous after all."

"I'm glad to hear that *your* confidence hasn't been shaken," Max said, truthfully. "I was afraid you might have lost your nerve."

"Bad rolls of the dice are inevitable, to borrow a line from my grandfather," Captain Stuart said. "It's what you make of those rolls - and how you recover from them - that shows what you're made of."

She tapped her fingers together, thoughtfully. "I checked and rechecked the records," she added. "There was no sign of *anything* before the enemy fleet uncloaked, Max; there were no reports of energy disturbances that we overlooked, nothing that might have suggested they were there before the shit hit the fan. The analysts think they actually had their drives stepped down and main power largely deactivated, just to make it harder for us to detect them."

"Brave," Max commented.

"Very brave," Captain Stuart agreed. "If we'd known they were there, Max, we would have slaughtered them before they managed to power up their shields and return fire. A hundred freighters, crammed with single-shot missile launchers, would have *obliterated* a fleet of battleships. They took that risk just to get at us!"

"And they would have succeeded, if you hadn't charged straight into the valley of death," Max pointed out. "You saved the fleet."

"I didn't overlook anything because there was nothing to overlook," Captain Stuart said. "We will take more precautions in future, just to be very sure we don't miss anything, but my nerve has not been harmed."

She smiled. "And you can put that on your next report before we leave the system."

"Aye, Captain," Max said. He smiled. "When are we leaving?"

"Two days from now," Captain Stuart said. "I'm just waiting on a very special ship."

— —

"CAPTAIN," BISCOE SAID. "The crew of the *Vengeance* is reporting that they are ready to depart."

Hoshiko looked up from her command chair. The former Tokomak ship was resting in the centre of the display, surrounded by the remaining seven ships of her squadron. She *was* pretty, Hoshiko had to admit, but her design lacked a certain practicality. A *human* ship of the same size and weight would have *much* more firepower crammed into her hull. She was surprised the Tokomak had rejected modular construction to such an extent, even on one of *their* ships. Repairing the ship had been a pain in the ass.

And if we didn't have a use for her, she thought, *we wouldn't have done anything more than turn her into a suicide-runner.*

"Very good," she said. "Communications, inform the squadron that we will depart in ten minutes, then signal Commander Rogers and inform him that he is now in command of the Grand Fleet."

"Aye, Captain," Lieutenant Bryon Yeller said.

Hoshiko sat back and forced herself to wait. She hadn't admitted it to anyone - with Commander Wilde gone, there was no one she could confide in - but the ambush had rattled her more than she cared to admit. The Druavroks had pulled off a successful ambush and her fleet had come far too close to total destruction. Launching a second mission against the same star system was chancy - she had no idea how many of the enemy ships were still there - but she needed to know she could still win. And the volunteer crew…

She winced, inwardly. Her grandmother had told her the stories, but she'd never quite believed that someone could *volunteer* for certain death. But then, the crew no longer had anything to live for. A chance of revenge was all they wanted.

"Take us out," she ordered, when the timer reached zero. "And fall into pursuit patterns once we're well clear of the star."

THIRTY-FOUR

Oklahoman Police arrested over a thousand individuals for treachery against both the United States and the Alliance for the Preservation of the United States; these individuals include liberals, communists, race-baiters and a number of politicians. The fate of these individuals has yet to be determined, but as a number of them are also on the Texan 'enemies' list it is quite likely that they will be extradited to Texas.
-Solar News Network, Year 54

The humans were clearly *vicious* prey.

Warlord Joist studied the display, feeling a grim sensation of dis-satisfaction. Ambushed, trapped, the humans had turned on their foes and fought like…they'd fought like Druavroks who *knew* there was nothing left for them, but to inflict as much damage as possible before they died like cornered beasts. And it had paid off for them; the main body of their fleet had escaped an inescapable ambush, while their devilishly capable human cruisers had inflicted vast damage during their passage through the ambushing fleet. *And*, to cap it all, they'd managed to escape alive.

The only advantage, as far as he was able to tell, was that the arrival of the ambush fleet had brought enough firepower to complete the conquest of Palsies. His forces had torn through the remaining orbital defences, soaking up losses as they struggled to overcome and destroy them and finally taken control of the high orbitals. This time, there had been no attempt to land troops and come to grips with their foe. The planet's cities had been nuked from orbit and every lone radio transmitter that dared squawk a signal into the void was smashed by a KEW. By the time a settlement fleet was dispatched from the homeworld, the planet would be largely denuded of its formal population and any survivors could be hunted down at leisure.

"Warlord," the sensor operator said. His voice was awed. "There is a ship of the *gods* approaching our system."

Warlord Joist started. If the Tokomak were on the way, he had to prepare a proper reception, a reception fit for the gods themselves. The sense of effortless mastery the Tokomak extruded demanded no less. And yet, a ship of the gods *now*? What did it mean? Had the Tokomak decided to intervene in the war? Or had they come to bless the cleansed world and open it up for settlement?

"Order the fleet to assume a welcoming formation," he said. "We must show full respect to our guests."

The sensor operator looked nervous. "My Lord, there is a flight of human ships in hot pursuit."

"Show me," Warlord Joist ordered. The display changed, showing a golden icon pulsing its way towards the system, followed by seven bright *red* icons. It looked, very much, as though the Tokomak were running to safety. How *dare* the humans chase them? "Order the fleet to assume a defensive position instead. We must cover the Tokomak as soon as they emerge from FTL."

"Understood," the communications officer said.

Warlord Joist barely noticed as he contemplated the implications. The humans attacking the Tokomak? There had been rumours, but all such rumours had to be nothing more than lies spread by weakling prey. What sort of fool would believe a tiny system could actually pose a threat to a race that ruled two-thirds of the galaxy? No, the prey lied to themselves to make themselves feel better about their role, while the predators of the galaxy knew better than to let themselves be deceived.

Let them come, he thought. *We will defend the Tokomak with our dying breath.*

— —

"TWENTY SECONDS TO emergence, Captain," the helmsman said.

"The squadron is in formation," Yeller confirmed. "We'll be following the *Vengeance* as soon as she leaves FTL."

"Make sure it looks like we fucked up," Hoshiko reminded the helmsman. "We don't want to actually *succeed* before the *Vengeance* has a chance to get into position."

She leaned back in her command chair as the final seconds ticked down to zero. The plan was chancy, she had to admit, but everything she'd read about the Druavroks suggested they'd fall for it without hesitation. Their *worship* of the Tokomak bordered on idolatry: it was unlikely, she'd been assured, that the Druavroks would fail to move to protect their former masters. Humans wouldn't have been so accommodating, but then humans wouldn't have been such ruthless servants either.

"Transit complete, Captain," Lieutenant Sandy Browne said. "*Vengeance* dropped out ahead of us."

Hoshiko nodded. The Druavroks had massed a powerful formation - twenty-five battleships - in position to cover the *Vengeance* as she emerged from FTL. They'd done a good job too, she noted; they weren't in *quite* the right position, but it was close enough to ensure she couldn't hope to run the *Vengeance* down before they overwhelmed her with missile fire.

And if I'd been genuinely interested in destroying the Vengeance, she thought, *I'd be really pissed at this moment.*

"Continue on present course," she ordered, as the *Vengeance* continued her passage towards the enemy fleet. "Prepare to bring us about when they open fire."

"Aye, Captain," Browne said.

Her console bleeped. "Captain, this is Henderson in Tracking," a voice said. "The planet has been bombarded."

Hoshiko swore under her breath as she looked at the report. The planet hadn't just been bombarded, it had been devastated. There had been over three hundred large cities on the planet, a handful larger than the largest megacity on Amstar, and now they were gone, blasted into blackened ruins. The Druavroks had nuked every last major settlement on the surface, judging by the pattern, then presumably sent down ground troops to finish the job. She had no idea just how warlike the planet's inhabitants had been, before the Druavroks had begun their offensive, but it was unlikely to matter. Most of them were dead and the remainder would soon join them, unless they knew how to live off the land…

She shuddered. It was a crime, a crime on a scale she couldn't even begin to grasp. There had been three billion sentients on the planet, a number beyond her ability to understand…for the first time in her life, she truly understood why one death was a tragedy and a million was nothing more than a statistic. Countless lives had been wiped out of existence in a single bloody spasm and there would be no one to put names and faces to even a handful of the dead. It was hard, so hard, to feel *anything* for the dead. There would be no Anne Frank on Palsies.

And the largest single asteroid in the Solar Union has a mere ten thousand residents, she thought, numbly. *How do we explain the death of over three billion sentients to our population?*

"The enemy fleet is moving forward to engage us," Biscoe reported. "They're charging weapons."

"Launch probes," Hoshiko ordered. She'd do what she could to ensure the dead were not forgotten, after the war. "I want a full shell of recon birds surrounding the squadron at all times, half of them going active. They are *not* to be allowed to sneak up on us again."

She sucked in her breath as the two fleets converged, the *Vengeance* running ahead and overheating her drives in a desperate attempt to escape. Lighting up the recon drones was *certain* to get them killed - the beancounters would make a fuss about the waste, when she got back home - but she was damned if she was risking a second ambush. The enemy had had plenty of time to set one up, if they wanted.

"The enemy are broadcasting welcoming messages to the *Vengeance*," Yeller said. "It reads very much like dreadful flattery, Captain."

"Oh, *good*," Hoshiko said.

She glanced at the live feed, then rolled her eyes. She'd met too many flatterers in her career, mostly men and women who thought she could ask her relatives to promote them, but none of them had ever literally promised to kiss her ass. The Druavroks, on the other hand, *had* offered to kiss the Tokomak's ass - as well as a number of other humiliating submissions to superior power. No doubt the beating the Tokomak had handed out, when the two races had met for the first time, had been truly epic. Centuries later, the Druavroks *still* hadn't recovered.

They must really have accepted the Tokomaks as gods, she thought. In truth, she'd heard it from the intelligence officers, but she hadn't wanted to believe it. And yet now the conclusion was inescapable. The Druavroks were practically crawling on their bellies before their masters. *We need to get them to think of us in the same way.*

"Open fire as soon as we enter missile range," she ordered. Opening fire at long range only gave the enemy more time to plot intercepts and deploy countermeasures, but for once it didn't really matter. All that mattered was keeping the Druavroks from noticing that the approaching Tokomak ship wasn't replying. "And then break away when they return fire."

"Aye, Captain," Biscoe said.

— —

"The humans are spitting fire," the tactical officer reported. "Their missiles are unusually fast."

"We already knew that," Warlord Joist snarled. He studied the display for a long moment, then relaxed slightly. The humans might have faster missiles than anyone else, at least for the time being, but they'd fired them far too early. "Deploy countermeasures, then return fire."

He licked his teeth as the Tokomak ship approached. He'd greeted them in the standard manner - he was their slave, after all, and so was everyone under him - and they had not replied, which didn't surprise him. He was not so important, after all, that they would rush to greet him. And besides, they *did* have to worry about being caught by the alarmingly-swift human ships.

"The human ships are breaking off," the tactical officer reported. "Their missiles will enter engagement range in twenty seconds."

"Engage them the moment they enter firing range," Warlord Joist ordered, coolly. His computers had had *more* than enough time to calculate how best to take the missiles down before they slammed into his ships. "But remember to cover the Tokomak ship."

"Of course, My Lord," the tactical officer said. "They didn't *fire* on the Tokomak ship."

Warlord Joist froze. Very few races in the galaxy would fire on a Tokomak ship, knowing that defeating one ship wouldn't be anything like enough to defeat the rest of their overwhelmingly powerful navy. And yet, if there was *any* truth in the rumours at all, the humans *had* engaged the Tokomak - and *won*! Maybe they hadn't fired on the incoming ship because the rumours were false, yet they'd definitely chased her into his arms. Their missiles, if fired in a single volley, could have overwhelmed her defences and blown her into atoms…

He stared at the icon on the display, thinking hard. It was a *Tokomak* ship. The humans had chased her, but not killed her…and they *could* have killed her. And that meant…

His mouth was suddenly dry. Obedience to the Tokomak was ingrained into his race, backed by the certain knowledge that only the Tokomak had the power to crush them like bugs. It wasn't *right* to question such a superior race, the only *predator* the Druavroks feared. And yet, if that ship hadn't been destroyed, it suggested the humans had not *wanted* to destroy the ship. And if that were the case…

"Contact the Tokomaks," he ordered. "Tell them…tell them that we need to verify their identity."

The communications officer turned to stare at him, his mouth snapping closed in shock. His crew stared too, unable to believe what they'd just heard. One did *not* question the Tokomak, one merely kowtowed. And yet…their shock snapped him out of his fitful trance, his claws clacking against his perch. Disobedience could not be tolerated. It was almost always the start of mutiny.

"Send the signal," he commanded, holding up his claws. "Tell them we need to verify their identity."

— —

CAPTAIN RUTHVEN BARROWS was privately surprised they'd managed to get so close to the looming battleships, although he had to admit that *he* would have hesitated to fire on a Tokomak ship too. His wife and two of his four daughters, like so many others, had been captured, killed and eaten on Amstar, while his remaining daughters had been very lucky to escape with their lives. He'd volunteered for the mission, *knowing* it was likely to be a suicide mission, because *someone* had to strike back at the Druavroks. The remainder of his family, already on their way to Sol, would be fine.

"Target their ships," he ordered. "And prepare to open fire."

He braced himself, feeling an odd calm overcoming him as the targeting solutions appeared in front of him. All of their active targeting sensors had been removed during the refit - even the Druavroks were likely to suspect something if they *knew* their ships were being targeted - but they weren't necessary. The passive sensors and the live feed from the squadron provided all the targeting data they could possibly require. And at such close range, the Druavroks would have bare seconds to react before the missiles started slamming into their hulls.

"They're demanding our identity, sir," the helmsman said. "No threats, yet…"

"Too late," Ruthven said. The barrage of missiles from the squadron was entering the enemy point defence range, allowing the enemy to open fire. They were distracted. "Fire."

Vengeance shuddered as her hull plates were blown off, followed by the first missiles fired directly towards the enemy ships. The Tokomak, for whatever reason, had covered their hull in a sheath that made it impossible to bolt additional weapons to the ship, but under the circumstances it didn't actually matter. He suspected there wasn't any *real* hope of escaping, once they'd opened fire. The enemy would return fire the second they overcame their shock.

"Missiles tracking their targets," the tactical officer said. "Impact in three…"

Ruthven smirked. "Burn, you bastards!"

"THEY OPENED FIRE on us!"

Warlord Joist had barely a second to react before the first missile slammed into his ship's shields, followed by a dozen more. His electronic servants did what they could, but it was already far too late. The Tokomak ship was spewing out hundreds of missiles, each one blazing forward on sprint mode. By the time they were tracked and a course predicted, they were already striking their targets. *And* the remaining missiles from the human ships were slipping through the sudden chinks in his defences.

"Four battleships have been badly hit," the communications officer reported. He sounded stunned, unable to quite believe what was happening. "The Tokomak ship is opening fire with energy weapons."

"Target her and open fire," Warlord Joist snapped. It was a *Tokomak* ship…but it had clearly been subverted. The humans had captured her and turned her into a weapon…and now she was limping forward with grim determination, clearly hoping to ram one of his ships before it was too late. "Blow her into dust!"

— —

"THEY'RE TARGETING US, sir!"

"I know, son," Ruthven said. It didn't *look* as though they'd have a chance to ram one of the enemy ships, but at least they'd inflicted a great deal of damage. Five battleships had been destroyed and seven more had been crippled. "It was a honour to serve..."

Fifty-seven missiles slammed into *Vengeance* and detonated, blowing the ship into dust.

— —

"THE TOKOMAK SHIP has been destroyed," the sensor officer reported.

"Take us in pursuit of the human ships," Warlord Joist snarled. "Don't let them get away!"

— —

"CAPTAIN," BISCOE REPORTED. "The enemy ships are lumbering after us."

Hoshiko nodded. It was a shame Captain Barrows hadn't lived long enough to ram one of the enemy ships, but his sacrifice had inflicted a great deal of damage on the enemy fleet. She thought, briefly, about sticking around and fighting a long-range missile duel, yet she knew it would probably prove futile. She'd need to close again to inflict any serious damage and that would expose her ships to *their* fire.

And we may even have started a religious war, she thought. *They might start fighting each other now that one of their commanders fired on a Tokomak ship*.

"Drop a gravity bomb, then take us into FTL," she ordered, calmly. "Direct course back to Amstar."

"Aye, Captain," Browne said. The display flickered and died as the ship jumped into FTL and raced away from the enemy ships. "They should be able to track us..."

"They know where we came from," Hoshiko said. She would have been astonished if the Druavroks *didn't* know Amstar was the centre of the Grand Alliance. "Let them give chase, if they wish."

"Aye, Captain," Browne said.

WARLORD JOIST STARED at the empty display. The humans had done it again! They'd tricked him...and now, no ship *dared* let a Tokomak ship close with them without checking the crew's identity first. But that was an offense against a superior race. Anyone who proposed it would be killed out of hand.

The mood in the compartment changed suddenly. He tasted the hostile scent in the air and looked up, baring his claws. His crew were looking at him, their beady eyes conveying a single dark emotion. He had stepped well over the line and now he needed to fight for his command...

He hopped off his perch, lifting his claws as he hissed a challenge in the very old tongue, the one they'd learned before the Tokomak had arrived. If he was lucky, the crew would back down rather than try to charge him. He *was* their superior, after all, and he had seen off a dozen challenges to his position...

The crew charged, hissing their rage and hatred. Warlord Joist killed the communications officer with one blow - the fool had left his neck exposed - but the movement allowed the tactical officer and the helmsman to bury their claws in his skin. He twisted in pain, cuffing the helmsman on the head and sending him to the deck, just before a pair of jaws latched on to his backside and bit, hard. There was a wave of pain...

...And then there was nothing, nothing at all.

THIRTY-FIVE

Federal troops, ordered to invade Oklahoma, mutinied today after their commanding officer was replaced by a political hack. Their new commanding officer has sent messages to both Washington and Austin announcing that his formation is reluctant to take part in the civil war, but is more than happy to serve as a border guard. It is unclear, as yet, if the Alliance for the Preservation of the United States will accept the offer.

-Solar News Network, Year 54

"Well," Griffin commented to himself. "It could be worse."

The Solar Union Naval Base was a modular structure, assembled from components that had been produced at Sol and shipped all the way to Martina. It was surrounded by a handful of automated weapons platforms - now part of a far greater defence network surrounding the planet itself - which were covered by five squadrons of alien warships, all from the Grand Alliance. And he - *he* - was in sole command.

He had no illusions. Captain Stuart's report on the Captain's Board was already making its way to Sol. It was unlikely he'd be allowed to remain in the sector, let alone in command of the naval base, once Fleet Command heard what he'd done. Captain Stuart might not have relieved him of duty, but Fleet Command would take a dim view of the whole affair and demand further punishment.

"Commander," Ensign Tabitha Swan said. She was a pale-skinned young woman, so young it was clear she'd only been out of the Academy a week before she'd been assigned to the naval base. "I have the latest reports from the planetary defence force."

Griffin allowed himself a tight smile. The only *good* news that had come out of the Grand Alliance's defeat was that Martina had finally evolved a workable united planetary defence force. It was going to give them headaches in the years to come - Griffin was old enough to remember NATO before it had collapsed into irrelevance - but for the moment it should be enough to protect their world against any reasonable attack. And, like Amstar, the longer the Druavroks waited to attack, the stronger the defences would become. There were nine fabbers in orbit around Martina and eight of them were steadily churning out new weapons, defences and starship components.

"Good," he said. "Have they finally ironed out the bugs on the frigate design?"

"Yes, Commander," Tabitha said. "They're planning to go into full production within the week."

"Let us hope it is enough," Griffin said. The Grand Alliance would eventually need Martina turning out cruisers and battleships, but the planet had never had a very strong shipbuilding industry, thanks to its disunited government. "And training programs?"

"Proceeding slowly," Tabitha informed him. "We're really needing to train the people to train the people at the moment, sir, and its slow going."

"Same old problem," Griffin said. He turned his attention to the display, where hundreds of industrial nodes hung in orbit around the planet. "Do you think there's any way we can speed the process up?"

"Only by cutting corners, sir," Tabitha said. "We *could* stick with the basics, the same training the Tokomak gave everyone, but they wouldn't be able to handle an unexpected problem."

Griffin nodded, curtly. He hadn't expected Tabitha to come up with anything - the vastly more experienced engineers at Amstar hadn't been able to come up with anything either - but it had been worth a try. Who knew? Maybe a junior officer, lacking the cynicism of her seniors, might be able to come up with something new. But then, Tabitha hadn't been ranked too highly at the Academy. If she had, she would have been assigned to starship duty.

Which is foolish of us, he thought, coldly. *Establishing a network of naval bases will become increasingly important as the years roll on and our influence grows.*

"I'm due to meet with the planetary council in three hours," he said. "Have Lieutenant Hassan come up with a plan for a whole new series of planetary defence exercises. I'll propose them to the council once we meet."

"Aye, Commander," Tabitha said.

She saluted and retreated, leaving Griffin alone with his thoughts - and the near-orbit display. Hundreds of thousands of freighters were moving in and out of the system, passing through the gravity points or dropping into FTL for the long voyage to their destinations. Unless he was *very* wrong, and he rather doubted it, some of them were probably spying for the Druavroks. They *had* to be aware of Martina's significance, particularly now that Captain Stuart had joined the war against them. No, had *galvanised* the war against them. The Druavroks *had* to understand just how important Martina was to their new enemies.

Assuming they can tell the difference between us, he thought, ruefully. The Druavroks seemed to be a united mass, but humans - and many alien races - were split into subgroups, some of which warred against the others. *They may assume we're from another colony world, rather than Sol.*

He shook his head. There was no way to know just how effective an intelligence net the Druavroks had, if they'd even bothered to establish one in the first place. The Tokomak could have told them the importance of gathering intelligence, but would the Druavroks have *listened*? They certainly seemed to hold every other race in absolute contempt, save for their former masters. It wasn't an attitude he understood, but it had worked for them until Captain Stuart joined the war. None of the other Galactics had been able to muster a fleet capable of beating the enemy in open battle.

And now I'm stuck here, he thought.

It wasn't a *bad* exile, as exiles went. There was work to do - vitally *important* work to do - and his conscience wouldn't allow him to slack off, even if he hadn't found it challenging as well as interesting. But, at the same time, he'd been dispatched to the rear, to serve as nothing more than a REMF. The cool contempt held throughout the Solar Navy for staff officers and military bureaucrats - particularly ones who held their posts for longer than a year - made it hard for him to just settle into his new role. And it didn't help that he knew the *rationale* for the contempt. The longer an officer remained away from the sharp end, the less he recalled what was actually *important*.

And it's time to stop feeling sorry for yourself, he told himself firmly, as the intercom bleeped. *You could have been sent back to Earth on a courier boat and you know it.*

He keyed the intercom. "Wilde."

"Commander, two warships have just come through Gravity Point Three," Lieutenant Hassan said. He was three years older than Tabitha, but his promotion had come at the price of a semi-permanent transfer to fixed naval bases. Thankfully, what he lacked in imagination he made up for with a plodding determination to cover all the bases. "They're claiming to be from Tis'll and requesting a meeting with the Grand Alliance's representative."

Griffin checked his implants. Tis'll was a small federation of planets, over ten thousand light years away in normal space. Without the gravity point, communication between Martina and Tis'll - or Sol - would be impossible. As it was, the latest update claimed that Tis'll hadn't expressed any interest in developing relationships with *anyone*.

"Invite them to enter high orbit," he said. He was curious to know what they had to say. "I'll speak to them personally before they are forwarded to Amstar."

"Aye, Commander," Hassan said.

"And check the hospitality records and find out what they can eat," Griffin added. "We may need to host them on the base."

He sighed, inwardly. The newcomers would understand, he was sure, if certain areas were deemed classified, but he doubted he could get away with not giving them a basic tour of the naval base. Maybe they were curious…or maybe they viewed the Grand Alliance as a potential threat, one that would eventually cut their access to Martina and the gravity points.

Or tax them through the nose, he thought, sardonically. *Now the Tokomak are gone, what's to stop the planetary council charging transit fees?*

"They're acknowledging, sir," Hassan said. "They'll be in high orbit in four hours, thirty-seven minutes."

"Good," Griffin said. It was ironic that he would have to make the case for joining the Grand Alliance to a group of aliens when he had his doubts about the whole concept, but there was no choice. "I'll contact the planetary council, then ready myself for the meeting."

"Yes, Commander," Hassan said.

— —

"I THINK WE may have a problem," Lieutenant Octavo said. "Take a look at *that*."

Thomas nodded, reluctantly. It had taken a week of prowling around the Tarsus System before they'd located a convoy they could use as cover to sneak into the system, but once they'd dropped out of FTL they'd been greeted with the sight of over two *hundred* battleships lying in wait, accompanied by over five hundred smaller ships. There was so much firepower gathered in orbit around the star, with nothing to defend, that Thomas *knew* Captain Stuart had been right. The Druavroks were planning an offensive.

And to think they told us that there were only ninety battleships in orbit, he thought, with grim amusement. It wouldn't matter a jot if *Rustbucket* ended up within firing range of ninety battleships or two hundred, but the larger fleet posed a far greater threat. *Someone must have miscounted.*

"Launch four recon probes," he ordered, "but keep them a safe distance from the battleships."

"Aye, sir," Lieutenant Octavo said. He glanced up from his console. "What do you think we can do about *that*?"

"I wish I knew," Thomas said. "We may have to slip out of the system and take word back to Amstar."

But even if they did, he had no idea what - if anything - the Captain could do about it. Two hundred battleships would require the entire Grand Fleet to handle, yet a straight fight in an uninhabited system would play to the enemy's strengths rather than their weaknesses. Could it be that the Druavroks were planning to lure the Grand Fleet into the system for a battle? A fleet of enemy warships, no matter the size, simply could not be ignored. They'd know that as well as their human opponents.

He frowned as more and more data flowed into the sensor arrays. The Druavroks weren't just preparing for an offensive, they were drilling heavily. He watched their ships engaging in mock battles, spitting out fire at imaginary enemies...it was impossible to be certain, but it looked very much as though they'd rigged the simulations to face missiles flying at two or three times the maximum speed. They'd be very well prepared to face human ships, he thought, as their command and control networks slowly revealed themselves. It looked, very much, as though they'd decentralised the whole system.

We taught them a lesson in the last encounter, he thought. *And they've learned from it.*

"I can't peg their command ship, sir," Lieutenant Octavo reported. "They keep swapping IFF codes. If there's a pattern I can't discern it."

Thomas nodded. The Tokomak had pioneered centralised control, with one command ship in charge of the whole network, but the Tokomak hadn't fought a serious war for centuries. Any *human* opponent - any opponent with a little common sense - would try to knock the command network down as quickly as possible and the simplest way to do *that* was to obliterate the command ship. Now, even *identifying* the command ship would prove impossible. The enemy might be smart enough not to place their commanders at the centre of the formation.

Of course, we might blow the command ship away without realising what we'd done, Thomas thought, ruefully. *And if they have redundancies built into their systems, we might not notice before it was far too late.*

"Just gather as much data as you can," he said. Two hundred battleships…where were they going? Amstar was the most logical target, but the defences were already formidable and growing by the day. How many battleships were the Druavroks prepared to throw away? "I think they'll be moving sooner rather than later."

Hours passed slowly, very slowly, as *Rustbucket* probed the edges of the enemy formation, searching for insights into their command network. The Druavroks kept exercising, drilling their ships against a foe with far greater technology than humanity. Thomas wondered, absently, just what it was doing to enemy morale, then dismissed the thought. The Druavroks would be far better prepared for humanity by testing themselves against a far greater, if simulated, enemy.

They'll be used to snagging missiles travelling at half the speed of light, he thought. *And our missiles only fly half so fast.*

"They're deploying more destroyers, sir," Lieutenant Octavo said. "They *may* have caught a sniff of us."

Thomas leaned forward. He'd been sure to keep their distance from the enemy fleet, but the Druavroks could easily have scattered stealthed sensor platforms around the system and *Rustbucket* might have passed too close to one of them without noticing. Even *Tokomak* platforms were almost impossible to detect with passive sensors, not unless the searcher got *very* lucky. But it seemed as though luck was on the wrong side today.

"Pull us back," he ordered, calmly. The enemy ships were settling into a search pattern, but there was something wrong about it. "See if you can predict their flight path…"

He smiled as it struck him. They'd been wrong. The Druavroks weren't searching for his ship, but carrying out a routine patrol of their formation. If they'd detected his ship, their destroyers would have charged towards the point of contact, hoping to overrun him before he brought up his drives and escaped into FTL. Five destroyers, after all, would be more than enough to kill a patrol boat.

"Hold us here," he ordered, tiredly. He'd have to go off watch soon, then use his implants to ensure he got some sleep. Without them, he'd be too nervous to close his eyes and actually allow sleep to overcome him. "Are the destroyers doing anything unusual?"

"They're just carrying out standard active sensor sweeps," Lieutenant Octavo reassured him, after a moment. "I have a solid lock on their hulls."

"For all the good it would do," Thomas said.

He frowned, inwardly. It proved, if nothing else, that the Druavroks weren't concerned about watching eyes. Normally, smaller ships were reluctant to use their active sensors in wartime unless the shit had already hit the fan. It was just too easy for a watching enemy to draw a bead on them from stealth. But then, with two hundred battleships in the system, the Druavroks had good reason to feel safe. Even the entire Grand Fleet might not be enough to win a straight battle.

And they don't have anything to attack or defend here, he thought. *They can just jump into FTL and run if the battle goes against them.*

He passed command to Lieutenant Fraser, then headed to his tiny cabin for a shower and a rest. Nothing had changed by the time he awoke, although long-range sensors reported two more squadrons of enemy battleships entering the system. He took another shower, feeling grimy after sleeping in his shipsuit, then walked back onto the bridge. Lieutenant Octavo joined him a moment later, looking disgustingly rested. Thomas had no idea how he did it.

And the Captain probably mastered the same trick years ago, he thought. It wouldn't be easy to return to being a mere ensign again, not when he'd held command of a courier boat and then a patrol boat. *I don't know how she does it.*

"Sir," Lieutenant Octavo said, once the enemy newcomers had arrived. "They're altering their formation. I think they're readying themselves to depart."

Thomas studied the display, then nodded in agreement. The Druavrok ships didn't have the practiced skill of a human fleet, or the endless perfection of a Tokomak formation, but there was no mistaking their intentions. They were definitely preparing to move. He checked the star chart, hastily calculating possible vectors. They might be intending to simply change course once they were out of detection range - a trick the Solar Union had used a hundred times - but assuming they wanted a least-time course there were still seven possible targets, including both Amstar and Martina.

"Keep us well clear," he ordered, as the enemy completed their formation. It looked as though 'hurry up and wait' was part of their lexicon too. "Give me a tracking coordinate as soon as we have one."

"It won't be reliable, sir," Lieutenant Octavo said. "They could change course…"

"I know," Thomas said. "Just give me what you have…"

He broke off as the enemy dropped into FTL, moving in a surprisingly tight formation. They must have learned it from the Tokomak, he considered, as the computers hastily updated their predictions. There could be no mistake. The Druavroks were heading directly for Martina, loaded for bear.

"Martina, sir," Lieutenant Octavo said. "They'll be entering the system within fourteen days."

Unless they change course, Thomas thought. But Martina made *sense*. Destroying the naval base would be annoying; occupying the gravity points would cut Captain Stuart off from Sol once and for all. *They must know where we come from.*

"Set course for Amstar," he ordered. The Grand Fleet had to be alerted. If the timing worked out, they might *just* reach Martina in time to trap the Druavroks against the planet. "Power up the drive and jump us into FTL as soon as possible."

"Aye, sir," Lieutenant Octavo said.

Thomas let out a long breath. Two hundred battleships was hardly a small force, but the Druavroks had had to call in ships from all over the sector to assemble it. If intelligence was correct, they were scraping the barrel for reinforcements…

…*And if that's true*, he told himself, *the next battle might be the last*.

THIRTY-SIX

The President of the United States, who assumed the position after the coup, has formally rejected the call for a new Constitutional Convention and full and free elections. In a speech before a very tame Congress, the President decried the neo-fascist state government of Texas and insisted that the federal government would take all necessary steps to bring the Texans to heel.

-Solar News Network, Year 54

"That's clever of them," Captain Ryman observed. "Sending that fleet to Martina forces our hand. We *have* to go to Martina…"

Hoshiko shook her head, watching the recordings for the fifth time. If she'd needed proof that the Druavroks were far from idiots - even if they *were* aliens - it was right in front of her, surrounded by glowing icons. The Druavroks might not be able to beat the Grand Fleet, but luring it into a deep-space engagement would give them their best chance at victory. Or, if she was wrong and they had *no* intention of offering battle, they'd detect the Grand Fleet hurrying towards Martina and beat a hasty retreat. There was no time to beat them to the system or do something clever to mask her approach.

"We're not going to Martina," she said, firmly. "That would be playing right into their hands."

She leaned forward, studying the holograms of her commanding officers. Two of them had voted against her, at the Captain's Board, and one had abstained...she wondered, absently, just who had cast the dissenting votes, then shrugged, dismissing the thought. It would all come out, she was sure, when Fleet Command held its inevitable inquiry into the whole affair. Until then, she had to assume they would follow her into the gates of hell, if necessary.

"They have drawn down the forces besieging a dozen worlds to put that fleet together," she said, nodding towards the intelligence reports. Tracking individual starships was tricky, but her intelligence analysts were very motivated. "And they have pulled reinforcements from their original cluster. They wouldn't have done that if they thought the reward wasn't worth the effort."

"Occupying Martina will give them control of the gravity points," Captain Ryman pointed out. "They'll cut you off from Sol."

"And allow them to destroy the base," Captain Macpherson added. "Losing the base and our trained personnel will be costly. The fabbers alone..."

"Yes, it will," Hoshiko agreed, cutting him off. "But Martina isn't the production capital of the sector, while holding the gravity points is a long-term issue. They will drag far more races and trade associations into the war if they try to block the gravity points. And, as for cutting our links to Sol, it *still* takes a year to get a message to Sol and back. We are on our own."

She took a breath. "There are two options here," she warned. "The first is that they are trying to tempt us into a battle on terms favourable to them. They have identified a target they think we must defend, something they took from the Tokomak playbook, and launched a massive force at it. If we engage them, we do so at a gross disadvantage, *despite* our advanced technology.

"The second is that they are planning to alter course - that they have *already* altered course - and head to another target. The Grand Fleet would be running around like a headless chicken while the bastards attack their *true* target - and, after what happened to Palsies, we cannot assume they intend to land ground troops."

She shuddered. The Galactics had grown used to horror, after the Tokomak-enforced peace had started to fall apart, but the near-complete genocide on Palsies had shocked the Grand Alliance. It had taken a great deal of careful diplomacy to talk the council out of ordering an immediate retaliatory strike against a Druavrok world, using stealthed missiles on ballistic trajectories to deliver a few tons of antimatter to the planet's surface. The entire population would have died, either within seconds of the blast or in the weeks to come as their world was rendered uninhabitable.

And if they scorch Martina clean of life, she thought grimly, *it will be impossible to keep the council from ordering the destruction of every enemy world.*

It was technically possible, she knew. The Tokomak had enforced high standards purely because rendering a world uninhabitable was *easy*. Hell, she was marginally surprised the Grand Alliance's members hadn't started retaliating in kind long before she'd become involved in the war, although it hadn't been easy for the different races to see that they had a common foe. *She* had no intention of committing genocide, but she had no idea what she'd do if the council ordered her to do it. If she resigned, the Grand Alliance would either fall apart or go ahead without Solarian involvement.

"But Captain," Captain Ryman said. "We cannot leave Martina to her fate!"

"The planet already has formidable defences - and those defences have a commander who knows how to use them," Hoshiko said. "However, the enemy has given us a window of opportunity I intend to exploit. The Grand Fleet is going to head to Druavrok Prime,"

She smiled, inwardly, at their astonished reactions. Druavrok Prime was the enemy homeworld - its true name was unpronounceable - and heavily defended, the sole Druavrok world to have heavy fixed defences.

They'd preferred to spend their resources on building up their fleet instead, she knew; their lack of attention to their rear was going to cost them dearly, if the war lasted long enough. But now, she had an opportunity to give them a beating they would never forget, a beating that might win the war in one fell swoop.

"We know how the Tokomak beat them," she added. "They attacked their homeworld and smacked them around, casually, until the Druavroks surrendered. Since then, the Druavroks were loyal servants; they never revolted, even when the Tokomak grip on the sector weakened badly. We need to crush them ourselves, crush them as badly as they were crushed by the Tokomak. It's the only way to win."

She allowed her smile to show on her face. "And even if they don't surrender, they have half of their industry orbiting the planet. We can take it out and cripple their ability to support their fleets, then hit two of their other worlds in quick succession. Their aggression is one thing, but without their industry they won't have the weapons or ships to be more than a minor nuisance. Their fleet will wither on the vine without regular supplies from home."

"They presumably have war stocks," Captain Mathewson commented. "They won't collapse into powerlessness at once."

"But those war stocks will run out," Hoshiko countered. "They'll run short of missiles very quickly, Captain, while we harass them across the sector. Their power will be broken once and for all if they refuse to surrender."

Captain Ryman scowled. "The council will want a say in the surrender terms," he said. "And..."

"We have to beat them first," Captain Macpherson snapped. "Captain...this plan is dangerous, very dangerous."

"I'm aware of that," Hoshiko said. Leaving Commander Wilde and his crews to face the enemy alone was risky. If the naval base were to be destroyed, regardless of what happened to the planet itself, she'd be in trouble when she returned home. Her family's enemies would claim she'd sent Commander Wilde to his death as a form of petty revenge. "But we don't have a choice."

She took a breath. "This is it," she insisted. "This is the chance we need to win the war in one fell swoop. I have no intention of missing this opportunity."

"But Martina will be left exposed," Captain Macpherson said.

"The risk has to be taken," Hoshiko said. She was surprised at his attitude. Had he planned to vote against her, only to be foiled when she'd put him in charge of the meeting? But there was no point in worrying about it now. "We'll send courier boats to Martina and every nearby system, warning them of the offensive and asking them to send warships - if they can spare them - to aid in the defence. If my calculations are accurate, we should be able to get some warning out before the fleet enters detection range."

"Barely," Captain Macpherson said.

"Commander Wilde will have at least three hours of warning before the enemy fleet arrives," Hoshiko said. Martina's sensor network might be based on Tokomak technology, but it *was* as elaborate as any other she'd seen in the sector. "He *will* have time to mount a defence."

She looked at Captain Macpherson. "Ready the fleet for departure," she said, firmly. "Recall all the crews on shore leave; inform them that we will be departing within four hours - sooner, if we can complete our preparations. I also want the fleet train to accompany us; we'll designate an RV point somewhere near Druavrok Prime so we can reload our missile tubes, if necessary. If the enemy refuses to surrender, we'll take the offensive right into their rear and start smashing their industrial nodes, one by one."

"Understood," Captain Macpherson said. He might have his doubts, but he knew his duty - and, presumably, that she wouldn't hesitate to relieve him of command if he tried any form of passive resistance. "I'll see to it at once."

Hoshiko nodded. "Captain Ryman, inform the council that we're going to be taking advantage of this opportunity," she added. "And that this could be the final mission of the war."

"Of course, Captain," Captain Ryman said. "Although, if you don't mind, I won't make *too* many promises. We need to crush the bastards first."

"True," Hoshiko agreed. She smiled as she looked from face to face. "We've come a long way since we first heard of the attempted genocide. Now, if everything works as planned, we have a chance to end the threat once and for all - and, in doing so, prove to the galaxy that humans are worthy allies. Dismissed!"

She rose as the holograms blinked out of existence, then made her way to her cabin. The steward was already waiting, holding a mug of coffee in one hand. Hoshiko nodded her thanks, took the mug and sat down on the sofa, keying her console to replay the sensor logs from *Rustbucket* once again. Ensign Howard had done a *very* good job.

And even if we're wrong about their destination, we still have a chance to stab a knife into their heart, she thought, as she clicked through to the star chart. *If worst comes to worst, we can beat a retreat from their homeworld, laying down covering fire as we go.*

She pushed the morbid thought aside as she tapped the console again. "Record," she ordered, curtly. "Commander Wilde. Sensor records from *Rustbucket* - details attached - have confirmed that the vast majority of the enemy's remaining mobile firepower is heading in your direction. Unless the enemy change course while in transit, they will reach your command in ten days. You must prepare at once for a major offensive.

"This opens an opportunity for the remainder of the fleet," she added, after a moment. For a moment, she found herself lost for words. What did one *say* to an officer one was abandoning to face a terrifyingly powerful threat? "The Grand Fleet will not be heading for Martina, but for Druavrok Prime. This may be our one chance to win the war outright."

She took a breath. "You are authorised to do whatever you feel is necessary to protect your command and defend Martina," she concluded. There was no point in trying to micromanage, not at such a distance. "I have sent messages to nearby star systems requesting support for your command, but I have no idea what you'll receive - if anything.

"For what it's worth, I'm sorry for leaving you in such an exposed position. I had no idea the enemy would gamble everything on a single attack aimed at you. Good luck."

It felt pathetic, somehow. She knew the risks - they *all* knew the risks - and yet she might have sent him to his death. Her grandfather would have known what to say, she was sure, but she didn't have the slightest idea what she could say to soften the blow. She'd chosen to risk leaving him to face the oncoming storm alone, while taking the fleet to strike a mortal blow at the enemy. Cold logic told her she should take advantage of the opportunity, that smashing the Druavroks was worth the loss of Martina, but she *liked* Commander Wilde.

"Send the message," she ordered. There would be time to make it up to him later, after the war was over. No doubt there would be plenty of time while Fleet Command argued over what should be done. "And attach copies of all the sensor records too."

— —

"I THOUGHT YOU'D be in Marine Country," Max said, as Hilde joined him in the observation blister. "Don't you have things to do?"

"There's very little for us to do now," Hilde said. The hatch closed beside her with an audible hiss, then locked. "The major intends to have us exercising constantly once we're on the move, but until then all we can really do is stay out of the way."

"Like me," Max said. The fleet was preparing to depart and he'd been told, in no uncertain terms, to keep his head down. Going to the observation blister had been a gamble, but he'd been going crazy in his cabin. "Don't they have a use for you?"

"Not at the moment," Hilde said. She smiled, rather dryly. "There's a joke in the corps, Max, about what happens to us marines when we're not needed. They put us in a stasis box, with a big sign telling people to break the glass in case of emergency. Right now, some of us would probably be better in stasis."

Max lifted an eyebrow. "I thought you would be spearheading an attack on the alien world...?"

"Apparently not," Hilde said. "If the Druavroks refuse to surrender, the Captain intends to smash their defences, spaceports and suchlike from orbit, then withdraw from the system. It doesn't call for anything from us."

"Oh," Max said. "Does that bother you?"

"I understand the practicalities," Hilde said. "But, at the same time, landing on an alien world...it would be one hell of a challenge."

Max nodded. The Druavrok homeworld, according to the files, was heavily defended, with orbital battlestations, ground-based planetary defence centres and a population ready to die to defend their world. If landing on Amstar had been bad, with mass attacks by enemy soldiers, landing on their homeworld was bound to be worse. And, with a sullen and unfriendly population, securing the planet was likely to be a nightmare. It would cost the Grand Alliance hundreds of thousands, perhaps millions, of lives...

And yet Hilde was right. It *would* be one hell of a challenge.

"It would be a costly one," he pointed out. "And really, what do we gain by landing a force on their homeworld?"

"That's the question," Hilde admitted. "If we wanted to exterminate them, we could just nuke the world from orbit."

Max felt sick. He'd had to put together a report on what the Druavroks had done to Palsies, making it clear that *no one* had provoked the Druavroks into committing mass genocide. No doubt, *someone* would try to argue that the Grand Alliance had pushed the Druavroks into doing something they wouldn't have done normally, but it wouldn't get very far in the Solar Union, where hard common sense was drilled into children from their very first day. The Galactics, on the other hand, might wonder just who was truly to blame. They knew the humans had been the first race to truly stand up to the Tokomak.

"Or just mine orbital space with self-replicating mines," he said. "They can remain trapped on the planet's surface indefinitely, once we take out their spaceports and defences."

"I know," Hilde said. She gave him an odd little smile. "But it would have been glorious."

"Not for the people on the surface," Max pointed out.

"We look for the chance to constantly test ourselves against the best the universe has to offer," Hilde said, ignoring him. "It's what we *are*. And yet, we keep asking ourselves if we live up to the standards set by the marines who landed on Iwo Jima, or the paratroopers who marched through Goose Green..."

"You do," Max said. "Really..."

Hilde met his eyes. "How would you know?"

She tapped her chest meaningfully. "I wouldn't be allowed to fight back then," she reminded him. "And not all of the *men* who joined us would be able to match the locals, not without genetic engineering that simply didn't exist..."

"It doesn't matter," Max said. "All that matters is what happens, here and now."

"I suppose," Hilde said. She smirked. "Can I carry you back to the cabin or would you like to walk?"

"Walk," Max said. "Maybe I should run."

"You should," Hilde agreed.

— —

"THE FLEET IS ready to depart," Yeller reported. "All ships are standing by."

"Take us out," Hoshiko ordered.

She sat back in her command chair, keeping her face impassive. The Druavroks would have to be psychic to guess what she had in mind, but they *had* managed to deduce her intention of hitting Palsies and plot a cunning ambush. It was just possible the enemy fleet intended to circle around and reinforce their homeworld's defences…

And if that happens, she told herself firmly, *we cut and run*.

"The fleet has entered FTL," Browne reported. "We're on a direct course for Druavrok Prime."

Hoshiko closed her eyes for a long chilling moment. Three weeks to Druavrok Prime, three weeks back…it would be one and a half months before she had the slightest idea what, if anything, had happened to Martina. And then…

No, she thought, rising. *There is nothing I can do now, but stay the course and pray I'm right*.

THIRTY-SEVEN

A famous news anchor was publicly assassinated in Washington DC, while interviewing the newly-appointed Director of Homeland Security. A message emailed to GNN immediately afterwards stated that Barbara Bosworth was murdered for spouting federal propaganda, rather than doing her duty as a reporter. Bosworth was particularly loathed by certain elements of the population for her treatment of conservative and religious figures…

-Solar News Network, Year 54

"There's a *what* coming in our direction?"

"An enemy fleet," Griffin said. He couldn't help feeling a flicker of sympathy for Lieutenant Hassan, but there was no time for shock. "A very *big* enemy fleet."

"The Grand Fleet has to come," Hassan said. "Sir…"

"The Grand Fleet will not be coming," Griffin said. The hell of it was that Captain Stuart might well be right to take the offensive, rather than come to Martina's rescue. But he still felt betrayed and abandoned. "We will have to fight on the assumption that there will be no reinforcements."

"But sir…"

"*That will do*," Griffin snapped. He took a moment to calm himself. Hassan didn't deserve to have the problem taken out on him. "I want you to order our irreplaceable technical staff onto a freighter, which is to hide in interplanetary space. If the battle goes badly and the system falls, they are to make their way to Amstar, where they will be of some use."

"Aye, sir," Hassan said. "Should we send a message to Sol?"

Griffin snorted. "Telling them *what*?"

He shook his head. "I'll put a ship through the gravity point if we lose the battle," he added, after a moment's thought. Too much depended on just what the Druavroks had in mind, but in their place he would certainly smash the planet's fabbers and orbital installations, even if he didn't land ground troops. "But they may intend to seize and blockade the gravity points themselves, rather than target the planet."

"Yes, sir," Hassan said.

Griffin's wristcom bleeped. "Commander, this is Ensign Swan," a voice said. "Tracking has detected a large fleet approaching on the predicted vector. ETA four hours and counting."

"They made good time," Griffin muttered. He cleared his throat. "Understood, Ensign. Pass the alert to the planetary government, then declare a state of emergency. All defences and warships are to prepare themselves for battle."

He rose to his feet. "I'm on my way," he added. "Lieutenant, you have your orders."

"Yes, sir," Hassan said.

Griffin cursed under his breath as he hurried through bland corridors - the naval base didn't feel lived in, not yet - and into the CIC. The warning from Amstar hadn't come in time to make any real difference, although the courier boat had almost burned out its drives in the desperate race to get there before the fleet. And the news wasn't good...he pushed his worries aside as he stepped into the chamber and looked at the display. A large flight of red icons were slowly crawling towards the system.

"The planetary government has declared a state of emergency," Tabitha said. "They're calling out the militia and putting civilians in bomb shelters."

Which won't be enough if the bastards render the planet uninhabitable, Griffin thought, grimly. *Martina may be about to die, no matter how much effort they spent in building up their defences.*

"Put the command network on full alert, then check the redundancies," he said, out loud. It wouldn't take the Druavroks long to realise that the defences were being controlled by the naval base, not if they'd already determined that the best way to keep Captain Stuart from receiving reinforcements was to block the gravity points. "I want them ready to take over if something happens to us."

"Aye, Commander," Tabitha said. "Our own shields and defences are ready..."

She paused. "Commander, two of the armed freighters just slipped into FTL and vanished!"

"Probably decided they didn't like the odds," Griffin commented. He had fifty-nine warships under his command, but none of them were any larger than a cruiser, while the Druavroks had at least two hundred *battleships* bearing down on them. The freighter crews had to know they were grossly outgunned. "Can you blame them?"

He leaned back in his command chair and waited, as patiently as he could. Reports flooded the system, reports of panic on the surface, reports of the government doing what it could to keep everyone calm, reports of officials insisting that the planet should surrender at once... he couldn't help thinking, when the chips were down, that most aliens were remarkably similar to humans. But then, the dictates of survival never actually changed. A race that didn't put its own interests first was doomed.

"They're still coming," Tabitha said. Her voice quavered. "Commander..."

Griffin frowned, inwardly. "Your first combat action?"

"Yes, sir," Tabitha said.

"It never gets any easier," Griffin said, with the private thought that Tabitha's first combat action was likely to be her last. If he'd been plotting an attack on Martina, he would have hammered the naval base first and disabled the command datanet. "But all you can do is brace yourself and remember your training."

He smiled, inwardly, as the hours slowly ticked down to zero. It never got any easier to go into battle for the first time, no matter the training. Training officers weren't actually *trying* to kill their charges, even during live fire exercises. There was always that thin margin of safety, a margin that no longer existed when the fighting became *real*. And combat wasn't a disease. Repeated exposure didn't make one immune. An experienced spacer could die as easily as a maggot fresh out of the Academy.

"Commander," Tabitha said. "I'm picking up several large forces approaching from several different directions."

"Show me," Griffin ordered.

He leaned forward as a new set of icons - several new sets - appeared on the display, advancing towards the system. He sent a command into the processor and plotted their course backwards to their most likely point of origin. It looked, very much, as though the Grand Alliance was sending help. And that meant the coming battle wasn't hopeless after all.

"I see," he said, out loud. "We need to hold the line, then."

"Yes, sir," Tabitha said.

Griffin leaned back in his command chair as the hours became minutes and the minutes became seconds. The relief forces might not be able to stop the Druavroks individually, but collectively they should be equal or greater to the approaching enemy force. And yet, if the Druavroks detected the relief force, they'd probably turn tail and run. He wouldn't blame them, but it would mean losing the chance to destroy - or cripple - their fleet.

"Order gravity bombs to be deployed as soon as the enemy drops out of FTL," he ordered. It was unlikely they'd be able to detect the relief forces already, but that would change when they finally arrived. "I want their sensors as badly scrambled as possible."

"Aye, sir," Tabitha said. "Twenty seconds to arrival."

"The freighter is standing by," Hassan said, stepping through the hatch. "They're well out of enemy detection range."

"Good," Griffin said. He motioned towards the secondary tactical console. "Take that, then stand at the ready. The enemy are about to appear."

He sucked in his breath as the enemy ships flashed into existence, wrapped in so much ECM that it was hard for his sensors to track and isolate individual ships. The Druavroks had *definitely* been learning, he noted; they'd make it harder for his missiles to lock onto their targets until they were much closer, although human advances in fire control would minimise the effect. He studied the display for a long moment, watching as the enemy fleet shook itself down. They'd managed to improve their operational patterns too.

"Launch a shell of drones," he ordered, coolly. The gravity bombs were already detonating, making it harder for the Druavroks to see the oncoming fleet. "And then stand by to open fire."

There was nothing subtle in the Druavrok advance, he noted, as the enemy closed on the planet's defenders. They were merely moving forward, trapping the defending warships against the planet. He cursed under his breath as the enemy ships launched drones of their own, making sure of their targeting solutions before opening fire. And then the display sparkled with deadly red icons.

"Enemy ships have opened fire, sir," Tabitha said. "They're targeting the warships."

"Order all ships to return fire," Griffin ordered. "And then execute evasive patterns."

He watched, grimly, as his freighters belched missiles, then dropped into FTL and vanished in the direction of the hidden fleet train. If the battle lasted long enough, they'd return with reloads of ammunition... thankfully, the gravity bombs would conceal their escape too. And if the defenders were *really* lucky, the enemy would assume that was all they were *meant* to do.

"Decoys are coming online now," Tabitha reported. "The enemy missiles aren't being diverted."

"They must have solid tactical locks," Hassan said, as the defenders started to spit point defence fire towards the oncoming storm. "The warships are pulling back, but it isn't fast enough."

"They're targeting the ships that deploy point defence," Griffin said. He studied the pattern for a long moment, puzzling over how the trick was done. No one, not even humanity, wasted *that* much effort on developing missile seeker heads. Anything close to true AI would be fantastically expensive. "Launch a second set of drones and sweep them through the enemy missile swarm."

"Aye, sir," Tabitha said.

Griffin watched, grimly, as his warships took a pounding. Their point defence was far better than their opponents, and they had the advantage of human-level command datalink, but the Druavroks had fired far too many missiles into the fray. Twenty-two warships were blown out of space, their defences battered down before the missiles completed their destruction and annihilated them. The remainder stumbled backwards, but the Druavroks kept coming, pushing them back against the planet. Even the loss of a dozen battleships to the swarm of missiles launched by the freighters didn't slow them down.

Of course it won't, he thought, grimly. He'd seen the Druavroks fight too many times to believe they could be deterred by casualties. They were happy to trade hundreds of starships in exchange for crushing their enemies. *Their blood is up by now.*

He glanced at the timer. They had to hold out for at least another hour before the reinforcements started to arrive, but he honestly didn't know if they *had* thirty minutes, let alone another hour. And then new red icons flickered into life on the display.

"Commander," Tabitha said. She sounded shocked. "I'm picking up small craft within the missile swarm."

"They must be feeding the missiles updated targeting information," Griffin said. It was a neat trick, although it wasn't unprecedented. The small craft were barely visible when compared to missiles blazing towards their targets. "Pass the word to the warships, Ensign. Take them out."

"Aye, Commander," Tabitha said.

Griffin forced himself to watch as the Druavroks pressed their offensive. Their fire became a great deal less accurate once the small craft were picked off and destroyed, but as they kept advancing they started to target the facilities in orbit. Griffin cursed, again, as their missiles slammed into some of the orbital defences, although now the orbiting weapons platforms could add their own fire to reinforce the remaining warships. Missile pods, floating in orbit well away from the shipping lanes, went online, launching flocks of missiles towards the enemy targets. For a moment, the Druavroks seemed to hesitate before resuming the offensive and launching a new spread of missiles...

"Commander," Tabitha snapped. "Those missiles are targeted on the planet!"

"Put them at the top of the targeting list," Griffin ordered. The Druavroks didn't seem to be aiming at any cities, which almost certainly meant antimatter warheads. One or two hits would be enough to slaughter most of the planet's population. "Everything else will have to cope on its own."

He gritted his teeth as the enemy belched another barrage of missiles. This time, they were targeting the remaining warships and the orbital defence network, *knowing* that the defences couldn't waste their fire covering themselves. The Druavroks might not be able to understand why he - and the other defenders - were concentrating on saving the planet, but that didn't keep them from trying to take advantage of it. There was nothing he could do about it either; all he could do was watch, helplessly, as his remaining warships died.

"They're targeting us," Tabitha said. "Missiles incoming. I say again, missiles incoming."

"Deploy decoys," Griffin ordered. Thankfully, the last of the planet-bound missiles had been swatted out of space. "And concentrate on hitting their battleships."

"Aye, Commander," Tabitha said.

Griffin watched, grimly, as the flight of missiles closed in on the naval base, the missiles slipping into terminal attack velocity as they approached. There would be no need to make any last minute course alterations, not against a target that couldn't move. But the naval base had heavy-duty shields to make up for its lack of manoeuvrability. Three missiles made it through the point defence to slam into the shields...

The station rocked, violently. "Three direct hits, sir," Hassan reported. "Shields at sixty percent!"

"Another wave of missiles incoming," Tabitha said. Griffin heard a note of panic in her voice and hastily tapped his console, ready to take over from her if necessary. "Point defence is attempting to intercept."

"Take them out, if you can," Griffin said. The Druavroks were hammering the planet's defences hard, even though they'd taken some nasty losses themselves. But they hadn't fired on the fabbers...that had to be a bad sign. They wanted the fabbers for themselves. "And keep firing!"

The station rocked again. Griffin didn't need Hassan to tell him that the shields were badly weakened, that the next barrage would probably be enough to finish them. He wondered, absently, if the Druavroks wanted the base intact, then dismissed the thought. They'd get neither the base nor the fabbers, thanks to him. He'd rigged the latter to blow if the Druavroks gained control of the system. It wouldn't be much of a consolation to the planet's inhabitants, who were very likely doomed, but if the Captain captured their homeworld or tore the guts out of their industry the Druavroks were screwed. The Grand Alliance would exterminate them before they could rebuild.

"They're closing in, Commander," Tabitha said. "I..."

"It's all right," Griffin said. The Druavroks had lost over fifty battleships and seventy more were damaged, including four that he doubted could be repaired economically. They wouldn't recover before it was far too late. "You've done well."

New icons flashed onto the display. "Commander," Hassan said. "Two squadrons of Grand Alliance warships have just arrived!"

"Warn them to combine their forces with the other incoming ships," Griffin snapped. They hadn't drilled for an attack on Martina, let alone organised a command network. "The Druavroks are too powerful for them to handle alone!"

"The Druavroks are altering course," Tabitha said. "They're heading away from the planet."

"More friendly squadrons have just arrived," Hassan said. "They're closing to missile range..."

The Druavroks must have expended most of their missiles, Griffin thought. He keyed the console, trying to run a projection. It was hard to be sure, but Battle Comp thought the Druavroks had expended at least eighty percent of their missiles. *They know they're at a major disadvantage.*

"Alliance ships have opened fire," Hassan reported. "Their missiles are human-grade."

God bless you, Captain, Griffin thought. The Druavroks had prepared for worse, according to the records, but their point defence network had already taken a beating. He was surprised they hadn't decided to beat a hasty retreat. *And if they stay here for more than a few minutes...*

He watched with grim satisfaction as the Grand Alliance ships closed in, firing barrage after barrage of missiles. The answering fire was slack, almost as if the Druavroks were badly stunned by the sudden shift in their fortunes. Maybe they were...they'd been on the verge of taking the system, only to be defeated by the sudden arrival of a whole new fleet. And to see so many races cooperating to put an end to them...it had to be a shock.

"Enemy ships are taking heavy damage," Hassan said. "I think their command network has come apart completely."

Griffin nodded in agreement. Each of the Druavrok ships was fighting its own battle, rather than coordinating with its fellows. It wasn't anything like enough to preserve them from the wave of missiles, each one sniffing out weaknesses in the point defence network and ripping them open to slam against their shields. One by one, the enemy ships died, a handful making their escape into FTL before it was too late. The remainder were systematically destroyed.

"That's the last of their ships, sir," Hassan said. He looked up, smiling coldly. "I think we won."

"I think so too," Griffin said, feeling tired. The battle had been savage, but surprisingly brief; the Grand Alliance, it was clear, had been a success after all. "Contact the fleet, ask them to assume position in high orbit. Then see what we can salvage from the remains of the defences."

"Aye, sir," Hassan said. "Do you want me to bring back the engineers?"

"Yes," Griffin said. He studied the display, taking in the clouds of debris where the planetary defences had been. Thankfully, the fabbers were still intact. "We're going to need them."

And let's hope that the Captain meets with success, he thought. He wanted - he needed - to tell her she'd been right. The Grand Alliance had saved Martina and taken a stand against the Druavroks. *If she does, we might just be able to put an end to this war.*

THIRTY-EIGHT

The killer of Barbara Bosworth appeared in Texas today to claim the reward for assassinating a person on the 'enemies' list. It is too early to tell if the reward will be forthcoming, but it is impossible to deny that the assassination has had a cooling effect on media-government relations. A number of reporters known for parroting the federal line, also mentioned on the list, have taken the opportunity to seek safety in Canada or the Solar Union.

-Solar News Network, Year 54

"We're entering detection range, Captain," Biscoe reported.

"Understood," Hoshiko said. Three weeks in FTL had done nothing to calm her fears, although the die had been cast the moment she'd made the decision to head to Druavrok Prime rather than move to defend Martina. "Bring the fleet to condition one, then standby."

She leaned back in her command chair, pushing her doubts out of her mind. The latest set of reports from her raiders had insisted that Druavrok Prime was heavily defended, although it wasn't clear just how many starships they had to back up the fixed defences. Surely, putting together such a large fleet to hit Martina must have forced them to draw ships from the rear, although there was no way to be sure. Galactic construction rates were far lower than humanity's, but the Druavroks had been in space for longer. They might have built far more battleships than she wanted to believe.

"Ten minutes, Captain," Biscoe said.

"Take us out of FTL at the planned emergence point," Hoshiko ordered. She would have preferred to drop out some distance from the planet, just so she could take a gander at what was waiting for her before it was too late to avoid a confrontation, but it was important to give the impression of inevitability. "And then take us straight towards the planet."

"Aye, Captain," Biscoe said.

Hoshiko nodded to herself, then glanced at the datanet status. The fleet had been reorganised, in the wake of their previous battle; she'd promoted several alien officers and given them command of mixed-race battlegroups. Thankfully, the urgent need to keep the Grand Alliance together had prevented any interracial bickering, although the pessimistic side of her suspected it was just a matter of time. There were old hatreds in the sector that had been in existence long before Christopher Columbus discovered America.

And that's why the Solar Union must not become involved on Earth, she thought, as the final seconds ticked down to zero. *We must look to the future, not to the past.*

She braced herself as the fleet dropped out of FTL and the display began to fill with red icons, hundreds surrounding the planet alone. The raiders hadn't exaggerated, she noted numbly; there were twenty-four battlestations orbiting the planet, protecting forty-seven fabbers and over a hundred smaller industrial nodes. It was odd to see a full-fledged *shipyard* orbiting a planet, but the Druavroks had five Galactic-standard shipbuilding facilities hanging over their homeworld. She couldn't help wondering why they'd taken the risk of allowing so many giant structures in orbit. A single accident could cause a global disaster.

They must be confident they can break up a falling piece of debris, she told herself, as newer icons flashed into existence. *But even that will leave tons of space dust in their atmosphere.*

"Captain," Biscoe said. "The enemy fleet is advancing on our position."

Hoshiko nodded as the enemy icons separated, a third leaving orbit and advancing towards the human ships. It was an impressive fleet, she had to admit; fifty battleships, a hundred smaller warships...and countless freighters, shuttles and other small craft. The latter, she suspected, were planning to ram her ships, rather than fire weapons they might not be carrying. She just hoped the Druavroks hadn't had time to cram antimatter into their hulls before her fleet arrived.

"Deploy the fleet into pattern alpha," she ordered. "And standby to open fire."

She took a breath. "Principle targets are the battleships," she added. "But watch the smaller craft. They're almost certainly kamikazes."

"Aye, Captain," Biscoe said.

"Fire on my command," Hoshiko said.

— —

IT WAS VERY quiet in the Great Hall.

The nine Great Lords of the Druavroks watched the display, silently reeling at the sight before them. Prey did not take the offensive, ever; prey did not seek to hunt down the predators and invade their lair. There were prey that were easy to take and prey that could be dangerous, even to a fully-armed predator, but no prey that actually chased the predator or moved in for the kill. It was impossible. It simply didn't happen, unless...

A sense of unease ran through the hall, carried by scent. One race *had* attacked the Druavroks, one race had invaded their system and hammered them so badly that they had forever lost the title of *prey*. Now, another race had invaded their system...no, *many* races, with many ships. The Great Lords couldn't believe just how badly the timing had worked out. They'd sent a fleet to take Martina and cleanse it of the unworthy prey, only to see a fleet appear in their own skies. How had things gone so badly?

None of them dared speak, yet. None of them dared suggest that perhaps they had been wrong all along, that perhaps the universe was divided into more categories than *predators* and *prey*. But the unspoken thought lingered on the air. The invaders had brought more than enough firepower to smash the orbital defences, claim the high orbitals and rain down fire on the homeworld itself. A chill ran through the room as the implications, still unspoken, danced through their heads. They had imposed the merciless logic of predators and prey on every other race, ever since the gods had departed. What mercy could they expect from prey who had become predators?

"The fleet is about to engage," a voice said. "The prey will be driven from our system."

Silently, the Great Lords hoped the speaker was right.

"THE ENEMY IS opening fire," Biscoe reported. "Their freighters are also launching missiles."

Hoshiko smiled, inwardly. *She'd* turned freighters into warships because there hadn't been any other choice, but she'd known their weaknesses right from the start. The Druavroks wouldn't have done the same unless they too had no choice. They had to have reached the end of the fleet they'd built up over the years. *And*, she noted, they hadn't managed to cram half as many missiles into freighter hulls as *her* crews.

No doubt they would have worked their way through the problem eventually, she thought, grimly. *It isn't quite as difficult as building an FTL generator.*

"Return fire," she ordered. "And then order our freighters to slip back into FTL and head to the RV point for reloading."

She watched, dispassionately, as her ships returned fire, launching a colossal salvo towards the enemy ships. Her tactical crews had pulled out all the stops, up to and including near-AI missile warheads to provide real-time targeting updates. The Druavroks were in for a very nasty surprise, she noted, as her missiles bunched up into assault formation and homed in on their targets. She'd fired enough missiles to smash each battleship twice over, unless...

"The enemy freighters are moving to block our missiles," Biscoe reported. "And their small craft are gunning their engines, advancing on our position."

"Alert the point defence crews," Hoshiko ordered, as the enemy missiles swept down on her fleet. "But their missiles have priority."

"Aye, Captain," Biscoe said.

Hoshiko gritted her teeth as the enemy missiles charged right into the teeth of her formation, despite the best efforts of her crews. Thousands died, but hundreds survived long enough to slam into their targets and detonate. Icons blinked once on the display and vanished, marking the loss of a dozen ships, while others stumbled out of formation, bleeding plasma and atmosphere from gaping wounds. She felt a stab of pain as *Spruance* died, while *Nimitz* took heavy damage...two more cruisers lost in her war. Their crews had deserved better than to die so far from home.

And then the small craft raged down on her formation. They *were* rammers, she realised, as one slammed into an alien battlecruiser. The enemy *hadn't* had time to load the ships with antimatter, she noted in relief, but they still did immense damage as they struck their targets and battered down their shields. The second wave of enemy missiles followed them, poking through holes in her point defence network and completing the destruction of nine more ships. She cursed under her breath as *Nimitz*, already crippled, followed *Spruance* into the netherworld. The only consolation was that some of the crew had managed to get to the lifepods before the cruiser was blown apart.

"They're targeting the second wave on our cruisers, Captain," Biscoe reported.

"Bunch up the point defence ships," Hoshiko ordered. Losing her remaining cruisers would be disastrous, particularly if the Grand Alliance still won the battle. "And continue firing."

She turned her attention to the Druavroks as her second salvo slammed home. The enemy fleet had already taken heavy losses, but the second salvo was lethal. One by one, the remaining enemy battleships were blown out of space with all hands. She silently saluted their bravery as they stood and fought, even though it was a dangerous mistake. They should have fallen back on the planet and linked their point defence into the planet's own defence network.

But that would have had our missiles slamming into their fabbers, she thought. It wasn't beyond the bounds of possibility that the Grand Alliance would lose the battle, yet inflict enough damage on the enemy that their ultimate victory would be assured. *They have good reason to want to keep the battle as far from their homeworld as possible.*

"The enemy fleet has been destroyed," Biscoe said, formally. "They do not appear to have even a *single* wave of small craft left."

"Lock missiles on the battlestations, then launch them on ballistic trajectories," Hoshiko ordered. She'd never have dared to take such liberties against a mobile fleet, but the battlestations couldn't dodge her fire. "Reconfigure the fleet. Any starships that have been disabled are to return to the RV point, if possible; the remainder is to form up and continue the advance."

"Aye, Captain," Biscoe said. "Our original fire groups have been quite badly disrupted."

"We'll just have to muddle through," Hoshiko said, tartly. She understood his concern - she would have preferred to delay matters until she could reorganise her formation properly too - but there was no time. The only way to win was to convince the Druavroks that they were doomed. "Continue firing."

She leaned back in her command chair and watched the missiles as they streamed from her ships. Ballistic trajectories were slow, but they had the great advantage of being undetectable until the missiles went active, allowing her to hit the battlestations from well outside their own range. They *could* launch missiles on ballistic trajectories themselves, if they wished, yet it would be easy for her to avoid them. She ordered the launch of another shell of recon drones, just in case the Druavroks *did* copy her, then settled down to wait. If everything went according to plan, the battlestations would be obliterated long before her fleet entered firing range.

And if that doesn't convince them to surrender, she thought, *we can start hitting their planetary defence centres from orbit.*

THE SCENT OF fear deepened as the enemy missiles started hammering the orbital battlestations, destroying them one by one. Some of the battlestations were attempting to return fire, but they were just spitting into the wind. The Great Lords watched in growing horror as, one by one, the battlestations died, debris scattering in all directions. A handful of chunks even started to fall towards the planetary surface, only to be blown apart by fire from the heavy PDCs. But that, the Great Lords noted, only ensured the enemy would know *precisely* where to target their fire, when they finally entered orbit.

They exchanged glances, each one reluctant to be the first to show any sign of weakness in front of their peers. Every one of them had fought their way to the top, literally; they had killed the previous occupants of their posts as they climbed the ladder to the very highest positions their system had to offer. Even now, they still fought to maintain their position against ambitious subordinates, to remain strong so that their subordinates would find more useful outlets for their talents than trying to overthrow their superiors. The slightest hint of weakness, the slightest suggestion that they might be losing their edge…it would be enough to ensure their death.

"The last of the battlestations has been destroyed," one said. The scent of despair grew stronger. "They are at liberty to destroy our industry, if they wish, or lay waste to our world."

It was a horrifying thought. They had been raised to believe that strength and determination was all that separated them from their rightful *prey*. The concept of a war won by mass production, by crushing the enemy under an endless stream of starships and missiles, was alien to them, even though it was how they'd been brought to heel by the Tokomak. But now, teeth and claws would be insufficient against the new threat, the new masters of the universe. Losing their industry would ensure their certain defeat.

"The people will fight," another said.

"The people will *die*," a third stated, flatly. He was old; the others, privately, suspected it wouldn't be long before he was overthrown and devoured by an eager subordinate. "They cannot stop the enemy from destroying this world."

They shared a long moment of horrified recognition. The Tokomak had crushed them - and, now, the humans were going to do the same. No, it was worse than that. The humans had somehow united over a dozen different races of prey and turned them into predators. No one, not even the Tokomak, had managed *that*. There was no way to avoid recognising that they were staring absolute disaster in the face.

"Then we submit," the third said. "Bare our throats and offer our submission to our new masters."

"The people will be horrified," the second said. It was a mark of his shock that he wasn't calling for a honour duel, even though the mere *suggestion* of surrender called for it. "They will demand our heads!"

"Then they will die," the third said. He waved a clawed hand towards the display, showing the advancing fleet. There was literally nothing in their path until they entered orbit, if they deigned to come close enough to allow the PDCs to target them. "Do you want to see warheads exploding on our worlds again?"

There was a long chilling pause. "Order the defences to stand down," the first said. No one argued with him. "And contact the enemy fleet. Tell them…tell them that we surrender."

"I'M PICKING UP a message from the planet's surface," Yeller said. "I think they're surrendering!"

Hoshiko blinked. "You *think?*"

"It's very...*florid,*" Yeller said. He frowned down at his console. "But yes, I think they're surrendering."

"Thank God," Hoshiko said.

She keyed her console, bringing up the message from the surface. It was *incredibly* flattering; she skimmed through nearly a hundred lines before she was convinced the Druavroks were actually offering to surrender, although their words were so colourful it was impossible to be sure. The offer to bare their throats was understandable, at least, but some of their other phases were difficult to parse. Were they literally offering to castrate themselves for her?

But their eunuchs become passive, she thought, remembering the doctor's dissection of a handful of alien corpses. *They may be offering to metaphorically castrate themselves.*

She looked at the tactical console. "Are they standing down?"

"Yes, Captain," Biscoe said. The display updated rapidly. "They've shut down the remaining defence platforms and deactivated their shields. We could finish the job in minutes, Captain, if we opened fire."

"Hold that thought," Hoshiko said. Tempting as it was, she wanted the industry intact if possible. Human settlers within the sector were going to need it. "Order the marines to secure the remaining orbital facilities. The crews are to be returned to the planet's surface, pending their ultimate disposition. And then..."

She hesitated. Her grandmother had told her stories of *her* grandfather, who'd fought in the Pacific War. Japan had surrendered, in the end, but hundreds of Japanese had vowed to fight on despite orders from the Emperor. It was sheer luck that they hadn't managed to prolong the war. If the Druavroks did the same thing, after offering a formal surrender, she doubted she could keep the Grand Alliance from turning their worlds into radioactive rubble.

"We'll secure the PDCs on the ground, then deal with their other worlds and enclaves," she added. Hopefully, no matter what had happened at Martina, they would surrender without further ado. "Do they want a formal ceremony?"

"Their Great Lords wish to grovel before you, it seems," Yeller said. He paused, studying the latest message from the surface. "I think…their Gal-Standard isn't bad, but some of their words don't translate well."

"We will be happy to hold a ceremony, once the planet is secure," Hoshiko said. She scowled at the thought of going down to the surface, then shook her head. Their Great Lords wouldn't want to grovel before anyone else, even a representative she picked personally. "Tell them I'll be on the ground once the PDCs are secure."

"Aye, Captain," Yeller said.

"And warn the crews not to let down their guard," Hoshiko added. She wanted to laugh in delight at ending the war, but she knew better than to take everything for granted. "This could just be a very deadly trick."

THIRTY-NINE

Texan-led forces from the Alliance for the Preservation of the United States invaded California in support of rural militias that have come under heavy attack from the remains of the state's government. The vast majority of the state's National Guard either melted away or defected, allowing the Alliance to seize key positions without a significant fight. Outside observers, however, have warned of a humanitarian crisis as the drought bites harder in the Californian cities.
-Solar News Network, Year 54

"Here they come," Thomas muttered.

He couldn't help feeling a flicker of fear as the Druavroks walked out of their enclave, their clawed hands held in the air. They looked like tiny dinosaurs, complete with gleaming white teeth and sharp claws; they carried no weapons, but he knew they didn't need them if they charged the small group of humans. And yet, as they approached, they threw their heads back and bared their throat, inviting the humans to cut them open. It was, to them, a very primal gesture of submission.

And if they were human, they'd be on their hands and knees, prostrating themselves before us, he thought, morbidly. It was hard to find any joy in the sight. *They're accepting us as their new masters.*

"They'll be off-world by the end of the day," Captain Ryman said, as the Druavroks walked past the humans and into the freighters waiting for them. "They're no longer welcome on Amstar."

Thomas nodded. Two months had passed since the Battle of Druavrok Prime, since the Druavroks had offered their unconditional surrender. The Grand Alliance had been working hard to clean up the mess since then, rounding up Druavrok forces and repatriating them back to their homeworlds. Very few multiracial worlds were willing to tolerate the Druavroks any longer, even though they *had* submitted. In the end, Thomas thought, a race that had intended to carry out a program of ethnic cleansing had wound up the victim of a very similar problem.

But at least they're not being killed, he thought. *We could have exterminated them from the universe and they know it.*

"I understand you volunteered to remain here," Captain Ryman said. "The Grand Alliance will be pleased to have you, I think."

"It struck me as a career opportunity," Thomas said. He'd been a *Captain*, to all intents and purposes. He didn't want to go back to being a mere ensign. "And the Grand Alliance made a very good offer."

Captain Ryman smiled. "The trick will be keeping it going, now that a dozen races have started to remember why they don't like each other very much," he said. "But I think we can handle it."

Thomas couldn't disagree. Captain Ryman and an ever-growing staff of humans and aliens had worked miracles, hammering out a treaty that bound the sector into a semi-united alliance of worlds. It was less united than the Tokomak Empire, he had to admit, but it was that very looseness that would ensure its success. That, perhaps, and the simple fact that the alliance would treat every intelligent race as an equal, rather than the caste system that had pervaded the Tokomak Empire.

And there's a need for mutual defence when - if - the Tokomak return, he thought. *Or if a new threat appears, now the empire is gone.*

"I'm sure you'll do fine," he said. "And there *will* be a human system within the sector?"

"The first settlers are already on their way," Captain Ryman agreed. "They'll have a dozen fabbers, taken from the Druavroks, to set up their own version of the Solar Union. Given time, and technological advancement, they may even merge with *our* Solar Union when the time comes."

"Yes, sir," Thomas said.

"Enjoy the peace while it lasts," Captain Ryman added. "We'll be starting anti-piracy patrols soon, as well as making contact with other worlds on the edge of the sector. Who knows what we might encounter next?"

"Yes, sir," Thomas said. "But whatever it is, I'm sure we can handle it."

— —

"THEY DESTROYED THEMSELVES," Max said. "They destroyed themselves rather than accept the orders to surrender."

He stood in the middle of a blackened wasteland, all that was left after the Druavrok enclave had used nuclear weapons to destroy itself. His suit blinked up warnings as he looked around, alerting him to high levels of background radiation. It wouldn't be safe, even for an enhanced human, to walk through the remains of the enclave without protection. But the Druavroks were gone.

"They were holding the line against every other race on the planet," Hilde said, from where she was watching him. "It must have terrified them to discover that they had been ordered to surrender, that they had been ordered to submit. They certainly didn't feel as though they'd lost."

Max thought he knew what they'd been feeling, but he didn't *understand*. The Druavroks had laid waste to their own enclave, rather than surrender; they must have known, on some level, that the orders were genuine. But they'd been holding out…they didn't want to just give up, after fighting for so long. They'd blown themselves up as a gesture of spite and defiance towards their own leaders, as well as those they considered to be prey.

"Madness," he said, finally.

"But it could have been worse," Hilde said. "And you know it."

"Yeah," Max agreed. "It could have been."

He closed his eyes in pain. There was no shortage of footage from the war, showing the Druavroks tearing through innocent villages, slaughtering and eating the defenders as casually as humans would eat cattle. And some of those victims had been human. There would be no sympathy for the Druavroks at home, no suggestion that they had been the innocent victims of human aggression. And yet, looking around the blackened ruins, he couldn't help feeling that it had been a terrible waste.

"Come on," Hilde said, gently. "We need to get back to the shuttle before night falls."

Max nodded and turned to follow her as she led the way out of the wasteland, gritting his teeth as more and more warnings flickered up in front of him. The Druavroks, as a final gesture of spite, had designed their nukes to create as much fallout as possible, ensuring that the planet's residents would have to spend years decontaminating the soil and cleaning up the mess. Perhaps their Great Lords would pay the bill, but even if they did it would still be hard to repair the damage they'd done. It was yet another reason, part of his mind noted, why living in space was far superior.

"So tell me," Hilde said. "Are you *really* going to Sparta?"

"Yes," Max said. "If they'll have me, I'll go."

"Good luck," Hilde said. "Just remember what I said about mental toughness."

"I remember," Max said. He'd have to work hard, very hard, to earn a place among the marines, but he was confident he could do it. "And yourself?"

"We're staying here for the moment," Hilde said. "There are other surrenders we have to take, if they actually see sense and surrender. If they don't, we'll have to hunt down and kill the renegades before they trigger off another war. And, after that…"

She sighed. "The Grand Alliance needs training officers for marines and groundpounders, so it looks like we're elected to take the job. It should be something different, if fun."

"I thought you said you didn't *like* training recruits," Max said.

"I don't," Hilde said. "But those are *marine* recruits. Here…we'll be putting units together from recruits from a dozen different races. There will be a whole series of interesting challenges to overcome."

Max had to smile. "You do realise they can't all go to the same toilets?"

"That's going to be one of the challenges," Hilde said. "Integrating the different races is going to be tricky, very tricky."

Max felt a sudden stab of regret. His affair with Hilde wasn't serious - it couldn't be serious, even if he stayed in the sector rather than heading back to Sol. She had her career and he had his…there was no way they could be together forever, even if such love existed outside romantic simulations and VR programs. And yet, part of him almost wished he could stay with her.

"I'll see you again, sometime," he mumbled. "And I'm sure there will be other reporters on their way out here."

"Just in time to miss the ending," Hilde agreed. By their most pessimistic calculations, Sol had received one or more of the original courier boats a month ago. "I guess you'll have fame and fortune once your recordings are widely distributed."

"There are more important things than fame and fortune," Max said. He shook his head in wry amusement. Six months ago, fame had been all-important. "And besides, there will be hundreds of commenters willing to take my recordings and pontificate on the meaning of it all."

He sighed as the shuttle came into view, waiting for them. "You never know," he added, thoughtfully. "You might see me again in a few months."

"Just try not to get killed at Sparta," Hilde warned. "It starts out hard, very hard, and gets harder as you go along."

— —

GRIFFIN ROSE TO his feet as Captain Stuart stepped into his office, looking pensive. He hadn't seen her since he'd left Amstar, although they'd exchanged messages frequently after the Druavroks had finally offered their surrender and submission. Now...he couldn't help feeling oddly nervous at seeing her again. By any reasonable standard, she'd not only won the war, she'd proved her point decisively. If his career wasn't in the crapper already, it sure as hell would be once Fleet Command had a chance to evaluate the outcome.

"Captain," he said.

"Please," the Captain said. "Call me Hoshiko."

"Hoshiko," Griffin said. It felt odd to address his superior by her first name, even in the privacy of his office. "Welcome to Martina."

Hoshiko smiled as she sat on his sofa. "You've done wonders with the place, Griffin."

Griffin nodded. If nothing else, the attack on Martina had spurred the planetary council into investing much more of the planet's GDP into defences, industrial nodes and a shipbuilding industry. Given time, Martina would rival a dozen other worlds in the sector, as well as being strong enough to beat off a fleet of enemy battleships. The disunity that had once kept the planet from becoming a major power in its own right was a thing of the past.

"I thank you," he said, awkwardly. "Would you care for tea? Or coffee?"

"Coffee would be fine," Hoshiko said. She crossed her legs as she leaned backwards. "I owe you an apology, Griffin."

"I owe you one too," Griffin said. "You were right."

"I could easily have been wrong," Hoshiko said. "I made the decision to leave Martina - and you - to its fate while taking the fleet to Druavrok

Prime. I did so knowing- *knowing* - that you would likely be facing the most powerful enemy fleet, a fleet that might well smash the defenders and scorch the entire planet. I knew that and I still made the decision to abandon you."

"It was the right call," Griffin said. "If you'd come here instead, you might well have scared them off and the war would have continued."

"Perhaps," Hoshiko said. "But I still feel bad about it."

"I think that proves you're human," Griffin said, dryly. He understood her feelings, all too well, but she'd been *right.* "You made a call, based on what you knew at the time; hindsight proves it was the *right* call. I don't think anyone will say that of me."

"You had every right to call a Captain's Board if you felt you had no other choice," Hoshiko said. "It was your duty."

"Hindsight will say that I made a dreadful mistake," Griffin said. "That I sacrificed my own career in an attempt to keep you from doing the right thing."

"It doesn't matter," Hoshiko said. "If you hadn't been here, who *knows* what would have happened? I dare say your victory here overrides your… tactical misjudgement."

She sighed. "I made a call back when we met Captain Ryman," she added. "Everything after that grew from that one moment. We needed to find allies, so I built the Grand Alliance, pushing our orders as far as they would go. I don't blame you for thinking that I went too far."

"Everyone else will," Griffin observed.

"Not I," Hoshiko said. She looked down at the deck. "I'm going to have to return to Sol, once the final stages of the mopping up are completed. The Druavroks, thankfully, aren't causing *too* many problems, but the rest of the Grand Alliance…"

"The war was easier to fight," Griffin agreed.

"I'm sure it will all be sorted out in good time," Hoshiko said. She met his eyes. "I'd like to leave you in command of the squadron, once I head home."

Griffin - barely - managed to keep himself from pointing out that the squadron now consisted of five ships, two badly damaged. One of the cruisers would probably have to be scrapped, according to the engineers. The vessel simply couldn't be repaired economically, they'd said; it would be cheaper to build another warship from scratch. But the commanding officer was resisting the demand, claiming that his vessel deserved a chance to fly again.

"I shouldn't have command," he said. "Even if I assume command of *Fisher*, Captain, there are four other captains who will be senior to me."

"I polled them," Hoshiko said. She gave him a smile that made him wish, suddenly, that he was thirty years younger. "They've agreed to accept you as squadron CO."

Griffin blinked in surprise, then sobered. "I doubt I will remain in command for long," he said, quietly. He had to struggle to keep the bitterness from his voice. "It won't be long before Fleet Command receives the dispatches we sent them, Captain. They'll order my relief for attempted mutiny."

"I'm not sure calling a Captain's Board *counts* as mutiny," Hoshiko said. "If anything, it was a perfectly *legal* attempted mutiny."

"That argument won't impress Fleet Command," Griffin said.

"I'm going in person to argue the case," Hoshiko said. "I suspect you'll have at least a year out here, Griffin. Even if they do dispatch reinforcements..."

She shrugged. "The other captains have agreed to accept you as squadron CO," she reminded him. "That's one hell of a vote of confidence."

Griffin scowled. It was...but why? Was it a reward for his defence of Martina or was it a stab at Hoshiko, who'd gambled everything on one roll of the dice? Or was it a tacit agreement to let bygones be bygones? He *had* had two supporters during the Captain's Board, after all.

"Maybe," he said. "And maybe pigs will fly."

"They do, on the moon," Hoshiko said, deadpan. "It will probably take Fleet Command years to decide what they're going to do about the whole situation, anyway. You'll have plenty of time to enjoy being in command."

"Paperwork and diplomacy," Griffin said. "Is there anything to enjoy?"

Hoshiko had to laugh. "Being the person who has to make the call," she said. "It can be enjoyable, if you're right."

"And if you're wrong," Griffin said, "you just have to learn from it."

"True," Hoshiko said. She rose and held out a hand. "I'm planning to stay here for two weeks, but if nothing blows up during the final stages of our operation I'll be taking a courier boat back to Sol. You'll assume command from that moment."

"I understand," Griffin said. He gripped her arm and shook it, firmly. "And thank you, Captain. It's been a honour."

"It's been an adventure," Hoshiko said. "But we did manage to do a great deal of good."

"Sure," Griffin agreed. "And now we get to clear up the mess."

HOSHIKO HAD HALF-HOPED, despite the awareness that she needed to return to Sol, that *something* would crop up and force her to delay her departure. There was no way to escape the fact that Fleet Command might well think she'd exceeded her orders, by forming the Grand Alliance in the first place, waging war on the Druavroks or passing human technology to a dozen different alien races. Hell, the mere introduction of human-style *education* would be enough to upset the *status quo* right across the sector. No matter what she said to Commander Wilde - and the rest of her crew - there was a very good chance she'd be put in front of a court martial board and charged with everything from misappropriation of government resources to outright treason. And if she was found guilty, she'd be marched to an airlock and thrown out into space.

She sighed as she rose from her command chair. "Commander - *Captain* - Wilde," she said. "The bridge is yours."

"Thank you, Captain," Wilde said. He'd been splitting his time, since the squadron had returned to Martina, between the cruiser and the naval base. Thankfully, training programs to provide more human manpower were well underway. "Good luck."

Hoshiko smiled, then turned to look around the bridge. Her crew had all been commended for service above and beyond the call of duty, although sorting out just who deserved what promotion was going to be one hell of a mess. No wonder several dozen officers had volunteered to remain with the Grand Alliance. It offered a faster path to promotion than anything they could reasonably hope to achieve in the Solar Union.

"Thank you, all of you," she said. She knew she'd done great things, but she couldn't have achieved any of them without her crew. They'd *all* pulled together and her report reflected that, although she'd done her best to make sure that any blame fell on her and her alone. "It's been a honour to serve."

And, with that, she strode off the bridge for the last time.

FORTY

A bomb blast destroyed the White House today, killing both the President and his handpicked Vice President. Details are sparse, but it looks like an inside job. So far, neither the remains of the federal government nor the Alliance for the Preservation of the United States have made any comment, but sources within the federal government believe that the government can no longer command the support of the American people or the military.

-Solar News Network, Year 54

Admiral Mongo Stuart watched coldly, very coldly, as Captain Hoshiko Stuart was shown into his office. He had considered himself used to surprise - he still recalled the day they'd captured an alien ship, starting the long path to the Solar Union - but he'd almost had a heart attack when the first reports from Martina reached Sol. They'd leaked too, thanks to that goddamned reporter; they'd only gotten worse as the months wore on. He honestly wasn't sure if he should be giving Hoshiko a medal or signing her death warrant.

And the public loves her, he thought, as she snapped to attention in front of him. *They see her as the second coming of Steve.*

"Stand at ease," he growled. She hadn't *precisely* been arrested, once she'd returned home, but she had been held in custody. He was the first person she'd met for five days. "Just between you and me, Hoshiko, just *what* were you thinking?"

Hoshiko met his eyes with admirable determination. "It's all in my report, Admiral."

"But I am asking *you*," Mongo snapped. "What were you thinking when you committed us to war against an unknown alien race?"

"I was thinking I had to do something to prevent a genocide," Hoshiko said. "My report includes a full analysis of the relevant sections of naval regulations..."

"Yes, you've had ample time to outline your justifications," Mongo said. "Let me see if I've got this straight. You launch an attack on an enemy squadron, then you launch an attack on an enemy world, *then* you attack two more squadrons in quick succession *and* send raiders deep into enemy space. In the meantime, as if that wasn't *quite* enough, you form an alliance with a dozen different races and present them with human technology as a free gift."

"As incentive to join the alliance," Hoshiko said, "and as the key to making them dangerous prey for the Druavroks."

"And then, you allow the enemy to attack your own naval base while taking the remainder of your fleet to the enemy homeworld and forcing them to surrender," Mongo continued. "And *now* you come home to inform us that we have a whole bunch of allies we didn't know we wanted or needed. You may have had permission to forge ties with alien races and worlds, Hoshiko, but an open offer of alliance is *well* beyond the scope of your orders."

"I do not believe what I did is in dispute," Hoshiko said, with the same maddening calmness he recalled from her grandmother. "However, I do believe it was both within the scope of my orders *and* the right thing to do."

"Clearly, we should have been more careful when we *wrote* your orders," Mongo snapped, curtly. "It was not your duty to get us involved in an alien war."

"Sir," Hoshiko said. "Permission to speak freely?"

Mongo nodded, once.

"The Druavroks were attempting genocide on a galactic scale," Hoshiko said. "They were targeting countless worlds, including ones with considerable populations of humans. I had orders to protect human settlements, where possible. The only way to do that, the only way to ensure the threat was removed for good, was to give the enemy a bloody nose. And the only way to do *that* was to form an alliance with other alien powers."

"As you stated in your report," Mongo said.

"It worked, sir," Hoshiko said. "The Druavroks are no longer a threat to the galaxy - and we have a whole alliance of friends."

"Yes, your *Grand Alliance*," Mongo sneered. "Do you expect Congress to ratify your treaty without a fuss?"

"I believe they should," Hoshiko said. "Right now, Admiral, the galaxy is in flux. The Tokomak Empire has been badly weakened, sectors are slipping out of its grasp…there is no longer a single authority forcing everyone to play nice. And *we* are a single solar system with some advanced technology, technology the Galactics will be able to match when they get their heads out of their assholes and start pushing the limits of their own systems. The idea that the Tokomak invented everything, that there is nothing more to invent, has been thoroughly discredited.

"We need allies, sir," she added. "Unless we come up with a superweapon that renders all previous starships completely useless, we're going to be massively outgunned when the Tokomak come at us again. Our manpower base is quite small, even with the AIs and other advances in automaton. The Grand Alliance may be the start of a united political structure to replace the Tokomak and ensure galactic peace."

Mongo lifted his eyebrows. "A United Federation of Planets?"

"Why not?" Hoshiko asked. "Admiral, there's a power void in the galaxy right now. If we don't move to replace the Tokomak, someone else will. And that someone might be one hell of a lot less benevolent than us."

"We can't impose our will on the sector, let alone the galaxy," Mongo said.

"We don't *have* to," Hoshiko said. "Admiral, the Tokomak set up a caste structure that kept everyone firmly in their place. The Grand Alliance, on the other hand, treats everyone as equals right from the start. There were hundreds of worlds applying to join when I left Martina, sir. The Grand Alliance is going to keep growing even if we don't take part."

"And what happens," Mongo asked, "when the problem of interstellar communications kicks in?"

"It won't," Hoshiko said. "The Grand Alliance isn't built to be centralised, Admiral; local authorities will have local authority. I'm not saying it will be perfect, but it will be one hell of an improvement on the Tokomak Empire."

"That's the argument currently being presented online," Mongo noted. "But what we do, regarding the Grand Alliance, isn't quite the same as what we do about you."

"I know, sir," Hoshiko said. She stood a little straighter. "The decision was mine, Admiral, and I take full responsibility."

"Fleet Command ordered a preliminary inquiry to begin as soon as we received the first reports," Mongo said. "It was not easy to determine *just* how to react, particularly once you returned to the system. There was a certain feeling that you pushed your orders about as far as they would go, but as every decision flowed naturally from the previous decision...

"On the other hand, your decisions could easily have caused a major crisis," he added, grimly. "And the next officer who follows the precedent you set could spark off a major war."

"Yes, Admiral," Hoshiko said.

"There's also the fact that you currently enjoy a great deal of public support," Mongo added, darkly. "The story has spread widely and the majority of the public, it seems, believes you did the right thing. Genocide, after all, is never pleasant. And you have a great many alien supporters, who might take it amiss if you were punished for saving their lives.

"It would be a different story, I suspect, if your squadron had been wiped out, but luck is on your side. Accordingly, we have been forced to dismiss all thoughts of putting you in front of a court martial."

Hoshiko relaxed, very slightly. If he hadn't been watching for it, Mongo knew, he wouldn't have seen it. She had to know just how badly it could have gone for her - and her crew - if she *had* been put on trial. As it was, the whole affair of the Captain's Board could be quietly swept under the carpet.

"It has been decided, therefore, that the naval base in the Martina Sector will be expanded and you, Captain Stuart, will be formally appointed as Ambassador to the Grand Alliance," he continued. "We will do our best to honour your commitments to the Grand Alliance, although it may be some time before we either join the alliance or invite our neighbours to join. The closest power blocs may be unwilling to sign up with us."

"They might change their mind, once they see the advantages it brings," Hoshiko said.

"They might," Mongo agreed. He leaned forward. "Off the record, Hoshiko, you do realise just how badly everything could have gone?"

"Yes, sir," Hoshiko said. "But it *didn't* go badly."

"This time, no," Mongo said. "But you took a terrible risk."

He smiled, faintly. "I rather think your grandfather would have approved."

"Thank you, Uncle," Hoshiko said.

Mongo nodded to himself. Whatever else happened, Hoshiko would probably never see command again, not unless she was recalled to the navy. Appointing her as Ambassador would give her the formal right to enter into proper negotiations - and she could have a staff who would keep her from going too far. *And* it would probably soften the blow a little.

"Tell me something," he said, before he dismissed her. "Why do you believe we shouldn't intervene on Earth, Hoshiko, when you intervened quite willingly in Galactic affairs?"

Hoshiko took a moment to compose her reply. "Admiral, we hold a door open for anyone who wants to leave Earth," she said. "They can enter the immigration settlements and remain there, if all they want is safety."

"There were riots there, only last month," Mongo commented. "The marines had to step in to restore peace."

"The point is, people can leave Earth," Hoshiko said. "If they want to stay and suffer, or fight to restore order, that's their choice. We cannot take that choice out of their hands."

"Some would say they don't truly have a choice," Mongo said.

"It isn't *that* long since we slapped Arabia for trying to forbid female emigration," Hoshiko pointed out. "We *enforce* those rules, sir. If someone wants to leave Earth, they can - and if they don't have the drive to leave, better they stay away from us."

She took a breath. "But the Druavroks weren't giving anyone a choice," she added. "As I saw it, the choice was between intervening or allowing them to slaughter billions upon billions of sentient people. And I took the decision to intervene."

"I see," Mongo said. "You do realise I cannot approve?"

"I understand," Hoshiko said.

"Good," Mongo said. "Because you *were* lucky. What you did was perhaps the single most reckless, the single most arrogant, decision taken since the Solar Union was founded. And it could have easily blown up in your face."

"I'm well aware of that, sir," Hoshiko said.

"I'm glad to hear it," Mongo said. "I'll see you again, once we handle the paperwork. And then you'll be on your way back to Martina."

He watched as she snapped off a salute, then turned and walked through the hatch. It hissed closed behind her.

"I always knew you liked her, Steve," he said. Behind him, another hatch opened. "She's very much like you."

"Yes," Steve Stuart agreed, as he stepped into the compartment. "She definitely takes after me."

Mongo smiled. "Setting up a whole new society?"

"Doing what she needs to do to preserve humanity - and sentient life," Steve agreed. "And isn't that what we're sworn to do, anyway?"

The End

AFTERWORD

A few months ago, it was reported that the United States, having expended billions of dollars in Syria, training forces to fight Islamic State, had very little to show for it. Reports I saw varied wildly, with the most extreme suggesting that the United States had no more than *five* loyalist fighters - or, somewhat more believable, that most of the fighters they'd trained had simply defected to Islamic State when they were asked to fight the Islamists, rather than the Syrian Government. Reactions varied too, with accusations that President Obama was secretly collaborating with Islamic State being merged with the suggestion that no Muslim could possibly be trusted to fight Islamists. In short, the entire program was a complete failure.

The United States has rarely enjoyed success in raising local formations to fight America's wars. In Iraq, early attempts to create an Iraqi Army and National Guard produced very limited results. Some units simply disintegrated when they were asked to go into combat, most notably in Fallujah, while others were rapidly infiltrated by religious fundamentalists and became militias. Shia-dominated units, in particular, wound up as nothing more than enforcement arms of Shia politicians, helping to prolong the war. And yet, during the Surge, America enjoyed a wave of success that, alas, was not capitalised on. What was different then?

Consider, if you will, a thought experiment. You are floating in the air over the White House, Washington DC, turning slowly so you can look in all directions. To the north, you have a peaceful ally; to the south, you have a containable problem; to the east and west you have vast oceans, presenting an impassable barrier to anyone wanting to invade the American coastline. You appear to be in a largely invulnerable position. Now, repeat the thought experiment while floating over Paris. All of a sudden, your position looks a great deal less secure; your eastern neighbour is having considerable problems with migrants, your neighbours on the other side of the Mediterranean are dangerously unstable and the EU, which you see as a way to buttress your position, is stumbling and may yet fall. The world looks profoundly different if you look at it from Paris, rather than Washington.

And if that's true of first-world nations, why would it *not* be true of small local factions?

The problem facing the United States - in both the Middle East and Afghanistan - is that the world looks profoundly different to the locals. They do not, for example, have much respect for borders, hence the United States' refusal to chase Taliban fighters over the border to Pakistan merely gives the insurgents useful safe havens. Nor do they agree, always, with the Americans when it comes to pointing at the enemy. The United States may be more concerned with Islamic State than the Syrian Regime, but the local fighters may have different ideas. To them, Islamic State is a potential ally while the Syrian Regime is a deadly threat. And that's why so many fighters defected when asked to fight Islamic State.

But there is a greater problem facing the United States - and anyone who wishes to build up a force of local sepoys. The United States has a nasty reputation as an untrustworthy ally, a force that expects its allies to be willing to commit suicide on its behalf. This tends to create distrust among the locals, who are quite happy to take all they can get from the United States, but less willing to commit themselves. Because the United States has this reputation, the locals are always watching for the moment the United States pulls out and abandons them to their enemies.

The United States manages, somehow, to be a permanent presence in the Middle East while being viewed as a *transient* power, one that will not be present after a certain point.

American politics influence this on both a macro and micro scale. On the micro scale, rules of engagement that hamper American forces, for example, convince the locals that the United States isn't actually sincere when it comes to supporting them. The absurd American insistence that irregulars comport themselves with great decency - a luxury allowed by vast American resources and technological capabilities - makes the locals roll their eyes - and decide, again, that the United States is not serious.

On the macro scale, things are worse. It is impossible to simplify the politics of the Middle East, let alone track how hundreds of different factions might interact. But consider this - the Kurds, not to put too fine a point on it, are the most loyal allies in the Middle East for the United States. However, they (understandably) want independence from the other powers in the region. This alienates them from Turkey, Iraq, Iran and Syria...and gives the United States a major problem when it tries to maintain a balancing act. Unsurprisingly, the United States is simply incapable of *maintaining* the balance, because the Kurds - and their enemies - are at such odds. Thus, even the Kurds watch the United States for signs of betrayal.

The key that made the Surge work was two-fold. First, the United States expanded its operations within Iraq, both moving additional combat troops into the country and settling up smaller patrol bases that made it easier to keep in touch with the local population. Second, the United States deliberately sought out allies among the Iraqi Sunnis (who had been marginalised during the Occupation, which drove them into the hands of AQ) and offered to support them. This forced the Shia to come to terms with the fact that the United States might have had enough of their blatant power grab and attempt to forge a power-sharing agreement with the Sunnis and Kurds. In short, the United States made a major commitment to Iraq's future.

But it didn't last. The United States chose to pull out of Iraq once it looked as though the country was on the way to recovery, thus weakening its commitment *before* Iraq was truly ready to stand on its own. And now the United States is seen, once again, as a betrayer.

Americans have a tendency to think in terms of presidential eras. The Bush Era replaced the Clinton Era, only to be replaced in turn by the Obama Era. But the rest of the world does not see it that way! Stabilising Iraq called for a far longer commitment than was actually made and, in the end, the task was only half-done. Whatever Obama's motivations in abandoning Iraq actually were, they don't matter to the locals. All that matters to them is, once again, that the United States abandoned people who depended on it.

This stands in interesting contrast to Britain's experience in both India and Malaya. Why was the British Empire so successful in raising sepoy troops?

As I see it, there were three major advantages that the United States lacks. First, there was never any *genuine* belief, at least not before 1919, that the British Empire would eventually collapse. The Raj's administrators didn't think of themselves as building and exploiting a temporary edifice; they thought they were building something for the ages. And this attitude was passed on to their subordinates.

This gave the British Empire a major advantage. The bureaucracy they built gave countless natives a stake in the system. They could and did call on thousands of native officials to keep the system running, eventually transferring the system to the natives upon independence. It was that bureaucracy that made the counter-insurgency campaign in Malaya such a success - and it was the *lack* of such a support structure that destroyed British efforts in Iraq.

Second, British officers assigned to sepoy troops were expected to go as close to native as possible. They spoke the language of their men, they understood their concerns and, to a very large extent, shared their lives as much as possible. Indeed, the British Empire was quite happy to make use of native races it had defeated in battle. (Sikhs and Ghurkhas were very welcome in the

Indian Army, allowing them a chance to win honour.) But they didn't have any illusions about their men either. They saw nothing wrong in soldiers taking gruesome trophies from the battlefield, if they wished.

They also had a degree of freedom of action that would be inconceivable to any modern-day American (or British) officer. In the days before the internet, before radio, before telegraph messages, it could take weeks or months to send a message to London and get a response, by which time the problem on the ground could have become a great deal worse. The officers on the spot had vast authority to handle problems, which they often did successfully before London knew what was going on. These days, politicians in Washington (few of whom have any real experience with the military) try to micromanage military operations. Even with the best of intentions, the need to keep the politicians in the loop imposes a time delay, delays that could easily become fatal.

Third, the loyalty of local sepoys was returned. British officers looked after their men who, when they retired, were sure of a pension and a place of honour in their community. (India never hunted for collaborators after independence, unlike many other colonised countries.) This was, intentionally or otherwise, an investment; the British Crown looked after its subjects, so the subjects returned its loyalty.

These days, both America and Britain have shown little loyalty to the incredibly brave men and women who risked everything to serve beside western troops. It was hard, very hard, for an Iraqi or Afghani interpreter to get a visa to emigrate to Britain or America, even though his life was in considerable danger at every moment. The failure to protect one's allies ensured that one would wind up with *few* allies - why should they join you, if you could not protect them?

WITH ALL OF this in mind, how might we move forward?

Truthfully, I have seen nothing in America (or Britain) that suggests the government, Republican or Democrat, is capable of the long-term thinking it needs to solve the growing chaos in the Middle East. The prospect of putting together a force capable of occupying the Middle East, from Tunisia to Pakistan, is a dream (or a nightmare) that will never be realised, certainly not with the current political realities. And yet, with the Middle East collapsing, we need to do something to stem the chaos. Putting together a force composed of local fighters may be the only way to keep Islamic State from growing into a far greater threat.

And yet, doing it may be impossible, because locals see the world differently from outsiders.

There are measures we can take to encourage locals to sign up with us. We can promise immigration rights to people who serve us faithfully, even to the point of taking their wives and children out of the country beforehand. We can provide training that is more suitable to their needs, provide weapons and equipment they can actually use and provide air cover and other measures without worrying about absurd ROE. And we can put officers on the ground with the authority to make whatever calls are necessary without reference to Washington.

And we can try to understand that they may not share our concerns.

But we will still have to overcome the problem of our reputation. Over the years, Washington has betrayed and abandoned too many foreigners who trusted it. (Right now, even America's oldest allies are doubtful of anything that comes out of Obama's mouth.) It would be grossly unwise for a Syrian, all too aware of just what Islamic State will do to his family if he takes up arms against him, to put his faith in the United States.

The problem with counterinsurgency - and nation-building - is that it takes *decades*. And, these days, the West wants everything at once, or it loses interest. And *that*, I suspect, is why so many of our counterinsurgency missions are doomed to fail.

Christopher G. Nuttall
Edinburgh, 2015

If you liked *The Black Sheep, you might like Desert Strike, by Leo Champion.*

It's about to go hot.

On the dry world of Arkin, the Zinj are taking over. A technologically-competent strain of Islam that make ISIS look like the Amish, they're challenged only by the nations of the West – and a divided West without much will to fight.

Among those who do have the will are fighter pilot Egan O'Connor, a working-class kid from a tough neighborhood, ready to test himself and serve his country. He's a chivalrous rookie ready for an honorable battle.

Jimmy Newland's a cavalry NCO who's earned his spurs. He's ready to fight but he doesn't want to; he's seen enough skirmishes to know how bad it can be. But he'll do his job if the cold war gets nastier – as it's about to.

And there's nothing chivalrous at all about Air Marshal Elisabeth Jaeger, a career intelligence officer promoted to field command. Twenty-five years ago she saw her husband murdered by the Zinj; she's spent the time since avenging him. As she's about do on a scale just a little bit broader than spywork…

Free Sample!

Warplanes raced east through the desert night, the Smoking Skulls' A and C Flights under the squadron commander personally.

The radio in O'Connor's earpiece, or at least the general-communications channel of it, was going crazy. From all he could understand, the situation had gone hot theater-wide over the timespan of a few minutes – the Zinj laagers moving out, every last one of them. Planes in the air, launched from the laagers and the towns they'd taken over to the east of what had been called the Brodie Line, although that was really just nine battalion-strength tank concentrations isolated from each other across perceived lines of Zinj laager supply.

Those armor battalions were coming under heavy air attack – Brusil with B and D Flights had been sent to help the nearest of those, 97/2 – as well as ground harassment.

Miners too. The Zinj were going all-out and not every vehicle from every laager was going against the Brodie Line tanks or their resupply convoys. But the civilians weren't anybody's particular problem right now but their own, as the cold war suddenly erupted in a blaze.

"OK," came Commander 'Icefish' Hauraki. "We're going in, as stated, to help out a convoy that left our very own base today. They are under attack from an approximately battalion-strength formation, themselves being company-strength plus what defenses the supply vehicles have. Enemy have since been reinforced with air support, Djinn at a minimum and possibly more."

"So we get shapes," came 'Sauron' Mordar. "Good. Ground scratches were getting boring."

"More than you might be bargaining for, Sauron. Didn't you hear when Jimmy-Jane said the latest intel says Murads could have been placed around here?"

"Met a couple of those this afternoon," said Lieutenant 'Shaker' Jamison, O'Connor's wing lead. "They're not so tough, sir. Cut and run blue-falcons they looked like to me."

"Don't count on these ones being the same. The Murads reported are known Djegouni, and the boys on the ground have seen hourglass flags. Same clan, they won't buddy-fuck each other like your incident earlier."

"Hourglasses schmourglasses," came back Mordar. "We can take them."

THE ZINJ WERE coming, a battalion-sized flood onto the convoy, elements splitting around to block their advance and cut them off. The great cumbersome overland trains were turning but not fast enough; they were hundreds of feet long, vast multi-jointed mechanical caterpillars, and they had not been designed for sharp turns.

"You ready?" Jimmy Newland asked TFC Barocce and the two in back. Red-headed beanpole Corporal Reiss was on the machine-gun. Sub-Corporal Mark Wagner, a short and wiry black-haired man, had a six-cylindered grenade launcher.

"Ready," said Reiss.

"Go," said Wagner.

"Hit it," said Barocce.

There was no time for dismounts. Doctrine said that the other two – in this case, Reiss and Wagner, with Newland taking Reiss' machine-gun position – would normally dismount.

A quick discussion with Lieutenant Ojibwe and Troop Sergeant Miser had had unanimous agreement that this was not going to be an infantry fight. Too many of them, too fluid a situation. This had become a fighting retreat back to Cone Hill and hope *that* place was still intact.

Barocce didn't say anything, just nodded.

"Let's do this thing. Over the dunes *now*, Rock!"

Barocce wheeled the Raider around and they crested the hill—

And the Zinj were close, a jeep no more than thirty yards away, others on its heels. Newland was already looking through the iron sights of his anti-materiel rifle, put a round – the heavy gun *boomed* and the shock wasn't helped by the confined armored space of the Raider – through the Zinj driver, a robed man in goggles. The man slumped, and *oh my fucking fuck I just killed someone* coursed through Newland's mind.

He'd just put a .55 round, designed for destroying engine blocks from a mile away, through a human chest at a hundred feet. He might have hurt someone before in the skirmishes; he definitely had killed a man now.

More explosions came as Wagner burped rounds out from his grenade launcher – fragmentation rounds, they looked like, bursting around the Zinj jeeps and technicals.

No. Zinj aren't people, he thought as Barocce wheeled the Raider back down into the cover of the dune. *Zinj are vermin. You've seen the people they've murdered. Zinj are pond scum.*

More Lancers coming up, meeting the Zinj with some real firepower. Another Zinj jeep crested the ridge – *my ridge*, Newland realized he was thinking of it as – and a second thereafter stopped a rocket, exploding in a blaze of flame.

Barocce took them around for another pass. Zinj, Zinj *everywhere*! Bullets ricocheted across the Raider's armor, glanced across the windshield. Reiss' machine-gun clattered back at them; Wagner's 40mm grenade launcher chugged out a couple of high-explosive rounds.

And coming in behind the Zinj were aircraft. Friendly-to-the-Zinj aircraft, apparently.

Oh fuck.

— —

FLYING OFFICER SECOND-CLASS Mabruk Idris Djegouni bared his teeth hungrily from behind the controls of his Djinn. He flew with eleven other of the dual-engined turboprops, hastily flown into one of the laagers just a few hours ago, refueled and sent into action *nobody* had expected this soon.

Big events were happening, he knew, but not a lot more than that. Everyone had known that the Zinj would eventually go all-out, that the infidel resistance would not remain so pathetic forever, as the Zinj pushed further and closer to the homelands of the Confederated Union and those nations too cowardly to even resist at the miserable level the CU had. But everyone Djegouni had always expected it to take longer; there were higher-level clan politics at work here, stuff it was far above Idris' station in life to think about.

Ahead of him were the vehicles from the cavalry battalion; a sea of them, sixty or seventy, with a few light tanks rumbling in behind them. Ahead of *them*, clearly visible in the star-spackled and double-mooned night, were the Confederated Union vehicles, fighting vehicles outnumbered five or six to one by their attackers.

They were arraying themselves into a swirling skirmish line, moving to block the attack and defend the supply vehicles. Those supply vehicles, three big long overland trains and a bunch of semi-trailers, were turning, but the turning radius of an overland train was something like a mile to do a half-circle. With one company of twenty or so jeeps moving in to cut off their retreat...

This was going to be a last stand, nothing more, on the enemy's part.

"Hit the trains," came the cold voice of squadron commander Hafiz. "Their defenders are just a detail. Remember the mission: cut their supply lines."

Idris armed rockets and aimed his plane for one of the overland trains.

Kill you. Then your protectors.

Think you can challenge the Zinj? Die, godless infidels.

— —

"FUCK. FUCK, FUCK, *fuck FUCK*!" came convoy commander Hammond's voice over the general radio channel as the enemy aircraft came in.

"Ditch them," Captain Bradford snarled from the shotgun seat of his Lancer. "Ditch the cargoes and blow them, get your men and your engines out of there. They're worth more!"

"Like hell, Bradford. My orders were to get this shit to 97/2. If we can't do that, we'll at least get this shit back to Cone Hill for another try."

You fucking idiot, Bradford thought.

In the other radio seat in back of Bradford's car, Corporal Jones was going "Mayday mayday, we have incoming air!"

"Hola, India Company," came a new voice. Jones gave it priority, put on the loudspeakers.

Above them, the attacking aircraft fired rockets into the overland trains. Something blew up in one of them; other explosions ripped up the ground around the convoy and its protectors. Something clanged *hard* against the Lancer's armor, a heavy piece of metal thrown by one of the high-explosive blasts.

"Who the hell's this?" Bradford demanded.

"Skull Six, Icefish Hauraki here. We're from the Air Force and we're here to help."

— —

"TWELVE IN ALL," came Icefish. "One flight circling high cover; we'll take them."

A Flight began to lift; the Vipers had been hugging the dirt at two thousand feet, trying to stay off the enemy radar and keep surprise.

"Sauron, you think you can handle a two to one fight? Sounds like Djinn, not Assads or Murads."

"Any day of the week," O'Connor spoke up. "We're jets, sir; they're just turboprops. They're multipurpose; we're fighters. Two to one is nothing."

There was laughter across the channel. Some of it – O'Connor was pretty sure one of those guys was 'Cock-Eye' Castle – seemed derisive.

"Don't knock the Djinn until you've fought them, *Meat*," came Icefish. "You might be able to go faster. Those things can turn on a tin lid."

The Confederated Union's last circulating coin, the quarter, was called the 'tin' or the 'tin lid' for how it looked, although it was only a bit over an inch in diameter.

"Use your speed. They get on your six, hit the burners, shake them off that way. Do *not* try to duel Djinn, they've got a stall speed like nothing," said Mordar.

"We can take them," said O'Connor, a little embarassed. *Fuck you, Cock-Eye.*

"Damn right we can," said Mordar. "Engage."

— —

Captain Steve Bradford watched his digital map with dismay, as reports came in and his RTOs in the back seat updated them. As he updated them, as the cumbersome road trains slowly made their way into a turn. The shortest of the three was three hundred yards long; the longest was four hundred and change. They'd take five minutes to do a hundred-and-eighty-degree turn, and right now Bradford wasn't sure they had one minute.

The first aircraft pass had been ineffective, mostly. One of the road trains' trunnions – the eight-foot-diameter wheels went in quads, a four-wheeled trunnion on each end of the seventy-foot-long carrier car – had been shot to crap and both axles were dragging, slowing the turn. The armor on others had been pecked, and something was burning on Landcrawler C.

Two of the semis, on the other hand, had been hit and were burning wreckage in the night. Another one was staggering along, something in the back of its trailer burning but the driver not just yet willing to give up.

Bail, idiot. Ditch it and bail with your cab intact!

Because those planes were coming back for another pass.

— —

Flying Officer Second-Class Mabruk Idris carefully lined up one of the overland trains in his rockets' sights as he came in again. Below was a firefight, the armored battalion engaging, the convoy and its protectors desperately fighting back—

And blips appeared on his radar. In the air, close and coming in.

The radio net erupted:

"Hostiles!"

"CU air about to engage," said Squadron-Colonel Hafiz.

Looked to be eight of them, four going high to engage his squadron's high cover. The CU were outnumbered three to two.

"Focus on the objective," ordered Idris' flight commander. "We've got them taken care of."

— —

Eight of the Djinn had been turning, about to make another pass on the convoy, when the Vipers showed up. The scene below was flashing lights and flares, burning vehicles and explosions. Tracer fire and missiles going in and out; a blazing candyland of red, white, yellow and green flashing back and forth across the rolling battlefield.

It was a bright double-moonlit, starlit night, and the visual accentuators on O'Connor's plane weren't truly necessary; he could see everything, look up and see more flashing tracers as the squadron commander and his flight engaged the enemy high cover.

His problem, C Flight's problem, was that they were outnumbered at dirt level by two to one.

Fuck that, he thought. The thing to do when you were outnumbered was to reduce a few of the other side!

"Break right, Shaker. Watch his back, Meat," said Mordar.

"Roger," said O'Connor and Jamison.

Four of the Djinn were turning to react to the Vipers. The other four were opening fire on the convoy, cannon blazing and rockets blasting from wing pods.

"Rip through them," said Jamison. "Take any shots you can but our job is to protect that damn convoy. We're going after the ones going after *it*."

Missile lock warning lit up. O'Connor banked right and accelerated, the Viper's engines growling under him as he pushed the throttle forwards.

One of the Zinj planes attacking the convoy was about to be in his sights. He pushed the cannon trigger; sent a burst at where it would be.

Hit! Hit! He clearly saw the shells spark off the Djinn, something on it exploding. The strafing aircraft turned to fight in the air, pushing for height and aiming.

Missile lock, and his threat indicator beeped *hard*. An oncoming Djinn; O'Connor pulled the stick back and hit the throttle again. The Djinn's missile fired, blazing a trail through the flame-lit semi-darkness, completely missed him.

Looking for Jamison – ah, there he was, higher up. O'Connor angled his jet back a bit more, going up to five thousand feet—

Missile lock.

Hit the chaff button, no idea where that Zinj was.

Cannon shells flashed past him. A Djinn was above him and on his six!

Well, he knew what to do in that case; throttle up, turning, evading. More cannon-shells flashed past. Another Djinn appeared ahead, turning; O'Connor aimed the plane slightly and opened fire. At least one of the cannon-shells struck. He banked left, aiming at the Djinn, firing more – and then a missile streaked into that plane, blew it apart in a blazing fireball.

"Looks like I just made ace," Mordar remarked.

I *want to make ace!* thought O'Connor. But for now, as he turned his plane and opened up on another Djinn, the chaos below irrelevant now to the fight in the air – as his missile-lock indicator lit up again and more fire came through his general vicinity – he had to stay alive!

— —

IDRIS TURNED, GOING for height, firing at a Viper that raced past him for a moment. The one he'd fired the missile at – ah, *there* he was, turning around to open fire on someone else.

He hit the rudder and ailerons, slowing his plane and turning tightly. Lined the infidel up in his sights and opened up—

— —

FIRE RIPPED INTO O'Connor's Viper, damage lights blazing and audio warnings shrieking. The plane slowed perceptibly and something scored across the top of his canopy. *Fuck.*

Zinj – there the bastard was, on his six and slightly above. Firing again. O'Connor hit the throttle and turned upwards, vertical, looping back; the Zinj banked left.

Burning wreckage fell from the sky above them; someone in the high-cover fight had scored a kill. Although those fights were merging now; O'Connor had seen one of the A Flight planes not too far above him.

He looped around the Zinj, hoping for a missile lock, getting one for just a moment and hitting the button.

A Skyfire heatseeking missile lanced out from the right-side wing of his Viper aiming at the Zinj no more than a mile away—

— —

Missile lock! went the warning indicator and it was so close Idris could *see* it. He hit the flare button and slammed his throttle forwards, both of his supercharged turboprop engines going to maximum as he banked the Djinn into a hard right turn.

A second or two later the missile blew past, distracted by the flare Idris had released. He kept with his turn, bringing his plane toward the Viper, racing head-on with Idris slightly below. He opened up, both of his wing-mounted Gatling guns sending streams of red tracers at the underside of the Viper as it flashed over him. Sparks showed that something had hit and then the Viper was past him.

No big. Idris turned, wheeling his Djinn around, aiming to get on the Viper's six – but where *was* the infidel?

— —

O'Connor had aimed his plane up, hitting the afterburner. He couldn't fly in as tight a circle as the Djinn, but he could apply more power and go faster. Now he looped down, firing for a moment at another Djinn that passed in front of him fighting someone else. Where was *his* one?

Ah. Turning upwards, in the lower right corner of O'Connor's canopy view. He aimed down, hit the cannon—

— —

THIRTY-MILLIMETER SHELLS POUNDED into the left wing, its left engine and then the top of the fuselage of Idris' plane. He didn't need digital indicators to know it was bad, because his left engine was burning.

Frantically his right hand pounded on the fire extinguisher button, although that was supposed to work automatically. His left hand focused on the stick—

His left-side engine exploded. Feeding power to the right-side, but he'd taken hits on the rudder and the left-wing control planes—

A part of the Djinn's left wing peeled away, no doubt damaged critically by the engine's explosion.

Fuck. Fucking infidel.

Idris hit the eject button.

— —

"GOT HIM!" O'CONNOR exalted as the Zinj pilot ejected, a parachute opening above him. He took his right hand from the throttle for just a moment to pound a fist in the air, a broad grin on his face.

He could see the Zinj pilot only a few hundred yards away, a dark dot under the parachute. Didn't want to fly too close, jet wash could mess with the parachute, but he aimed to within a couple of hundred yards, slowing the plane and waggling his wings a couple of times in salute.

"You flew well with what you had," O'Connor said.

Missile lock came the warning.

This fight wasn't over. He hit afterburners, banked away from the defeated enemy warrior, went looking for the next Zinj.

— —

'ICEFISH' HAURAKI LOOKED at his radar, filtered the chaos of radio communications for a moment to make sense of what had been happening here. The two fights had merged as the Zinj ground attackers had fought for height; the combat had disintegrated into a blazing twenty-plane furball.

But his Skulls had been more successful than not, so far. From what he could gather six – half – of the Zinj planes were down, for the loss of only one of his own.

Of course, one was too many. He hoped 'Rumble' Yoko had ejected successfully and would make it back somehow.

A Zinj crossed his sights about a mile away and he opened up, turning his plane and his cannon to aim the shells into the bastard's flight path.

And it looked like they were running, exchanging height for eastwards speed and fleeing.

"Chase them?" asked Mordar. As she would. His indicators showed she was already turning—

One of the fleeing Zinj exploded. Somebody – Castle? – on the radio net cheered.

"No. We've got something on the ground. Let's help those cavalry. Dollar, you and Junkie stay high cover in case they come back; Junkie's wing lead. Sauron, I'm joining C Flight downstairs. Good job everyone, but this ain't over – there's a convoy on the ground that needs to make it home."

16797943R00224

Printed in Great Britain
by Amazon